# NEVER LOOK AWAY

A THRILLER

# LINWOOD BARCLAY

DELL BOOKS • NEW YORK

*Never Look Away* is a work of fiction. Names, characters, places, and incidents either are the product of the author's imagination or are used fictitiously. Any resemblance to actual persons, living or dead, events, or locales is entirely coincidental.

2011 Dell Mass Market Edition

Copyright © 2010 by Linwood Barclay
Excerpt from *The Accident* © 2011 by Linwood Barclay

All rights reserved.

Published in the United States by Dell, an imprint of The Random House Publishing Group, a division of Random House, Inc., New York.

DELL is a registered trademark of Random House, Inc., and the colophon is a trademark of Random House, Inc.

Originally published in hardcover in the United States by Delacorte Press, an imprint of The Random House Publishing Group, a division of Random House, Inc., in 2010.

This book contains an excerpt from the forthcoming book *The Accident* by Linwood Barclay. This excerpt has been set for this edition only and may not reflect the final content of the forthcoming edition.

ISBN 978-0-553-59174-3
eBook ISBN 978-0-440-33918-2

Cover design: Carlos Beltran
Cover art: Blacksheep
Cover photograph: Juergen Stein/Getty Images

Printed in the United States of America

www.bantamdell.com

9 8 7 6 5 4 3 2 1

Dell mass market edition: August 2011

*For Neetha*

"He's really out of it."

"Look for a key."

"I told you, I've been through his pockets. There's no goddamn handcuff key."

"What about the combination? Maybe he wrote it down somewhere, put it in his wallet or something."

"What, you think he's a moron? He's going to write down the combination and keep it on him?"

"So cut the chain. We take the case, we figure out how to open it later."

"It looks way stronger than I thought. It'll take me an hour to cut through."

"You can't get the cuff over his hand?"

"How many times do I have to tell you? I'm gonna have to cut it off."

"I thought you said it would take forever to cut the cuff."

"I'm not talking about the cuff."

# PROLOGUE

"I'M SCARED," ETHAN SAID.

"There's nothing to be scared about," I said, turning away from the steering wheel and reaching an arm back to free him from the kiddie seat. I reached under the pad where he'd been resting his arms and undid the buckle.

"I don't want to go on them," he said. The tops of the five roller coasters and a Ferris wheel could be seen well beyond the park entrance, looming like tubular hills.

"We're not going on them," I reminded him for the umpteenth time. I was starting to wonder whether this excursion was such a good plan. The night before, after Jan and I had returned from our drive up to Lake George and I'd picked Ethan up at my parents' place, he'd had a hard time settling down. He'd been, by turns, excited about coming here, and worried the roller coaster would derail at the highest point. After I'd tucked him in, I slipped under the covers next to Jan and considered discussing whether Ethan was really ready for a day at Five Mountains.

But she was asleep, or at least pretending to be, so I let it go.

But in the morning, Ethan was only excited about the trip. No roller-coaster nightmares. At breakfast he was full of questions about how they worked, why they didn't have an engine at the front, like a train. How could it get up the hills without an engine?

It was only once we'd pulled into the nearly full parking lot shortly after eleven that his apprehensions resurfaced.

"We're just going on the smaller rides, the merry-go-rounds, the kind you like," I said to him. "They won't even let you go on the big ones. You're only four years old. You have to be eight or nine. You have to be this high." I held my hand a good four feet above the parking lot asphalt.

Ethan studied my hand warily, unconvinced. I don't think it was just the idea of being on one of the monstrous coasters that scared him. Even being near them, hearing their clattering roar, was frightening enough.

"It'll be okay," I said. "I'm not going to let anything happen to you."

Ethan looked me in the eye, decided I was deserving of his trust, and allowed me to lift the padded arm up and over his head. He worked his way out of the straps, which mussed up his fine blond hair as they squeezed past his head. I got my hands under his arms, getting ready to lift, but he squirmed free, said, "I can do it," then slithered down to the car floor and stepped out the open door.

Jan was around back, taking the stroller out of the trunk of the Accord, setting it up. Ethan attempted to get in before it had been locked into the open position.

"Whoa," Jan said.

Ethan hesitated, waited until he'd heard the definitive click, then plopped himself into the seat. Jan leaned over into the trunk again.

"Let me grab something," I said, reaching for a backpack.

Jan was opening a small canvas bag next to it that was actually a soft-sided cooler. Inside were a small ice pack and half a dozen juice boxes, cellophane-wrapped straws stuck to the sides. She handed me one of the juice boxes and said, "Give that to Ethan."

I took it from Jan as she finished up in the trunk and closed it. She zipped up the cooler bag and tucked it into the basket at the back of the stroller as I peeled the straw off of the sticky juice box. It, or one of the other juices in the cooler, must have sprung a tiny leak. I took the straw from its wrapper and stabbed it into the box.

Handing it to Ethan, I said, "Don't squeeze it. You'll have apple juice all over yourself."

"I know," he said.

Jan reached out and touched my bare arm. It was a warm August Saturday, and we were both in shorts, sleeveless tops, and, considering all the walking we had ahead of us, running shoes. Jan was wearing a long-visored ball cap over her black hair, which she had pulled back into a ponytail and fed through the back of the cap. Oversized shades kept the sun out of her eyes.

"Hey," she said.

"Hey," I said.

She pulled me toward her, behind the stroller, so Ethan couldn't see. "You okay?" she asked.

The question threw me off. I was about to ask her the same thing. "Yeah, sure, I'm good."

"I know things didn't work out the way you'd hoped yesterday."

"No big deal," I said. "Some leads don't pan out. It happens. What about you? You feel better today?"

She nodded so imperceptibly it was only the tipping of the visor that hinted at an answer.

"You sure?" I pressed. "What you said yesterday, that thing about the bridge—"

"Let's not—"

"I thought maybe you were feeling better, but when you told me that—"

She put her index finger on my lips. "I know I've been a lot to live with lately, and I'm sorry about that."

I forced a smile. "Hey, we all go through rough spots. Sometimes there's an obvious reason, sometimes there isn't. You just feel the way you do. It'll pass."

Something flashed in her eyes, like maybe she didn't share my certainty. "I want you to know I appreciate . . . your patience," she said. A family looking for a spot drove by in a monster SUV, and Jan turned away from the noise.

"No big deal," I said.

She took a deep, cleansing breath. "We're going to have a good day," she said.

"That's all I want," I said, and allowed myself to be pulled closer. "I still don't think it would hurt, you know, to see someone on a regular basis to—"

Ethan twisted around in the stroller so he could see us. He stopped sucking on the juice box and said, "Let's go!"

"Hold your horses," I said.

He settled back into his seat, bouncing his legs up and down.

Jan leaned in and gave me a quick kiss on the cheek. "Let's show the kid a good time."

"Yeah," I said.

She gave my arm a final squeeze, then gripped the handles of the stroller. "Okay, buster," she said to Ethan. "We're on our way."

Ethan stuck his hands out to the sides, like he was flying. He'd already drained his juice box and handed it to me to toss in a wastebasket. Jan found a moistened towelette for him when he complained about sticky fingers.

We had several hundred yards to get to the main entrance, but we could already see people lined up to buy tickets. Jan, wisely, had bought them online and printed them out a couple of days earlier. I took over stroller duty while she rooted in her purse for them.

We were almost to the gates when Jan stopped dead. "Nuts."

"What?"

"The backpack," she said. "I left it in the car."

"Do we need it?" I asked. It was a long trek back to where we'd parked.

"It's got the peanut butter sandwiches, and the sunscreen." Jan was always careful to goop Ethan up so he didn't get a burn. "I'll run back. You go ahead, I'll catch up to you."

She handed me two slips of paper—one adult ticket and one child—and kept one for herself.

She said, "I think there's an ice-cream place, about a hundred yards in, on the left. We'll meet there?"

Jan was always one to do her research, and must have memorized the online map of Five Mountains in preparation.

"That sounds good," I said. Jan turned and started back for the car at a slow trot.

"Where's Mom going?" Ethan asked.

"Forgot the backpack," I said.

"The sandwiches?" he said.

"Yeah."

He nodded, relieved. We didn't want to be going anywhere without provisions, especially of the sandwich variety.

I handed in my ticket and his, bypassing the line to purchase them, and entered the park. We were greeted with several junk food kiosks and about a dozen stands hawking Five Mountains hats and T-shirts and bumper stickers and brochures. Ethan asked for a hat and I said no.

The two closest roller coasters, which had looked big from the parking lot, were positively Everest-like now. I

stopped pushing the stroller and knelt down next to
Ethan and pointed. He looked up, watched a string of
cars slowly climb the first hill, then plummet at high
speed, the passengers screaming and waving their hands
in the air.

He stared, eyes wide with wonder and fear. He
reached for my hand and squeezed. "I don't like that,"
he said. "I want to go home."

"I told you, sport, don't worry. The rides we're going
on are on the other side of the park."

The place was packed. Hundreds, if not thousands, of
people moving around us. Parents with little kids, big
kids. Grandparents, some dragging their grandkids
around, some being dragged by them.

"I think that must be the ice-cream place," I said,
spotting the stand just up ahead.

I got behind the stroller and started pushing. "Think
it's too early for ice cream?" I asked.

Ethan didn't respond.

"Sport? You saying no to an ice cream?"

When he still didn't say anything, I stopped to take a
look at him. His head was back and to the side, his eyes
closed.

The little guy had fallen asleep.

"I don't believe it," I said under my breath. Not even
at the first merry-go-round and the kid was already
comatose.

"Everything okay?"

I turned. Jan had returned, a bead of sweat trickling
down her neck. The backpack was slung over her shoulder.

"He's nodded off," I said.

"You're kidding me," she said.

"I think he passed out from fear after getting a close
look at that," I said, pointing to the coaster.

"I think I've got something in my shoe," Jan said. She

navigated the stroller over to a concrete ledge surrounding a garden. She perched herself on the edge, nudging Ethan and the stroller to her left.

"Feel like splitting a cone?" she asked. "I'm parched."

I guessed what she was thinking. We could share a treat now, while Ethan dozed. He'd get plenty of junk before the day was out, but this would be something just for us.

"Dipped in chocolate?" I asked.

"Surprise me," she said, putting her left foot up on her knee. "Need money?"

"I got it," I said, patting my back pocket. I turned and strolled over to the ice-cream stand. It was the soft white stuff that comes out of a machine. Not my favorite in the world—I like the real thing—but the young girl who took my order did manage a skillful twirl at the top. I asked her to dip it in the vat of chocolate, which clung like skin to the ice cream as she presented it to me.

I took a tiny bite out of it, cracking the chocolate, and instantly regretted it. I should have let Jan have the first bite. But I'd make up for it through the week. On Monday, come home with flowers. Later in the week, book a sitter, take Jan out to dinner. This thing Jan was going through—maybe it was my fault. I hadn't been attentive enough. Hadn't made the extra effort. If that was what it was going to take to bring Jan around, I was up to it. I could put this marriage back on the rails.

I didn't expect to see Jan coming straight for me when I turned. Even with the sunglasses over her eyes, I could still tell she was upset. There was a tear running down one cheek, and her mouth was set in a terrible grimace.

Why the hell wasn't she pushing the stroller? I looked beyond her, to where I thought she'd been sitting.

She came up to me quickly, clapped her hands on the sides of my shoulders.

"I only looked away for a second," she said.

"What?"

"My shoe," she said, her voice shaking, uneven. "I was getting—the stone—I was getting the stone out of my shoe, and then I looked—I looked around and—"

"Jan, what are you talking about?"

"Someone's taken him," she said, almost in a whisper, her voice nearly gone. "I turned and he—"

I was already moving past her, running over to where I'd last seen them together.

The stroller was gone.

I stepped up onto the ledge Jan had been sitting on, scanned the crowds.

*It's just a mix-up. This isn't what it looks like. He'll be back in a second. Someone grabbed the wrong stroller.*

"Ethan!" I shouted. People walking past glanced at me, kept on going. "Ethan!" I shouted again.

Jan was standing below me, looking up. "Do you see him?"

"What happened?" I asked quickly. "What the hell happened?"

"I told you. I looked away for a second and—"

"How could you do that? How could you take your eyes off him?" Jan tried to speak but no words came out. I was about to ask a third time how she could have allowed this to happen, but realized I was wasting time.

I thought, instantly, of that urban legend, the one that got called into the newsroom once or twice a year.

"I heard from a friend of a friend," the calls usually began, "that this family from Promise Falls, they went down to Florida, and they were at one of the big theme parks in Orlando, and their little boy, or maybe it was a little girl, got snatched away from his parents, and these people took him into the bathroom and cut his hair and made him look different and smuggled him out of the park but it never got in the papers because the park owners don't want any bad publicity."

There was never, ever anything to it.

*But now . . .*

"Go back to the main gate," I told Jan, trying to keep my voice even. "If someone tries to take him out, they'll have to go through there. There should be somebody from park security there. Tell them." The ice-cream cone was still in my hand. I tossed it.

"What about you?" she asked.

"I'll scout out that way," I said, pointing beyond the ice-cream stand. There were some restrooms up there. Maybe someone had taken Ethan into the men's room.

Jan was already running. She looked back over her shoulder, did the cell phone gesture to her ear, telling me to call her if I found out anything. I nodded and started running the other way.

I kept scanning the crowds as I ran to the men's room entrance. As I entered, breathless, the voices of children and adults and hot-air hand dryers echoed off the tiles. There was a man holding up a boy, smaller than Ethan, at one of the urinals. An elderly man was washing his hands at the long bank of sinks. A boy about sixteen was waving his hands under the dryer.

I ran past all of them to the stalls. There were six of them, all doors open except for the fourth. I slapped on the door, thinking it might open.

"What?" a man shouted from inside. "I'll be another minute!"

"Who's in there?" I shouted.

"What the hell?"

I looked through the crack between the door and the frame, saw a heavyset man sitting on the toilet. It only took a second to see that he was in there alone.

"Fuck off!" the man barked.

I ran back out of the restroom, nearly slipping on

some wet tiles. Once I was back out in the sunlight, saw all the people streaming past, I felt overwhelmed.

Ethan could be anywhere.

I didn't know which way to head off, but going in any direction seemed a better plan than just standing there. So I ran toward the base of the closest roller coaster, the Humdinger, where I guessed about a hundred people were waiting to board. I scanned the lineup, looked for our stroller, or a small boy without one.

I kept running. Up ahead was KidLand Adventure, the part of Five Mountains devoted to rides for children too young for the big coasters. Did it make sense for someone to have grabbed Ethan and brought him here for the rides? Not really. Unless, again, it was some kind of mix-up, someone getting behind a stroller and heading off with it, never bothering to take a look at the kid sitting inside. I'd nearly done it myself once at the mall, the strollers all looking the same, my mind elsewhere.

Up ahead, a short, wide woman, her back to me, was pushing a stroller that looked an awful lot like ours. I poured on the speed, pulled up alongside her, then jumped in front to get a look at the child.

It was a small girl in a pink dress, maybe three years old, her face painted with red and green spots.

"You got a problem, mister?" the woman asked.

"Sorry," I said, not even getting the whole word out before I'd turned, still scanning, scanning, scanning—

I caught sight of another stroller. A blue one, a small canvas bag tucked into the back basket.

The stroller was unattended. It was just standing there. From my position, I couldn't tell whether it was occupied.

Out of the corner of my eye, I caught a glimpse of a man. Bearded. Running away.

But I wasn't interested in him. I sprinted in the direction of the abandoned stroller.

*Please, please, please . . .*

I ran around to the front of it, looked down.

He hadn't even woken up. His head was still to one side, his eyes shut.

"Ethan!" I said. I reached down, scooped him out of the stroller, and held him close to me. "Ethan, oh God, Ethan!"

I held him out where I could see his face, and he was frowning, like he was about to cry. "It's okay," I said. "It's okay. Daddy's here."

I realized he wasn't upset because he'd been snatched away from us. He was annoyed at having his nap interrupted.

But that didn't stop me from telling him, again, that everything was okay. I hugged him close to me, patted his head.

When I held him out again, his lip stopped trembling long enough for him to point at the corner of my mouth and ask, "Did you have chocolate?"

I laughed and cried at the same time.

I took a moment to pull myself together, then said, "We have to find your mother, let her know everything's okay."

"What's going on?" Ethan asked.

I got out my phone, hit the speed dial for Jan's cell. It rang five times and went to message. "I've got him," I said. "I'm coming to the gate."

Ethan had never had such a speedy stroller ride. He stuck out his hands and giggled as I pushed him through the crowds. The front wheels were starting to wobble so much I had to tip the stroller back, prompting him to laugh even more.

When we got to the main gate, I stopped, looked around.

Ethan said, "I think maybe I want to try the big coaster roller. I'm big enough."

"Hold on, partner," I said, looking. I got out my phone again. I left a second message: "Hey, we're right here. We're at the gate. Where are you?"

I moved us to the center of the walkway, just inside the gate, where the crowds funneled in to get to the rides.

Jan wouldn't be able to miss us here.

I stood in front of the stroller so Ethan could watch me. "I'm hungry," he said. "Didn't Mom come? Did she go home? Did she leave the backpack with the sandwiches in it?"

"Hold on," I said.

"Can I have *just* peanut butter? I don't want the peanut-butter-with-jam ones."

"Just cool your jets a second, okay?" I said. I was holding my cell, ready to flip it open the instant it rang.

Maybe Jan was with park security. That'd be fine, even though Ethan had been found. Because there was somebody running around this park, taking off with other people's kids. Not a good thing.

I waited ten minutes before placing another call to Jan's cell. Still no pickup. I didn't leave a message this time.

Ethan said, "I don't want to stay here. I want to go on a ride."

"Just hang on, sport," I said. "We can't go off without your mom. She won't know where to find us."

"She can phone," Ethan said, kicking his legs.

A park employee, identifiable by his khaki pants and shirt with the Five Mountains logo stitched to it, walked past. I grabbed his arm.

"You security?" I asked.

He held up a small walkie-talkie device. "I can get them," he said.

At my request, he called in to see whether anyone

from security was helping Jan. "Someone needs to tell her I've found our son," I said.

The voice coming out of the walkie-talkie was scratchy. *"Who? We got nothing on that."*

"Sorry," the park employee said and moved on.

I was trying to tamp down the panic. Something was very wrong.

Someone tries to take your kid. A bearded man runs away.

Your wife doesn't come back to the rendezvous point.

"Don't worry," I said to Ethan, scanning the crowds. "I'm sure she'll be here any minute now. Then we'll have some fun."

But Ethan didn't say anything. He'd fallen back asleep.

# PART ONE
## TWELVE DAYS EARLIER

# ONE

"YEAH?"

"Mr. Reeves?" I said.

"Yeah?"

"This is David Harwood at the *Standard*," I said.

"Yeah, David." This was the thing with politicians. You called them "Mister" and they called you by your first name. Didn't matter whether it was the president of the United States or some flunky on the utilities commission. You were always Bob or Tom or David. Never Mr. Harwood.

"How are you today?" I asked.

"What's on your mind?" he asked.

I decided to counter curt with charm. "Hope I didn't catch you at a bad time. I understand you just got back. What was it, just yesterday?"

"Yeah," Stan Reeves said.

"And this trip was a—what? A fact-finding mission?"

"That's right," he said.

"To England?"

"Yeah," he said. It was like pulling teeth, getting anything out of Reeves. Maybe this had something to do with the fact that he didn't like me very much. Didn't like the stories I'd been writing about what could end up being Promise Falls' newest industry.

"So what facts did you pick up?" I asked.

He sighed, as if resigned to answering a couple of questions, at least. "We found that for-profit prisons have been operating in the United Kingdom successfully for some time. Wolds Prison was set up to be run that way in the early nineties."

"Did Mr. Sebastian accompany you as you toured the prison facilities in England?" I asked. Elmont Sebastian was the president of Star Spangled Corrections, the multimillion-dollar company that wanted to build a private prison just outside Promise Falls.

"I believe he was there for part of the tour," Stan Reeves said. "He helped facilitate a few things for the delegation."

"Was there anyone else from the Promise Falls council who made up this delegation?" I asked.

"As I'm sure you already know, David, I was the council's appointee to go to England and see how their operations have been over there. There were a couple of people from Albany, of course, and a representative from the state prison system."

"Okay," I said. "So what did you take from the trip, bottom line?"

"It confirmed a lot of what we already know. That privately run correctional facilities are more efficient than state-run facilities."

"Isn't that largely because they pay their people far less than the state pays its unionized staff, and that they don't get nearly the same benefits as state employees?"

A tired sigh. "You're a broken record, David."

"That's not an opinion, Mr. Reeves," I said. "That's a well-documented fact."

"You know what else is a fact? It's a fact that wherever unions have their clutches in, they've been taking the state to the cleaners."

"It's also a fact," I said, "that privately run prisons

have had higher rates of assaults on guards, and prisoner-on-prisoner violence, largely due to reduced staffing levels. Did you find this to be the case in England?"

"You're just like those do-gooders out at Thackeray who lose sleep when one inmate tears into another." Some of the faculty at Thackeray College had banded together to fight the establishment of a private prison in Promise Falls. It was becoming a cause célèbre at the school. Reeves continued, "If one prisoner ends up sticking a shiv in another prisoner, you want to explain to me exactly how that hurts society?"

I scribbled down the quote. If Reeves ever denied it later, I had him on my digital recorder. The thing was, making this comment public would only boost his popularity.

"Well, it would hurt the operators of the prison," I countered, "since they get paid by the state per inmate. They start killing each other off, there goes your funding. Do you have any thoughts on Star Spangled Corrections' aggressive congressional lobbying for stiffer penalties, particularly longer sentences for a variety of crimes? Isn't that a bit self-serving?"

"I've got a meeting to get to," he said.

"Has Star Spangled Corrections settled on a site yet? I understand Mr. Sebastian is considering a few of them."

"No, nothing definite yet. There are a number of possible sites in the Promise Falls area. You know, David, this means a lot of jobs. You understand? Not just for the people who'd work there, but lots of local suppliers. Plus, there's a good chance a facility here would take in convicted criminals from outside our area, so that means family coming here to visit, staying in local hotels, buying from local merchants, eating in local restaurants. You get that, right?"

"So it'd be like a tourist attraction," I said. "Maybe they could put it next to our new roller-coaster park."

"Were you always a dick, or is it something they teach in journalism school?" Reeves asked.

I decided to get back on track. "Star Spangled's going to have to come before council for rezoning approval on whatever site they pick. How do you plan to vote on that?"

"I'll have to weigh the merits of the proposal and vote accordingly, and objectively," Reeves said.

"You're not worried about the perception that your vote may have already been decided?"

"Why would anyone perceive such a thing?" Reeves asked.

"Well, Florence for one."

"Florence? Florence *who*?"

"Your *trip* to Florence. You extended your trip. Instead of coming back directly from England, you went to Italy for several days."

"That was . . . that was all part of my fact-finding mission."

"I didn't realize that," I said. "Can you tell me which correctional facilities you visited in Italy?"

"I'm sure I could have someone get that list to you."

"You can't tell me now? Can you at least tell me how many Italian prisons you visited?"

"Not offhand," he said.

"Was it more than five?"

"I don't think so."

"Less than five, then," I said. "Was it more than two?"

"I'm really not—"

"Did you visit a single correctional facility in Italy, Mr. Reeves?"

"Sometimes you can accomplish what you need to accomplish without actually going to these places. You set up meetings, meet off-site—"

"Which Italian prison officials did you meet with off-site?"

"I really don't have time for this."

"Where did you stay in Florence?" I asked, even though I already knew.

"The Maggio," Reeves said hesitantly.

"I guess you must have run into Elmont Sebastian while you were there."

"I think I did run into him in the lobby once or twice," he said.

"Weren't you, in fact, Mr. Sebastian's guest?"

"Guest? I was a guest of the hotel, David. You need to get your facts straight."

"But Mr. Sebastian—Star Spangled, Inc., to be more precise—paid for your airfare to Florence and your accommodation, isn't that correct? You flew out of Gatwick on—"

"What the fuck is this?" Reeves asked.

"Do you have a receipt for your Florence stay?" I asked.

"I'm sure I could put my hands on it if I had to, but who saves every single receipt?"

"You've only been home a day. I'm guessing if you have one it hasn't had a chance to get lost yet."

"Look, my receipts are none of your fucking business."

"So if I were to write a story that says Star Spangled Corrections paid for your Florence stay, you'd be able to produce that receipt to prove me wrong."

"You know, you got a hell of a lot of nerve tossing around accusations like this."

"My information is that your stay, including taxes and tickets to the Galleria dell'Accademia and anything out of your minibar, came to three thousand, five hundred and twenty-six euros. Does that sound about right?"

The councilman said nothing.

"Mr. Reeves?"

"I'm not sure," he said quietly. "It might have been about that. I'd have to check. But you're way off base, suggesting that Mr. Sebastian footed the bill for this."

"When I called the hotel to confirm that your bill was being looked after by Mr. Sebastian, they assured me that everything was covered."

"There must be some mistake."

"I have a copy of the bill. It was charged to Mr. Sebastian's account."

"How the hell did you get that?"

I wasn't about to say, but a woman who didn't like Reeves very much had phoned from a blocked number earlier in the day to tell me about the hotel bill. I was guessing she worked either at city hall or in Elmont Sebastian's office. I couldn't get a name out of her.

"Are you saying Mr. Sebastian didn't pay your bill?" I asked. "I've got his Visa number right here. Should we check it out?"

"You son of a bitch."

"Mr. Reeves, when this prison proposal comes before council, will you be declaring a conflict of interest, given that you've accepted what amounts to a gift from the prison company?"

"You're a piece of shit, you know that?" Reeves said. "A real piece of shit."

"Is that a no?"

"A goddamn piece of shit."

"I'll take that as a confirmation."

"You want to know what really gets me?"

"What's that, Mr. Reeves?"

"This high-and-mighty attitude from someone like you, working for a newspaper that's turned into a fucking joke. You and those eggheads from Thackeray and anyone else you got on your side getting your shorts in a knot because someone might outsource running a prison, when you outsource fucking reporting. I remember when the Promise Falls *Standard* was actually a paper people had some respect for. Of course, that was before its circulation started going to shit, when it actually had *journalists* reporting on local events, before the Russell family started farming out some of its reporting duties to offshore help, getting reporters in goddamn India for Christ's sake to watch committee meetings over the Internet and then write up what happened at them for a fraction of what it would cost to pay reporters here to do the job. Any paper that does something like that and still thinks it can call itself a newspaper is living in a fool's paradise, my friend."

He hung up.

I put down my pen, took off my headset, hit the stop button on my digital recorder. I was feeling pretty proud of myself, right up until the end there.

The phone had only been on the receiver for ten seconds when it rang.

I put the headset to my ear without hooking it on. "*Standard.* Harwood."

"Hey." It was Jan.

"Hey," I said. "How's it going?"

"Okay."

"You at work?"

"Yeah."

"What's going on?"

"Nothing." Jan paused. "I was just thinking of that movie. You know the one? With Jack Nicholson?"

"I need more," I said.

"Where he's a germaphobe, always takes plastic cutlery to the restaurant?"

"Okay, I know the one," I said. "You were thinking about that?"

"Remember that scene, where he goes to the shrink's

office? And all those people are sitting there? And he says the line, the one from the title? He says, 'What if this is as good as it gets?'"

"Yeah," I said quietly. "I remember. That's what you're thinking about?"

She shifted gears. "So what about you? What's the scoop, Woodward?"

# TWO

MAYBE THERE WERE CLUES earlier that something was wrong and I'd just been too dumb to notice them. It's not like I'd be the first journalist who fancied himself a keen observer of current events, but didn't have a clue when it came to the home front. But still, it seemed as though Jan's mood had changed almost overnight.

She was tense, short-tempered. Minor irritants that would not have fazed her in the past now were major burdens. One evening, while we were getting ready to make up some lunches for the next day, she burst into tears upon discovering we were out of bread.

"It's all too much," she said to me that night. "I feel like I'm at the bottom of this well and I can't climb out."

At first, because I'm a man and don't really know—and don't really want to know—what the hell's going on with women in a physiological sense, I thought maybe it was some kind of hormonal thing. But I realized soon enough it was more than that. Jan was, and I realize this is not what you'd call a clinical diagnosis, down in the dumps. Depressed. But depressed did not necessarily mean depression.

"Is it work?" I asked her one night in bed, running my hand on her back. Jan, with one other woman, managed the office for Bertram's Heating and Cooling. "Has something happened there?" The latest economic slowdown meant fewer people were buying new air conditioners or furnaces, but that actually meant more repair work for Ernie Bertram. And sometimes, she and Leanne Kowalski, that other woman, didn't always see eye to eye.

"Work's fine," she said.

"Have I done something?" I asked. "If I have, tell me."

"You haven't done anything," she said. "It's just . . . I don't know. Sometimes I wish I could make it all go away."

"Make what all go away?"

"Nothing," she said. "Go to sleep."

A couple of days later, I suggested maybe she should talk to someone. Starting with our family doctor.

"Maybe there's a prescription or something," I said.

"I don't want to take drugs," Jan said, then quickly added, "I don't want to be somebody I'm not."

After work on the day she called me at the paper, Jan and I drove up together to pick up Ethan at his grandparents' place.

My mother and father, Arlene and Don Harwood, lived in one of the older parts of Promise Falls in a two-story red-brick house that was built in the forties. They didn't buy until the fall of 1971, when my mother was pregnant with me, and they'd had the place ever since. Mom had made some noises about selling it after Dad retired from the city's building department four years ago, arguing that they didn't need all this space, a lawn to cut, a garden to maintain, that they could get along just fine in a condo or an apartment, but Dad wouldn't have any of it. He'd go mad cooped up in a condo. He had his workshop out back in a separate two-car garage, and spent more time in there than in the house, if you didn't count sleeping. He was a relentless putterer, always looking for something to fix or tear down and do all over again. A door or cupboard hinge never had a chance to squeak twice. Dad practically carried a can of WD-40 with him at all times. A stuck window, a dripping tap, a running toilet, a jiggly doorknob—none of them stood a chance in our house. Dad always knew exactly what tool he needed, and could have strolled into his garage blindfolded to lay his hands on it.

"He drives me nuts," Mom would say, "but in forty-two years of marriage I don't think we've had even one mosquito get through a hole in a screen."

Dad's problem was that he couldn't understand why everyone else wasn't as diligent about their duties as he was with his. He was intolerant of other people's mistakes. As a city building inspector, he was a major pain in the ass to every Promise Falls contractor and developer. Behind his back they called him Don Hardass. When he got wind of that, he had some business cards made up with his new nickname.

He found it difficult not to share his wisdom about how to make this a more perfect world, in every respect.

"When you leave the spoons to dry like this without turning them over, the water ends up leaving a mark," he'd say to my mother, holding up one of the offensive items of cutlery.

"Piss off," Arlene would say, and Don would grumble and go out to the garage.

Their squabbling masked a deep love for each other. Dad never forgot a birthday or anniversary or Valentine's Day.

Jan and I knew, when we left Ethan with his grandparents, as we did through the week when we both went to work, that he wasn't going to be exposed to any hazards. No frayed light cords, no poisonous chemicals left where he could get his hands on them, no upturned carpet edges he could run and trip on. And their rates just happened to be more reasonable than any nursery schools in the area.

"Mom called me after you," I said to Jan, who was driving in her Jetta wagon. It was nearly five-thirty. We'd rendezvoused at our house so we could pick up Ethan in one car, together.

Jan looked over, said nothing, figured I'd continue. "She said Dad's really done something over the top this time."

"She say what?"

"No. I guess she wanted to build the suspense. I got hold of Reeves today, asked him about his hotel bill in Florence."

Jan said, without actually sounding all that interested, "How's that story coming?"

"Some woman called me anonymously. She had some good stuff. What I need to know now is how many others on the council are taking bribes or gifts or trips or whatever from this private prison corporation so that they'll give them the nod when the rezoning comes up for a vote."

"And you thought all the fun'd be over when Finley dropped out of politics." A reference to our former mayor, whose night with a teenage hooker didn't sit well with his constituents. Maybe, if you were Roman Polanski, you could screw someone a third your age and still win an Oscar, but if you were Randall Finley, it kind of played hell with your bid for Congress.

"Yeah, well, that's the thing about politics," I said. "When one dickhead leaves the scene, half a dozen others rush in to fill the vacancy."

"Even if you get the story," Jan said, "will they print it?"

I looked out my window. I made a fist and tapped it lightly on my knee. "I don't know," I said.

Things had changed at the *Standard*. It was still owned by the Russell family, and a Russell still sat in the publisher's chair, and there were various Russells scattered about the newsroom and other departments. But the family's commitment to keeping it a real newspaper had shifted in the last five years. The overriding concern now, with declining revenues and readership, was survival. The paper had always kept a reporter in Albany to cover state issues, but now relied on wires. The weekly book section had been killed, reduced to a page in the back end of Style. The editorial cartoonist, tremendously gifted at lampooning and harpooning local officials, was given the heave-ho, and now we picked up any number of national, syndicated cartoonists who'd probably never even heard of Promise Falls, let alone visited it, to fill the hole on the editorial page. Oh yeah, the editorials. We used to run two a day, written by staffers. Now, we ran "What Others Think," a sampling of editorials from across the country. We didn't think for ourselves more than three or four times a week.

We no longer had our own movie critic. Theater reviews were farmed out to freelancers. The courts bureau had been shut down, and only the most newsworthy trials got covered, provided we happened to know they were on.

But the most alarming indicator of our decline was sending reporting jobs offshore. I hadn't thought it was possible, but when the Russells heard about how a paper in Pasadena had pulled it off, they couldn't move quickly enough. They started with something as simple as entertainment listings. Why pay someone here fifteen to twenty bucks an hour to write up what's going on around town when you could email all the info to some guy in India who'd put the whole thing together for seven dollars an hour?

When the Russells found how well that worked, they stepped it up. Various city committees had a live Internet video feed. Why send a reporter? Why even pay one to watch it from the office? Why not get some guy named Patel in Mumbai to watch it, write up what he sees, then email his story back to Promise Falls, New York?

The paper was looking to save money any way it could. Advertising revenue was in free fall. The classified section had all but disappeared, losing out to online services like Craigslist. Many of the paper's clients were becoming more selective, banking on fewer but costlier radio and TV spots instead of full- or even half-page ads. So what if you hired reporters to cover local events who'd never even set foot in your community? If it saved money, go for it.

While it wasn't surprising to find that kind of mentality among the paper's bean counters, it was pretty foreign in the newsroom. At least until now. As Brian Donnelly, the city editor and, more important, the publisher's nephew, had mentioned to me only the day before, "How hard can it be to write down what people say at a meeting? Are we going to do a better job of it just because we're sitting right there? Some of these guys in India, they take really good notes."

"Don't you ever get tired of this?" Jan asked, hitting the intermittent wipers to clear off some light rain.

"Yeah, sure, but I'm beating my head against the wall with Brian."

"I'm not talking about work," Jan said. "I'm talking about your parents. I mean, we see them every day. Your parents are nice enough and all, but there's a limit. It's like we're being smothered or something."

"Where's this coming from?"

"You know we can never just drop Ethan off or pick him up at the end of the day. You have to go through the interrogation. 'How was your day?' 'What's new at work?' 'What are you having for dinner?' If we'd just put him in day care, they wouldn't give a shit, they'd just kick him out the door and we could go home."

"Oh, that sounds better. A place where they don't actually have any interest in your kid."

"You know what I'm saying."

"Look," I said, not wanting to have a fight, because I wasn't sure what was going on here, "I know most days you get off work before I do, so you've been doing pickup duty, but in another month it won't even matter. Ethan'll be going to kindergarten, which means we won't be taking him to my parents' every day, which means you won't have to endure this daily interrogation you suddenly seem so concerned about." I shook my head. "It's not like we can take turns dropping him off at *your* parents' place."

Jan shot me a look. I regretted the comment instantly, wished I could take it back.

"I'm sorry," I said. "That was a cheap shot."

Jan said nothing.

"I'm sorry."

Jan put her blinker on, turned in to my parents' driveway. "Let's see what your dad's done now."

Ethan was in the living room, watching *Family Guy*. I walked in, turned off the set, called out to Mom, who was in the kitchen, "You can't let him watch that."

"It's just a cartoon," she said, loud enough to be heard over running water.

"Pack up your stuff," I told Ethan, and walked back into the kitchen, where Mom stood at the sink with her back to me. "In one episode the dog tries to have sex with the mother. In another, the baby takes a machine gun to her."

"Oh, come on," she said. "No one would make a cartoon like that. You're really turning into your father." I gave her a kiss on the cheek. "You're wound too tight."

"It's not *The Flintstones* anymore," I said. "Actually,

cartoons now are better. But a lot of them are *not* for four-year-olds."

Ethan shuffled into the kitchen, looking tired and a little bewildered. I was surprised he wasn't asking about food. Mom had probably already given him something.

Jan, who had come in a few seconds after me, knelt down to Ethan. "Hey, little man," she said. She looked into his backpack. "You sure you have everything here?"

He nodded.

"Where's your Transformer?"

Ethan thought for a moment, then bolted back into the living room. "In the cushions!" he shouted.

"What's Dad done this time?" I asked.

"He's going to get himself killed," Mom said, taking a pot from the sink and setting it on the drying rack.

"What?"

"He's out in the garage. Get him to show you his latest project. So, Jan, how was work today? Things good?"

I walked through the light rain to the garage. The double-wide door was open, Dad's blue Crown Victoria, one of the last big sedans from Detroit, parked in there. My mother's fifteen-year-old Taurus sat in the driveway. Both cars had kid safety seats in the back for when they had Ethan.

Dad was tidying his workbench when I walked in. He's taller than me if he stands up straight, but he's spent most of his life looking down—inspecting things, trying to find tools—so that he's permanently round-shouldered. He still has a full head of hair, which is something of a comfort to me, even if his did start going gray when he was barely forty.

"Hey," he said.

"Mom said you have something to show me."

"She needs to mind her own business."

"What is it?"

He waved a hand, which I wasn't sure was a dismissal or surrender. But when he opened up the passenger door and took out something to show me, I realized he was going to share his latest project.

It was several white pieces of cardboard, about the size of a piece of regular printer paper. They looked like they might be the card sheets they slide into new shirts. Dad saved all that stuff.

He handed the small stack to me and said, "Check it out."

Written on each one, in heavy black marker, all in capitals, was a different phrase. They included TURN SIGNAL BROKEN?, STOP RIDING MY ASS, TAILLIGHT OUT, HEADLIGHT OUT, SPEED KILLS, STOP SIGNS MEAN STOP, and GET OFF THE PHONE!

They looked like the cue cards you used to see the crew holding up for Johnny Carson.

Dad said, "The STOP RIDING MY ASS one I did with bigger letters because they've got to be able to see it through my rear window, and I'm up in the front seat. But if they're tailgating that close, they'll probably see it."

I looked at him, at a loss for words.

"How many times you seen some jackass do something stupid and you wish you could tell him? I keep these in the car, pick out the right one, hold it up to the window, maybe people will start to realize their mistakes."

I'd found some words. "You installing bulletproof glass?"

"What?"

"You flash these, someone's going to shoot you."

"That's crazy."

"Okay, so let's say it's you. You're driving down the road and someone shows a sign like that to you."

Dad studied me. "That'd never happen. I'm a good driver."

"Work with me."

He pushed his lips in and out a moment. "I'd probably try to run the son of a bitch off the road into the ditch."

I took the cards from him and ripped them, one by one, in half, then dropped them in the metal garbage bin. Dad sighed.

Jan came out the back door with Ethan. They walked up the side of the house to the Jetta and Jan started getting Ethan strapped into the safety seat.

"Guess we're going," I said.

"Your problem," Dad said, "is you're afraid to shake things up. Like that new prison they want to build. That'd be a real shot in the arm for the town."

"Sure. Maybe we could get a nuclear waste storage facility while we're at it."

I got into the Jetta next to Jan. She backed out, pointed us in the direction of our house. Her jaw was set firmly and she wouldn't look at me.

"You okay?" I asked.

Jan said nothing all the way home, and very little through dinner. Later, she said she would put Ethan to bed, something we often did together.

I went upstairs as she was tucking our son in.

"You know who loves you more than anyone in the whole world?" she said to him.

"You?" Ethan said in his tiny voice.

"That's right," Jan whispered to him. "You remember that."

Ethan said nothing, but I thought I could hear his head moving on his pillowcase.

"If someone ever said I didn't love you, that wouldn't be true. Do you understand?"

"Yup," Ethan said.

"You sleep tight and I'll see you in the morning, okay?"

"Can I have a drink of water?" Ethan said.

"No more stalling. Go to sleep."

I slipped into our bedroom so I wouldn't be standing there when Jan came out.

# THREE

"CHECK IT OUT," SAID Samantha Henry, a general assignment reporter who sat next to me in the *Standard* newsroom.

I wheeled over on my chair and looked at her computer monitor. Close enough to read it, but not so close she might think I was smelling her hair.

"This just came in from one of the guys in India, who was watching a planning committee meeting about a proposed housing development." The committee was grilling the developer about how small the bedrooms appeared to be on the plans. "Okay, so read this para right here," Samantha said, pointing.

"'Mr. Councilor Richard Hemmings expressed consternation that the rooms did not meet the proper requirements for the swinging of a cat.'" I stared at it a moment and grinned. "I should call my dad and ask if that's actually written somewhere in the building code. 'A bedroom must be large enough that if you are standing in the center, grasping a cat by the tail, its head will not hit any of the four walls when you are spinning with your arm fully extended.'"

"Stuff's coming in like this every day," Samantha said. "What the fuck do they think they're doing? You saw the correction we ran the other day?"

"Yeah," I said. The city did not actually own any barns, and no city employees had actually closed the barn doors after the horses had left. It was bad enough our reporters in India were unfamiliar with American idioms, but when they got past the copy desk right here in the office, something was very, very wrong.

"Don't they care?" Samantha asked.

I pushed away from the monitor, leaned back in my chair, and laced my fingers behind my head. I always felt a little more relaxed when I moved away from Sam. The thing we had was a long time ago, but you started sharing a computer screen too often and people were going to talk.

It felt like the chair's back support was going to fail, and I shifted forward, put my hands on the arms. "You have to ask?"

"I've never seen anything like this," she said. "I've been here fifteen years. I asked the M.E.'s assistant for a new pen and she wanted to see an empty one first. Swear to God. Half the time, you go in the ladies' room, there's no goddamn toilet paper."

"I hear the Russells may be looking to sell," I said. It was the number one rumor going around the building. "If they can pare down the costs, get the place showing a profit, they'll have an easier time unloading the place."

Samantha Henry rolled her eyes. "Seriously, who'd buy us in this climate?"

"I'm not saying it's happening. I just heard some talk."

"I can't believe they'd sell. This place has been run by one family for generations."

"Yeah, well, it's a very different generation running it now than ten years ago. You won't find ink running through the veins of anyone on the board these days."

"Madeline used to be a reporter," Samantha said, referring to our publisher. She didn't need to remind me how Madeline got her start here.

"Used to be," I said.

What with papers shutting down all over the country, everyone was on edge. But Sam, in particular, was worried about her future. She had an eight-year-old daughter and no husband. They'd split up years ago, and she'd never gotten a dime of support from him. A former *Standard* staffer, he'd left to work on a paper in Dubai. It's pretty hard to chase a guy down for money he owes you when he's on the other side of the planet.

When she was newly divorced, with a baby, Sam put up a brave front. She could do this. Still have her career and raise a child. We didn't sit next to each other back then, but we crossed paths often enough. In the cafeteria, at the bar after work. When we weren't trading reporters' usual complaints about editors who had held or cut their stories, she let down her guard about how tough things were for her and Gillian.

I guess I thought I could rescue her.

I liked Sam. She was sexy, funny, intellectually challenging. I liked Gillian. Sam and I started spending a lot of time together. I started spending a lot of nights at Sam's. I fancied myself as more than a boyfriend. I was her white knight. I was the one who was going to make her life okay again.

I took it pretty hard when she dumped me.

"This is too fast," she told me. "This is how I fucked things up last time. Moving too quickly, not thinking things through. You're a great guy, but . . ."

I went into a funk I don't think I really came out of until I met Jan. And now, all these years later, things were okay between Sam and me. But she was still a single mother, and things had never stopped being a struggle.

She lived paycheck to paycheck. Some weeks, she didn't make it. She'd had the labor beat for years, but the paper could no longer afford to devote reporters to specific issues, so now she reported to general assignment, and couldn't predict the hours she'd be working. It played hell with her babysitting. She was always scrambling to find someone to watch her daughter when a last-minute night assignment landed on her desk.

I didn't have Sam's week-to-week financial worries, but Jan and I talked often about what else I could do if I found myself without a job. Unemployment insurance only lasted so long. I—and Jan for that matter—was worth more dead since we signed up for life insurance a few weeks back. If the paper folded, I wondered if I should just step in front of a train so Jan would be up $300,000.

"David, you got a sec?"

I whirled around in my chair. It was Brian Donnelly, the city editor. "What's up?"

He nodded his head in the direction of his office, so I got up and followed him. The way he made me trail after him, without turning or chatting along the way, made me feel like a puppy being dragged along by an invisible leash. I wasn't even forty yet, but I saw Brian was part of the new breed around here. At twenty-six, he was management, having impressed the bosses not with journalistic credentials but with business savvy. Everything was "marketing" and "trends," "presentation" and "synergy." Every once in a while, he dropped "zeitgeist" into a sentence, which invariably prompted me to say "Bless you." The sports and entertainment editors were both under thirty, and there was this sense, at least among those of us who had been at the paper for ten or more years, that the place was gradually being taken over by children.

Brian slipped in behind his desk and asked me to close the door before I sat down.

"So, this prison thing," he said. "What have you really got?"

"The company gave Reeves an all-expenses-paid vacation in Italy after the UK junket," I said. "Presumably, when Star Spangled's proposal comes up before council, he'll be voting on it."

"*Presumably.* So he's not actually in a conflict of interest yet, is he? If it hasn't come up for a vote. If he abstains or something, then what do we really have here?"

"What are you saying, Brian? If a cop takes a payoff from a holdup gang to look the other way, it's not a conflict until the bank actually gets robbed?"

"Huh?" said Brian. "We're not talking about a bank holdup here, David."

Brian wasn't good with metaphors. "I'm trying to make a point."

Brian shook his head, like he was trying to rid his brain of the last ten seconds of conversation. "Specifically about the hotel bill," he said, "do we have it a hundred percent that Reeves didn't pay for it? Or that he isn't paying back Elmont Sebastian? Because in your story," and now he was looking at his computer screen, tapping the scroll key, "you don't actually have him denying it."

"He called me a piece of shit instead."

"Because we really need to give him a chance to explain himself before we run with this," Donnelly said. "If we don't, we could get our asses sued off."

"I gave him a chance," I said. "Where's this coming from?"

"What? Where's *what* coming from?"

I smiled. "It's okay, I get it. You're getting leaned on by She Who Must Be Obeyed."

"You shouldn't refer to the publisher that way," Brian said.

"Because she's your aunt?"

He had the decency to blush. "That has no bearing on this."

"But I'm right about where this is coming from. Ms. Plimpton sent the word down," I said.

While born a Russell, Madeline Plimpton had been married to Geoffrey Plimpton, a well-known Promise Falls realtor who'd died two years ago, at thirty-eight, of an aneurysm.

Madeline Plimpton, at thirty-nine, was the youngest publisher in the paper's history. Brian was the son of her much older sister Margaret, who'd never had any interest in newspapers, and had instead pursued her dream of having a property worthy of the annual Promise Falls Home and Garden Tour. She managed to be on it every year, which I would never suggest, not for a moment, was because she was tour president.

Brian had never actually worked as a reporter, so you almost couldn't blame him for not understanding the thrill of nailing a weasel like Reeves to the wall. But Madeline, when she was still a Russell, had worked as a general assignment reporter alongside me more than a decade ago. Not for long, of course. It was part of her crash course in learning the family business, and in no time she was moving up the ranks. Entertainment editor, then assistant managing editor, then M.E., all designed to get her ready to be publisher once her father, Arnett Russell, packed it in, which he had done four years ago. The fact that Madeline had, however briefly, worked in the trenches made her willingness to turn her back on journalism—to tiptoe around the Reeves story—all the more disheartening.

When Brian didn't deny that his aunt was pulling the strings here, I said, "Maybe I should go talk to her."

Brian held up his hands. "That'd be a very bad idea."

"Why? Maybe I can make a better case for this story than you can."

"David, listen, trust me here, that's not a good plan. She's this close to—"

"To what?"

"Forget it."

"No. She's this close to what?"

"Look, it's a new era around here, okay? A newspaper is more than just a provider of news. We're an . . . an . . . entity."

"An entity. Like in *Star Trek*?"

He ignored that. "And entities have to survive. It's not all about saving the world here, David. We're trying to get out a paper. A paper that makes money, a paper that has a shot at being around a year from now, or a year after that. Because if we're not making money, there's not going to be anyplace to run your stories, no matter how important they may be. We can't afford to run anything that's not airtight, not these days. We've got to be sure before we go ahead with something, that's all I'm telling you."

"She's this close to what, Brian? Firing me?"

He shook his head. "Oh, no, she couldn't do that. She'd need some sort of cause." He sighed. "How would you feel about a move to Style?"

I settled back in my chair, absorbed the implications. Before I could say anything, Brian added, "It's a lateral move. You'd still be reporting, except it would be on the latest trends, health issues, the importance of flossing, that kind of shit. It wouldn't be something you could file a grievance over."

I breathed in and out a few times. "Why's Madeline so worked up about the prison story? If I was writing about another Walmart coming into town, I could see her freaking out over lost ad dollars, but I kind of doubt Star Spangled Corrections is going to be running a bunch of full-page ads about weekly specials. 'License plates fifty percent off!' Or maybe, 'Need your rocks split? Call the Promise Falls Pen.' Come on, Brian, what's she upset about? She buying the argument that this is going to mean jobs? More local jobs means more subscribers?"

"Yeah, there's that," Brian said.

"There's something else?"

Now Brian took a few slow breaths. There was something he was debating whether to tell me.

"David, look, you didn't hear this from me, but the thing is, if this prison sets up here, the *Standard* could wipe all its debts, have a fresh start. We'd all be able to feel a lot more secure about our jobs."

"How? Are they going to get inmates to write the stories? Let them start covering local news for free as part of their rehabilitation?" Even as I said it, I thought, *Not too loud. Give the bosses around here an idea—*

"Nothing like that," Brian said. "But if the paper sold Star Spangled Corrections the land to build their prison, that would help the bottom line."

My mouth was open for a good ten seconds. I'd been a total moron. Why had this never occurred to me? The twenty acres the Russell family owned on the south side of Promise Falls had for years been the rumored site of a new building for the *Standard*. But that talk stopped about five years ago when earnings began to fall.

"Holy shit," I said.

"You didn't hear it from me," Brian said. "And if you go out there and breathe a word of this to anyone, we're both fucked. Do you understand? Do you understand why anything we run has to be nailed down, I mean *really* nailed down? If you find something good, really good, she won't have any choice but to run it, because if she doesn't, the TV station'll find out and they'll go with it, or the *Times Union* in Albany will get wind of it."

I got up from my chair.

"What are you going to do, David? Tell me you're not going to do anything stupid."

I surveyed his office, like I was sizing it up for redecorating. "I'm not sure this room meets the cat-swinging code, Brian. You might want to look into that."

I sat at my desk and stewed for half an hour. Samantha Henry asked me five times what had happened in Brian's office, but I waved her off. I was too angry to talk. Despite Brian's warning not to, I was seriously considering walking into the publisher's office, asking her if this was what she really wanted, that if we had to abandon our principles to save the paper, was the paper really worth saving?

In the end, I did nothing.

Maybe this was how it was going to be. You came in, you churned out enough copy to fill the space, didn't matter what it was, you took your paycheck, you went home. I'd worked at a paper like that—in Pennsylvania—before coming back to the hometown rag. There'd always been papers like that. I'd been naïve enough to think the *Standard* would never turn into one of them.

But we were hardly unique. What was happening to us was happening to countless other papers across the country. What might buy us some time was the Russell family's ace in the hole—a huge tract of land it hoped to sell to one of the country's biggest private prison conglomerates.

If things didn't work out here, maybe I could get a job as a bull. Wasn't that what inmates called guards?

I picked up the phone, hit the speed dial for Bertram Heating and Cooling. If I couldn't save the state of journalism, maybe I could put a bit of effort into my marriage, which had been showing signs of wear lately.

A voice that was not Jan's said, "Bertram's." It was Leanne Kowalski. She had the perfect voice for someone working at an air-conditioning firm. Icy.

"Hey, Leanne," I said. "It's David. Jan there?"

"Hang on." Leanne wasn't big on small talk.

The line seemed to go dead, then Jan picked up and said, "Hey."

"Leanne seems cheery today."

"No kidding."

"Why don't we see if my parents can hang on to Ethan for a couple of extra hours, we'll go out for a bite to eat. Just the two of us. Rent a movie for later." I paused. "I could get into *Body Heat*." Jan's favorite film. And I never got tired of the steamy love scenes between William Hurt and Kathleen Turner.

"I guess," she said.

"You don't sound very excited."

"Actually, yeah," said Jan, warming to the idea. "Where were you thinking for dinner?"

"I don't know. Preston's?" A steakhouse. "Or the Clover?" A bit on the pricey side, but if the newspaper business was going into the dumper, maybe we should go while we could still afford it.

"What about Gina's?" Jan asked.

Our favorite Italian place. "Perfect. If we go around six, we probably won't need a reservation, but I'll check just to be sure."

"Okay."

"I could pick you up at work, we'll go back for your car later."

"What if you get me drunk so you can take advantage of me?"

That sounded more like the Jan I knew.

"Then I'll drive you to work in the morning."

Taking a shortcut through the pressroom on the way to the parking lot, I spotted Madeline Plimpton.

It was the pressroom that most made this building feel like a real newspaper. It was the engine room of a battleship. And if the *Standard* ever ceased to be a paper, these monstrous presses—which moved newsprint through at roughly fifty feet per second and could pump out sixty thousand copies in an hour—would be the last thing standing, the final thing to be moved out of here. We'd already lost the composing room, where the paper's pages had been, literally, pasted up. It had vanished once editors started laying out their own pages on a computer screen.

I saw Madeline up on the "boards," which was pressman-speak for the catwalks that ran along the sides, and through, the presses, which were not actually massive rollers, but dozens upon dozens of smaller ones that led the never-ending sheets of newsprint on a circuitous route up and down and over and under until they miraculously appeared at the end of the line as a perfectly collated newspaper. The machinery had been undergoing some maintenance, and a coverall-clad pressman was directing Madeline's attention to the guts of one part of the presses, which ran from one end of the hundred-foot room to the other.

I didn't want to pass up this opportunity to speak to her directly, but I knew better than to clamber up the metal steps. The pressmen could be a bit sensitive about that sort of thing. They weren't as hard-line as they used to be, but the men—and handful of women—who ran and maintained the presses were staunch unionists. If someone from anywhere else in the paper got up on the boards without their permission—especially management—it suddenly got a lot easier to carry on a conversation. The presses would stop dead. And they wouldn't start running again until the trespassers left.

But the pressmen, while still a force to be reckoned with, had softened with the times. They knew newspapers were in a tough period from which they might never recover. And the people who worked in this room found it difficult to dislike Madeline Plimpton. She'd always been able to connect with the average working guy, and knew the names of everyone who worked in here.

Madeline was in her publisher's outfit: a navy knee-length skirt and matching jacket that was not only impervious to printer's ink, but set off her silver-blonde hair. She was a curiosity in some ways. Designer duds, but down here on the boards, I wondered if, in her heart, she wouldn't have been more comfortable in the tight jeans she'd worn as a reporter. She'd look just as good in them today as she did then. I'd only seen Madeline age in the time since her husband had died, and even after that she'd managed to keep any new lines in her face to a minimum.

I managed to catch her eye when she glanced down.

"David," she said. It was normally deafening in here, but the presses weren't currently in operation, so I could hear her.

"Madeline," I said. Considering that we'd come through the newsroom together, years earlier, it had never occurred to me to call her by anything other than her first name. "You got a minute?"

She nodded, said something to the pressman, and descended the metal staircase. She knew better than to ask me to join her up there. The boards were not a place to hang out.

Once she was on the floor, I said, "This Reeves story is solid."

"I'm sorry?" she said.

"Please," I said. "I get what's going on. We like this new prison. We don't want to make waves. We act real nice and play down local opposition to this thing and we get to sell them the land they need to build."

Something flickered in Madeline's eyes. Maybe she'd figure out Brian had told me. Fuck him.

"But this will end up biting us in the ass later, Madeline. Readers, they may not get it right away, but over time, they'll start figuring out that we don't care about news anymore, that we're just a press release delivery system, something that keeps the Target flyer from getting wet, a place where the mayor can see a picture of himself handing out a check to the Boy Scouts. We'll still carry car crashes and three-alarm fires and we'll do the annual pieces on the most popular Halloween costumes and what New Year's resolutions prominent locals are making, but we won't be a fucking newspaper. What's the point in doing all this if we don't care what we are anymore?"

Madeline looked me in the eye and managed a rueful smile. "How are things, David? How's Jan?"

She had that way about her. You could blow your stack at her and she'd come back with a question about the weather.

"Madeline, just let us do our jobs," I said.

The smile faded. "What's happened to you, David?" she asked.

"I think a better question would be, what's happened to you?" I said. "Remember the time you and I were covering that hostage taking, the one where the guy was holding his wife and kid, said he was going to kill them if the police didn't back off?"

She didn't say anything, but I knew she remembered.

"And we got in between the police and the house, and we saw everything that went down, the cops storming the place, beating the shit out of that guy, even after they'd found out he didn't have a gun. Just about killed him. And the story we put together after, laying it all out just like it happened, even though we knew it was going to cause a shit storm with the police, which it sure as hell did when it ran. You remember the feeling?"

Her eyes went soft at the memory. "I remember." She paused. "I miss it."

"Some of us still care about that feeling. We don't want to lose it."

"And I don't want to lose this paper," Madeline Plimpton said. "You go to bed at night worried about whether your story will run. I go to bed worried about whether there's going to be a paper to run it in. I may not sit in the newsroom anymore, but I'm still on the front line."

I didn't have a comeback for that.

I parked out front of Bertram's a little after five-thirty. Leanne Kowalski was standing in the parking lot like she was waiting for someone.

I nodded hello as I got out of the Accord and headed for the door. "How's it going, Leanne?" I said. I'd met her enough times to have known better than to ask.

"Be a lot better if Lyall ever turns up," she said. Leanne was one of those people who seemed to have only two moods. Annoyed, and irritated. She was tall and skinny, narrow hipped and small breasted, what my mother would call scrawny. Like she needed some meat on her bones. While she kept her black, lightly streaked hair short, she had bangs she had to keep moving out of her eyes.

"No wheels today?" I asked. There was usually an old blue Ford Explorer parked next to Jan's Jetta any time I drove by.

"Lyall's clunker's in the shop, so he borrowed mine," she said. "I don't know where the hell he is. Was supposed to be here half an hour ago." She shook her head and rolled her eyes. "Honest to God."

I offered up an awkward smile, then pulled on the office door handle, a cool blast of A/C hitting me as I went inside.

Jan was turning off her computer and slinging her purse over her shoulder.

"Leanne's her usual cheerful self," I said.

Jan said, "Tell me about it."

We both happened to look out the window at the same time. Leanne's Explorer had just careened into the lot. I could see Lyall's round face behind the windshield, his sausagelike fingers gripped to the wheel. There was something bobbing about inside, and it took me a moment to realize it was a large dog.

Instead of getting in the passenger side, Leanne went to the driver's door and yanked it open. She was pretty agitated, waving her hands, yelling at him. We couldn't make out what she was saying, and as curious as we were to hear it, we didn't want to venture outside and run the risk of getting in the middle of it.

Lyall slithered out of the driver's seat. He was almost bald and heavyset, and his tank top afforded us a generous glimpse of his armpits. He slunk around the front of the Explorer, Leanne shouting at him across the hood the entire time.

"Must be fun to be him," I said as Lyall opened the passenger door and got in.

"I don't know why she stays with him," Jan said. "All she does is bitch about him. But you know, I think she actually loves the loser."

Leanne got behind the wheel, threw the Explorer into reverse, and kicked up dust as she sped off down the road. Just before Leanne backed out, I saw Lyall give her a look. It reminded me of a beaten dog, just before it decides to get even.

Gina showed Jan and me to our table. Her restaurant had about twenty tables, but it was early and only three of them were taken.

"Mr. Harwood, Mrs. Harwood, so nice to see you

again," she said. Gina was a plump woman in her sixties whose eatery was a legend in the Promise Falls area. She, and she alone, possessed the recipe to the magical tomato sauce that accompanied most of the dishes. I hoped it was written down someplace, just in case.

"When did you tell your parents we'd be coming for Ethan?" Jan asked around the time we got our minestrone.

"Between eight and nine."

She had her spoon in her right hand, and as she reached with her left for the salt her sleeve slipped back an inch, revealing something white wrapped about her left wrist.

"They're really good with him," she said.

That seemed something of a concession, given how she'd been talking about my parents only the other day.

"They are," I said. It looked like a bandage wrapped around her wrist.

"Your mom's in good shape. She still has lots of energy," Jan said. "She's, you know, youthful for her age."

"My dad's pretty good, too, except for being a bit, you know, insane."

Jan didn't say anything for a moment. Then, "It's good to know that if something . . . if something happened to me—or to you—they'd be able to help out a lot."

"What are you talking about, Jan?"

"It's just good to have things in place, that's all."

"Nothing's going to happen to you or to me," I said. "What's that on your wrist?"

She left her spoon in the bowl and pulled her sleeve down. "It's nothing," she said.

"It looks like a bandage."

"I just nicked myself," she said.

"Let me see."

"There's nothing to see," she said. But I had reached

across the table, taken hold of her hand, and pushed the sleeve up myself. The bandage was about an inch wide and went completely around her wrist.

"Jesus, Jan, what did you do?"

She yanked her arm away. "Let go of me!" she said, loud enough to make the people at the other tables, and Gina by the front door, glance our way.

"Fine," I said quietly, taking my hand back. Keeping my voice low, I said, "Just tell me what happened."

"I was cutting some vegetables for Ethan and the knife slipped," she said. "Simple as that."

I could see injuring your finger while cutting up carrots, but how did a knife jump up and get your wrist?

"Just drop it," Jan said. "It's not . . . what it looks like. I swear, it was totally an accident."

"Jesus, Jan," I said, shaking my head. "These days, lately, I don't know . . . I'm worried sick about you."

"You don't have to be concerned," she said curtly and studied her soup.

"But I am." I swallowed. "I love you."

Twice she started to speak and then stopped. Finally, she said, "I think, sometimes, it would be easier for you if you didn't have both of us to worry about. If it was just you and Ethan."

"What the hell are you talking about?"

Jan didn't say anything.

I was frantic with concern, but there was anger, too, creeping into my voice. "Jan, answer me honestly here. What kind of thoughts are going through your head lately? Are you having—I don't know how to put this—self-destructive thoughts?"

She kept looking at the soup, even though she wasn't eating it. "I don't know."

I had this feeling that we had reached a moment. One of those moments in your life when you feel the ground moving beneath you. Like when someone calls and says a loved one has been rushed to the hospital. When you get called in by the boss and told they won't be needing you anymore. Or you're in a doctor's office, and he's looking at your chart, and he says you should sit down.

You're finding out something that's going to make everything that happens from here on different from everything that has gone before.

*My wife is ill,* I thought. *Something's happened to her. Something's come undone. Something's wrong with the circuitry.*

"You don't know," I said. "So you *might* be thinking about hurting yourself in some way."

Her eyes seemed to nod.

"How long have you been having thoughts like this?"

Jan's lips went out, then in, as she considered the question. "A week or so. These thoughts come in, and I don't know why they're there, and I can't seem to get rid of them. But I feel I'm this huge burden to you."

"That's ridiculous. You're everything to me."

"I know I'm a drag on you, like an anchor."

"That's crazy." I immediately regretted my choice of word. "Look, if you've been feeling this way a week or so . . . what's brought this on? Has something happened? Something you haven't told me about?"

"No, nothing," she said unconvincingly.

"Has something happened at work?" After seeing Leanne going at it with Lyall, I wondered whether she was dragging Jan down somehow. "Is it Leanne? Is she making your life hell, too?"

"She's . . . she's always been hard to deal with, but I've learned to cope," Jan said. "I can't really explain it. I just started feeling this way. Feeling that I'm a burden, that I have no purpose."

"That's ridiculous," I said. "You know what I think? I think maybe you need to talk to—"

"I don't want to hear this," Jan said.

"But if you just talked—"

"What, so they could put me away? Lock me up in some loony bin?"

"For God's sake, Jan. Now you're just being paranoid." And again, I managed to pick a word I really should have avoided.

"Paranoid? Is that what you think I am?"

I sensed Gina approaching.

"That's what you'd like, isn't it?" Jan said, her voice rising again. "To be rid of me for good."

Gina stopped, and we both looked at her.

"I'm sorry," Gina said. "I was just going to—" she pointed at the soup bowls, "take those away, if you were finished."

I nodded, and Gina removed them.

To Jan, I said, "Maybe we should go home and—"

But Jan was already pushing back her chair.

# FOUR

I DIDN'T SLEEP MUCH that night. I tried to talk to Jan on the way home, and before we went to bed, but she wasn't interested in having any further conversations with me, particularly when I brought up the topic of her seeking some kind of professional help.

So I was pretty weary the following morning, walking with my head hanging so low on my way into the *Standard* building that I didn't even notice the man blocking my path until I was nearly standing on his toes.

He was a big guy, and he seemed ready to burst out of his black suit, white shirt, and black tie. Over six feet tall, he had a shaved head and there was a tattoo peeking out from his shirt collar, but not enough for me to tell what it was. I put his age at around thirty, and the way he carried himself suggested that he was not to be messed with. He wore the suit as comfortably as Obama sporting bling.

"Mr. Harwood?" he said, an edge to his voice.

"Yes?"

"Mr. Sebastian would be honored if you would join him over coffee. He'd like a moment to have a word with you. He's waiting down at the park. I'd be happy to drive you."

"Elmont Sebastian?" I said. I'd been trying for weeks to get an interview with the president of Star Spangled Corrections. He didn't return calls.

"Yes," the man said. "By the way, my name is Welland. I'm Mr. Sebastian's driver."

"Sure," I said. "What the hell."

Welland led me around the corner and opened the door of a black Lincoln limo for me. I got into the back, settled into a gray leather seat, and waited while he got in behind the wheel. If this car had a glass partition, it wasn't in position, so I asked Welland, "Have you worked long for Mr. Sebastian?"

"Just three months," he said, pulling out into traffic.

"And what were you doing before that?"

"I was incarcerated," Welland said without hesitation.

"Oh," I said. "For very long?"

"Seven years, three months, and two days," Welland said. "I served my time at one of Mr. Sebastian's facilities near Atlanta."

"Well," I said as Welland steered the car in the direction of downtown.

"I'm a product of the excellent rehabilitation programs Star Spangled facilities offer," he said. "When my sentence ended, Mr. Sebastian took a chance on me, gave me this job, and I think it says a lot about the stock he puts in second chances."

"Do you mind my asking what you were serving time for?"

"I stabbed a man in the neck," Welland said, glancing into the mirror.

I swallowed. "Did he live?" I asked.

"For a while," Welland said, making a left.

He stopped the car by the park that sits just below the falls the town takes its name from. Welland came around, opened the door, and pointed me in the direction of a picnic table near the river's edge. A distinguished-looking, silver-haired man in his sixties was seated on the bench with his back to the table, tossing popcorn to some ducks. When he spotted me and rose from the bench, I could see he was as tall as Welland, although more slender. He smiled broadly and extended a large sweaty hand.

I made a conscious effort not to wipe my hand on my pants.

"Mr. Harwood, thank you so much for coming. It's a pleasure to be able to speak to you at last."

"I've been available, Mr. Sebastian," I said. "You're the one who's been hard to get hold of."

He laughed. "Please, call me Elmont. May I call you David?"

"Of course," I said.

"I love feeding the ducks," he said. "I love watching them gobble it down."

"Yeah," I said.

"When I was a boy, I had a summer job working on a farm," he said, tossing more kernels, watching the ducks lunge forward and fight over them. "I grew to love God's creatures back then."

He turned and pointed to the table, where a couple of take-out coffees sat in a box filled with creams, sugars, and wooden sticks. "I didn't know what you took in yours, so it's black. Help yourself to what you need."

He turned himself around and tucked his legs under the table as I took a seat opposite him. I didn't reach for a coffee, but did go into my pocket for a notepad and pen. "I've left several messages for you."

Sebastian glanced across the park lawn at Welland, who was standing guard by the limo. "What do you think of him?" he asked.

I shrugged. "Model citizen."

Another laugh. "Isn't he, though? I'm very proud of him."

"Why did you pay for Stan Reeves's trip to Florence?" I asked. "Is that standard policy? To reward people in advance who'll be voting on your plans?"

"That's good." He nodded. "You get right to it. I appreciate that. I like directness. I'm not one to pussyfoot around."

"If you can find another way to say it, you can put off answering my question even longer."

Elmont Sebastian chuckled and pried off one of the coffee lids and poured in three creams. "As it turns out, this is exactly why I was hoping to meet with you. To deal with that question. I brought you here to show you something."

He reached into his suit jacket and withdrew an envelope that had his name written on it. The flap was tucked in, not glued. He pulled it back, withdrew a check, and handed it to me.

Was this how Elmont Sebastian operated? He cut reporters checks to back off?

I took it in my hand and saw that it was not made out to me, but to him. And it was written on the personal account of Stan Reeves, in the amount of $4,763.09. The date in the upper right corner was two days ago.

"I know you think you were onto something where Councilor Reeves is concerned," he said. "That he accepted a free side trip to Italy from me, but nothing could be further from the truth. I had already rented a couple of rooms in Florence, expecting to entertain friends, but they had to cancel at the last minute, so I said to Mr. Reeves, while we were still in England, that he was welcome to take the extra room. And he was pleased to do so, but he made it very clear to me that he was not able to accept any gifts or gratuities. That would put him in an untenable position, and of course I understood completely. But the reservation was all paid for, so we made arrangements that he would settle up with me upon his return. And there's the check that proves it."

"Well," I said, handing it back, "I'll be damned."

Elmont Sebastian smiled, revealing an uneven top row of teeth. "I would have felt terrible had you gone ahead with a story that impugned the reputation of Mr. Reeves. And myself, for that matter, but I am used to having my name besmirched by the press. But to see Mr. Reeves harmed—it would have been my fault entirely."

"Isn't it great that that's all cleared up," I said.

He returned the check to its envelope and slipped it back into his coat. "David, I'm very concerned you may not appreciate what my company is trying to do. I get the sense from your stories you think there's something inherently evil about a private prison."

"A for-profit prison," I said.

"I'm not denying it," Sebastian said, taking a sip of coffee. "Profit is not a dirty word, you know. Nothing immoral with rewarding people financially for a job well done. And when it turns out to be a job that serves the community, that makes this country a better place to live, well, what's wrong with that, exactly?"

"I'm not on a one-man crusade, Mr. Sebastian." He looked hurt, my not calling him by his first name. "But there are a lot of people around here who don't want your prison coming to Promise Falls. For a whole host of reasons, not the least of which is that you're taking what has traditionally been a government responsibility and turning it into a way to make money. The more criminals that get sentenced, the better your bottom line. Every convict sent to your facility is like another sale."

He smiled at me as though I were a child. "How do you feel about funeral home directors, David? Is what they do wrong? They make money out of death. But they're providing a service, and they're entitled to make money doing that. Same for estate lawyers, the florists you call to send flowers to loved ones, the man who cuts the lawn at the cemetery. What I do is, David, is make America a better place. The good citizens of this country are entitled to feel safe when they go to bed at night, and they're entitled to feel that way knowing they're getting the best bang for their tax dollar. That's what I do, with all the facilities I run across a great many of these wonderful United States of America. I help people sleep at night, and I help keep their taxes down."

"And all you get out of it is, if last year is any indication, a $1.3 billion payoff."

He shook his head in mock sadness. "Do you work for free at the *Standard*?" he asked.

"Your company's actively involved in trying to see minimum sentences raised across the board. You're telling me your only motive there is to make Americans sleep safe at night?"

Sebastian glanced at his watch. I thought it might be a Rolex, but the truth was, I'd never seen a real Rolex. But it looked expensive.

"I really must be going," he said. "Would you like me to make a copy of the check for the purposes of your story?"

"That won't be necessary," I said.

"Well then, I guess I'll be off." Sebastian rose from the bench and started walking across the grass back to his limo. He brought his take-out cup with him, but even though he walked right past an open waste bin, he handed it to Welland to dispose of. Welland opened the door for him, closed it, got rid of the cup, and before getting into the driver's seat he looked at me. He made his hand into a little gun, grinned, and took a shot at me.

The limo drove off. It was looking very much like they weren't going to be giving me a lift back to the paper.

# FIVE

TEN DAYS AFTER OUR dinner at Gina's, Jan got us tickets to go to Five Mountains, the roller-coaster park. It seemed the perfect metaphor for her moods since our dinner at Gina's. Up and down, up and down, up and down.

She'd been doing her best to be herself around Ethan in the ten days since she'd said I'd be happy to be rid of her, and my tactful suggestion that she might be paranoid. If Ethan had noticed his mother was not well, he hadn't been curious enough to ask what was up. He usually asked whatever question came into his head, so that told me he really hadn't noticed. Jan had taken a couple of days off from work in the last week, but I'd still taken Ethan to my parents', thinking maybe what she needed was time to herself. She'd never actually come out and said she wanted to kill herself, but I still felt a low-level anxiety when I thought about her home alone.

The day after Gina's, I snuck out of the office for a hastily booked afternoon appointment with our family doctor, Andrew Samuels. When I called, I told the nosy receptionist, who always wanted to know why you were seeing the doctor, I had a sore throat.

"Going around," she said.

But when I was alone in the office with Dr. Samuels, I

said, "It's about Jan. She's not herself lately. She's down, she's depressed. She said she thinks Ethan and I would be better off without her."

"That's not good," he said. He had some questions. Had something happened recently? A death in the family? Financial problems? Trouble at work? A health matter she might not have told me about?

I had nothing.

Dr. Samuels said the best thing was for me to suggest she come and see him. You couldn't diagnose a patient who wasn't there.

I started pushing her to go talk to him. At one point, I said that if she refused to go, I'd go see him without her, never letting on I'd already done it. She was furious. But later she came into the kitchen and told me she'd made an appointment to see him the following day, which she was taking off.

The next evening, I asked how it had gone. I tried hard not to make it the first thing I asked when I saw her.

"It was good," Jan said without hesitation.

"You told him how you've been feeling?"

Jan nodded.

"And what did he say?"

"Mostly he just listened," she said. "He let me talk. For a long time. I'm sure I ran into the next appointment, but he didn't rush me at all."

"He's a good guy," I said.

"So, I told him how I've been feeling, and I guess that's about it."

Surely there was more. "Did he have any suggestions? Did he write you out a prescription or anything?"

"He said there were some drugs I could try, but I told him I didn't want anything. I've already told you that. I'm not going to become some drug addict."

"So did he do *anything*?"

"He said I'd already taken the first positive step by coming to see him. And he said there were some people who were better at this sort of thing—"

"Psychiatrists?"

Jan nodded. "He said he'd refer me to one if I wanted."

"So you said yes?"

Jan eyed me sharply. "I said no. You think I'm crazy?"

"No, I don't think you're crazy. You don't have to be crazy to go see a psychiatrist." I'd almost said "shrink."

"I'm going to try to deal with this on my own."

"But those thoughts you were having," I said. "About whether to harm yourself." I couldn't bring myself to say "suicide."

"What about them?"

"Are you still having those?"

"People have all kinds of thoughts," she said, and walked out of the room.

That same day Jan ordered the tickets, an email arrived in my in-box at work:

"We spoke the other day. I know you're looking into Star Spangled Corrections and how they're trying to buy up all the votes on council. Reeves is not the only one they've treated to trips or gifts. They've gotten to practically everyone, so there's no way this thing is not going to go through. I've got a list of what's being paid out and who's getting it. I don't dare phone you or say who I am in this email, but I'm willing to meet you in person and give you all the evidence you need for this. Meet me tomorrow at 5:00 p.m. in the parking lot of Ted's Lakeview General Store. Take 87 north to Lake George, up by the Adirondack Park Preserve. Take 9 North, which goes for a ways alongside 87. There's an area where the woods opens up, and that's where Ted's is. Don't come early and hang around and don't wait long for me. If I'm not there by 5:10, it probably means something has happened and I'm not coming. I'll tell you this much: I'm a woman, which you probably figured out when I called you, and I will be in a white pickup."

I read it through a couple of times, sitting at my desk in the newsroom. Rattled, I signed out, went to the cafeteria for a coffee, took a couple of sips, left it there, and returned to my desk.

"You okay?" Samantha Henry, at her desk next to mine, asked. "I said hello to you twice and you ignored me."

The Hotmail address it had been sent from was a random series of letters and numbers that offered no clues about the author. I made a couple of notes, then deleted the email. Then I went into the deleted emails and made sure it was purged from the system. Maybe I was paranoid, but ever since learning that the paper's owners had an interest in selling land to Star Spangled Corrections, I'd been looking over my shoulder a bit more.

I didn't trust anyone around here.

"Holy shit," I said under my breath.

Someone had dirt on the members of Promise Falls council who were accepting bribes, gifts, kickbacks, whatever you wanted to call them, from Elmont Sebastian's prison corporation.

My story on Reeves's Florence vacation had never made the paper. His check to Sebastian was obviously written after he'd found out I knew about his Florence trip, but it was enough to bury the story as far as Brian was concerned, and I wasn't sure I blamed him. I needed something that really nailed Reeves and possibly other council members to the wall.

This anonymous email might just be it.

I certainly had no confidence in Brian to champion my stories on this issue. Only a couple of days earlier, in an editorial that wasn't actually written in some far-flung part of the country and wired to us, the Promise Falls *Standard* proclaimed that a private prison would bring not only short-term construction jobs to a recession-weary town, but long-term employment. If the citizens of Promise Falls expected to be protected from those who would break the law, they could hardly adopt a "not in my backyard" attitude when it came to hosting a facility that would lock up those lawbreakers. And as for the prison being privately run, the paper had taken a "let's see" attitude. "This concept, while it has met with mixed results in other jurisdictions, deserves a chance to prove itself here."

The piece had Madeline Plimpton's fingerprints all over it.

It made me sick to my stomach to read it.

I went to Google Maps to find the rendezvous point. Even though I had no doubt I was going to head up to Lake George, I had to admit the email was short on specifics. I still didn't know who this woman was, or whom she worked for. Someone at city hall? Could it be a clerk? An administrative assistant? Someone in the mayor's office who saw everyone come and go? Some pissed-off prison guard from one of Sebastian's other facilities? Whoever she was, she knew about Reeves and his free hotel stay in Florence. Maybe it was someone right in his office. The guy was widely regarded as an asshole; it wasn't hard to imagine one of his staff sticking a knife in his back.

I guessed I'd have to wait until I got to Lake George to find out.

\* \* \*

"I've bought us tickets to go to Five Mountains," Jan said when she phoned in the afternoon.

"You what?"

"The park north of town? The one we drive by with all the roller coasters?"

"I know what it is." Everyone knew about Five Mountains. It had opened just outside Promise Falls in the spring to much fanfare.

"You don't want to go?" she asked. "I already bought the tickets online. I don't think there's any way to take them back."

"No, no, it's okay," I said. "I'm just surprised." One minute, she was talking like someone who wanted to kill herself, the next she was booking tickets to a theme park. "You booked tickets for all three of us?"

"Of course," she said.

"Those coasters are huge. They won't let Ethan on them."

"They've got that area for little kids, with the merry-go-rounds and everything."

"I guess." Then, a worry. "You didn't book these for tomorrow, did you?" It wasn't like Ethan was in school yet. He could go any day, and for all I knew Jan was planning to take the next day off, assuming I might be persuaded to do the same.

"No, they're for Saturday," she said. "Is that a problem?"

"No, that's perfect. It would have been hard for me to go tomorrow."

"What's up tomorrow?"

I lowered my voice so Sam, who was tapping away at her computer, wouldn't hear. "I have to meet somebody."

"Who?"

"I don't know. I got this anonymous email, a woman

claiming to have the goods on Reeves and some of the other councilors."

"Oh my God, that's just what you've been waiting for."

"Yeah, well, I don't know whether it'll pan out."

"You meeting her in some dark alley or something?"

"I'm driving up to Lake George."

Jan didn't say anything for a moment.

"What is it, hon?"

"Nothing. I was just, I was just thinking of taking one more mental health day tomorrow. It's really slow in the office. If we were having a real heat wave, the phone'd be ringing off the hook with A/C service calls, but the weather's been not so bad, so it's pretty quiet."

I hesitated just for second. "Why don't you ride up with me?" I could use the company, and given Jan's dark thoughts lately, it would be a way to keep tabs on her for the day. Not that I was going to offer that up as a reason for her to join me.

"I couldn't do that," Jan protested. "Wouldn't that freak out your contact, you not coming alone?"

I thought about that. "If she asks, I'll just tell her. You're my wife. We made a day of it. Combined meeting a source with a drive in the country. If anything, it should put her more at ease."

Jan didn't sound entirely convinced. "I suppose. But if this is some secret Deep Throat kind of meeting, are we going to be safe?"

I managed a chuckle. "Oh, it's going to be very dangerous."

I didn't think it would take much more than an hour to drive to Lake George, and even though I was supposed to meet this person at five, I thought it made sense to get on the road at three. The woman in the note had made it clear that there was only about a ten-minute window for us to connect. I was to be there at five, and if she hadn't shown up within ten minutes, I was to turn around and go home.

Jan decided to keep Ethan with her for most of the day, then drive over and drop him off at my parents' around two. It didn't seem to matter how many times we imposed on them, they didn't mind. Mom adored him, and loved the novelty of having a male under her roof who'd actually do what she asked. Dad was talking about setting up a train set in the basement for Ethan to play with when he was over, although I suspected Dad was using Ethan as a cover story. Dad probably needed a project, and he'd always loved model trains, the big Lionel engines that made a huge racket and spewed smoke. I couldn't imagine Mom being crazy about the idea, but if it kept Dad from making more instructional signs for his fellow motorists, she'd probably be on board.

I got to the house about quarter to three, thinking Jan might be waiting for me on the front porch—we live in an old part of town where they still have such things—but she wasn't there. I bounded up the steps, opened the screen door, and called out Jan's name.

"You all set?" I said.

"Up here!" she said.

I bounded up the single flight, talking the entire way. "I think if we hit the road now, we might be in Lake George in time to grab a bite to eat or a coffee or something before I meet with—"

I walked into our bedroom. Jan was in the bed, under our covers, her head resting on her crooked arm.

"What—are you sick?" I asked.

She threw back the covers to reveal that she was naked. "Do I look like I'm sick?" she asked.

"Well," I said, smiling, "even in August you're bound to catch cold if you head up to Lake George like that."

"If you really want to get up there in time to get coffee, I suppose I could throw on my clothes and we could go right now."

"To be honest," I said, "I had coffee this morning."

Fifteen minutes later, we were on the road.

For the first twenty miles, I was starting a conversation in my head that wasn't going anywhere.

"You seem better," I wanted to say to Jan.

"You haven't been as down the last day or two," I nearly said.

"It's good to see you like this," I contemplated telling my wife.

But I said nothing out of fear of jinxing things. If Jan was coming out of this downturn, I didn't want to fuck it up by making a big deal out of it. I worried she might get defensive, accuse me of watching her every little tic, overanalyzing her every word. Which, of course, was exactly what I'd been doing for a couple of weeks now.

So I decided to act as though there was nothing out of the ordinary. That Jan wasn't taking a day off work because she'd been so troubled. She was just playing hooky. Keeping me company on my way to an interview.

I'd brought along my pen and notepad and digital recorder. If possible, I wanted to get this woman's revelations on tape—okay, it's not really tape anymore, but I'd yet to find another way to say this that didn't sound funny. But I had my doubts she'd want to have her voice recorded.

I had the recorder tucked into my pocket just in case.

"Not bad traffic," I said as we headed up the interstate.

Jan turned slightly sideways in her seat, not an easy thing to do in the Jetta. She alternated looking at me, the scenery, the road behind us.

"There's something I should tell you," she said.

I suddenly got that feeling again, the one I'd had in the restaurant. "What?" I said.

"Something . . . I did," she said.

"What did you do?"

"Actually, it's more like something I didn't do," she said, looking out the rear window, then back out the front.

"Jan, tell me what's going on," I said.

"You know that day we took a drive in the country?"

I shook my head. "We do that a lot."

"I can't even remember the name of the road, but it's a place I can find, you know? Like, make a right turn at the white house, keep on going until you go past the red barn, that kind of thing?"

"You've always been able to find your way around," I said. "You just don't have much of a memory for street names or road numbers."

"That's right," she said. "So I don't know if I can even tell you where I was, I mean, the road or anything. But you know that back road, it's well paved but it's out in the country and it doesn't get a lot of traffic? On the way to the garden center?"

That narrowed it down a bit.

"And you come up to this bridge? You know where the road narrows a bit to go over it, and even though there's still a line down the middle, if there's a truck coming the other way you slow down and let it go through first?"

Now I knew exactly where she was talking about.

"And it goes over the river there, and the water's moving really fast over the rocks?"

I nodded.

Jan glanced out the back window again, then looked at me. "So I drove up there the other day, parked the car, and I walked out to the middle of the bridge."

*I don't want to hear this.*

"I stood there for the longest time," Jan said. "I

thought about what it would be like to jump, wondered if a person could survive a fall like that. It's not all that far, but the rocks, they're pretty jagged down there. And then I thought, if I'm going to jump off a bridge, I should just use the one that goes over Promise Falls. Remember you told me that story, about the student who did that a few years ago?"

"Jan," I said.

"I stood up on the railing—it's made of concrete and it's quite wide. I stood there for a good thirty seconds, I'm guessing, and then climbed back down."

I swallowed. My mouth was very dry. "Why?" I asked. "What made you not do it?"

*Because she loves us. Because she couldn't imagine leaving Ethan and me behind.*

She smiled. "There was a car coming. A farmer's truck, actually. I didn't want to do it in front of anyone, and by the time I was back down, the moment had passed."

*I have to take her to a hospital. I need to turn around and drive her to a hospital and have her checked in. That's what I need to do.*

"Well," I said, trying to conceal my alarm, "it's a good thing that truck came along."

"Yeah," she said, and smiled, like what she'd told me was no big deal. Just something she'd thought about, and then the moment had passed.

I asked, "What did the doctor say when you told him about this?"

"Oh, this happened since I saw him," she said offhandedly. She reached out and touched my arm. "But you don't have to worry. I feel good today. And I feel good about tomorrow, about going to Five Mountains."

That was supposed to be reassuring? So what if she felt good right now? What about an hour from now? What about tomorrow?

"There's something else," Jan said.

I gave her a look that said, "What?"

"It might be my imagination," she said, glancing out the rear window again, "but I think that blue car back there has been following us ever since we left our place."

# SIX

IT WAS MAYBE A quarter of a mile behind us, too far to be sure what make of car it was, definitely too far to read a license plate. But it was some kind of American sedan, General Motors or Ford, in dark blue, with tinted windows.

"It's been following us since we left?" I said.

"I'm not positive," Jan said. "It does kind of look like a million other cars. Maybe there was one blue car behind us when we were driving out of Promise Falls, and that's a different blue car."

I was doing just under seventy miles per hour, and eased up slightly on the accelerator, letting the car coast down to just over sixty. I wanted to see whether the other car would pull into the outside lane and pass us.

A silver minivan coming up on the blue car's tail moved out and passed it, then slid into the long space between us.

"I can't quite see it," I said, glancing at both my side and rearview mirrors, while not taking my eyes off the road ahead. Even slowing down, we were gaining on a transport truck.

Jan was about to turn around in her seat but I told her not to. "If someone's following us, I don't want them to know we've spotted them."

"Aren't they going to figure that out since we've slowed down?"

"I've only slowed a little. If he's on cruise control or something, he's going to catch up to us pretty soon."

The van had moved back into the passing lane and whipped past us and the truck ahead. I looked in the mirror. The blue car loomed larger there, and I could see now that it was a Buick with what appeared to be New York plates, although the numbers were not distinct, as the plate was dirty. "He's catching up," I said.

"So maybe it's nothing," Jan said, sounding slightly relieved. "And it is a pretty long highway, without that many exits. It's not like he can just turn off anywhere."

I put on my blinker to move over a lane. Slowly we overtook the truck.

"That's true," I said, but I wasn't feeling any less tense. I was puzzling out the implications if in fact the blue car was tailing us.

It would seem to indicate that someone knew I was meeting with this anonymous source. I couldn't think of any other possible reason why anyone would want to follow me.

And if someone was tailing me to this rendezvous, it meant, in all likelihood, that the email the woman had sent me had been intercepted, found, something. Maybe it had been found on her computer. Or she'd told someone she was going to meet with a reporter.

Could this be a setup? But if so, who was doing it? Reeves? Sebastian? What would be the point of that?

I passed the truck, moved back into the right lane. Now I couldn't see the car at all, and I had to maintain my speed or the truck was going to have to pull out and pass me. Gradually, I put some distance between the truck and us.

Jan was checking the mirror on her door. "I don't see him," she said. "You know what? I think—you're going to love this—maybe I'm just a bit paranoid today. God knows, with everything else I've been feeling, that might actually make sense."

Which was worse? To find out we were being followed, or that Jan, already troubled with on-again, off-again depression, was starting to think people were following her?

The blue car passed the truck, moved in front of it.

"He's back," I said.

"Why don't you speed up a bit," Jan suggested. "See if he does the same."

I eased the car back up to seventy. Gradually, the blue car shrank in my rearview mirror.

"He's not speeding up," Jan said. "You see? It's just me losing a few more marbles. You can relax."

By the time we got off at the Lake George exit, I'd stopped checking my mirror every five seconds. The car was probably back there, but it had fallen from sight. Jan was visibly relieved.

It was 4:45 p.m., and my sense of the Google map I'd printed out before we'd left told me we were only five minutes away from Ted's Lakeview General Store. We wound our way up 9 North. I wasn't pushing it. I didn't want to arrive too early, and I didn't want to somehow speed past Ted's without seeing it.

As it turned out, it would have been hard to miss. It was the only thing along that wooded stretch of highway. It was a two-story white building set about fifty feet back from the road, a full set of self-serve gas pumps out front. I hit the blinker, came slowly off the main road, tires crunching on some loose gravel.

"So this is it," Jan said. "We just wait?"

I looked at the dashboard clock. Five minutes before five. "I guess." There were some parking spots off to one side, an old Plymouth Volare in one of them. I swung the car around in front of them, backed in alongside the Volare so I'd have a good view of the highway in both directions, then powered down the windows and turned off the engine.

There wasn't a lot of traffic. We'd be able to spot an approaching white pickup long before it turned in to the lot.

"What do you think this source is going to have for you?" Jan asked.

I shrugged. "I don't know. Private memos? Printouts of emails? Recorded phone calls? Maybe nothing. Maybe there're just things she wants to tell me. But it'll be a lot better if she has some actual proof. The *Standard*'s not going to run a word if I haven't got this thing cold."

Jan rubbed her forehead.

"You okay?"

"Just getting a headache. I've had one most of the way up. I feel like I could nod right off, to tell you the truth."

"You got some aspirin or Tylenol or something?"

"Yeah, in my purse. I'm going to go in, get a bottle of water or something else to drink. You want anything?"

"An iced tea?" I said.

Jan nodded, got out of the car, and went into the store. I kept my eyes on the road. A red Ford pickup drove past. Then a green Dodge SUV. A motorcyclist.

My dashboard clock read 5 p.m. on the dot. So she had ten minutes from now to show up.

Whoever she was.

A truck loaded with logs rumbled past. A blue Corvette convertible, top down, went screaming by, heading for Lake George.

Then, coming from the north, a pickup truck.

It was a couple of hundred yards away, pale in color. The way the afternoon sun was filtering through the trees, I wasn't sure whether it was white, pale yellow, or maybe silver.

But as the truck approached, I could see that it was a Ford, and that it was white.

The truck's turn signal went on. It waited for a Toyota Corolla coming from the south to get past, then turned into the lot. The truck rolled up to the self-serve pumps.

My heart was pounding.

The driver's door opened, and a man in his sixties stepped out. Tall, thin, unshaven, in a plaid work shirt and jeans. He slipped his credit card into the pump and started filling up.

He never once looked in my direction.

"Shit," I said.

I looked back out to the highway, just in time to see a blue Buick sedan drive by.

"Hello," I said under my breath.

The car was driving under the speed limit. Slow enough to take in what was going on at Ted's Lakeview General Store, but fast enough not to look like he was going to stop.

The thing was, I didn't know that it was a "he." The windows were well tinted. It might have been more than one "he." It might have been a "she."

The car kept heading north and eventually disappeared.

It was 5:05 p.m.

Jan came out of the store, a Snapple iced tea in one hand, a bottle of water in the other. She was talking even before she opened the passenger door.

"I'm in there and I'm thinking, what if he sees his contact and ends up driving away, leaving me here?"

"There's been no sign," I said. The white pickup at the pump had left before Jan returned. "But there was one interesting thing."

"Yeah?" she said, handing me my iced tea and cracking the plastic cap on the water.

"I saw what I think was our blue Buick driving by."

Jan said, "You're shittin' me."

"No. It was headed north and kept on going."

"Do you know for sure it was the same car?"

I shook my head. "But there was something about it as it drove past. Like whoever was inside was scanning this place."

Jan found some Tylenols and popped them into her mouth, then chased them down with the water. She looked at the clock. "Four minutes left," she said. "Is that clock right?"

I nodded. "But her clock might not be, so I'll hang in a few minutes extra. There's still time for her to show up."

I drank nearly half the iced tea in one gulp. I hadn't realized, until the cold liquid hit my tongue, just how parched I was. We sat for another five minutes, saying nothing, listening to the cars go by.

"There's a pickup," Jan said. But it was gray, and it did not turn in.

"From the north," I said, and Jan looked.

It was the blue Buick. Maybe two hundred yards away.

I opened my door.

"What are you doing?" Jan asked. "Get back in here."

But I was already heading across the parking lot. I wanted a better look at this car. I wanted a look at the license plate. I reached into my pocket and took out my digital recorder. I didn't have to write down the plate number. I could dictate it.

"David!" Jan called out. "Don't do it!"

I ran to the shoulder, recorder in hand. I turned it on. The Buick was a hundred yards away, and I could hear the driver giving more gas to the engine.

"Come on, you fucker," I said as the car closed the distance.

It was close enough now to read the plate. I'd forgotten it was plastered with dried mud. As the car zoomed past the general store, I waited to get a look at the back bumper, but that plate was muddied up as well—save for the last two numbers, 7 and 5, which I spoke breathlessly into my recorder. The car moved off at high speed and disappeared around the next bend.

I clicked off the recorder, put it in my pocket, and trudged back to the car.

"What were you thinking?" Jan asked.

"I wanted to get the plate," I said. "But it was covered up."

I got back into the car, shook my head. "Fuck," I said. "It was the same car, I'm sure of it. Someone knows. Someone found out about this meeting."

Which was why I wasn't surprised when, by 5:20 p.m., no woman in a white pickup had showed up at Ted's Lakeview General Store to give me the goods on Reeves and the rest of the Promise Falls councilors.

"It's not going to happen," I said.

"I'm sorry," Jan said. "I know how important this was to you. Do you want to hang in for a while longer?"

I gave it five more minutes, then turned the key.

On the way home, Jan's headache didn't get any better. She angled her seat back and slept most of the way. When we were almost to Promise Falls, she woke up long enough to say she didn't feel well and asked if I could drop her at home before I went to get Ethan.

By the time I got back with our son, Jan was in bed, asleep. I tucked him in myself.

"Is Mommy sick?" he asked.

"She's tired," I said.

"Is she going to be okay for tomorrow?"

"Tomorrow?" I said.

"We're going to the roller coasters," he said. "Did you forget?"

"Yeah, I guess I did for a minute there," I said, feeling pretty tired myself.

"Do I have to go on the big ones? They scare me."

"No," I said. "Just the fun rides, not the scary ones." I put my lips to his forehead. "We want it to be a good day."

I kissed him good night and went down the hall to our bedroom. I thought about asking Jan whether a trip to Five Mountains was really a good idea, but she was asleep. I undressed noiselessly, hit the light, and got under the covers.

I slid my hand down between the sheets until I found Jan's. I linked my fingers into hers, and even in sleep, instinctively, she returned the grip.

I felt comforted by the warmth of it. I didn't want to let go.

"I love you," I whispered as I slept next to my wife for the last time.

# PART TWO

# SEVEN

"WHERE'S MY SON?" I asked.

I was sitting in the air-conditioned reception area of the Five Mountains offices. They were tucked away, camouflaged, behind the old Colonial street front just in from the main gates. There were a number of people there. The park manager, a thirtyish woman with short blonde hair named Gloria Fenwick, a man in his twenties who was identified as her assistant and whose name I had not caught, and a woman barely twenty who was the Five Mountains publicity director. They were all dressed smart casual, unlike the other park employees in attendance, who were dressed identically in light tan shirts and slacks with their names embroidered on their chests.

But I wasn't asking any of them about Ethan. I was speaking to an overweight man named Barry Duckworth, a police detective with the Promise Falls department. His belly hung over his belt, and he was struggling to keep his sweat-stained white shirt tucked in.

"He's with one of my officers," Duckworth said. "Her name's Didi. She's very nice. She's just down the hall with him, getting him an ice cream. I hope that's okay?"

"Yeah, sure," I said. "How is he?"

"He's good," Duckworth said. "He seems fine. But I

thought it would be better if we had a chance to talk without your son here."

I nodded. I was feeling numb, dazed. It had been a couple of hours since I'd seen Jan.

"Tell me again what happened after you went out to the car," Duckworth said. Fenwick, her assistant, and the park publicist were hovering nearby. "I wonder if I might be able to speak to Mr. Harwood alone?" he asked them.

"Oh, sure, of course," said Fenwick. "But if you need anything . . ."

"You already have people reviewing the closed-circuit TV?" he asked.

"Of course, although we don't really know who or what we're looking for," she said. "If we had a picture of this woman, that would help a lot."

"You've got a description," he said. "Mid-thirties, five-eight, black hair, ponytail pulled through a baseball cap with . . . Red Sox on the front?" He looked at me for confirmation and I nodded. "Red top, white shorts. Look for someone like that, anything that seems out of the ordinary."

"Certainly, we'll do that, but you also know that we don't really have all the public areas equipped yet with closed circuit. We have cameras set up on all the rides, so we can see any technical problems early."

"I know," Duckworth said. "You've explained that." Now he looked at them and smiled, waiting for them to clear out. Once they had, he pulled out one of the reception chairs so he could sit looking straight at me.

"Okay," he said. "You went out to the car. What kind of car is it?"

I swallowed. My mouth was very dry. "An Accord. Jan's Jetta we left at home."

"Okay, so tell me."

"Ethan and I waited by the gate for about half an

hour. I'd been trying to reach my wife on her cell, but she wasn't answering. Finally, I wondered whether she might have gone back to the car. Maybe she was waiting for us there. So I took Ethan back through the gates and we went to the car, but she wasn't there."

"Was there any sign that she might have been there? That she'd dropped anything off there?"

I shook my head. "She had a backpack, with lunch things and probably a change of clothes for Ethan, with her, and I didn't see it in the car."

"Okay, then what did you do?"

"We came back to the park. I was thinking maybe she showed up when we went out to the parking lot. We showed our tickets again so we could get back in, then waited around just inside the gate, but she didn't show up."

"That was when you approached one of the park employees."

"I'd talked to one earlier, who asked security if Jan had been in touch, and she hadn't. But then, when we came back from the car, I found someone else, asked him if they had any reports of anything, like maybe Jan had collapsed, or fallen, you know? And he said he didn't think so, and he got on his radio, and when he couldn't turn up anything, I said we had to call the police."

Barry Duckworth nodded, like that had been a good idea.

"I need a drink of water," I said. "Are you sure Ethan's okay?"

"He's fine." There was a water fountain in the reception area. The detective got up, filled a paper cone with water, and handed it to me before sitting back down.

"Thank you." I drank the water in a single gulp. "Are you looking for that man?"

"What man is that?" he asked.

"The man I told you about."

"The one you saw running away?"

"That's right. I think he might have had a beard."

"Anything else you can tell me about him?"

"It was just for a second. I really didn't get a close look at him."

"And you think this man was running away from your child's stroller."

"That's right."

"Did you see this man take the stroller?"

"No."

"You didn't see him pushing it away?"

"No."

"How about when you found the stroller, was he holding on to it, standing by it, anything?"

"No, I told you, I just caught a glimpse of him running through the crowd when I found Ethan," I said.

"So he could have just been a man running through the crowd," the detective said.

I hesitated a moment, then nodded. "I just had a feeling."

"Mr. Harwood," Duckworth said, then stopped himself. "Your name. David Harwood. It seems familiar to me."

"Maybe you've seen the byline. I'm a reporter for the *Standard*. But I don't cover the police, so I don't think we've met."

"Yeah," Duckworth said. "I knew I knew it from someplace. We get the *Standard* delivered."

Suddenly something occurred to me. "Maybe she went home. Could she have gone home? Maybe she took a taxi or something?"

I expected Duckworth to leap up and have someone check, but he said, "We've already had someone go by your house, and it looks like no one's home. We knocked on the door, phoned, looked in the windows. Nothing seemed out of the ordinary."

I looked down at the floor, shook my head. Then, "Let me call my parents, see if she might have gone there."

Duckworth waited for me to fish out my cell and place the call.

"Hello?" My mother.

"Mom, it's me. Listen, is Jan there?"

"What? No. Why would she be here?"

"I'm just—we kind of lost contact with each other. If she shows up, would you call me right away?"

"Of course. But what do you mean, you lost—"

"I have to go, Mom. I'll talk to you later."

I flipped the phone shut and put it back into my pocket. Duckworth studied me with sad, knowing eyes.

"What about her own family?" he asked.

I shook my head. "There isn't anyone. I mean, not anyone she'd go see. She's an only child and she's estranged from her family. Hasn't seen them in years. For all I know, her parents are dead."

"Friends?"

Again, I shook my head. "Not really. No one she spends time with."

"Work friends?"

"There's one other woman in the office, Leanne Kowalski, at Bertram's Heating and Cooling. But they aren't close. Leanne and Jan don't really connect."

"Why's that?"

"Leanne's a bit rough around the edges. I mean, they get along, but they don't have girls' nights out or anything."

The detective wrote down Leanne's name just the same.

"Now, some of these questions may seem insensitive," Duckworth said, "but I need to ask them."

"Go ahead."

"Has your wife ever had episodes where she wandered off, behaved strangely, anything like that?"

I took probably one second longer to answer than I should have. "No."

Duckworth caught that. "You're sure?"

"Yes," I said.

"How about—and my apologies for asking this—an affair? Could she be seeing anyone else?"

I shook my head. "No."

"Have the two of you had any arguments lately? Cross words between you?"

"No," I said. "Look, we should be out looking for her, not sitting around here."

"There are people looking, Mr. Harwood. You sure you don't have a picture of her on you? A wallet shot? On your cell phone?"

I rarely used my phone for pictures. "I have some at home."

"By the time you get home, maybe we'll have found her," he said reassuringly. "If not, you have some you could email me?"

"Yes."

"Okay, so, in the meantime, let's put our heads together to see whether there's a way to narrow down this search."

I nodded.

Duckworth said, "Let's go back to my earlier question. The one about whether your wife has had any episodes lately."

"Yes?"

"What weren't you telling me there? I could see it in your eyes, you were holding something back."

"Okay, I was telling you the truth, she's never wandered off or done anything like that. But there is something . . .

this is very hard for me to even think about, let alone talk about it."

Duckworth waited.

"Are there any bridges around here?" I asked.

"I'm sorry?"

"Not big ones, like on the interstate, but smaller ones, over creeks or anything?"

"I'm sure there are, Mr. Harwood. Why would you be asking that?"

"The last couple of weeks, my wife . . . she hasn't totally been herself."

"Okay," he said patiently.

"She's been feeling . . . depressed. She's said some things. . . ."

I felt myself starting to get overwhelmed.

"Mr. Harwood?"

"I just need . . . a second." I held my hand tightly over my mouth. I had to hold it together. I took a moment to focus. "The last couple of weeks, she's been having these thoughts."

"Thoughts?"

"About . . . harming herself. Suicidal thoughts. I mean, I don't think she's actually tried to do it. Well, she had this bandage on her wrist, but she swears that was just an accident when she was peeling vegetables, and she did go out to this bridge, but—"

"She tried to jump off a bridge?" Duckworth asked straightforwardly.

"She drove out to one, but she didn't jump. A truck came along." I felt I was rambling. "Jan's been feeling like . . . like everything was too much. She told me the other night she thought Ethan and I would be better off without her."

"Why do you think she would say something like that?"

"I don't know. It's like her brain just short-circuited

these last few days. It was yesterday she told me about driving out to that bridge, standing on the railing until the truck showed up."

"That must have been very hard to hear."

I nodded. "It was." I was holding back tears. "Very."

"Did you suggest that she go talk to someone?"

"I already had. I'd been to see our doctor, Dr. Samuels." Duckworth seemed to recognize the name and nodded. "I told him about the changes in Jan's behavior, and he said she should see him. So I talked her into it, and she saw him the other day, but this was before the bridge incident. She says she did that after she went to see the doctor."

"Was she on any kind of medication?"

"No. In fact, I asked her about that. I was hoping he might prescribe something for her, but she said she didn't want drugs changing who she was. She said she could deal with this without taking anything."

"Would you excuse me a moment?" Duckworth said, reaching into his jacket for his cell phone. He slipped outside the door before placing a call. I couldn't hear everything he said, but I made out the words "creek" and "suicide."

I just sat there, rubbing my hands together, wanting to get up and leave that room, do something besides wasting my time while—

Duckworth came back in, sat back down.

"Do you think it's possible that's what she did?" he asked. "That she may have taken her own life?"

"I don't know," I said. "I hope to God not."

"We're doing an extensive search of the grounds, of the park itself," he said. "As well, we're searching beyond the park, looking at the other cars out there, talking to people."

"Thank you," I said. "But I'm confused about one

thing." I shook my head. "I'm confused about a lot of things."

"What is it?"

"My son. Why did someone run off with my son?"

"I can't say," Duckworth said. "It's a good thing he's okay."

I felt a minor wave of relief. It was true. At least Ethan was safe. There was no indication anyone had done anything to him.

"Isn't it a hell of a coincidence that someone would take off with Ethan at the same time as my wife goes missing?" I asked.

The detective nodded thoughtfully. "Yes," he said.

Fenwick, the park manager, had reappeared. "Detective?" she said.

"Yeah?"

"We have something you might want to see."

"What?" I said. I was on my feet. "You've found her?" But she wouldn't look at me, only Duckworth.

"What?" I asked again.

She led Duckworth, with me following, to a cubicle with fabric-covered partitions. The young publicist was sitting at a computer with some grainy black-and-white images on the screen.

She said, "Our people in security were reviewing some images from the gate around the time the Harwoods arrived."

I looked at the screen. The camera must have been mounted just inside the park, looking at the gate. I recalled that there were half a dozen booths, lined up in a row, where guests bought tickets, or showed the ones they'd bought online. The image on the screen showed one booth, and there, in the crush of people arriving for a day of fun, were Ethan and I.

"It was actually not that tricky," the young woman at the keyboard said. "They entered the name 'Harwood' into the system, which brought up the ticket info, and that showed the time of entry into Five Mountains."

"Yeah, thàt's us," I said, pointing.

"Where's your wife?" Duckworth asked me.

I started to point, then said, "She wasn't with us then. Ethan and I entered the park on our own."

Duckworth's eyes seemed to narrow. "Why was that, Mr. Harwood?"

"She forgot the backpack. We were almost to the gate, and then she remembered, and she told us to go on ahead, we'd meet up later by the ice-cream place."

"And that's what you did? You and your son came in on your own?"

"That's right."

"But that's not the last time you saw your wife."

"No, she came in later and joined us."

Duckworth nodded, then said to the publicist, "Can your people get some pics from the area of the ice-cream stand?"

She half-turned in her chair. "No," she said. "We don't have any cameras there at this point. Just on the gates and the rides. Our plan is to put in more cameras, in more locations, but we're still relatively new, you understand, and we've been prioritizing where CCTV is concerned."

Duckworth didn't say anything. He studied me for a moment before saying he wanted to check in with his people. He was moving for the door.

"I want to get Ethan," I said.

"Absolutely," he said, nodding his head in agreement. Then he went into the hall and closed the door behind him.

# EIGHT

BARRY DUCKWORTH WALKED DOWN the hall and turned into a room gridded with cubicles. The Promise Falls police detective guessed that on a weekday, these desks would be filled with people conducting the business end of things for Five Mountains park, but unlike the workers who actually ran the rides and sold the tickets and emptied the trash, they got Saturday and Sunday off.

The park manager didn't have to be called in. Five Mountains was still a new attraction in the upper New York State area, and Saturdays were always the busiest. Fenwick had called in her publicist the moment she suspected this could turn into a public relations nightmare for the park. If Jan Harwood had somehow wandered into the mechanism of a roller coaster, or drowned in one of the shallow waterways that ran through the grounds, or choked on a Five Mountains hot dog, they needed to be on top of that.

As if that weren't enough, there was this business of a kid in a stroller being wheeled away from his parents. Once that news started getting out there, hold on to your hat, buster. Before you knew it, parents would be hearing that some tot had been carved up for body parts at the face-painting booth.

There were only two people in this other office. Didi Campion, a uniformed officer in her mid-thirties, and

Ethan Harwood. They were sitting across from each other on office chairs, Campion leaning over, her arms on her knees, Ethan sitting on the edge of his chair, legs dangling.

"Hey," Duckworth said.

All that remained of an ice-cream treat Ethan had been eating was an inch of cone. His tired eyes found Duckworth. The child looked bewildered and very small. He said nothing.

"Ethan and I were just talking about trains," Didi Campion said.

"You like trains, Ethan?" Duckworth asked.

Ethan nodded. He drew his lips in, like he was doing everything he could not to say anything.

"We're going to get you back with your dad in just a minute," Duckworth said. "That okay with you?"

Another nod.

"Would you mind if I talked with Officer Campion over here for just a second? We're not going anyplace."

Ethan looked from Duckworth to Campion and his eyes flashed with worry. Duckworth could see that the boy had already formed an attachment to the policewoman.

"I'll be right back," Campion assured him and touched his knee.

She got out of the chair and joined Duckworth a few feet away.

"Well?" he asked her.

"He wants to see his parents. Both of them. He's asking where they are."

"What else did he tell you? What about the person who took him away in his stroller?"

"He doesn't know anything about it. I think he slept through the whole thing. And he said he and his father were waiting and waiting for his mother to come but she didn't."

Duckworth leaned in. "Did he say when he last saw her?"

Campion sighed. "I don't know if he quite got what I was trying to ask him. He just keeps saying he wants to go home, that he doesn't want to go on any of the roller coasters, not even the small rides. And he wants his mom and dad."

Duckworth nodded. "Okay, I'll take the kid back to his father in just a second." Campion took that as a sign that they were done, and she went back to sit with Ethan.

The door edged open. It was Fenwick. "Detective?"

"Yes."

"I know you have your own people out combing the grounds, but Five Mountains personnel have searched every square inch of the grounds and they're reporting back that they haven't found any sign of this woman. I mean, in any kind of distress. No woman passed out in any restrooms, not in any of the areas that are off-limits to guests, no indication that she fell or came to any kind of harm anywhere at all. I really think, at this point, it would be best if the police presence in the park were scaled back. It's making people nervous."

"Which people?" Duckworth asked.

"Our guests," Fenwick said defensively. "They can't help but think something's wrong, with all these police around. They'll start thinking terrorists have put bombs on the roller coasters or something like that."

"How about the parking lot?" Duckworth asked.

"It's been searched," Fenwick said confidently.

Duckworth held up a finger and got out his cell, punched in a number. "Yeah, Smithy, how ya doin'. I want someone at the exit scoping out every car as it leaves. See if there's anyone in any of them matches the description of this missing woman. You see someone like that, if she's acting funny, you hang on to that car till I get there."

Fenwick looked like she'd bitten into a lemon. "Tell me you're not going to search every car that leaves here."

"No," he said, but he wished he could. He wished he had the authority to make everyone pop their trunk as they left for home. Duckworth had a feeling that anything he did about cars in the lot amounted to doing too little too late. If Jan Harwood had run into trouble, if someone had stuffed her into a trunk, they could have left the lot a couple of hours ago. But you did what you could.

"This is terrible, just terrible," Fenwick said. "We don't need this kind of publicity. If this woman wandered off because she has mental problems or something, that's hardly our fault. Is that man planning to sue us? Is this some setup to get money out of us?"

"Would you like me to convey your concerns to Mr. Harwood?" Duckworth asked. "I'm sure, as a writer for the *Standard,* he'd love to do a piece on your outpouring of sympathy for his situation."

She blanched. "He works for the paper?"

Duckworth nodded.

Fenwick moved around the detective and dropped to her knees in front of Ethan. "How are you doing there? I bet you'd love another ice-cream cone."

Duckworth's cell, which was still in his hand, rang. He put it to his ear. "Yeah."

"It's Gunner here, Detective. I'm down in the security area. We patched that video of the guy and his kid going through the gates a few minutes ago up to the main office."

"I just saw it."

"They couldn't pick out the wife in those, right?"

"That's right. Mr. Harwood says his wife had gone

back to the car to get something and told him to go on ahead."

"Yeah, okay, so she would have come into the park a few minutes later, then, right?"

"Yeah," Duckworth said.

"So what we did before was, because the Harwoods ordered their tickets online, and printed them out, we were able to pinpoint at what time those tickets got scanned and processed at the gate."

"I got that."

"So then we thought, we'll look for when the third ticket, the wife's, got processed at the gate, and then when we had that we could find the closed-circuit image for that time."

"What's the problem?" Duckworth asked.

"Nothing's coming up."

"What do you mean? You saying she never came into the park?"

"I don't know. Here's the thing. I've got them checking their ticket sales records, all the stuff that gets bought in advance online, and they only show two tickets being purchased on the Harwoods' Visa. One adult and one kid."

# NINE

THE DOOR OPENED AND Ethan ran in. I scooped him up in my arms and held on to him tight, patted the back of his head.

"You okay?" I asked. He nodded. "They were nice to you?"

"I had an ice cream. A lady wanted to get me another, but Mom would be mad if I had two."

"We never really had any lunch," I said.

"Where's Mommy?" Ethan asked, but not with any sense of worry.

"We're going home now," I said.

"Is she home?"

I glanced at Duckworth, who had followed Ethan into the room. There was nothing in his expression.

"Let's just go home," I said. "And then maybe we'll see Nana and Poppa."

Still holding Ethan, I said to Duckworth, my voice low, "What do we do now?"

He breathed in and then exhaled, his belly going in and out. "You head home. First thing, you send me a picture. If you hear anything, you get in touch with me." He had already given me his card. "And we'll call if there are any developments."

"Of course."

"Maybe start making up a list, anyone your wife

might have called, anyone she might have gotten in touch with."

"Of course," I said.

"Tell me again how you bought your tickets for today?"

"I told you. From the website."

"You ordered them?"

"Jan did," I said.

"So it wasn't actually you who sat down at the computer to do it, it was your wife."

I didn't understand the point of this. "That's what I just said."

Duckworth seemed to be mulling this over.

"Is there something wrong?" I asked.

"Only two tickets were bought online," he said. "One adult ticket, one child."

I blinked. "Well, that doesn't make much sense. There must be some mistake. She was in the park. They wouldn't have let her in the gate without a ticket. There's been some kind of mix-up."

"And I'm asking them to look into that. But if it turns out only one adult ticket was purchased, does that figure?"

It didn't. But if that was what had happened, I could think of at least one possible explanation.

"Maybe Jan made a mistake," I offered. "Sometimes, ordering online, it's easy to do that. I was booking a hotel online once, and the website froze up for a second, and when I got the confirmation it said I'd booked two rooms when I only wanted one."

Duckworth's head went up and down slowly. "That's a possibility."

The only problem with my theory was that, on the way into Five Mountains, Jan had taken out of her purse all our tickets. She had handed me mine and one for Ethan, and made a point of keeping one for herself so she could get into the park after she went back to the car for her backpack.

She hadn't mentioned any ticket problem when she'd found us inside the gate.

I was about to mention this to Duckworth, but stopped myself, because I suddenly had another theory that was too upsetting to discuss aloud, certainly not in front of Ethan, who had wrapped his arms around my neck.

Maybe Jan never bought a ticket because she was thinking she might not be around to use it. Maybe that piece of paper she was flashing wasn't a ticket after all.

*No point buying a ticket if you know you're going to kill yourself.*

But could Jan have seriously thought that if she killed herself, we'd head off to Five Mountains to celebrate?

"Something?" Duckworth said.

"No," I said. "I just, I don't know what to say. I really need to get Ethan home and get that picture to you."

"Absolutely," he said and moved aside to let me leave.

Leaving Five Mountains was a surreal experience.

Once I had Ethan in his stroller, we exited the offices and were back in the park, not far from the main gate. We were surrounded by the sounds of children and adults laughing. Balloons bobbed and, when the children holding them loosened their grips on the strings, soared skyward. Upbeat music blared from food stands and gift shops. Above us, roller-coaster passengers screamed with terrified delight.

Fun and pandemonium everywhere we looked.

I held on tight to the stroller handles and kept on pushing. We went past a couple of Promise Falls uniformed cops, but they were doing more ambling than searching. Perhaps there was no place else to look.

At least not here.

Ethan swung around and tried to eye me from his stroller seat. "Is Mommy home?" It had to be the fifth time he'd asked.

I didn't answer. First of all, I didn't have an answer to his question. And second, I did not have high hopes. I couldn't shake the feeling that something very bad had happened to Jan. That Jan had done something very bad to herself.

*Don't let it be true.*

Once we got to the car, I placed Ethan in his seat, buckled him in, dumped his toys within reach. "I'm hungry," he said. "Can I have a sandwich?"

"A sandwich?"

"Mom put sandwiches in her backpack."

There was no backpack. Not now.

"We'll get something to eat when we get home," I said. "Just hang in there. It won't take long."

"Where's Batman?"

"What?"

Ethan was sorting through his action figures. Spider-Man, Robin, Joker, Wolverine. A melding of the Marvel and DC universes. "Batman!"

"I'm sure he's there," I said.

"He's gone!"

I searched around his safety seat and down in the crevices of the car upholstery.

"Maybe it fell out," Ethan said.

"Fell out where?" I asked.

He just looked at me, like I was supposed to know.

I searched under the front seats, thinking Batman could have fallen and gotten tucked under there.

Ethan was crying.

"Damn it, Ethan!" I shouted. "You think we don't have enough to worry about right now?"

I reached my hand an inch farther and got hold of something. A tiny leg. I pulled out Batman and handed it to Ethan, who took the Caped Crusader happily into his hands, then tossed it onto the seat next to him to play with something else.

There was a huge traffic backup getting out of Five Mountains. Everyone was being stopped by the police on their way out, a cop peering inside, doing a walk-around like it was a border crossing. It took us twenty minutes to reach the exit, and I powered down my window when the cop leaned forward to talk to me.

"Excuse me, sir, we're just doing a check of cars as they leave. Just take a moment." No explanation offered.

"I'm the guy," I said.

"I'm sorry?"

"My wife is the one you're looking for. Jan Harwood. I have to get home so I can email a photo of her to Detective Duckworth."

He nodded and waved us on.

From the back seat, Ethan said, "The police lady told me a joke."

"What?"

"She said you would like it because you're a reporter."

"Okay, what is it?"

"What's black and white and red all over?"

"I give up," I said.

"A newspaper," Ethan said and cackled. He waited a beat, and said, "I don't get it." Another pause. "Is Mom making dinner?"

As we came in the door Ethan shouted, "Mom!"

I was about to join in and shout out Jan's name, but I decided to wait and see whether Ethan got a reply.

"Mom?" he yelled a second time.

"I don't think she's home," I said. "You go in and watch some TV and I'll just make sure."

He trundled off obediently to the family room while I did a quick search of the house. I ran up to our bedroom, checked the bathroom, Ethan's bedroom. Then I was back to the main floor and down the steps into our unfinished basement. It didn't take more than a second to realize she wasn't there. The only place left to check was the garage.

There was a connecting door between the kitchen and the garage, and as I put my hand on it I hesitated.

Jan's Jetta had been in the driveway when we'd pulled in. So her car was not in the garage.

*So at least she couldn't have—*

Open the damn door, I told myself. I turned the knob and stepped into the one-car garage. It was as messy and disorganized as always.

And there was no one in it.

There were two large plastic Rubbermaid garbage containers in the corner. It had never occurred to me before that they were each large enough to hold a person, but my mind was going places it had never gone before. I approached the cans, put my hand on the lid of the first one, held it there a moment, and then lifted it off.

Inside was a bag of garbage.

The second can was empty.

Back in the kitchen, I found our laptop, folded shut, beside the phone, half buried in mail from the last couple of days and a handful of flyers.

I took it over to the kitchen table, hit the on button, and drummed my fingers waiting for it to do its thing. Once it was up and running, I opened the photo program. We had gone to Chicago last fall, and it was the last time I'd moved pictures from the digital camera into the computer.

I looked through the photos. Jan and Ethan standing under the passenger jet at the Museum of Science and Industry. Another one of them in front of the Burlington

Zephyr streamlined passenger train. The two of them wandering through Millennium Park, eating cheese corn from Garrett's, their fingers and mouths orange with cheese powder.

Most of the pictures were of Jan and Ethan, since I was the one who usually took the pictures. But there was one shot of Ethan and me together, down by the water, sailboats in the background, him sitting on my lap.

I zeroed in on two shots that were particularly good of Jan. Her black hair, longer last fall than now, partly covered the left side of her face, but not enough to obscure her features. Her brown eyes, soft cheekbones, small nose, the almost imperceptible L-shaped scar on the left side of her chin, the one she got falling off a bike when she was in her teens. At her throat, a slender necklace with a small pendant designed to look like a cupcake, with diamondlike frosting and cake of gold, something Jan had had since she was a child.

I dug Detective Duckworth's card from my pocket and sent the picture to the email address that was embossed on it. I added two more pictures—not quite as good, but from different angles—to the email, just to be sure he had enough.

I added a note to the last one. "I think the first shot shows her best, but I added a couple more. I'm going to look for more and will send them to you. Please call if you hear anything." I also printed out a couple dozen copies of that first shot.

I reached over for the phone and set it on the kitchen table. I didn't want to wait for Duckworth to check his emails. I wanted him to know he had the photos now, so I dialed his cell.

"Duckworth," he said.

"It's David Harwood," I said. "I just sent you the pictures."

"You're home?"

"Yes."

"Any sign of her? Phone message, anything?"

There'd been no flashing light, and there were no new email messages. "Nothing," I said.

"Okay, well, we'll get those pictures of your wife out right away."

"I'll talk to the *Standard*," I said, thinking that my next call would be to the city desk. There was still time to get Jan's picture in the Sunday edition.

"Why don't you let us handle that," Duckworth said. "I think it might be better if any releases about this are funneled through a single source, you know?"

"But—"

"Mr. Harwood, it's only been a few hours. In a lot of cases we don't even move on a missing-persons case this quickly, but given some of the circumstances, the fact that it happened at Five Mountains, well, that kind of raised the priority level, if you get what I'm saying."

I listened.

"The fact is, your wife might just walk in the door tonight and this will all be over. That happens, you know."

"You think that's what's going to happen this time?"

"Mr. Harwood, we don't know. I'm just saying we might want to give this a few more hours before we issue a release. I'm not saying we won't, I'm just saying we'll revisit this in another hour or so."

"In an hour or so," I said.

"I'll be in touch," he said. "And thank you for these pictures. This is a real help. Absolutely."

I found Ethan on the floor, sitting on his haunches, watching *Family Guy*.

"Ethan, you're not watching that." I picked up the remote and killed the TV. "I've told you not to watch that!"

He whispered, "I'm sorry." His lower lip protruded.

It was the second time I'd screamed at him since all of this had started. I took him into my arms, pulled him in close to me. "I didn't mean to yell at you. I'm sorry."

I looked into his face and tried to smile. "You okay?"

He nodded, sniffed. "When's Mommy coming home?" he asked, probably thinking she wouldn't be so mean to him.

"I just sent some pictures of Mommy to the police so if they see her they can tell her we're here waiting for her."

"Why are the police looking for her? Did she rob something?" Worry washed over his face.

"No, she didn't do anything like that. The police aren't looking for her because she did a bad thing. They're looking for her to help her."

"Help her what?"

"Help her find her way home," I said.

"She should have taken her car," Ethan said.

"What?"

"She has the TV map in it."

The navigation screen.

"I don't know if it's that kind of lost," I said. "You know what I think we should do? I think we should head over to see Nana and Poppa, see what they're up to."

"I just want to stay here in case Mom comes home."

"I'll tell you what," I said. "We'll write her a note so she knows where we are. Would you help me with that?"

Ethan ran up to his room and returned with some blank paper and his box of crayons.

"Can I write it?" he asked.

"Sure," I said.

I set him up at the kitchen table. He got his face right down to the paper, watching the path of his crayon.

He'd been working on his letters, even though he wasn't yet in school.

He randomly printed several capital letters, some of them backward.

"Great," I said. "Now let's go." When he wasn't looking, I wrote at the bottom of the page: *Jan. Gone to my parents with Ethan. PLEASE call.*

I had to wait while he ran around gathering a different collection of figures and cars. I wanted to get moving, but didn't have it in me to speak harshly to him again.

I got him belted in once again and we drove across town to my parents' house. I didn't often arrive unannounced. I usually gave them some sort of courtesy call. But I knew I couldn't talk to them on the phone about this.

"When we get there, you go on in and watch TV. I need to talk to Nana and Poppa for a while."

"But not *Family Guy,*" Ethan said.

"That's right," I said.

My mother happened to be looking out the front window when we pulled into the driveway. Dad was holding the door open by the time Ethan was bounding up the stairs to the porch. He slipped past my father and ran into the house.

Dad stepped out, Mom right behind him. Dad was looking at the car.

"Where's Jan?" he asked.

I collapsed into my father's arms and began to weep.

# TEN

DR. ANDREW SAMUELS HATED to think of himself as a cliché, but couldn't shake the feeling that that's exactly what he was.

He was a doctor, and he was golfing. Cops ate donuts, postal workers shot each other, and doctors played golf.

He hated golf.

He hated everything about it. He hated the walking, he hated having to put on sunscreen when it was a blistering hot day. He hated waiting for the dumb bastards on the next green dicking around, taking their time when he was ready to shoot. He hated the tacky clothes you were expected to wear. But more than anything else, he hated the whole idea of it, using up thousands upon thousands of acres of land so men and women could chase around little balls and drop them into tiny holes in the ground. What a fucking ridiculous idea.

But despite his feelings about the game, Samuels had an expensive set of clubs and the spiked shoes and he even maintained a membership at the Promise Falls Golf and Country Club because it was more or less expected in this town that if you were the mayor or a doctor or a lawyer or a prominent businessman, you were a member. If you weren't, all anyone could assume was that you were sliding inexorably to the bottom of the Promise Falls food chain.

So here he was, on a glorious Saturday afternoon, on

the fifteenth hole with his wife's brother, Stan Reeves, a Promise Falls councilman, first-class gasbag, and all-around asshole. Reeves had been suggesting for months that they get out and play eighteen holes, and Samuels had been able to hold him off up to now, but had finally run out of excuses. No more out-of-town trips, no weddings, and, sadly, no weekend funerals to attend.

"You're slicing a bit to the right, there," Reeves said after Samuels took his tee shot. "Watch me."

Samuels put his driver back into his bag and pretended to watch his brother-in-law.

"You see how the center of my body never moves when I'm swinging? Let me just do it for you in slow motion here."

*Only three holes left after this one,* Samuels thought. You could see the clubhouse from here. He could get in his cart, cut across the seventeenth and eighteenth fairways, and be back in the air-conditioned restaurant in four minutes, an ice-cold Sam Adams in front of him. It was, he admitted, the one thing he liked about the game.

"Did you see that?" Reeves said. "Perfect drive. I don't even know where yours ended up."

"Somewhere," Samuels said.

"This is good, huh?" Reeves said. "We don't do this enough."

"It's been a while," Samuels said.

"Takes your mind off things. I'm sure you've got your share of stress being a doctor, but let me tell you, running a city, that's a twenty-four/seven kind of thing, you know?"

Reeves was such a jerk, it made Samuels wonder whatever happened to the former mayor, Randall Finley.

"I don't know how you do it," Samuels said.

And then his cell rang.

"Aw, come on, you didn't leave that on, did you?" Reeves whined.

"Hang on," Samuels said, reaching eagerly into his pocket for his phone. *Let it be an emergency,* he thought. He could be at the hospital in fifteen minutes.

"Hello?" he said.

"Dr. Samuels?"

"Speaking."

"My name's Barry Duckworth, a detective with the Promise Falls police."

"Detective, how are you today?"

Reeves perked up at the mention of the word.

"Not too bad. I gather you're out on the course some-place. I called your service and they told me and gave me your number when I leaned on them."

"No problem. What's up?"

"I'd like to talk to you in person. Now."

"I'm at the Promise Falls Golf and Country Club, fif-teenth hole."

"I'm already at the clubhouse."

"I'll be right there." He put the phone back into his pocket. "You'll have to finish without me, Stan."

"What's going on?"

Samuels put up his hands in mock bafflement. "I guess I'm going to get a taste of what it's like for you, this being on call at all hours."

"Hey, if you take the cart, I'm going to have to—"

But Samuels was already driving away.

Barry Duckworth was outside waiting by the pro shop, where golfers dropped off their carts. He shook hands with Dr. Samuels, who said, "Can I buy you a drink?"

"Don't have time," Duckworth said. "I need to ask you about one of your patients."

Samuels's bushy gray eyebrows shot up momentarily. "Who?"

"Jan Harwood."

"What's happened?"

"She's disappeared. She and her husband, David Harwood, and their son went to spend the day at Five Mountains, and she went missing."

"Dear God," said Samuels.

"A thorough search has been done of the park, although I'd still like to take another run at it." Duckworth led Samuels into the building's shade, not just to get out of the heat, but to distance themselves from other golfers who might be listening.

"Mr. Harwood thinks it's possible his wife may have killed herself."

Samuels nodded, then shook his head. "Oh, this is just terrible. She's a very nice woman, you know."

"I'm sure she is," Duckworth said. "Mr. Harwood said she's been depressed the last couple of weeks. Mood swings, talking about how the rest of her family would be better off without her."

"When was this?" Samuels asked.

"A day or two ago, if my understanding of what Mr. Harwood said is correct."

"But it's still possible that she's just missing, that she hasn't killed herself or anything," the doctor said. "You haven't found her."

"That's right. That's why there's a sense of urgency about this."

"What is it I can do for you, Detective?"

"I don't want to violate patient-doctor confidentiality here, but if you have any idea where she might go, what she might do, just how serious the threat is that she might kill herself, I'd really appreciate it."

"I don't think I can be much help here."

"Please, Dr. Samuels. I'm not asking you for personal details, just something that might help us find this woman before she does any harm to herself."

"Detective, if I knew anything, I'd tell you, I really would. I wouldn't stand behind some privacy shield. I want you to find her, alive and well, as much as any-one."

"Did she tell you anything, anything at all, that would indicate to you whether she might take her own life, or whether she was just, I don't know, trying to get attention?"

"She didn't tell me anything, Detective."

"Nothing? A place she might go to think things over?"

"She didn't tell me anything because she hasn't been to see me."

The detective blinked. "Say again?"

"I saw her . . . maybe eight months ago? Just routine. But she didn't come see me about being depressed or sui-cidal. I wish she had."

"But Mr. Harwood says he went to see you about her. That you told him to convince his wife that she should make an appointment with you."

"That's all true. David came in last week, very con-cerned. And I told him I needed to talk to her myself to make an assessment, and possibly refer her to someone else for counseling."

"And she never came in?"

The doctor shook his head.

"Because Mr. Harwood," Duckworth said, "told me she saw you."

Samuels shook his head. "I kept waiting for her to make an appointment, but she never did. This is just ter-rible. I should have called her myself, but then she would have known her husband had been to see me. Oh shit. If I'd called her, maybe we wouldn't be having this conversation now."

# ELEVEN

ONCE I'D PULLED MYSELF together, Mom and Dad and I sat down at the kitchen table to talk things out. Ethan was in the living room, having a heated discussion with the various vehicles he owned from the *Cars* cartoon movie.

"Maybe she's just gone to think things over," Dad said. "You know how women can be sometimes. They get a bee in their bonnet and have to go sort things out for a while. I'm sure she'll be getting in touch any minute now."

Mom reached out a hand and placed it over mine. "Maybe if we put our heads together, we can think about where she might have gone."

"I've been doing that," I said. "She wasn't home, she didn't come here. I don't know where to begin."

"What about her friends?" Mom asked, but even as she asked it she must have known what my answer would be.

"She doesn't really have any close ones," I said. "She's never been a joiner. She probably talks more to Leanne at the office than anyone else, and she doesn't even like her."

Ethan walked in, ran a toy car across the table, going "Vroom!"

"Ethan," I said, "scoot." He did two laps of the

kitchen, "vrooming" the whole time, then returned to the living room.

"We should call her anyway," Mom said, and I agreed that was a good idea. I didn't know her number, so Mom grabbed the book and opened it to the K's.

She found a listing for an L. Kowalski and I dialed as she called out the number to me.

Two rings and then, "Yep?"

"Lyall?"

"Yep."

"Dave Harwood here. Jan's husband."

"Yeah, sure, Dave. How's it going?"

I dodged the question. "Is Leanne there?"

"She must be out shopping," he said. He sounded hungover. "And taking her time getting back. Anything I can help you with?"

Did I want to get into it with him, about Jan's disappearance? There was nothing in Lyall's voice to suggest he had even an inkling anything was wrong, but he must have found it odd that I'd be calling for his wife.

"That's okay," I said. "I'll try her later."

"What's this about?"

"I wanted to bounce a gift idea off her, something for Jan."

"Okay," he said, satisfied. "I'll tell her you called."

Everyone was quiet for a moment after I hung up the phone. Then Dad said, very matter-of-factly and just a little too loud, "I just can't believe she'd kill herself."

"For God's sake, Don, keep your voice down," Mom hissed at him. "Ethan's just in the other room."

It wasn't likely Ethan would have heard over all the car noises he was making.

"Sorry," Dad said anyway. He had a habit of talking louder than he had to, and it had nothing to do with hearing loss. He heard everything fine, but always assumed no one else was ever really listening. With Mom, it was often the case. "But still, she doesn't seem the type to have done it."

"The last couple of weeks, though," I said, "this change came over her."

Mom used her hand to wipe away a tear running down her cheek. "I know what your father is saying, though. I just didn't see any signs."

"Before a couple of weeks ago, I hadn't either," I said. "But I'm guessing they must have been there and I wasn't paying attention."

"Tell me again what she said to you at the restaurant," Mom said.

I took a moment. It was hard to say these things out loud without getting choked up. "She said something along the lines of I'd be happy if she was gone. That Ethan and I would be better off. Why would she say something like that?"

"She wasn't in her right mind," Dad said. "Any fool can tell that. For the life of me, I can't figure what she'd be unhappy about. She's got a good husband, a wonderful boy, you've got a nice house, you both got good jobs. What's the problem? I'm telling you, I just don't get it."

Mom sighed, looked at me. Her face said, *Pay no attention to him.* She turned to Dad and said, "Just because you've got a man and a roof over your head doesn't mean your life is perfect."

He made a face. "What are you getting at?"

Mom shook her head and looked at me. "I didn't think he'd get that one." It was her attempt to lighten the mood.

"I was only making a point," Dad said. He frowned, stared down at the table. It was then that I noticed his eyes were welling up with tears.

"Dad," I said, clutching his hand.

He pulled it away, got up from the table, and walked out of the kitchen.

"He doesn't want to show how upset he is," Mom said. "Any time you have problems, it tears him apart."

I wanted to get up and go after him, but Mom held on to my hand. "He'll be back in a minute. Give him a second to pull himself together."

In the other room, I heard him say to Ethan, "Hey, kiddo. Did I show you the train catalogues I picked up?"

Ethan said, "I'm watching TV."

"How much does Ethan know?" Mom asked me.

"Not much. He knows his mother hasn't come home, and he knows the police are looking for her. He thought that meant she'd robbed a bank or something, but I told him she hadn't done anything like that."

Mom smiled in spite of everything, but only for a moment.

Something had been niggling at me. "There's somewhere I have to go," I said.

"What? Where?"

"That bridge."

"Bridge?"

"The one Jan talked about jumping from. I mentioned to the police that they should check bridges near the park, and I think they did, but the one she told me about, it's up that road that goes to Miller's Garden Center, west of town."

"I know the one."

"The police won't have checked it. I never mentioned it specifically."

"David," Mom said, "call the police and let them check."

"I don't know how soon they'll get to it. I have to do something now. You'll watch Ethan?"

"Of course. Take your father."

"No, that's okay."

"Take him," she said. "It will make him feel like he's doing something, too."

I nodded. "Hey, Dad," I called into the living room. He came back, composed. "Take a ride with me."

"Where we goin'?"

"I'll explain on the way."

We took my car, which made Dad fidgety. He'd never been a good passenger. If he wasn't behind the wheel, he figured there was a pretty good chance we were going to die.

"You got a red up there," he said.

"I see it, Dad," I said, taking my foot off the gas as we approached the light. It turned green before we got there, and I tromped on it.

"You get bad mileage that way," Dad said. "Hitting the accelerator hard, then hitting the brake instead of slowing down gradual. That's what sucks up the gas."

"You've said."

He glanced over at me. "Sorry."

I gave him a smile. "It's okay."

"How you holding up?"

"Not so good," I said.

"You can't give up hope," he said. "It's way too early for that."

"I know," I said.

"So you know just where this bridge is?"

"Pretty sure," I said. We were out of Promise Falls now, heading west. Only a couple of miles out I found the county road I was looking for. Two-lane, paved. The road went through a variety of topography. There was wide-open farmland, then dense woods, followed by more farmland. The bridge spanned a creek that flowed through a heavily treed area.

"Up ahead," I said.

It wasn't much of a bridge. Maybe fifty or sixty feet across, asphalt over cement, with three-foot-high concrete railings along the sides. I pulled the car as far onto the shoulder as I could this side of the bridge and killed the ignition.

It was quiet out there except for the sound of the water running under the bridge. We got out of the car and walked to the center of it, Dad staying close to me.

I went to the west side first and looked down. It wasn't more than twenty feet down, not much of a drop, really. The creek was shallow here, rocks cropping up above the surface. It probably wasn't much more than a foot deep any place under the bridge. A summer or two back, when we hadn't had any rain for weeks, this creek bed was dry for a spell.

I looked at the water, hypnotized almost as it coursed around the rocks. Everything was serene.

"Best check out the other side, huh?" Dad said, touching my arm. We crossed the road and leaned up against the opposite railing.

There wasn't a body in the creek. And if someone did jump off this bridge, there wasn't enough depth, or force, to move one farther downstream. If someone took his life jumping off this bridge, he'd be found.

"I just want to get a good look underneath," I said. It wasn't possible to see everything that was under the bridge while standing on it.

"You want me to come?" Dad asked.

"Just stay here."

I ran to the end, then cut around and worked my way down the embankment. It didn't take more than a moment, and once there all I found were a few empty beer cans and some McDonald's wrappers.

"Anything?" Dad shouted.

"No," I said, and climbed back up to the road.

The thing was, a person would probably survive a jump off this bridge, unless they plunged headfirst.

"This is a good thing, right?" said Dad. "Isn't it?"

I said nothing.

"You know what else I was thinking?" Dad said. "She didn't leave any note. If she was going to do something to herself, she'd have left a note, don't you think?"

I didn't know what to think.

"If I was gonna kill myself, I'd leave a note," he said. "That's what people do. They want to say goodbye somehow."

"I don't think people always do that," I said. "Only in the movies."

Dad shrugged. "Maybe there were some other people she wanted to see before she did anything too rash."

"Like who?" I asked.

"I don't know. Like, maybe her own family."

"She doesn't have any family. At least not any that she talks to anymore."

Dad knew Jan was estranged from her parents, but it must have slipped his mind. If he'd thought about it a moment, he would've recalled that it was never an issue whose folks we spent every Christmas with.

"Maybe that's where she went," Dad said. "Could be she felt she needed to look them up after all these years and make some sort of peace with them. Tell them what she thinks of them, something like that."

I stood on the bridge, looking off into the woods.

"Say that again?" I said.

"She could be trying to find her family. You know, after all these years, she wants to clear the air or something. Give them a piece of her mind."

I walked over and surprised him with a pat on the shoulder. "That's not a bad idea," I said.

"I'm not just good-looking," Dad said.

# TWELVE

ERNIE BERTRAM WAS SITTING on the front porch of his Stonywood Drive home, nursing a long-necked bottle of beer, when the black car pulled up at the curb. The owner of Bertram's Heating and Cooling knew an unmarked police cruiser when he saw one. The tiny hubcaps, the absence of chrome. An overweight man in a white business shirt with tie askew got out of the cruiser. He stood, then reached back into the car for his jacket, which he pulled on as he walked up the driveway. The man glanced at Bertram's van, then looked up to the porch.

"Mr. Bertram?" he said.

Bertram stood up and set his beer on the wide railing. "What can I do for you?" He was about to add "Officer," but considering that this man wasn't wearing a uniform, he wasn't sure that was appropriate.

"Detective Duckworth, Promise Falls police," he said, mounting the steps. "Hope I'm not disturbing you."

Bertram pointed to a wicker chair. "Just finished dinner. Have a seat."

Duckworth did. "Get ya a beer?" Bertram asked, grabbing his own from the railing and sitting back down. Duckworth noticed that the man had unbuttoned the top of his pants and let his zipper down an inch. A little post-dinner pressure release.

"Thanks, but no," he said. "I need to ask you a couple of questions."

Bertram's eyebrows went up. "Sure."

"Jan Harwood works for you, isn't that right?"

"That's right," he said.

"I don't suppose you've heard from her today?"

"Nope. It's Saturday. Won't be talking to her till Monday morning."

The front door eased open. A short, wide woman in blue stretch pants said, "You got company, Ern?"

"This is Detective . . ."

"Duckworth," he said.

"Detective Duckworth is with the police, Irene. He can't have beer, but maybe you could have a lemonade or something?"

"I've got some apple pie left over," Irene Bertram said.

Detective Duckworth considered. "I probably could be persuaded to have a slice," he said.

"With ice cream? It's just vanilla," she said.

"Sure," he said. "I wouldn't mind that at all."

Irene retreated and the door closed. Ernie Bertram said, "It's just a frozen one you heat up in the oven, but it tastes like it was homemade."

"Sounds good to me," Duckworth said.

"So what's this about Jan?"

"She's missing," the detective said.

"Missing? Whaddya mean by missing?"

"She hasn't been seen since about midday, when she was with her husband and son at Five Mountains."

"Son of a bitch," Ernie said. "What's happened to her?"

"Well," said Duckworth, "if we knew that, we'd probably have a better chance of finding her."

"Missing," he said, more to himself than to Duckworth. "That's a hell of a thing."

"When's the last time you talked to her?" Duckworth asked.

"That'd be Thursday," he said.

"Not yesterday?"

"No, she took Friday off. She's been taking a few days off here and there the last couple of weeks."

"Why's that?"

Ernie Bertram shrugged. "Because she could. She had some time built up, so she asked if she could take an occasional day, instead of everything all at once."

"So they weren't sick days," Duckworth said.

"No. And it was okay with me because it's been a fairly quiet summer. Which is actually not that okay. Haven't sold an air conditioner in two weeks, although it is getting late in the season. You sell them mostly in the spring or early summer, when it starts getting hot. But with this recession, homeowners aren't willing to put down a couple thousand or whatever for a new unit. Paying the mortgage is hard enough, so they're getting as much out of their old ones as they can. And the last few days haven't been that scorching, so there hasn't been that much to do repair-wise."

"Uh-huh," said Duckworth.

The door opened. Irene Bertram presented Barry Duckworth with a slab of pie that had a scoop of ice cream next to it the size of a softball.

"Oh my," he said.

"Jan's missing," Ernie said to his wife.

"Missing?" she said, plunking herself down in a third chair.

"Yup," Ernie said. "Gone."

"Gone where?"

"She was up at that new roller-coaster park and disappeared." He zeroed in on Duckworth. "She get thrown off one of the coasters?"

"No, nothing like that," he said.

"Because those things, they're not safe," Bertram said.

Duckworth put a forkful of apple pie into his mouth, then quickly followed it with some ice cream so he could let the flavors mingle. "This is amazing," he said.

"I made it myself," Irene said.

"I already told him," Ernie said.

"You bastard," she said.

"How would you describe Ms. Harwood's mood the last few weeks?" the detective asked Ernie Bertram.

"Her mood?"

Duckworth, his mouth full of a second bite of pie, nodded.

"Fine, I guess. What do you mean, her mood?"

"Did she seem different? Maybe a bit down, troubled?"

Bertram took another drag on his beer. "I don't think so. Although I'm on the road a lot. I'm not in the office much. The girls could be turning tricks out of there and I wouldn't know it."

"Ernie!" said Irene, punching him in the shoulder.

"That was just a joke," he said to Duckworth. "They're fine women who work for me."

"You shouldn't make jokes like that," Irene said.

"So if, say, Jan Harwood had been depressed of late, you might not have noticed," Duckworth said between forkfuls.

"Only one depressed in that office is Leanne," he said. "Has been ever since she showed up five years ago."

"But not Ms. Harwood?"

"If anything," Bertram said, suddenly very thoughtful, "I'd say she was more excited."

"Excited?"

"Well, maybe that's the wrong word. Agitated? That's not right, either. But acting like something was just around the corner."

Duckworth set down his fork and rested the plate on the broad arm of the wicker chair. He noticed that the ice cream was melting, and if he didn't deal with it soon, it would start dribbling over the edge of the plate.

"What was just around the corner?"

"Beats me. But when she came to me, asking about taking a day off here and there, or maybe just half a day, there was something—I don't know how to describe it— like she was looking forward to something, expecting something."

Irene said, "Ernie is very good at reading people. You go into people's homes, fixing their furnaces and air conditioners, you get to know what people are really like."

Duckworth smiled at her, as though he actually appreciated the contribution.

"How much time had she taken off lately?" Duckworth asked.

"Let me think . . . Leanne—the other girl at the—"

"They don't call them girls anymore, Ernie," Irene said. "They're women. And you got some ice cream about to make a break for it there."

Duckworth used his fork to move the melting ice cream away from the edge, then mashed another forkful of pie into it and popped it into his mouth.

"Anyway," Ernie said, "Leanne might have an idea how many days. There was yesterday, and another day earlier in the week, and a couple the week before."

Duckworth had taken out his notepad and was writing things down. When he was done, he looked up and said, "I want to go back to something you said a moment ago."

"Yeah?"

"About Jan being excited. Tell me more about that."

Ernie thought. "Maybe it was a bit like when women are getting ready for something. Like a trip, or having relatives in to visit."

"But you wouldn't have characterized her as suicidal at all?"

Irene put a hand to her breast. "Oh my. Is that what you think happened?"

"I'm just asking," Duckworth said.

Ernie said, "I don't think so. But who knows how people think, what they keep bottled up inside."

Duckworth nodded. He finished off the last of the pie and ice cream in three more bites.

"Where did they go yesterday?" Ernie asked.

"Where did who go yesterday?" Duckworth asked.

"Jan and David. They went on some outing yesterday. Jan mentioned it before she left work on Thursday."

"You sure you don't mean their trip to Five Mountains today?"

He shook his head. "She said David was taking her somewhere Friday. It was all really mysterious, she said she couldn't talk about it. I got the idea that maybe it was a surprise or something."

Duckworth made another scribble on his pad, then put it into his jacket. He was about to thank Ernie for his time and Irene for the pie when a phone rang inside the house.

Irene jumped up and went inside.

When Duckworth rose out of his chair, Ernie did the same. "David must be beside himself," Ernie said. "Wondering what's happened to his wife."

Duckworth nodded. "Of course."

"I sure hope you find her soon," he said.

Irene was at the door. "It's Lyall," she said.

Ernie shook his head. "What's he want?"

"He hasn't seen Leanne all day. Actually, not since yesterday."

Duckworth felt a jolt. "Leanne Kowalski?"

Ernie went into the house and picked up the receiver

sitting by the phone on the front hall table. Duckworth followed him in.

"Lyall?" Ernie listened a moment, then said, "Nope, I didn't. . . . Since when? . . . That's a long time to be shopping, even for a woman. Did you hear about Jan? Police are here—"

"May I take that?" Duckworth said and took the phone away from Ernie. "Mr. Kowalski, this is Detective Barry Duckworth with the Promise Falls Police Department."

"Yeah?"

"What's this about your wife?"

"She's not home."

"When were you expecting her?"

"Hours ago. She went out to do some shopping. At least that's what I think. That's what she usually does on a Saturday. She was going to the mall and then she was going to do the groceries."

"Your wife and Jan Harwood work together?"

"Yeah, at Ernie's. Can you put him back on? I want to ask whether he called her in on an emergency or something."

"He didn't," Duckworth said.

"What's this about Jan? Her husband called here a while ago looking for her. What are you doing at Ernie's place? Everything okay there?"

Duckworth had his notepad out again. "Mr. Kowalski, what's your address?"

# THIRTEEN

THERE WAS SOMETHING I'D never been totally honest about with Jan.

It wasn't that I lied to her. But there was something I'd done I'd never told her about. If she'd ever flat out asked about it, maybe then I would have lied. I think I might have had to. She'd have been too furious with me.

It wasn't that I cheated on her. I'd never done anything like that, not even close. This had nothing to do with another woman.

One time, about a year ago, I drove by her house.

This would be the house she grew up in, her parents' place, a nearly three-hour drive from Promise Falls. It was in the Pittsford neighborhood of southeast Rochester, on Lincoln Avenue. A long, narrow two-story. The white paint was peeling from the walls, and a couple of the black shutters—one on the first floor and one on the second—hung crookedly. The screening in the metal storm door was frayed, and there were chunks of brick missing from the chimney. But while the house needed some attention, it was far from derelict.

I had been driving back from Buffalo, where I'd gone to interview a city planner who felt that conventional ideas to slow residential traffic—speed bumps, four-way stops—didn't do anything but anger drivers to the point of road rage, and thought roundabouts, traffic circles, and landscaped medians were a better way to go. It was on the way back that I decided to take 490 north off 90 and head into the Rochester neighborhood I knew to be the one where Jan grew up.

I think I knew, even before leaving for Buffalo, I was going to take this side trip.

It never would have been possible if we hadn't had the leak behind the bathroom sink several days earlier.

Jan was at work and I had taken the day off as payback for several late-night city council meetings I'd recently covered—this was before we'd turned that beat over to Rajiv or Amal or whoever in Mumbai. I'd gone down to the unfinished side of our basement, where the furnace and hot water tank are, and noticed a steady drip of water coming down from between the studs. That was where the copper pipes turned north to feed the upstairs bathroom.

I did what I always did when I had a household emergency. I called Dad.

"Sounds like maybe you've got a pinhole leak in one of your pipes," he said. "I'll be right over." He couldn't disguise the joy and excitement in his voice.

He showed up half an hour later with his tools, including a small propane torch for welding.

"It's going to be in the wall somewhere," he said. "The trick is finding it."

We thought we could hear a hissing sound behind the bathroom sink, about a foot up from the floor. It was a pedestal sink, so it was easy to get up close to the wall for a listen.

Dad pulled out a saw with a pointed end on the blade that would allow him to stab right into the drywall and start cutting.

"Dad," I said, looking at the floral wallpaper and not looking forward to tearing it all up, "would it be worth going in from the other side?"

"What's over there?" he asked.

"Hang on," I said. As it turned out, the linen closet was on the opposite side of the wall from the bathroom sink. I opened it and started clearing out everything on the floor below the first shelf—a basket for dirty laundry, a stockpile of toilet paper and tissue boxes—until the wall was clear. I thought, if the pipe could be reached from here, it made more sense to hack through in a place where it wouldn't be noticed.

Once I had everything out, I got down on my hands and knees and crawled into the closet and listened for the leak.

The baseboard that ran along the inside of the closet looked loose along the back. I touched it, and noticed that it seemed to be fitted into place and not nailed. I got my fingers in behind it, and felt something.

It was the top edge of a letter-sized envelope, which was perfectly shaped to hide behind baseboarding. I worked the envelope out. There was nothing written on it, nor was it sealed, but the flap was tucked in. I opened it, and inside I found a single piece of paper and a key.

I left the key inside and removed the paper, which was folded once, and was an official document of some kind.

It was a "Certificate of Live Birth."

Jan's birth certificate. All the details she had never wanted to share with me were on this piece of paper. Of course, I already knew her last name was Richler—rhymes with "tickler"—but she'd gone to great lengths never to speak her parents' names or even say where they lived.

Now, at a glance, I knew that her mother's name was Gretchen, that her father's name was Horace. That she had been born in the Monroe Community Hospital in Rochester. There was an address for a house on Lincoln Avenue.

I committed the details of the document to memory, folded it and put it back into the envelope. I didn't know what to make of the key. It was a type I didn't recognize. It didn't appear to be a house key. I left it in the envelope, and put it back where I'd found it, pushing the baseboard back into place.

By the time I got around the other side of the wall, Dad had already made a hole. "I'm in!" he said. "And there's your leak right there! You want to turn off the main valve?"

Before the Buffalo trip, I went to the online phone directories and found only five Richlers listed in the Rochester area, and only one of them was an H. Richler.

He was still listed as living on Lincoln Avenue.

That told me at least one of Jan's parents was still alive, if not both. If Horace Richler was dead, it was possible his wife, Gretchen, had left the listing unchanged.

I made a call from my desk at the *Standard* in a bid to clear that up. I dialed the Richler number and a woman who sounded as though she could be in her sixties or seventies answered. Gretchen, I was betting.

"Is Mr. Richler there?" I asked.

"Hang on," she said.

Half a minute later, a man said tiredly, "Hello."

"Is this Hank Richler?"

"Huh? No. This is Horace Richler."

"Oh, sorry. I've got the wrong number."

I offered another apology and hung up.

It was hard not to be curious about them when Jan had so steadfastly refused to talk about them.

"I don't want anything to do with them," she'd said over the years. "I don't ever want to see them again, and I don't imagine they'll be too destroyed if they never see me."

Even when Ethan was born, Jan was adamantly opposed to letting her parents know.

"They won't give a rat's ass," she said.

"Maybe," I said, "knowing that they have a grand-child will change things. Maybe they'll think it's time for some sort of reconciliation."

She shook her head. "Not a chance. And I don't want to talk about it anymore."

What I'd learned since first meeting Jan at a jobs placement office when I was interviewing some unemployed people for a story six years ago was that her unnamed father was a miserable son of a bitch, and her mother spent most of her time drunk and depressed.

Jan didn't like to talk about it. The story of her parents, and her life with them, spilled out in bits and pieces over the years.

"They blamed me for everything," Jan said one Saturday night two years ago when my parents had taken a very young Ethan for a sleepover. We'd gone through three bottles of wine—a rare event considering that Jan drank very little—and there'd been every indication we were headed upstairs for some long-overdue debauchery. Unexpectedly, Jan began to talk about a part of her life she'd never shared with me.

"What do you mean, they blamed you?" I asked.

"Him, mostly," Jan said. "For fucking up their lives."

"What, by being a kid? By existing?"

She looked at me through glassy eyes. "Yeah, pretty much. Dad had a nickname for me. Hindy."

"Hildy?"

"No. Hindy."

"Like the language?"

She shook her head, took another sip of wine, and said, "No, with a 'y.' Short for 'Hindenburg.' Not just because I went through a bit of a pudgy period, but because he thought of me as his own personal little fucking disaster."

"That's horrible."

"Yeah, well, that was true love compared to my tenth birthday."

I was going to ask, but decided to wait.

"He promised to take me to New York to see an actual Broadway musical. I always dreamed of going there. I'd watch the Tonys when they were on TV, saved copies of the Sunday Arts section of *The New York Times* whenever I found one, looking at all the ads for the shows, memorizing the names of the stars and the reviews. He said he got tickets for *Grease*. That we were going to take the bus down. That we were going to stay in a hotel. I couldn't believe it. My father, he'd been so indifferent to me for so long, but I thought maybe, because I was ten . . ."

She had another sip of wine.

"So it got to be the day that we were supposed to go. I got my bag all packed. I picked out just what I was going to wear to the theater. A red dress and black shoes. And my father, he wasn't doing anything to get ready. I told him to get moving, and he smiled, and he said, 'There's no trip. No bus ride. No hotel. No tickets for *Grease*. Never was. Disappointment's a bitch, isn't it? Now you know how it feels.'"

I was speechless. Jan smiled and said, "Bet you think I caught a lucky break. You'd rather die than sit through *Grease*."

I found some words. "How'd you deal with that?"

She said, "I went to another place."

"Where? Relatives?"

"No, no, you don't get it," she said. Jan put her hand to her mouth. "I think I'm going to be sick."

The next morning she refused to talk about it.

She did tell me, over time, that she left home at seventeen and for nearly twenty years had had no contact with either of her parents. She had no brothers or sisters who might have let her know, whether she wanted to or not, what had happened to her mother and father.

For all she knew, they were both dead.

Except I knew they weren't, because of the phone call I'd made.

I'd never told Jan about what I'd found behind the baseboard. I didn't want her to know I'd violated her privacy. I was troubled that she'd gone to such lengths to keep me from knowing about her background, but maybe she was right not to trust me. Finding the birth certificate was leading me to do the very thing she had always wanted to prevent.

Driving back from Buffalo, I took a detour to the north and found the Lincoln Avenue home, and stared at its peeling paint and shutters askew, as if some meaning could be drawn from it all. I wondered whether one of the two second-story windows had been Jan's bedroom, or if her room had been at the back of the house.

I pictured her as a child, going in and out of that front door, perhaps playing in the front yard. Jumping rope on the sidewalk, playing hopscotch on her driveway. Maybe those images were too idyllic. Perhaps, growing up in a household where love was displaced by anger and resentment, such simple pleasures were elusive. Maybe for Jan, every time she came out that door was like being released from prison. I could picture her running to a friend's house, returning home only when she had to.

Staring at the house really didn't tell me anything. I don't know what I was expecting.

Then her parents showed up.

I had been parked across the street and two houses down, so I didn't attract the attention of Horace and Gretchen Richler as they got out of their twenty-year-old Oldsmobile.

Horace opened his door slowly and put his foot on

the ground. It took some effort for him to turn in his seat and bring himself out. He was slowed by arthritis or something similarly disabling. He was in his late sixties or early seventies, a few wisps of hair, a couple of liver spots. He was short and stocky, but not fat. Even at this age, it looked like you'd have to take a good run at him to knock him over.

He didn't look like a monster. But then, monsters often don't.

Horace was going around to the trunk as Gretchen got out. She moved slowly, too, although she wasn't quite as creaky as her husband. Even though he was out of the car before her, she was to the trunk before him, and waited for him to fit the key into the lock and pop it.

There wasn't a lot to her. She was tiny, under five feet, probably no more than eighty or ninety pounds. Wiry. She reached into the trunk and looped her fingers through the handles of half a dozen plastic grocery bags, lifted them out and headed for the door. Her husband closed the trunk and followed, carrying nothing.

They went into the house, and they were gone.

They didn't appear to have spoken a word between them. They'd run their errands, and they'd come home.

Was there anything I could read into what I'd seen? No. And yet I was left with the impression that these were two people going through the motions, living out the rest of their lives a day at a time without purpose. While I picked up no hostile body language from Horace toward Gretchen, I did detect an overall sadness about them.

*I hope you're sad*, I thought. *I hope you're fucking miserable for what you did.*

When the Oldsmobile had pulled into the driveway, I'd initially had an impulse to get out, march over, and tear into Horace Richler. I wanted to tell him what a terrible man he was. I wanted to tell him that a man who would abuse his daughter—even if that abuse was limited to emotional—didn't deserve to be called a father. I wanted to tell him that his daughter had turned out well despite his attempts to sabotage her. I wanted to tell him that he had a wonderful grandson, but because he'd been such a miserable bastard he was never going to meet him.

But I didn't tell him anything.

I watched Horace Richler go into the house with his wife, Gretchen. I watched the door close behind them.

Then I drove home, and never told Jan about the stop I had made along the way.

# FOURTEEN

I THOUGHT ABOUT MY visit to the Richler home on the way back from the bridge with Dad.

What if Jan had been wanting, for years, to say to her parents what I'd wanted to say when I'd parked out front of their home? What if the way her father had treated her had been eating her up for years, in ways she'd never let on? Revealing how much her father's actions still hurt her might have made her feel vulnerable. And yet, Jan had told me over the past two weeks how fragile, how potentially self-destructive she had been feeling.

I just didn't know anything anymore.

I tried to put myself in Jan's position. *I'm in a bad place, thinking about taking my own life. Before I do such a thing, do I want to confront my father, tell him what I think of him? Tell my mother she should have stood up for me? Tell both of them how they ruined my life before I end it?*

I shuddered.

"You okay there?" Dad asked.

"Yeah," I said.

"It's a good thing," he said. "That we didn't find her there. Under that bridge. That's a good thing. Because if that's the place she was talking about doing herself in, well, stands to reason that she didn't."

Dad was trying really hard. Driving out to that

bridge, it had been a long shot at best. The fact that Jan wasn't there just meant that Jan wasn't there. The fact was, we didn't know where she was. But I didn't want to make my father feel bad by dismissing his hunt for a silver lining.

"I suppose," I said. "I suppose." Jan had also mentioned the much taller bridge in downtown Promise Falls, but if she'd tried something there, I told myself, there would have been witnesses. The police would have heard almost immediately.

Dad pointed up ahead. "You see that? Guy didn't signal. How hard is it to put your blinker on? Christ almighty."

Not long after that, we were riding behind a driver who moved into the oncoming lane in preparation for a left turn into a driveway, allowing us to scoot past.

"What the hell is that?" Dad said. "People in the country pull that stunt all the time. What if someone was passing us, or someone suddenly showed up in the oncoming lane? I swear to God, how do these people get their licenses?"

When I didn't respond to either of these observations, Dad decided to dial it down a bit. Finally, he said, "So, you been thinking about my idea? About Jan looking up her parents?"

"Yeah, I have."

"You got any way to get in touch with them? Your mother's told me Jan doesn't talk about them, that she's never even told you who they are or where they live."

"I think I could find them," I said.

"Yeah? How would you go about that?"

"They live in Rochester," I said. "I know the address."

"So she did tell you?"

"Not exactly," I said.

"Well, if I was you, I'd call them up, see if she's been in

touch. If they're in Rochester, Jan would have had plenty of time to drive there by now."

In what? I was in my car, and Jan's was at home.

"How long a drive is it? Three, four hours?"

"Under three," I said.

"So when we get back, we'll give them a call. It's long distance but I don't care about that."

That was a major concession on Dad's part. He hated long-distance calls being made on his phone.

I glanced over and smiled. "Thanks, Dad. But I'm afraid the moment I say Jan's name, they'll hang up on me."

He shook his head at the thought of it. "How can parents be like that?"

"I don't know."

"I mean, you didn't always do what we wanted but we never disowned you," Dad said, forcing a smile. "You could be a real pain in the ass sometimes."

"I don't doubt it."

"You have to let your kids make their own decisions in life, good or bad."

"Is that why you're so reluctant to offer advice?" I asked.

Dad shot me a look. "Smart-ass."

We were getting back into Promise Falls, only a few blocks from my parents' house. It was nearly dark, and the streetlights had come on. I felt a sense of imminent doom as we rounded the corner, expecting to see one or more police cars parked out front. But there were no unfamiliar cars parked at the curb.

My mother was standing at the door. She opened it and came out as we pulled into the driveway. She had a hopeful, expectant look on her face, but I shook my head.

"Nothing," I said. "We didn't find Jan."

"So she wasn't—she didn't—"

"No," I said. "Any news here? Anything from the police?"

She shook her head. We all went into the house, where I saw Ethan on the third step of the stairs, preparing to jump.

"Ethan, don't—"

He leapt down to the main floor, hitting it with a thump. "Watch!" he said, ran up to the third step, and did it again.

"He's been a madman," Mom said. "I let him have half a glass of Coke with his macaroni."

Mom always liked to blame Ethan's rowdiness on something he'd had to eat or drink. It had been my experience that it didn't much matter.

I gave her a kiss and went into the kitchen to use the phone. I had Detective Duckworth's card in my hand and dialed his cell.

"Duckworth."

"It's David Harwood," I said. "I know you'd probably have called if you knew anything, but I wanted to check in."

"I don't have any news," Duckworth said. His voice sounded guarded.

"You still have people searching?"

"We do, Mr. Harwood." He paused. "I think, if there are no developments overnight, if Mrs. Harwood doesn't come home, we should put out a release in the morning."

I pictured her coming through the door here, into my parents' house. There was a loud thunk from the other room as Ethan hit the floor again.

"Okay, good," I said. "How about a news conference?"

"I don't know that we're at that stage," he said. "I think a picture and a description of your wife and the circumstances of her disappearance will do for now."

"I think we need a news conference," I said.

"Let's see where we are in the morning," he said. There was something in his voice. It sounded controlled, held back.

"I might not be here in the morning," I said.

"Where are you going to be?"

"Jan's parents are in Rochester."

Mom's eyes widened when I said it. I'd never told her about the trip I'd made to see Jan's childhood home.

With Duckworth, I continued, "She hasn't had any contact with them in probably twenty years. They didn't come to our wedding, they've never met their grandson. But I'm thinking, what if Jan decided to go see them? What if, after all this time, she had some reason to get in touch that she didn't share with me? Maybe she just wanted to finally tell them what she thinks of them."

Duckworth was quiet, saying only, "I suppose."

"I'd phone them, but I'm worried about doing this any way but face-to-face. I mean, they've never set eyes on me. What are they going to think, some guy phones them and says he's their son-in-law and oh, by the way, their daughter's missing and is there any chance she might have dropped by? And if Jan is there, and doesn't want me to know, I'm worried that if I call, she'll take off."

"Maybe," Duckworth said with little conviction.

From the other room, Mom shouted at Ethan, "Enough!"

I said, "I'm probably going to hit the road in a couple of minutes, get a hotel in Rochester, and see Jan's parents first thing in the morning."

Instead of addressing my plans, Duckworth said, "Tell me again about your wife and Leanne Kowalski."

The question threw me. "I told you. They work together. That's about it."

"What time did you and your son get to Five Mountains, Mr. Harwood?"

Why did he ask it that way? Why didn't he ask when Ethan and I and *Jan* got to Five Mountains?

"I guess it was about eleven, maybe a little after. Didn't they have it right down to the minute, when they scanned our ticket at the gate?"

"I think you're right," Duckworth said.

"Is something going on?" I asked. "Please tell me if something's going on."

"If I have any news, Mr. Harwood, I'll be in touch. I have your cell number."

I hung up the phone. Mom and Dad were both standing there, watching me.

"Jan told you about her parents?" Mom asked.

"I figured it out."

"Who are they?"

"Horace and Gretchen Richler," I said.

"Does Jan know you know?"

I shook my head. I didn't want to get into this. I leaned against the kitchen counter. I was exhausted.

"You need to get some rest," Mom said.

"I'm going to Rochester," I said.

"In the morning?"

"No, now." I realized it was suddenly very quiet. "Where's Ethan?"

"He collapsed on the couch," Mom said. "Thank God."

"Can he stay here for the night?"

"You can't drive anywhere now," Mom protested. "You'll drive off the road."

"Why don't you make me a thermos of coffee to go while I say good night to Ethan," I said.

Without waiting for any further protest, I went into the living room, where Ethan was resting his head on the end of the couch. He'd pulled a throw around himself.

"Gotta go, sport," I said. "You're staying here for the night."

No reaction. His eyes suddenly looked heavy. "I'll bet Mommy's at the mall."

"Maybe so," I said.

"Okay," he said, and his eyelids drifted down like flower petals closing for the night.

# FIFTEEN

BARRY DUCKWORTH CLOSED THE phone and said
to Lyall Kowalski, "Sorry about that."

"Was that Jan's husband?" he asked. He and the detective were sitting in his living room. Lyall was in a
black T-shirt and dirty, knee-length shorts with pockets
all over them. Duckworth wondered whether Lyall had
gone prematurely bald at age thirty-five, or whether he
shaved his head. Some guys, once they started losing
some hair, decided to go the whole nine yards with it,
make a fashion statement.

Even before he saw the pit bull coming out of the
kitchen, Duckworth knew there was a dog here. The
house was permeated with the smell of pooch.

"Yes, that was him," Duckworth said.

"Has he seen my wife?"

"No," Duckworth said, but thinking, *At least he's not
saying he has*. There were things about this case that
were starting to bother him, even before he'd learned
that Jan Harwood's workmate was missing, too.

"Tell me again what time your wife left the house,"
Duckworth said.

Lyall Kowalski was leaning forward on the couch, elbows on his knees. "Okay, so she was actually gone before I got up. I got in kind of late last night and was
sleeping in."

"Where had you been?"

"I was at the Trenton." A local bar. "With some friends. We had a few, and Mick gave me a lift home."

"Mick?"

"Mick Angus. We work together at Thackeray."

"What do you do at the college, Mr. Kowalski?"

"We're both in building maintenance."

"So you got home when?"

Lyall scrunched up his face, trying to remember. "Three? Or maybe five."

"And your wife was here when you got home?"

"As far as I know," he said, nodding.

"What do you mean, as far as you know?"

"Well, there's no reason to think that she wasn't."

"I don't understand."

"I didn't actually talk to her. I didn't make it as far as the bedroom. I camped out on the couch."

"Why'd you do that?"

"Leanne gets kinda bitchy when I come home drunk. Actually, she's kind of bitchy even when I'm sober. Plus, I kinda forgot I was supposed to take her out to dinner last night. So I didn't want to have to deal with that, so I didn't get into bed with her."

"Were you at the Trenton all night?"

"I think so. Except after they closed, I had a couple of drinks in the parking lot with Mick."

"Who drove you home?" Duckworth said disapprovingly.

Lyall waved his hands at Duckworth, like it was no big deal. "Mick can drink a lot and still drive better than most people sober."

"Where were you supposed to go for dinner?"

"Kelly's?" he said, like he was asking Duckworth for confirmation. "I know I said something on Thursday about taking her there for dinner but it slipped my mind."

"Did you talk to your wife at all last night, while you were at Trenton's?"

"My cell was dead."

"So you fell asleep on the couch. Did you see your wife in the morning?"

"Okay, that's the thing? I think I might have heard her saying something to me while I was sleeping it off, but I can't exactly swear to it."

"So what does your wife usually do on a Saturday?"

"She kind of has a routine. She goes out around eight-thirty. Most weekends, she goes out by herself, even if I haven't been out with my buds the night before. I've offered to go with her sometimes, but only because I know she'll say no. She kinda likes to go on her own. I don't take any offense or anything."

"Where does she go?" Duckworth asked.

"To the malls. She likes to go to all of them. Every damn one between here and Albany. She likes Crossgates and Colonie Center. How much clothes and shoes and jewelry and makeup does one woman need?"

"She drops a lot of money on Saturdays?"

"I don't know how she affords it. We're kind of on a limited budget," Lyall said. "What I don't get is if all the malls have exactly the same stores, what's the point in going to one after another?"

"I don't know," Duckworth said, thinking it was the first thing Lyall Kowalski had said that bordered on insightful.

"So after she's done with the malls, she makes the grocery her last stop, because she doesn't want all her Lean Cuisines melting while she's wandering around JCPenney."

"But you don't actually know where, exactly, she would have gone."

"No."

"Where does she buy groceries?"

Lyall shrugged. "Grocery store?"

The dog, built like a three-foot cross section of a punching bag with legs, walked through the room, nails clicking on the uncarpeted wood floor. He collapsed on a square of area rug in front of an empty chair.

"If this were like other Saturdays, what time would you be expecting her back?"

"Three or four? Five at the latest."

"When did you get up?"

"Around one," Lyall said.

"And did you try calling your wife at all?"

"I tried her cell, but it goes straight to message. And she hasn't called here to say she was going to be late or anything."

Duckworth nodded slowly. He asked, "When was the last time you actually saw or spoke to your wife, Mr. Kowalski?"

He thought a moment. "I guess, middle of yesterday? She called me from work to check what time we were going out for dinner." He winced, as if someone had stuck a pin in his arm.

"So you didn't speak to her later yesterday or last night, not at all?"

Lyall shook his head.

"And you didn't actually talk to her this morning?"

Another shake.

"When Mick dropped you off here last night, did you notice whether Leanne's car was here?"

"I wasn't all that observant at the time."

"For all you know," Duckworth said, "she wasn't even here last night."

"Where would she be if she wasn't here?"

"I don't know. What I'm asking is whether you can actually say, with any certainty, that your wife was here when you got home in the middle of the night, or was here this morning."

He looked slightly dumbstruck. "I'm just assuming she was here. Wouldn't make sense for her not to be here."

"Do you have a list of the bank and credit cards your wife uses?"

"What for?" he asked.

"We could check, see where she used them, it would tell us where she's been."

Lyall scratched his head. "When Leanne buys anything, she tends to use cash."

"Why's that?"

"We kinda had our cards canceled."

Duckworth sighed. "Has Leanne ever done this before? Gone out and not come back until late, or maybe stayed over with a friend for the night? Is it possible—and I'm sorry to have to ask this—that she might have a boyfriend?"

Lyall shook his head, clenched his fists, and pressed his meaty lips together. "Shit no, I mean, no, she wouldn't do that."

Duckworth sensed something. "Mr. Kowalski?"

"She's my girl. She's not going to mess around on me. No way."

"Has she ever done anything like that before?"

He waited a beat too long before answering. "No."

"I need you to be straight with me here," Duckworth said. "This kinda stuff, it happens to the best of us."

Lyall's lips moved in and out. Finally, he said, "It was years ago. We were going through a rough patch. Not like now. Things are pretty good now. She had a thing with some guy she met in a bar. Just a one-nighter, that was all there was to it. Some guy passing through."

"Who was the man?"

"I never knew. But she told me. Not to confess, but to stick it to me, you know? Saying things like if I wasn't going to show her a good time, there was plenty of guys who would. I cleaned up my act after that."

Duckworth looked around the room, then let his eyes settle back on Lyall.

The man was on the verge of tears. "I'm real scared something's happened to her. Like maybe she had a car accident or something. Have you checked on that? She drives a Ford Explorer. It's blue and it's, like, a 1990, so it's kind of eaten up with rust."

"I don't have any report of an accident involving that make of vehicle," Duckworth said. "Mr. Kowalski, how close are your wife and Jan Harwood?"

He blinked. "They work together."

"Are they friends? Do they get together after work? Have they ever, I don't know, gone on a girls' weekend away?"

"Shit no," he said. "Just between you and me, Leanne thinks Jan's a bit stuck-up, you know? Think she's better than everybody."

Last thing, Duckworth asked Lyall Kowalski some basic questions, wrote down the answers in his notebook.

"What's your wife's date of birth?"

"Uh, February ninth. She was born in 1973."

"Her full name?"

Lyall sniffed, then said, "Leanne Katherine Kowalski. Well, her name before she met me was Bothwick."

Duckworth kept scribbling. "Weight?"

"Whoa. One-forty? No, one-twenty? She's kind of skinny. And she's around five-six or -seven."

"Hair?"

"Black. It's kinda short, with some streaks in it."

Duckworth asked for a picture. The best Lyall could come up with was a wedding photo of the two of them, a ten-year-old shot of them jamming wedding cake into each other's mouths.

Before he pulled away from the curb out front of the Kowalski house, Duckworth got out his phone, waited for someone to answer, and said, "Gunner."

"Yeah, hey, Detective."

"You still at Five Mountains?"

"I've been here all day," he said. "Just finishing up now."

"How'd it go?"

"Okay, so, the first thing we did was check a couple more times to see if we could track down that third ticket bought online."

"Right."

"We thought maybe there was a glitch in the system, but we've pretty much ruled that out. If she came into the park, she didn't do it with a ticket purchased over the Internet."

"Okay," Duckworth said.

"Then, with the pictures the husband provided, we spent the rest of the day looking at all the people coming in and going out through the gates, trying to spot the wife. We narrowed it down to the time frame basically established from when the husband and the kid got there, and when he called the police."

"I'm with ya."

"It's not easy. There's so many people, sometimes you can't make them out, sometimes they're wearing hats that cover half their face, so the thing is, she might have been there and we didn't see her. But we looked for a woman matching her description, dressed the way the husband described her."

"And nothing."

"Nothing. If she's there, we can't find her."

"Okay, look, thanks, I appreciate it. Go home."

"You don't have to ask me twice," he said.

"Is Campion still around?"

"Yeah, she's been here all day. I can see her outside the door."

"You wanna put her on?"

Duckworth heard Gunner put down the phone and call out to Officer Didi Campion. Twenty seconds later, the phone was picked up.

"Campion here."

"It's Barry, Didi. Long day, huh?"

"Yes, sir."

"I want to ask you again about the time you spent with the kid this morning."

"Sure."

"Did he actually say the mother was there with them at the park?"

"What do you mean?"

"Had the boy seen Mrs. Harwood that morning?"

"He was asking about her. He was asking what had happened to her. I certainly got the sense he'd seen her at the park."

"Do you think—how do I put this—he could have been convinced his mother had been there even if she hadn't?"

"You mean like, the dad says we're just going to meet your mom now, your mom just went into the bathroom, something like that?"

"That's kind of how I was thinking," Duckworth said.

Campion said, "Hmmm."

"I mean, the kid's only what, four years old? Tell a four-year-old enough times that he's invisible and he'll start believing it. Maybe the dad made him think his mother was there even if she wasn't."

"The kid was kind of dozy," Campion said. "Like, tired, not stupid."

"This Harwood guy, he says the three of them are going to Five Mountains for the day, but he only gets two tickets. He says his wife has been talking suicide, tells us his wife went to the doctor about it, but turns out she never went."

"She didn't?"

"No. I talked to Dr. Samuels today. And her boss, who runs the heating and cooling company? He says he didn't see any signs that she was depressed the last couple of weeks. If anything, she was excited about something. Kind of, I don't know, anticipating something."

"Weird."

"So far, the only person who's saying the wife's suicidal is the husband. Doctor never saw her, her boss says she was fine."

"So the husband, he's laying the groundwork."

"This Bertram guy, the wife's boss, said Harwood took his wife for a drive someplace on Friday. When Bertram asked her where they were going, she said it was a secret or something, a surprise."

"So where you going with this, Detective?"

"You still on shift?"

Campion sighed. "I'm kind of doing a double. Wanna make it a triple? Having a life is hugely overrated."

"You've put out news releases before, right?"

"I've worked that end, yeah."

"I told Harwood we'd put out a release tomorrow, but I think we need to put one out tonight. Shake the bushes, you know? We've still got time to make the eleven o'clock news. Something simple. A picture of Jan Harwood, believed last seen in the vicinity of Five Mountains. Police seeking any information about the woman's whereabouts, contact us, blah blah blah, the usual drill."

"I'm on it," Campion said.

Duckworth thanked her and closed the phone. He was starting to wonder whether Jan Harwood ever even made it to Five Mountains. He was starting to wonder just what her husband might have done with her.

How the hell that fit in with Leanne Kowalski, he had no idea. But two women who worked together, going missing at the same time—that was one hell of a coincidence. He decided to put his focus, for now, on Jan Harwood. Maybe he'd turn up Leanne Kowalski along the way.

# SIXTEEN

I WAS ABOUT A half an hour out of Rochester when my cell rang.

"It was on the news," Mom said. "They had it on the TV."

"What?" I said. "What did they have?"

"They had a picture of Jan, and that the police were looking for help to find her. That's good, right, that they did that?"

"Yeah," I said slowly. "But the detective, he said they were going to make a decision about that tomorrow. I wonder what made him change his mind. How much did they say?"

"Not much," my mother said. "They gave her name and age and height and what she was last seen wearing."

From some distance away, my father shouted, "Eye color!"

"That's right. They said what color eyes she has and hair and that kind of thing."

"And where it happened?"

"Just a mention," Mom said. "It said she was last seen near Five Mountains. But they didn't have anything about that man trying to take Ethan. Shouldn't they have had something on that?"

I said, "I wonder why Detective Duckworth didn't call me. You'd think, if he was deciding to change the timing of the release, he would have let me know."

I wondered how long it would be before someone from my own paper called, asking what the hell was going on, how the *Standard* could get scooped on the disappearance of the spouse of one of its own staff members. Even if we didn't have an edition until the next day, it could have gone up on the website.

I didn't have time to worry about that now.

"Are you almost there?" Mom asked. Dad yelled, "Tell him to keep drinking coffee!"

"Pretty close," I said. "I was going to get a hotel, go see Jan's parents in the morning, but now I'm thinking maybe I should just knock on the door tonight. I can't lay in my hotel all night thinking about her. I have to do something right away."

I didn't hear anything on the other end.

"Mom?"

"I'm sorry. I was just nodding. I guess I was thinking you could see me." She laughed tiredly.

"How's Ethan?"

"I just left him on the couch. I'm afraid if I move him he'll wake up and never settle down again. Your father and I are going to turn in now. But if something happens, if you have any news, you call us, okay?"

"I will. You too."

Before putting the phone back into my jacket, I considered calling Detective Duckworth and asking him why he'd decided to go ahead with releasing Jan's picture now. But I was almost to Rochester, and I needed to focus on my upcoming meeting with Jan's parents.

I wasn't exactly looking forward to it, not after all the things Jan had said about them. But I wasn't there to criticize them for how they'd raised Jan. I wasn't there to lay blame, decide who was right and who was wrong.

I wanted to know if they'd seen Jan. Plain and simple. Had she been there? Had she called them? Did they have any idea where she might be?

Just after midnight I got off 90 and headed north on 490. Not long after that, I got off at the Palymra Road exit and quickly found my way to Lincoln Avenue.

The streetlamps were the only thing casting any light at 12:10 a.m. You might have thought, on a Saturday night, that there might have been a house or two with the lights on, a party going on. But maybe this was a street made up mostly of older residents. No lights on after ten on a Saturday night.

I rolled down the street and came to a stop out front of the house I had seen only once before. The Oldsmobile was in the driveway. The house was dark save for one light over the front door.

I killed the engine and sat in the car a moment, listening to the engine tick as it cooled.

I wondered if Jan could be in that house.

If Jan had returned here, it was hard to imagine the kind of confrontation she was likely to have had that could have ended with an invitation to spend the night.

"Let's do this," I said under my breath.

I got out of the car and closed the door as quietly as I could. No sense waking any more people on Lincoln than I had to. I walked across the empty street, up the driveway, and onto the front porch of the home of Horace and Gretchen Richler.

I stood in the glow of the single bulb, looking for a doorbell button. I found it mounted in the right side of the door frame and pushed on it, hard, with my thumb.

No bell went off inside the house, at least none that I could hear. I glanced over at the metal mailbox hanging from the wall, noticed the "No Flyers or Junk Mail!" sticker. Maybe the Richlers didn't like to be troubled with nuisance callers or mail. One way to deal with that was to disconnect the doorbell.

Or it could just be broken. To be certain, I leaned on

the button a second time, but still heard nothing from inside the house.

I opened the metal storm door and saw a tarnished brass knocker on the main door. I rapped it five times. I didn't know whether it would wake the Richlers, but it sounded like five gunshots out here on the porch.

When I didn't see any lights going on after fifteen seconds, I did it again. I was about to do it a third time when I could see, through the window, light cascading down the stairs.

Someone was up.

I rapped two more times, lightly, so they wouldn't think whoever was at the front door had taken off before they'd made the decision to come downstairs. In another moment Horace Richler appeared, in a bathrobe and pajamas, what hair he had pointing in several directions.

Before he got to the door, he shouted, "Who is it?"

"Mr. Richler?" I called out. Not shouting, but loud enough that I hoped he could hear me through the door. "I need to speak to you."

"Who the hell is it? You know what time it is? I gotta gun, you know!"

If he really did, it wasn't in his hands at this moment.

"My name is David Harwood! Please, I need to speak to you! It's very important."

There was someone else coming down the stairs now. It was Gretchen Richler, in a nightgown and robe, her hair also in disarray. I could just make out her asking her husband who it was, what was going on.

"It's about Jan!" I said.

I thought I saw Horace Richler hesitate for a second as he reached for the door, wondering if he heard me correctly. I heard a deadbolt turn back, a chain slide, then the door opened about a foot.

"What the hell is this all about?" Horace Richler

asked, his wife pressed up against his back. I didn't know whether she was using her husband to protect herself, or to keep me from seeing her in her nightclothes. Probably both.

"I'm so sorry to wake you up, Mr. Richler, Mrs. Richler. I truly am. I wouldn't do this if it weren't an emergency."

"Who are you?" Gretchen Richler asked. Her voice was high and scratchy, like an old record playing too fast.

"My name's David Harwood. I'm Jan's husband."

The two of them stared at me.

"It would never have been my choice for us to meet this way, believe me. I've driven here tonight from Promise Falls. Jan's missing and I'm trying to find her. I thought, maybe, there was a chance she might come here to see you."

They were still both staring. Horace Richler's face, at first frozen, was turning into a furious scowl.

"You've made some kind of mistake, mister," he said. "You better get your ass off my goddamn porch."

"Please," I said. "I know there's some history between you and your daughter, that you haven't talked to her in a long time, but I'm worried that something bad has happened to her. I thought, if she didn't actually come here, she might have called, or you might have an idea where she might go, some old friends she might try to get in touch with."

Horace Richler's face grew red with fury. His fists were clenching at his sides.

"I don't know who you are or what the fuck your game is, but I swear to God, I may be an old man, but I'll kick your ass all the way down Lincoln Avenue if I have to."

I wasn't ready to give up.

"Tell me I haven't got the right house," I said. "You're Horace and Gretchen Richler and your daughter is Jan."

Gretchen came out from behind her husband and spoke to me for the first time.

"That's right," she whispered.

"My daughter's dead," Horace said through gritted teeth.

The comment hit me like a two-by-four across the side of the head. Something horrible had happened. I'd gotten here too late.

"My God," I said. "When? What happened?"

"She died a long time ago," he said.

I breathed out. At first, I thought he'd meant something had just happened to Jan. Then I assumed he meant that because he and his daughter were estranged, it was as though Jan was dead to him. "I know you may feel that way, Mr. Richler. But if you ever loved your daughter, you need to help me now."

Gretchen said, "You don't understand. She really is dead."

I felt the wallop all over again. I really had gotten here too late. Had Jan already been to see her parents? Had she taken her life here? Was that her final act of revenge against them? To come to Rochester and kill herself in front of them?

I managed to say, "What are you talking about?"

"She died when she was a little girl," Gretchen said. "When she was only five years old. It was a terrible thing."

# PART THREE

# SEVENTEEN

THE WOMAN OPENED HER eyes. She blinked a couple of times, adjusting to the darkness.

She was in bed, on her back, staring up at the ceiling. It was warm in the room—there was an air conditioner humming and rattling somewhere, but it wasn't up to the job—and in her sleep she had thrown off her covers down to her waist.

She reached down and touched her stomach to see whether she had broken out in a sweat. Her skin was cool, but slightly clammy. She was taken aback for a moment to discover she was naked. She'd stopped sleeping in the nude a long time ago. Those first few months of marriage, sure, but after a while, you just want something on.

Light from the tall streetlamps out by the highway filtered through the bent and twisted window blinds. She listened to the relentless traffic streaming by. Big semis roaring through the night.

She tried to recall where, exactly, she was.

She slipped her legs out from under the covers, sat up, and placed her feet on the floor. The cheap industrial carpet was scratchy beneath her toes. She sat on the side of the bed for a moment, leaning over, head in her hands, her hair falling in front of her eyes.

She had a headache. She glanced over at the bedside

table, as if some aspirin and a glass of water might magically be there, but all she could see in the minimal light were some crumpled bills and change, a digital clock that was reading 12:10 a.m., and a blonde wig.

That told her she'd only been asleep for an hour at the most. She'd gotten into the bed around half past ten, tossed and turned and looked up at the stained tiles overhead until well after eleven. At some point, clearly, she'd nodded off, but the last hour of sleep had not been a restful one.

Slowly she stood up, took two steps over to the window, and peered between the blinds. It wasn't much of a view. A parking lot, about a quarter of the spots taken. A sign tall enough to be seen from the interstate advertising "Best Western." Off in the distance, more towering signs. One for Mobil, another for McDonald's.

The woman went to the door, checked that it was still locked.

She padded softly across the room and pushed open the door to the bathroom. She went inside and felt for the light switch, waiting until she had the door closed behind her before flicking it on.

The instant, intense illumination stung her eyes. She squinted until she got used to it, then gazed at her naked reflection in the oversized mirror above the counter.

"Yikes," she whispered. Her black hair was stringy, her eyes dark, her lips dry.

There was a small, open canvas toiletries bag on the counter by the sink. A few things had not been returned to it, including a toothbrush, some makeup, a hairbrush. She opened the bag wider, rooted around inside.

"Yes," she said when she had found what she wanted. She had a travel-sized bottle of aspirin. She unscrewed the cap and tapped two tablets into her palm. She put them in her mouth, then leaned over a running faucet to scoop some water into her hand. She got enough into her mouth to swallow the pills. She tilted her head back to ease their passage down her throat, then cupped more water into her hand just to drink. She reached for a towel to dry her hand and chin.

She glanced down at a bandage on the inside of her right ankle and grimaced. That cut wouldn't have healed yet. A couple more days should do it.

At that point, her stomach growled, loud enough that it seemed to echo off the tiles of the tiny room. Maybe that was why she had the headache. She was hungry. She'd had very little to eat the whole day. Too on edge. Wasn't sure she'd be able to keep anything down.

The McDonald's was probably one of those twenty-four-hour ones. Truckers had to have someplace to eat in the dead of night. A Big Mac would do it. She could imagine the wonderful blandness of it. There was nothing left to eat in the motel room. Not so much as a few Doritos or half a Mars bar. They'd picked up some junk to eat along the way, but she'd hardly touched it.

Hungry as she was, she wasn't going to venture out of this motel room. Best to stay put, at least for now. She might end up drawing more attention to herself at night, a woman alone, than she would in the middle of the day.

She put her hand on the bathroom doorknob, flicked off the light before turning it. Now her eyes had to adjust in reverse, getting used to the darkness so she wouldn't stumble over anything on her way back to the bed.

She returned to the window, half expecting to see the blue Ford Explorer out there. But that had been ditched long ago, and far from here. It would surely be found eventually, and it was hard to know whether that would end up being a good thing or bad. Lyall probably would have called the police by now. Useless as he was, he'd notice eventually that his wife hadn't returned home. Drinking to all hours, staying out late with his friends, never helping out around the house, and that damn smelly dog. The Explorer had reeked of that beast. At least Lyall wasn't a mean drunk. Every once in a while, he got this look, like maybe he wasn't going to take it anymore. But it never lasted long. The guy didn't have it in him to fight back.

Someone stirred in the other half of the bed she'd been sleeping in moments earlier.

She turned away from the window. There wasn't much else to do but try to get back to sleep. Maybe, once the aspirin kicked in, she'd be able to nod off. She looked at the clock: 12:21 a.m.

There was no reason to get up early. No job to go to anymore. No one to make breakfast for.

She sat gently on the side of the bed, raised her legs ever so slowly and tucked them under the covers, lowered her head onto the pillow, trying her best not to breathe. If there was anything good about motel beds, this was it. The mattresses seemed to be resting on concrete, not box springs, and you could usually get in and out of bed without disturbing your partner's sleep.

But not this time.

The person on the other side of the bed turned over and said, "What's going on, babe?"

"Shh, go back to sleep," she said.

"What's going on?"

"I had a headache. I was looking for aspirin."

"There's some in the little case there."

"I found them."

A hand reached out and found her breast, kneading the nipple between thumb and forefinger.

"Jesus, Dwayne, I tell you I've got a headache, and then you cop a feel?"

He withdrew the hand. "You're just stressed out. It's going to take you a while to get over this whole Jan thing."

The woman said, "What's to get over? She's dead."

# EIGHTEEN

"SO YOU BETTER GET off my porch and hit the fucking road," Horace Richler said to me.

"I . . . I don't understand," I said, standing at the open front door, looking into the faces of Horace and his wife, Gretchen.

"Too goddamn bad," he said, and started putting his weight behind the door to close it.

"Wait!" I said. "Please! This doesn't make any sense."

"No kidding," Horace said. "You wake us up in the middle of the night asking for our dead daughter, you're damn right it makes no sense."

He nearly had the door closed when Gretchen said, "Horace."

"Huh?"

"Hang on a minute." The door didn't open any farther, but it didn't close, either. Gretchen said to me, "Who did you say you are again?"

"David Harwood," I said. "I live in Promise Falls."

"And your wife's name is Jan?"

Horace interrupted. "Christ's sake, Gretchen, the guy's a lunatic. Don't encourage him."

I said, "That's right. Jan, or, you know, Janice. She's Janice Harwood now, but before we got married she was Jan Richler."

"There must be lots of Jan Richlers in the world," Gretchen said. "You've come to the wrong house."

I had the palm of my hand on the door, hoping it wouldn't close farther. "But her birth certificate says that her parents are Horace and Gretchen, that she was born here in Rochester."

The two of them stared at me, not quite sure what to believe.

It was, surprisingly, Horace who asked, "What's her birthday?" There was a defiant tone in his voice, like he wasn't expecting me to know the answer.

I said, "August 14, 1975."

It was as if the air had been let out of both of them. Horace acted as though he had taken a blow to the chest. He folded in on himself and his head drooped. He let go of the door, turned away, and took a step back into the house.

Gretchen's face had fallen, but she held her spot at the door.

"I'm sorry," I said. "This is as much a shock to me as it is to you."

Gretchen shook her head sadly. "This is very hard on him."

"I don't know how to explain this," I said. My knees felt weak, and I realized that I was trembling slightly. "My wife has been missing since early today—since Saturday, around the middle of the day. She just vanished. I've been trying to think of anyone she might have gotten in touch with, and that's why I came here to see you."

"Why would your wife have our daughter's birth certificate?" Gretchen asked. "How is that possible?"

Before I could even attempt to come up with an explanation, I said, "Would it be all right if I came in?"

Gretchen turned toward her husband, who'd been listening without actually looking at us. "Horace?" she said. All he did was raise a hand dismissively, an act of surrender, suggesting it was up to his wife whether I'd be allowed inside.

"Come in, then," she said, opening the door wider.

She led me into a living room filled with furniture that I was guessing had been handed down to them from their own parents. Only the drab couch looked less than twenty years old. What splashes of color there were came from pillows smothered in crocheted covers crudely resembling flowers. Scattered across the couch and chairs, they were like stamps on old manila envelopes. Cheap landscapes hung so high on the wall they nearly lined up with the ceiling.

I took a seat first in one of the chairs. Gretchen sat down on the couch, pulling her robe tightly around her. "Horace, come on, lovey, sit down."

There were some framed family photos in the room, most of them featuring one or both of the Richlers, often with a boy. If the pictures could have been arranged in chronological order, I'd be able to see this boy's progression from age three to a man in his early twenties. There was one picture of him—as an adult—in uniform.

Gretchen caught me looking. "That's Bradley," she said.

I nodded. I might normally have offered up a comment, that he was good-looking, a handsome fellow, which was true. But I was feeling too shell-shocked for pleasantries.

Reluctantly, Horace Richler came over to the couch and sat down next to his wife. Gretchen rested her hand on his pajama-clad knee.

"He's dead," Horace said, seeing that I'd been looking at the picture of the young man.

"Afghanistan," Gretchen said. "One of those I.E.D.s."

"I'm so sorry."

"He was killed along with two Canadians," she said. "Almost two years ago now. Just outside Kabul."

The room was quiet for several seconds.

"So that's both our children," Gretchen said.

Hesitantly, I said, "I don't see any pictures of your daughter." I was desperate to see what she had looked like, even as a five-year-old. If it was Jan, I was sure I'd know it.

"We . . . don't have any out," Gretchen said.

I said nothing, waiting for an explanation.

"It's . . . hard," she said. "Even after all these years. To be reminded."

Another uncomfortable silence ensued, until Horace, whose lips had already been going in and out in preparation, blurted, "I killed her."

I said, barely able to find my voice, "What?"

He was looking down into his lap, seemingly ashamed. Gretchen gripped his knee harder and put her other hand to his shoulder. "Horace, don't do this."

"It's true," he said. "It's been enough years that there's no sense beating around the bush."

Gretchen said to me, "It was a terrible, terrible thing. It wasn't Horace's fault." Her face screwed up, like she was fighting back tears. "I lost a daughter and a husband that day. My husband's never been the man he was once, not in thirty years. And he's a good man. Don't let anyone tell you any different."

I asked, "What happened?"

Gretchen started to speak, but Horace cut her off. "I can tell it," he said, as though this was part of his penance, to confess. "I've lost a daughter and I've lost a son. What the hell difference does it make anymore?"

He reached inside himself for the strength to continue.

"It was the third of September, 1980. It was after I'd come home from work, after Gretchen had made dinner.

Jan and one of her little friends, Constance, were playing in the front yard."

"Arguing more than playing," Gretchen interjected, and I looked at her. "I'd been watching them through the window. You know how little girls can be."

Horace continued, "I was going to meet my friends after dinner. Bowling. I was in a league back then. The thing is, I'd got home late, ate my dinner fast as I could, because I was supposed to be meeting up with everyone at six, and it was already ten past when I finished dinner. So I ran out to the car and jumped in and backed out of the driveway like a bat out of hell."

I waited, a sick feeling in the pit of my stomach.

"It wasn't his fault," Gretchen said again. "Jan . . . was pushed."

"What?" I said.

"If I hadn't been going so fast," Horace said, "it wouldn't have mattered. You can't go blaming this on that other little girl."

"But it is what happened," Gretchen said. "The girls were having a fight, standing by the driveway, and Constance pushed Jan into the path of the car just as Horace started backing up."

"Oh my God," I said.

Horace said, "I knew right away I'd hit something. I slammed on the brakes and got out, but . . ."

He stopped, made his hands into tight fists, as though that could keep the tears from welling up in his eyes. It worked for him, but not for Gretchen.

I tried to swallow.

"The other little girl started to scream," Gretchen said. "It was her fault, but can you really blame a child? Kids, they don't know the consequences of their actions. They can't anticipate."

"She wasn't driving the car," Horace said. "I was the one behind the wheel. I should have been watching. I was the one who should have been anticipating. And I wasn't. I was too worried about getting to a fucking bowling alley on time." He shook his head. "And the hell of it is, they never did a damn thing to me. Said it wasn't my fault, it was an accident, just one of those horrible things. I wish they'd done something to me, but maybe it wouldn't have made any difference. Anything they might have done, short of killing me, wouldn't have stopped me from wanting to punish myself even more."

"Horace tried to take his life," Gretchen said. "A couple of times."

He looked away, embarrassed by that revelation more than the one he'd made himself. When he didn't say anything further, it was clear this was the end of the story.

"That child who pushed Jan, her life was ruined that day, too. I know she deserves some pity," Gretchen said. "But I never had any for her, or her parents. Not surprisingly, they moved away after that. Sometimes, I think we should have done the same thing."

"There's not a single time I get in the car I don't think about what I did," Horace said. "Not a single time, not in all these years."

This was the saddest room I'd ever been in.

I was definitely a mess. Listening to Horace Richler tell how he ran over his own daughter with his car would have been devastating enough. But the implications of his story were overwhelming me.

He was talking about Jan. The Jan on my wife's birth certificate.

But Horace's Jan had been dead for decades. And my Jan was, at least up until today, alive.

My wife had Horace and Gretchen Richler's child's name. She had her birth certificate.

But it was glaringly obvious that they could not be the same person.

I was dumbstruck. I was so numbed by what I'd been told that I didn't even know what to ask next.

"Mr. Harwood?" Gretchen said. "Are you okay?"

"I'm sorry. I . . ."

"You don't look well. You've got bags under your eyes and don't look like you've had any sleep in a long time."

"I don't . . . I don't know what to make of this."

"Well," said Horace, trying to put some bluster back into his voice, "we don't exactly know what the hell to make of you, either."

I tried to focus. I said, "A picture. Could I please see a picture of Jan?"

Gretchen exchanged glances with her husband before deciding my request was reasonable. She got up and crossed the room to an old-fashioned rolltop desk and chair in the corner. She sat down, opened the door, and reached in.

She must have stolen a look at the picture every once in a while, because it took her no time at all to put her hands on it. I could understand, from Horace's point of view, why the picture was not on display. Did you want your daughter, the one you'd killed, looking at you every day?

It was a black-and-white portrait shot, the kind that might have been taken at Sears, about three by five inches. Slightly faded, one of the corners bent.

She handed it to me. "This was taken about two months . . . before," she said.

Jan Richler had been a beautiful child. An angelic face, dimples, bright eyes, curly blonde hair.

I searched the photo for any hints of my wife. Maybe something in the eyes, the way the mouth turned up at the corner. The line of her nose.

I tried to imagine this picture on a table covered with photos of other children. I looked for anything in the shot that would make me pick it up and say, "That's her, that's the girl I married."

There was nothing.

I handed the picture back to Gretchen Richler. "Thank you," I said quietly.

"Well?" she said.

"I know it seems ridiculously obvious to say that's not my wife," I said, "but that's not my wife."

Horace made some kind of grunting noise.

"May I show you a picture?" I said, reaching into my jacket. It was one of the copies I'd printed out of the snapshot I'd emailed to Detective Duckworth, taken in Chicago.

Horace took the picture first, gave it nothing more than a glance, then handed it to Gretchen.

She gave the picture the attention I thought it warranted, considering this was a woman with her daughter's name and all. She studied it at arm's length at first, then brought it up close, giving it a kind of microscopic examination, before putting it down on the table.

"Anything?" I said.

"I was just . . . noticing how beautiful your wife is," she said, almost dreamily. "I like to think that if our Jan had lived, she would have been as pretty as your wife here." She picked it up to hand it to me, then reconsidered. "If this woman, your wife, is using our daughter's name, maybe she has some ties to this area. In case I saw her, should I hang on to this?"

I had other printed copies. I supposed it was possible Jan might yet show up here, although I now couldn't imagine why, and it would be good for her image to be fresh in the Richlers' minds. "Sure," I said.

She took the picture and put it in the drawer with her daughter's, and stood there with her back to us.

Horace said, "And that woman, she says we're her parents?"

"She's never talked about you by name," I said. "I figured it out from her birth certificate."

Gretchen turned slowly and said, "Didn't it seem odd that she's never taken you to meet her parents?"

"She's always said she's been estranged from her family. That was why I came here. I thought, maybe, she was trying to reestablish contact. Say her piece. Something. Because for the last couple of weeks she's been very troubled. Depressed. I wondered if she could be, I don't know, exorcising her demons. Confronting things that have troubled her for years."

"Would you excuse me for a minute?" Gretchen asked, her voice shaking slightly.

Neither of us felt the need to give her permission. After she had climbed the stairs and we heard a door close, Horace said to me, "You think you're over it, and then something comes along and opens up the wound all over again."

"I'm sorry," I said.

"Yeah, well, whatever," Horace said.

I nodded my regrets and attempted to stand up. I was a bit shaky on my feet.

"I hope you're not thinking of getting behind the wheel of a car," Horace said.

"I should be okay," I said. "I'll stop for a coffee or something on the way."

"You look so tired even coffee may not help," he said, the first time since I'd come here that he sounded at all conciliatory.

"I need to get back home, see my boy. I can pull over and grab a few winks if I have to," I said.

From the top of the stairs, Gretchen said, "How old is your son? He looks about three in that picture with your wife."

I watched as she descended, slowly coming into view. She seemed to have pulled herself together in the last couple of minutes. "He's four," I said. "His name is Ethan."

"How long have you been married?"

"Five years."

"How's it going to help your son if you fall asleep at the wheel and go into a ditch?"

I knew she was right. "I may find a place to stay," I said.

Gretchen pointed to the couch, where Horace still sat. "You'd be more than welcome to stay here."

The couch, with its bright crocheted pillows, suddenly looked very inviting.

"I don't want to put you out," I said.

"Please," she said.

I nodded gratefully. "I'll be gone first thing in the morning."

Horace, his brow furrowed, had his face screwed up tight. "So if you don't mind my asking," he said, "if your wife is going around saying she's Jan Richler but she's not, then who the hell is she?"

The question had already been forming in my mind, but I'd been trying to ignore it.

Horace wasn't done. "And how could she do that to our little girl? Take her name from her? Hasn't she suffered enough?"

# NINETEEN

SUNDAY MORNING, THE DUCKWORTHS' clock radio went off at 6:30.

The detective didn't move. He didn't hear the newscaster say that it was going to be a cloudy day, or that it was only going to be in the high 70s, or that it might rain on Monday.

But Maureen Duckworth heard everything because she was already awake, and had been for some time. A nightmare—another one involving their nineteen-year-old son, Trevor, who was traveling around Europe with his girlfriend, Trish, and hadn't phoned or sent them an email or anything in two days, which was typical of him, never giving a thought to how much his mother worried—woke her around four. In this dream, her son had decided to go bungee jumping off the Eiffel Tower, except somehow while he was on the way down he was attacked by flying monkeys.

She knew there were a lot of things that could happen to a kid away from home, but had to admit this particular scenario was unlikely. She persuaded herself that this nightmare held no special meaning, that it wasn't an omen, that it was nothing more than a stupid, ridiculous dream. Having done that, she might normally have gotten back to sleep, had her husband's snoring not been almost loud enough to shake the windows.

She gave Barry a shove so that he'd roll off his back

and onto his side, but it didn't do a damn bit of good. It was like sleeping next to a chain saw.

She twisted in the earplugs she kept next to her bed for just such emergencies, but they were about as effective as heading out naked in a snowstorm with nothing on but lip balm.

She had, in fact, been staring at the clock radio when it read 6:29, and was counting down the seconds in her head, waiting for it to come on. She was off by only two seconds.

She'd gotten Barry to try those strips that stick to the top of the nose, supposedly open up the nasal passages, but they didn't do anything. Then she bought him some anti-snoring capsules he could take just before going to bed, but they struck out as well.

What she really thought would help would be if he lost a little weight. Which was why she'd been serving him fruits and granola at breakfast, packing him a lunch with plenty of carrot sticks, and cutting back on fried foods and butter at dinner.

She got out of bed and collected dirty clothes in the room. The clothes she'd taken off the night before, the slacks and shirt Barry had tossed off after coming in late from work. He'd put in an extra-long day, looking for this woman who went missing at the roller-coaster park.

She looked at the slacks. What was that on them? Was that ice cream? Mixed in with some kind of pie?

"Barry," she said. He didn't move. "Barry," she said, a little louder so she could be heard over the snoring.

She walked around to his side of the bed and touched his shoulder.

He snorted, opened his eyes. He blinked a couple of times, heard the radio.

"Yeah, okay," he said. "I didn't even hear that come on."

"I did," Maureen said. "You sure you have to go in today?"

He moved his head sideways on the pillow. "I want to see if that release we put out last night turned up anything."

"You want to tell me what this is?" she said, holding the stained trousers a few inches from his nose.

He squinted. "I was working vice undercover. Had to get a hand job in the line of duty."

"You wish. That's ice cream, isn't it?"

"Maybe," he said.

"Where'd you have ice cream?"

"The missing woman? I went to see her boss. You've seen that Bertram Heating and Cooling truck?"

"Yeah."

"Him. His wife got me some pie."

"With ice cream."

"Yeah."

"What kind of pie?"

"Apple."

Maureen Duckworth nodded, as if she suddenly understood. "I'd eat apple pie for breakfast if we had it."

"What do we have?"

"You're getting fruit and some fiber," she said.

"You know torture's not allowed now, right? New regime and all."

The phone rang.

Maureen didn't react. The phone could ring anytime, day or night, around here. "I'll get it," she said. She picked up the receiver on her side of the bed. "Hello. . . . Yeah, hi. . . . No, don't worry about it, I was already up. . . . Sure, he's here. . . . We're just bringing in the hoist to get him out of bed."

She held out the phone. Barry leaned across the bed to grab it.

"Duckworth," he said.

"Hey, Detective. You got a pen?"

Barry grabbed the pen and paper that were always sitting by the phone. He wrote down a name and a number, made a couple of notes. "Great, thanks," he said and hung up.

Maureen looked at him expectantly.

"We got something," he said.

Duckworth waited until he was showered and dressed and had a cup of coffee in his hand before he dialed the number from the phone in the kitchen.

Someone picked up after two rings. "Ted's," a man said.

"Is this Ted Brehl?" Duckworth asked.

"That's right."

"Did I pronounce that right?"

"Like the letters for the blind, right."

"This is Detective Barry Duckworth, Promise Falls police. You called in about half an hour ago?"

"Yeah. I saw that thing on the news last night. When I got up this morning, came in to open the store, I thought maybe I should give you a call."

"Where's your store?"

"Up by Lake George? On 87?"

"I know the area. Real pretty up there."

Maureen put a bowl of granola, topped with bananas and strawberries, in front of her husband.

"Yeah, so, I saw that woman."

"Jan Harwood."

"Yeah, she was in here."

"When was that?"

"Friday. Like, must have been around five?"

"Five in the afternoon?"

"That's right. She came in to buy some water and iced tea."

"Was she alone?"

"She came into the store alone, but she was with a man, her husband, I guess. He was out in the car." Ted Brehl's description of it matched the vehicle owned by David Harwood.

"So they just stopped to buy some drinks and then left?"

"No, they sat out there for quite a while, talking. I looked out a couple of times. I looked out again around five-thirty, and they were gone."

"You're sure it was her?"

Brehl didn't hesitate. "Oh yeah. I mean, I might normally have forgotten, but she struck up a conversation with me. And she's a nice-looking lady, the kind you remember."

"What did she talk about?"

"I'm trying to remember how she put it. She said she'd never been up this way before, first of all, at least not that she could remember. I asked her where she was going, and she said she didn't exactly know."

"She didn't know?"

"She said her husband wanted to take her for a drive in the country, up into the woods. She said maybe it was some sort of surprise or something, because he'd told her not to tell anyone they were going."

Duckworth thought about that.

"What else did she say?"

"That was about it, I guess."

"How was her mood?"

"Mood?"

"Was she happy? Depressed? Troubled?"

"She seemed just fine, you know?"

"Sure," Duckworth said. "Listen, thanks for calling. I might be in touch again."

"Okay. Just wanted to help."

Duckworth hung up the phone, then looked down at

his cereal. "You got some sugar or whipped cream I can put on this?" he asked.

Maureen sat down opposite him and said, "It's been two days." Barry knew instantly she was talking about their son, Trevor. He reached out and held her hand.

# TWENTY

I WOKE EARLY ON the Richlers' couch, but that was okay because they were early risers themselves. I heard Horace Richler banging around the kitchen shortly after six. From my vantage point, I could see him standing at the sink in slippers and robe. He ran some water into a glass and popped a couple of pills into his mouth, then turned and shuffled back toward the stairs.

Once he was gone, I threw off the crocheted blanket that Gretchen had told me she'd made herself. It was so huge I marveled that anyone under two hundred years of age could have stitched it. Even though I'd packed a small bag, I'd opted to sleep in my clothes, taking off only my jacket and shoes before I'd put my head down on an honest-to-God bed pillow, not a crocheted one, that Gretchen had provided.

"I'm sorry about not having anything better than the couch," she'd said. "You see, no one sleeps in our son's room. We've left it just the way it was. And the guest bedroom has kind of turned into storage, you know? We don't get a lot of company." She'd thought a moment. "I don't think we've ever had any overnight guests, to tell you the truth. You might be our first, ever."

I could have used a shower, but I didn't want to push it. I grabbed my travel kit and went into the first-floor bathroom at the back of the house and shaved, brushed my teeth, and wet my hair enough to get the bumps flattened. When I came back out, I smelled coffee.

Gretchen was dressed and in the kitchen. "Good morning," she said.

"Good morning."

"How did you sleep?"

"Pretty good," I said. Even though I'd gone to bed troubled and on overload, my body had been exhausted and I'd conked out right away. "How about you?"

She smiled, like she didn't want what she had to say to hurt my feelings. "Not so great. Your news, it was disturbing. And it brought back a lot of bad memories for us. Especially for Horace. I mean, we both took the loss of Jan hard, but when you consider how it happened, he . . ."

"I understand," I said. "I'm sorry. I had no way of knowing."

"Something like this, it touches so many people. Us, our relatives, the school Jan went to. Her kindergarten teacher, Miss Stephens, had to take a leave for a week, she was so upset. All the kids in her class were devastated. The little girl who pushed her . . . If it happened today, they'd have probably put her in therapy. Maybe her parents did, who knows. Mr. Andrews, the school principal, he got them to put up a little plaque at the school in Jan's memory. But I could never go look at it, and Horace, he couldn't bear to see it. He didn't want the fuss, except he wished they'd have put him in jail or something, like he said. So a lot of people, they were affected by this."

"And then me," I said.

"And then you. Coffee?"

"Please."

"Except with you," Gretchen said, "it's different."

She filled a mug with coffee from a glass carafe while I waited for her to continue.

"You didn't know our Jan. Not ever. You don't know any of us. And yet, here you are, sitting here, connected to us somehow."

I poured some cream into the coffee, watched the liquids interact without stirring, and nodded. "And I don't know exactly how," I said.

Gretchen put both hands flat on the countertop, a gesture that seemed to foretell an important announcement, or at the very least, a direct comment. "Mr. Harwood, what do you really think has happened to your wife?"

"I don't know," I said honestly. "I'm worried that she may have harmed herself."

Gretchen took half a second to understand what I was getting at. "But if she hasn't, and you find her alive . . ." Gretchen was struggling with something here.

"Yes?"

"Let's say you find her, and she's okay, is it going to be the same?"

"I'm not sure I follow."

"Your wife can't be Jan Richler. Isn't that clear to you?"

I looked away.

"If she's not the woman you've always believed she was, how are things going to be the same?"

"Perhaps," I said slowly, "there's just been some kind of a mix-up. Maybe there's an explanation for this that's not immediately obvious."

Gretchen kept her eyes on me. "What kind of explanation?"

"I don't know."

"Why would anyone take on someone else's identity? Why would they do that?"

"I don't know."

"And why, of all the people whose identity someone could take, why take my daughter's?"

I couldn't say it again.

"Horace was right, last night, when he asked how someone could do that to our girl. How could someone use her like that? All she is to us now is a name, and a memory. And all these years later, someone tries to steal that from us?"

"I'm sure Jan—" My wife's name caught in my throat. "I'm sure there's an explanation. If, for some reason, my wife had to take a name that was not her own, I'm sure she would never have intended any harm to you or your husband or the memory of your daughter."

What the hell was I talking about? What possible scenario was I trying to envision?

"Suppose," I said, thinking out loud, and very slowly, "she had to change her identity for some reason. And the name she had to take, that she was given, say, happened to be your daughter's."

Gretchen eyed me skeptically. I looked down at my untouched coffee.

"Horace couldn't sleep last night," she said. "It was more than just being upset. He was angry. Angry that someone would do such a thing. Angry at your wife. Even without knowing her."

"I just hope," I said, "that there'll be a chance for you to tell her face-to-face what you think."

Before I left, just in case Jan somehow turned up here, I wrote down my home and cell numbers and address, as well as my parents' number and address.

"Please get in touch," I said.

Gretchen placated me with a smile, like she knew she wasn't going to have any news for me.

My cell rang on the way home. It was Mom.

"What's happening?" she asked. "We've been worried sick, wondering why you haven't called."

"I'll be home in a few hours," I said.

"Did you find her?"

"No."

"What about the Richlers? Did you find them?"

"Yes," I said.

"Did Jan go see them? Have they heard from her?"

"No," I said. I didn't want to get into it. I was almost afraid to ask how Ethan was, given his rambunctious nature, but did anyway.

"He's fine. We thought a truck hit the house this morning, but it was just him jumping on the stairs. Your father's got him in the basement now to—"

"Locked up?"

Mom actually laughed. "He and your father are in the basement talking about building a train set."

"Okay. I'm going to go by the house on the way. Then I'll come and pick up Ethan."

"I love you," Mom said.

"Love you, too."

The interstate's a pretty good place to let your mind wander. You can put your car on cruise, and your brain as well, if you want. But my thoughts were all over the place. And they all circled around one thing.

Why did my wife have the name and birth certificate of a child who had died years ago at the age of five?

It was more than some crazy coincidence. This wasn't a case of two people having the same name by chance. Jan's birth certificate details had led me to the Richlers' front door.

I thought about the things I'd speculated to Gretchen. That maybe Jan had been required to take on a new identity.

I tried to work it out. Jan Richler, the Jan Richler I'd married, the woman I'd been with for six years, the woman I'd had a child with, was not really Jan Richler.

It was hardly a secret that if you could find the name of someone who'd died at a young age, there was a good chance you could build a new identity with it. I'd worked in the news business long enough to learn how it could be done. You applied for a new copy of the deceased's birth certificate, since birth and death certificates were often not cross-referenced, certainly not several decades ago. With that, you acquired other forms of identification. A Social Security number. A library card. A driver's license.

It wasn't impossible for someone to become someone else. My wife had become Jan Richler, and when she met and married me, Jan Harwood.

But before that, she had to have been someone else.

And what was the most likely reason for someone to shed a past life and start up a new one?

Two words came to mind immediately: *Witness protection.*

"Jesus Christ," I said aloud in the empty car.

Maybe that was it. Jan had witnessed something, testified in some court case. Against whom? The mob? Was it ever anyone but the mob? Bikers, maybe? It had to be someone, or some organization, with the resources to track her down and exact revenge if they managed to do it.

If that was the case, the authorities would have had to create a new identity for her.

It was the kind of secret she might feel she could never tell me. Maybe she was worried that if I knew, it would expose me—and more important, Ethan—to risks we couldn't even imagine.

No wonder she'd hidden her birth certificate. The last thing she wanted me to do was nose around and blow her cover. Not because of what it would mean to her, but because of what it might mean to us, as a family.

And if she was a protected witness, relegated to living out a new life in some new location, what, if anything, did it have to do with her disappearance?

Had someone figured out where she was? Did she believe she was about to be discovered? Did she run to save herself?

But if she did, why couldn't she have found a way to tell me something?

Anything?

And if Jan's life was in danger, was I doing the right thing in trying to find her? Would I end up leading the person or persons who wanted to do her harm right to her?

Assuming, of course, that any of my theories about Jan being in the witness protection program were anything other than total horseshit.

I'd have to tell Barry Duckworth what I'd learned. He'd no doubt have connections, people he could talk to who might be able to reveal whether Jan—under another name—had ever been a star witness in an important trial. Maybe—

My phone rang. I'd left it on the seat next to me so I could grab it quickly.

"Yeah?"

"Dave?"

"Yes."

"David, Jesus, you're the biggest story on the news and you don't let your own goddamn paper know about it?"

Brian Donnelly, the city editor.

"Brian," I said.

"Where are you?"

"I-90. I'm coming back from Rochester."

"Man, this is terrible," he said.

"Yeah," I said. "Jan's been gone since about—"

"I mean, shit, by the time the cops issued their release, the paper had already gone to bed, so TV and radio have it, but we haven't got anything in the edition, and it's about one of our own people! Madeline's totally pissed. What the hell? You couldn't call us with this?"

"Sorry, Brian," I deadpanned. "I don't know what I was thinking."

"Look, I want to put Samantha on the line, she can get some quotes from you for the main story, but I want to know whether you could write a first-person. 'Mystery Hits Close to Home for *Standard* Reporter.' That kind of thing. I don't mean to come across as an asshole or anything, but—"

"No worries there," I said.

"But a first-person perspective would be really good. We haven't gotten much from the cops about what actually happened, and you could give us some of that, and you know, this kind of play, it might help you find . . . uh, find . . ."

"Jan," I said.

"Exactly. So if you—"

I flipped the phone shut and tossed it back over on the passenger seat. A few seconds later it rang again. I flipped it open and put it to my ear.

"Dave? It's Samantha here."

"Hi, Sam."

"I just heard what Brian said to you. My God, I am so sorry. He's the King of Doucheland. I can't believe he said those things."

"Yeah, he's something."

"Is Jan still missing?"

"Yes."

"Can you talk about it? Is there anything you can say, for the record?"

"Just . . . that I'm hoping she'll be home soon."

"The cops are being real weird about it, I have to tell you," she said.

"What do you mean?" I asked.

"They're just not saying much. Duckworth's the head of the investigation. You know him?"

"Sam."

"Oh yeah, stupid question. He's releasing very few details, although we learned that something happened at Five Mountains, right?"

"Sam, I'm on the way home. I'm going to see Duckworth when I get back, and maybe then we'll have a better idea what we're dealing with. I honestly hadn't expected them to release anything until this morning. The news last night, that caught me off guard."

"Okay, off the record. How are you holding up?"

"Not so good."

"Listen, I'll call you later, okay? Give you some time to get your shit together."

"Thanks, Sam."

I pulled into my driveway shortly before noon.

Once I was in the door, I called out Jan's name. Just in case.

Nothing.

For the last twenty miles, all I could think about was the birth certificate I had found. I needed to see it again. I needed to prove to myself that I hadn't imagined it.

Before I went upstairs, I checked to see whether there were any phone messages. There were five, all from different media outlets asking for interviews. I saved all of them, thinking at some point I might be willing to give as many as I could if it meant more people would know Jan was missing.

Then I went upstairs.

I opened the linen closet and dragged out everything

from the bottom. I crawled into the closet and pried away the baseboard along the back wall with a screwdriver I'd found in the kitchen drawer.

The envelope, the one that had contained a birth certificate for Jan Richler, and a key, was gone.

# TWENTY-ONE

SHE WAS ACTUALLY ASLEEP when the man in the bed next to her threw back the covers and padded across the bristly carpet to the bathroom. She'd stared at the ceiling for a long time after getting back under the covers, wondering whether she'd ever nod off. Thinking about what she'd done, the life she'd left behind.

The body they'd buried.

But at some point, it happened. Her anxiety surrendered, at last, to weariness. If only it had been a restful sleep.

Like her, Dwayne had slept naked. Dwayne Osterhaus was a thin, wiry man, just under six feet tall, with a small tattoo of the number "6" on his right buttock. It was, he believed, his lucky number. "Everyone picks seven, but I like six." His lean, youthful body was betrayed by his thinning gray hair. Maybe prison did that to you, she thought, watching him with one eye open as he crossed the room. Turned you gray early.

He closed the bathroom door, but she could still hear him taking a leak. Went on forever. She reached for the remote and clicked on the TV, thumbed the volume button to drown him out. It was one of the morning news shows out of New York. The two hosts, a man and a woman, were jabbering on about which couples were in the lead to get married on live TV.

The bathroom door opened, filling the room with the sound of a flushing toilet.

"Hey," he said, glancing at the set. "I thought I heard voices out here. You're awake." She hit the mute button as he crawled back into the bed.

"Yeah, I'm awake."

"How'd you sleep?"

"Lousy."

"Me, any time I woke up, I kept listening for the sounds of other guys breathing, snoring, having a middle-of-the-night wank. As much as that can fuck up your sleep, the sounds all start blending together, you know, and you get used to them. I guess it's a bit like when you live in New York or something, and you hear horns honking all night, after a while you don't notice it. Then you go sleep someplace where all the noises are gone, at least the ones you know, you really notice the difference. That's how it was when I woke up. I thought, hey, where the fuck am I? Lot of truck traffic on the highway all goddamn night, but that's not what I'm used to. You still got your headache?"

"What?"

"In the night, you had a headache. You still got it?"

"No," she said, and immediately regretted it.

Dwayne shifted closer to her under the covers, slipped his hand down between her legs.

"Hey," she said. "You've been away so long you think you have to get to the main event right away. No one's marching you back to a cell in five minutes."

"Sorry," he said. She'd mentioned this before, but in a different context. At last night's dinner at the Big Boy just off the interstate, he'd had his meal half eaten before she had her napkin unfolded and on her lap. He was shoveling it in like the restaurant was in flames, and he wanted his fill before his hair caught fire. When she mentioned it to him, he explained he'd gotten into the habit of finishing his food before someone else tried to grab it away from him.

He moved his hand away, lightly played with one of her nipples. She turned to face him. Why not be a bit accommodating? she thought. Play the role. She reached down to take him in her hand. She wondered what he might have done in prison. Had he had sex with men? She knew he wasn't that way, but half a decade was a long time to go without. You made do. Had he? Maybe she'd ask him sometime. Then again, maybe not. A guy might be touchy about that kind of thing, asking whether he'd engaged in a bit of knob gobbling while he was away.

Not that it mattered to her one way or the other. She was just curious. She liked to know things.

Dwayne figured thirty seconds of foreplay was more than enough to get her motor running. He threw himself on top of her. The whole thing was over in a minute, and for that she was grateful.

"Wow, that was great," she said.

"You sure?" he asked. "I kind of, you know, could have gone longer, babe, but it just happened."

"No, you were terrific," she said.

"Listen," he said, propping himself up on his elbow, "what should I call you now? I need to get used to something other than your regular name. Like if we're in public. I guess I could call you Blondie." He nodded toward the wig on her bedside table and grinned. "You look hot as shit when you're wearing that, by the way."

She thought a moment. "Kate," she said.

"Kate?"

"Yeah," she said. "From now on, I'm Kate."

Dwayne flopped onto his back and stared at the cracked plaster overhead. "Well, *Kate,* sometimes I can't believe it's over. Seemed more like a hundred years, you know? Other guys, they just did their time, day after day after day, and it's not like they didn't want it to be over, but it wasn't like they had anything waiting for them when they got out. Me, every day I just kept thinking about what my life would be like when I finally got the fuck out of there."

"I guess not everybody had waiting for them what you had waiting," said Kate.

Dwayne glanced over. "No shit," he said. "Plus, I had you waiting, too."

Kate had not been foolish enough to think he'd been talking about her in the first place.

"I know you probably still think I'm the stupidest son of a bitch on the planet," he said.

She said nothing.

"I mean, we were all set, and then I get picked up for something totally unrelated. You don't think I wasn't kicking myself every single day, asking myself how I could be so fucking stupid? The thing is, that guy provoked me. I never should have gone down for that. It was justifiable. My lawyer sold me out, that's what he did."

She'd heard it before.

"A guy takes a swing at you with a pool cue, what, exactly, are you supposed to do? Stand there and let him hit you in the head with it?"

"If you'd paid him the money you owed him, it wouldn't have come to that," she said. "Then he wouldn't have taken a swing at you, and you wouldn't have picked up the eight ball and driven it right into his forehead."

"Good thing the son of a bitch came out of his coma before sentencing," Dwayne said. "They'd have sent me away forever."

Neither of them said anything for a couple of minutes. Dwayne finally broke the silence with "I have to admit, babe, every once in a while, I'd get a bit worried."

"About what?" she asked.

"That you wouldn't wait. I mean, it's a long time. Even when it's something good at the end, it's a long time."

Kate reached over and lazily traced circles around his nipples. "I don't want to make it sound like I had it as bad as you," she said, "but I was kind of in a prison of my own while you were in yours."

"You were smart, I gotta hand it to you, the way you did it, getting a new name, disappearing so fast."

The thing was, she'd already had that in place, even though she hadn't started using it right away. Just seemed like a good idea. Planning ahead and all that. Even she hadn't expected to be needing it so soon.

Dwayne had already been going by another name around the time it all went down—not that he had all the documents Kate had—and was confident if that guy started asking around, things wouldn't get traced back to him. When he got arrested for the assault, it was his real name that went in the paper, so no major worries there. But once things went south, even before Dwayne did the dumbass thing with the eight ball, she started playing it safe. With so much waiting for her at the end of the rainbow, she didn't want to end up dead before she got there. She didn't want to leave anything to chance. Not when she realized the courier had lived.

"So this guy," Dwayne said.

"What guy?"

"Whaddya mean, what guy? The guy you married. That guy."

"What about him?"

"What was he like?"

She wasn't going to answer, then said, "He loved me. In spite of everything."

"But what was he like?"

"He's . . . never realized his potential."

Dwayne nodded. "That's what I'm about. Realizing my potential. You're going to have a much brighter future with me, that you can count on. You know what I'd like to do? I'd like to live on a boat. You're so totally fucking free. You don't like where you are, you cast off, you go someplace else. And you get to see a whole lot of the world. What about you? You want to live on a boat?"

"I've never really thought about it," she said, and stopped running her finger on his chest. Now she was looking at the ceiling, too. "I think I might get seasick. One time, when I was a kid, my parents took that ferry across Lake Michigan and I puked over the side." She paused and became briefly reflective. "I like the idea of an island, though. Someplace with a beach, where you could sit all day and watch the waves roll in. A piña colada in my hand. No one to bother me, pick on me, ask me for anything. Just a place where I could go and live the rest of my life in peace."

Dwayne hadn't listened to a word. "I'd like to get a big one. A boat with whaddyacallems, staterooms or something. Little bedrooms. And they're not like sleeping on some fucking submarine or something. It'd be a nice size bed. And every night, when you're going to sleep, you hear the water banging up against the boat, it's real relaxing."

"Banging?" she said.

"Maybe not banging. Lapping? Should I have said 'lapping'?"

"Have you ever even been on a boat before?" Kate asked him.

Dwayne Osterhaus screwed up his face momentarily. "I don't think you have to have done something to know you'd like it. I never been in the sack with Beyoncé, but I got a pretty good idea I'd enjoy it."

"She's been waiting for your call," she said. She threw back the covers. "I'm going to take a shower."

Walking to the bathroom, she wondered what had happened in the years since she'd last been with Dwayne. Something was different. Sure, he was no rocket scientist when she was with him before, but there'd been compensations. Living on the edge, the almost constant, awesome sex, the thrill of taking chances, not knowing what the next day would bring.

Dwayne seemed to fit the bill back then. He suited her purposes. He helped her get the things she needed. It was no surprise that he'd be different now. A guy gets sent up for a few years, he's not going to be the same guy when he gets out.

Maybe it wasn't just him. Maybe someone else had changed.

"I need some breakfast," he said. "Like a Grand Slam, you know? The whole thing. Eggs, sausage, pancakes. I'm goddamn starving."

At Denny's, they got a low-rise booth next to a man who was taking two small children out for breakfast. The man, his back to Dwayne, was telling the boys—they looked to be twins, maybe six years old—to sit still instead of getting up and standing on the seat.

The waitress handed them their menus and Dwayne said, smiling ear to ear, "*Kate* and me could use some coffee." While the waitress went for the pot, Dwayne grinned and said, "I thought I'd start getting used to it."

"You say it like that, she's going to know there's something fishy about it," she said.

The waitress set two mugs on the table, filled them, then reached into the pocket of her apron for creams.

Dwayne said to Kate, "I'm thinking sausage, bacon, and ham. You should get that, too, put some meat on your bones." He grinned at the waitress. "You keep these coffees topped up, ya hear?"

"You bet," she said. "You know what you want or you need a few minutes?"

"I want a donut!" one of the boys shouted behind Dwayne.

"We're not getting donuts," the father said. "You want some bacon and eggs? Scrambled the way you like them?"

"I want a donut!" the boy whined.

Dwayne was grinding his teeth as he ordered his Grand Slam with extra meat, while Kate ordered as basic an order of pancakes as was possible. "No home fries, no sausage, just pancakes," she said. "Syrup on the side."

As the waitress walked away, Dwayne glanced over his shoulder at the kid who was annoying him, then leaned toward Kate and whispered, "I think your wig's a bit cockeyed."

She reached up and adjusted it, trying to make it look like she was just patting her own hair, making sure everything was in place.

"You look good like that," he said. "You should keep it that way. You should dye it."

"And if the cops somehow figure out they're looking for a blonde, what am I supposed to do? Dye it again? I'd rather get myself a couple more wigs."

Dwayne smiled lasciviously. "You could wear a different one every night."

"That how they do it inside?" she asked. "Guy's a redhead one night, brunette the next, takes your mind off the fact he's a man?"

She couldn't believe she'd said it.

Dwayne's eyes narrowed. "Excuse me?"

"Forget it," she said.

"There something you want to ask me?" he asked.

"I said forget it."

The twins, when they weren't whining because their father wouldn't let them order french fries for breakfast, were jabbing at each other. The father yelled at them both to stop it, prompting each to accuse the other of starting it.

Dwayne's eyes were boring into Kate.

"I said forget it," she said.

"You think I'm a faggot?" he asked.

"No," she said.

"'Cause a person might do things and still not be a faggot," he said.

*No more wondering now,* she thought.

"You want to go places you shouldn't?" he asked. "I can do that, too, *Kate.*"

"Dwayne."

"How's it feel, putting your friend in the ground?"

"She wasn't my friend," she said.

"You worked in the same office together."

"She wasn't my friend. And I get it. We're even. I'm sorry."

"He did it first!" one of the boys whimpered.

Dwayne closed his eyes. Through gritted teeth, he said, "Fucking kids."

"It's not their fault," she said, relieved to be able to channel Dwayne's thoughts to the kids, and away from her comment. "They have to be taught how to behave in a restaurant. Their dad should have brought something for them to do, a coloring book, a video game, something. That's what you do."

Dwayne took a few deep breaths, inhaling and exhaling through his nose.

The waitress served the father and twins, and a moment later, brought plates for Kate and Dwayne. He was on it like a bear on a bag of trash.

"Eat your breakfast," the father said behind Dwayne.

"I don't *want* to," said one twin.

The other one suddenly showed up at the end of Kate and Dwayne's table. He inspected their breakfast until Dwayne said, "Piss off."

Then the boy began strolling up to the cash register. The father twisted around in his booth and said, "Alton, come here!"

Dwayne looked at Kate and mouthed, *"Alton?"*

She poured some syrup on her pancakes, cut out a triangle from one and speared it with her fork. There'd been plenty of things to lose her appetite over in the last twenty-four hours, but she was hungry just the same. Had been since the middle of the night, when she'd stood at the window looking at the McDonald's sign. And she had a feeling that she needed to eat fast, that they might not be staying here much longer.

Dwayne shoveled more food into his mouth, put the mug to his lips, mixed everything together. His mouth still full, he said, "What were the odds, huh?"

She couldn't guess where his mind was. Was he talking about the odds that they would be here, today, getting ready to do the thing they'd been waiting so long to do?

When she didn't answer, he said, "That we'd run into her? That she'd see us?"

"Alton, come back here right now!"

"But I gotta say," Dwayne continued, "I think we turned a bad situation into a positive."

"Whatever."

*"Alton, I'm warning you, you better get back here!"*

"My eggs are icky!" said the twin still at the table.

Dwayne spun around, put one hand on the father's throat, drove him down sideways and slammed his head onto the bench. The man's arm swept across the table, knocking coffee and a plate of eggs and bacon all over himself and the floor. His eyes were wide with fear as he struggled for breath. He batted pitifully at Dwayne's arm, roped with muscle, pinning the man like a steel beam. The boy at the table watched, speechless and horrified.

Dwayne said, "I was going to have a word with your boys, but my girl here says it's your fault they act like a couple of fucking wild animals. You need to teach them how to behave when they're out."

She was on her feet. "We need to go," she said.

# TWENTY-TWO

"WHEN WAS THIS AGAIN?" Barry Duckworth asked.

Gina tried to think. "Around the beginning of last week? Maybe Monday or Tuesday? Wait, not this past week, but the week before."

"I'm not saying you have to do this now," the detective said, getting a whiff of pizza dough baking in the oven, "but if I needed you to find the receipt for that night, do you think you could?"

"Probably," she said. "Mr. Harwood usually pays with a credit card."

"Okay, that's good. Because at some point I may need to know exactly when this happened." Duckworth was already thinking about Gina on a witness stand, how a defense attorney would slice her up like—well, that pizza he thought he could smell cooking—if she couldn't remember when the incident took place.

"So Mr. and Mrs. Harwood are pretty regular customers at your restaurant here?"

Gina hesitated. "Regular? Maybe every three weeks or so. Once a month? I really wonder if I've done the right thing."

"About what?"

"About calling the police. I think maybe I shouldn't have done this."

Duckworth reached across the restaurant table, covered

with a white cloth, and patted her hand. "You did the right thing."

"I didn't even see it on the news at first, but my son, who works here in the kitchen, he saw it, and he said, 'Hey, isn't that those people who come in here once in a while?' So he showed me the story on the TV station's website, and I saw that it was Mrs. Harwood, and that's when I remembered what had happened here that night. But now that I've called the police, I think I may have done a terrible thing."

"That's not true," the detective said.

"I don't want to get Mr. Harwood in trouble. I'm sure he'd never do anything to hurt his wife. He's a very nice man."

"I'm sure he is."

"And he always leaves a fair tip. Not, you know, huge, but just about right. I hope you're not going to tell him that I spoke to you."

"We always do our best to be discreet," Duckworth said, promising nothing.

"But my son, he said I should call you. So that's what I did."

"Tell me what the Harwoods are usually like when they're here."

"Usually, they're very happy," she said. "I try not to listen in on my customers. People want to have their private conversations. But you can tell when a couple are having a bad evening, even if you can't hear exactly what they are saying. It's how they lean back in their chairs, or they don't look at each other."

"Body language," Duckworth said.

Gina nodded enthusiastically. "Yes, that's it. But the last time they were here, forget about the body language. I could hear what they were saying. Well, at least what she was saying."

"And what was that?"

"They'd been talking about something that couldn't have been good, because they both looked very upset. And I was coming over to the table, and that was when she said to him something like 'You'd be happy if something happened to me.'"

"Those were her words?"

"It might have been different. Maybe she said he'd be happy if she was dead. Or he was rid of her. Something like that."

"Did you hear Mr. Harwood say anything like that to her?"

"Not really, but maybe that was what he said to her just before she got so upset. Maybe he told her he wished she was dead. That's what I was thinking."

"But you didn't actually hear him say that?" Duckworth asked, making notes.

Gina thought. "No, but she was very upset. She got up from the table and they left without having the rest of their dinner."

Duckworth sniffed the air. "I can't imagine leaving here without eating."

Gina smiled broadly. "Would you like a slice of my special pizza?"

Duckworth smiled back. "I guess it would be rude to say no, wouldn't it?"

When he got back into his car, after an astonishing slice of cheese-and-portobello-mushroom pizza, Duckworth made a couple of calls.

The first was to his wife. "Hey," he said. "Just called to see what was going on."

"Not much," Maureen said.

"No emails or anything?"

"He's five or six hours ahead, so he has to be up by now."

"Don't be too sure."

"Don't worry. Just do your thing. Did you eat the salad I packed you?"

"I won't lie. I'm still a little hungry."

"Tomorrow I'll put in a banana."

"Okay. I'll call you later."

The second call was to see whether Leanne Kowalski had come home. He didn't call her husband—he didn't want to get into a discussion with him right now—but he knew he'd be able to find out what he needed to know by calling headquarters.

She had not come home.

The detective felt it was time to step up efforts where she was concerned. Someone needed to be working exclusively on that while he worked the Harwood disappearance, and they'd need to compare notes several times through the day to see where the two cases intersected, assuming they did. He put in a call to the Promise Falls police headquarters to see what could be done on that front.

Duckworth was thinking he might need to take a drive up to Lake George before the day was over, but there was at least one other stop he wanted to make first.

Along the way, he thought about how this was coming together:

David Harwood called the police to tell them his wife had gone missing during a trip to Five Mountains. But there was no record of her entering the park. Tickets to get him and his son in were purchased online, but there was no ticket for his wife.

*This is what trips them up. They try to save a few bucks and end up in jail for the rest of their lives.*

*You think they're too smart to make a mistake that dumb. And then you think about that bozo who helped bomb the World Trade Center back in 1993, gets caught*

*when he's trying to get his deposit back on the rental
truck that carried the explosives.*

The surveillance cameras at the amusement park
failed to turn up any images of Jan Harwood. Not con-
clusive, Duckworth thought, but not a very good sign
for Mr. Harwood. They'd have to go over the images
more thoroughly. They'd have to be sure.

David Harwood's story that his wife was suicidal
wasn't passing the sniff test. No one he'd spoken to so
far shared his assessment of Jan Harwood's mental
state. Most damning of all—Harwood's tale that his
wife had been to see her doctor about her depression,
and Dr. Samuels's report that she'd never shown up.

Now, Gina's story about Jan Harwood telling her husband he'd be pleased if she weren't in the picture anymore—what the hell was that about?

And the Lake George trip. David Harwood hadn't
mentioned anything about that. A witness had put Jan
Harwood in Lake George the night before she disappeared. The store owner, Ted Brehl, reported that Jan
had said she didn't know where she was headed, that
her husband was planning some sort of surprise. And
her boss, Ernie Bertram, had backed this up, saying that
Jan was headed on some sort of "mysterious" trip with
her husband Friday.

Was it possible Ted Brehl was the last person to see
Jan Harwood? Not counting David Harwood, of
course. Duckworth was becoming increasingly convinced that David Harwood was the last person to see
his wife alive.

And he was getting a gut feeling no one else ever
would.

Arlene Harwood tried to keep busy. Her husband, who
could sometimes get underfoot and be—let's be honest
here—a real pain in the ass when he started telling her

how to do things, was entertaining Ethan. That was good. Don had gone into the garage and found an old croquet set, and with Ethan's help had set it up in the backyard. But Ethan quickly adopted a playing style that had little to do with hitting the wooden balls through the hoops. Just whacking the balls in any old direction kept him occupied, and Don quickly abandoned plans to teach his grandson the game's finer points.

Arlene, meanwhile, went from one activity to another. She did some dishes, she ironed, she paid some bills online, she tried to read the paper, she flipped through the TV channels. The one thing she did not do, at least not for more than a minute or so, was use the phone. She didn't want to tie up the line. David might call. Maybe the police.

Maybe Jan.

When she wasn't feeling desperately worried for her daughter-in-law, she was thinking about her son and grandson. What if something had happened to Jan? How would David deal with it? How would Ethan deal with losing a mother?

She didn't want to let her mind go there. She wanted to think positively, but she'd always been a realist. Might as well prepare yourself for the worst, and if things turned out better than you'd expected, well, that was a bonus.

She racked her brain trying to figure out where Jan might have gone, what might have happened to her. The thing was, she'd always had a feeling that she'd never shared with her son or her husband. She certainly couldn't tell Don—he'd never be able to keep his mouth shut about how she felt. But there was something about Jan that wasn't quite right.

Arlene Harwood couldn't say what it was. It might have had something to do with how Jan handled men, and didn't handle women. David had fallen for her hard soon after he met her while doing a story for the *Standard* on people looking for jobs at the city employment office. Jan was new to town, looking for work, and David tried to coax some quotes out of her. But Jan was reserved, didn't want her name in the paper or to be part of the piece.

Something about her touched David. She seemed, he once disclosed to his mother, "adrift."

Although she wouldn't be interviewed for the piece, she did disclose, after some persistent questioning from David, that she lived alone, didn't have anyone in her life, and had no family here.

David had once said if it hadn't been so corny, he would have asked her how a woman as beautiful as Jan could be so alone. Arlene Harwood had thought it a question worth asking.

When David finished interviewing other, more willing subjects at the employment office, he spotted Jan outside waiting for a bus. He offered her a lift, and after some hesitation, she accepted. She had rented a room over a pool hall.

"That's really—I mean, it's none of my business," David said, "but that's not really a good place for you to live."

"It's all I can afford at the moment," she said. "When I get a job, I'll find something better."

"What are you paying?" he asked.

Jan's eyes widened. "You're right, it's none of your business."

"Tell me," he said.

She did.

David went back to the paper to write his story. After he'd filed it, he made a call to a woman he knew in Classified. "You got any rentals going in tomorrow I can get a jump on? I know someone looking for a place. Let me give you the price range."

She emailed him copies of four listings. On the way home, he parked across from the pool hall, went upstairs and down a hallway, knocking on doors until he found Jan.

He handed her the list he'd printed out. "These won't be in the paper until tomorrow. At least three of these are in way better parts of town than this, and they're the same as what you're paying now." He tried to peer past her into her room. "Doesn't look like you'd have that much to pack."

"Who the hell are you?" Jan asked him.

That weekend, he helped her move.

Someone new to rescue, his mother thought, after Samantha Henry made it clear she could manage on her own, thank you very much.

It was a short courtship. (Arlene grimaced to herself; there was a word nobody used anymore. "Courtship." Just how old was she, anyway?) But damn it all, things did move fast.

They were married in a matter of months.

"Why wait?" David said to his mother. "If she's the right one, she's the right one. I've been spinning my wheels long enough. I've already got a house." It was true. He'd bought it a couple of years ago, having been persuaded by the business editor that only saps paid rent.

"Jan wants to rush into this, too?"

"And remind me how long you knew Dad before you got married?"

"Got you there," Don said, walking in on the conversation. They'd gone out for five months before eloping.

The thing was, Don had loved Jan from the first time David brought her home. Jan ingratiated herself effortlessly with David's father, but did she really make the same effort with his mother? Maybe Arlene was imagining it, but it struck her that Jan had a natural way with men. She got them to give her what she wanted without their even realizing it.

*No great mystery there,* Arlene thought. Jan was unquestionably desirable. She had the whole package. Not a supermodel's face, maybe, but the full lips and eyes, the pert nose, went together well. Her long legs looked great in everything from a tight skirt to tattered jeans. And she had a way of communicating her sex appeal without it being tarty. No batting of the eyelashes, no baby girl voices. It was just something she gave off, like a scent.

When David first started bringing her around, Don made an absolute fool of himself, always offering to take her coat, freshen her drink, get her another sofa cushion. Arlene finally spoke to him. "For Christ's sake," she said one evening after David and Jan went home. "What's wrong with you? What's next? You gonna give her a back rub?"

Don, awakened to the fact that he'd gone overboard, managed to tone it down from that point on, but never stopped being entranced by his son's girlfriend and future wife.

Arlene, however, was immune to that kind of charm. Not that Jan had ever been anything but cordial with her. (*"Cordial"? There I go again,* Arlene thought.) But Arlene felt the girl knew that what worked with men wouldn't pass muster with her.

What kind of girl, Arlene wondered, cuts off all ties with her family? Sure, not everyone came from a home as loving as the one she made, but come on. Jan didn't even let her parents know when Ethan was born. How bad did parents have to be not to let them know they had a grandson?

Jan must have had her reasons, Arlene told herself. But it just didn't seem right.

The doorbell rang.

Arlene was only steps away from the door at the time, going through the front hall closet, wondering how many years it had been since some of the coats at the ends had been worn, whether it was time to donate some of them to Goodwill. Startled by the sound, she clutched her chest and shouted, "My God!"

She closed the closet so she could see the front door. Through the glass she spotted an overweight man in a suit and loosened tie.

"You scared me half to death," she said as she opened the door.

"I'm sorry. I'm Detective Duckworth, Promise Falls police. You're Mrs. Harwood?"

"That's right."

"David's mother?"

"Yes."

"I'm heading the investigation into your daughter-in-law's disappearance. I'd like to ask you some questions."

"Oh, of course, please come in." As Duckworth crossed the threshold she asked, "You haven't found her, have you?"

"No, ma'am," he said. "Is your son home?"

"No, but Ethan's here. He's out back playing with his grandfather. Did you want me to get him in here?"

"No, that's okay. I met Ethan yesterday. He's a handsome young fellow."

Normally, Arlene Harwood might have swelled with pride. But she was too anxious about why the detective was here. She pointed to the living room couch, then realized several of Ethan's action figures were scattered there.

"That's okay," Duckworth said, moving them out of the way. "My son's nearly twenty and still collects these things." He sat down and waited for Arlene to do the same.

"Should I get my husband?" she asked.

"We can talk for a moment, and then maybe I'll have a chat with him. This is the first I've had a chance to talk to you."

"If there's anything I can do—"

"Oh, I know. Your son . . . this must be a terrible time for him right now."

"It's just dreadful for all of us. Ethan, he doesn't really understand how serious it is. He just thinks his mother has gone away for a little while."

Duckworth found an opening. "You have some reason to think that's not the case?"

"Oh, I mean, what I meant was . . . I mean, we are hoping that's all this is. But it's so unlike Jan to just take off. She's never done anything like that before, or if she has, David's certainly never mentioned it." She bit her lip, thinking maybe that came out wrong. "I mean, not that he keeps things from me. He counts on us a lot for support. We—my husband and I—look after Ethan all the time, now that we're retired. He doesn't go to day care, and he'll be starting school next month."

"Of course," Barry said. "Have you noticed anything out of the ordinary with Jan lately? A change in mood?"

"Oh my, yes. David's been saying the last couple of weeks Jan has seemed very down, depressed. It's been a tremendous worry to him. Did he tell you Jan talked about jumping off a bridge?"

"He did."

"I can't imagine what might have triggered it."

"So you observed this yourself, this change in Jan's mood?"

Arlene stopped to consider. "Well, she's not here all that much. Dropping off Ethan in the morning, picking him up at night. We usually only have time to say a few words to each other."

"Keeping in mind that you've only seen her for short

periods, would you agree that Jan's been troubled lately?"

"Well," she hesitated, "I think Jan always puts on her best face when she's around her in-laws. I think if she was feeling bad, she might try not to show it."

"So you can't point to any one incident, say, where Jan acted depressed?"

"Not that I can think of."

"That's okay. I'm just asking all kinds of questions here, and some of them, I have to admit, may not make a lot of sense, you know?"

"Of course."

"Do you know whether Jan and Leanne Kowalski ever talked about taking a trip together? Were they close friends?"

"Leanne? Isn't that the girl who works in the office with Jan?"

"That's right."

"No, I'm afraid I don't know. I don't really know who Jan socializes with. You'd do better asking David about that."

"That's a good idea," he said. "Now, I'm just trying to nail down Jan's movements in the day before she went missing."

"Why is that important?" Arlene Harwood asked.

"It just gives us a better idea of a person's habits and their behavior."

"Okay."

"Do you know what Jan was doing on the Friday before she went to the Five Mountains park?"

"I don't really know. I mean—oh wait, she and David went for a drive."

"Oh yes?" Duckworth said, making notes. "A drive where?"

"I'm trying to remember. But David asked if we would look after Ethan longer that day, because he had to go someplace and Jan was going to go along with him."

"Do you know where they were going? What they were going to do?"

"I'm not sure. You really should ask David. Do you want me to get him on the phone? He's on his way back from Rochester right now."

"No, that's okay. I just wondered if you had any idea."

"I think it had something to do with work. He's a reporter for the *Standard*, but you probably already know that."

"I do, yes. So you think he was going somewhere on a story. An interview?"

"I really can't say. I know he's been working on that new prison that's supposed to come to town. You know about that?"

"I've heard about it," Duckworth said. "Isn't it unusual for your son to take his wife along with him when he's working?"

Arlene hesitated and shrugged. "I don't really know."

"So, he asked you to babysit Ethan until they got back from this trip?"

"That's right."

"When was that?"

"In the evening. Before it got dark. David came by to pick up Ethan."

"David and Jan," Duckworth said.

"Actually, just David," Arlene said.

"Jan waited in the car?"

"No, David came by on his own."

Duckworth nodded, like there was nothing odd about this, but he had a strange tingling going on in the back of his neck. "So why would that be? Wouldn't it make sense for the two of them to drop by here on the way home and pick up Ethan?"

"She wasn't feeling well," Arlene said.

"I'm sorry?"

"David told me. He said Jan wasn't feeling well during the drive back, so he dropped her at their place, and then he came over here for Ethan."

"I see," Duckworth said. "What was wrong with her?"

"A headache or something, I think David said."

"Okay. But I guess she felt well enough in the morning to go to Five Mountains. How did she seem to you then?"

"I didn't see her in the morning. They went straight to the park," Arlene said. Outside, the sound of a car door closing. Arlene got up and went to the window. "It's David. He should be able to help you with these questions."

"I'm sure he will," Duckworth said, getting to his feet.

# TWENTY-THREE

WHEN I PULLED UP in front of my parents' house, I spotted an unmarked police car at the curb.

My pulse quickened as I parked behind it. I was out of the car in a second and took the steps up to the porch two at a time. As I was swinging open the door, I found Barry Duckworth standing there.

"Mr. Harwood," he said.

"Has something happened?" I asked. I'd only run a few steps but felt out of breath. It was an adrenaline rush.

"No, no, nothing new," he said. Mom was standing just behind him, her eyes desperate and sorrowful. "I was driving by and decided to stop. Your mother and I were having a chat."

"Have you found out anything? Did they search the park again? Did anything turn up on the surveillance cameras? Has—"

Duckworth held up his hand. "If there are any developments, I promise you'll be the first to know."

I felt deflated. But the truth was, I was the one with news.

"I need to talk to you," I said to him.

"Sure."

"But I want to see Ethan first," I said. I could hear his laughter coming from the backyard. I started to move past the detective, but he reached up and held my arm.

"I think it would be good if we could talk right now," he said.

My eyes met his. Even though he'd said there was nothing new, I could tell he was holding something back. If he'd had good news, he would have just told me.

"Something *has* happened," I whispered to him. "Don't tell me you've found her."

"No, sir, we have not," he said. "But it would help if you'd come down to the station with me."

I had that feeling you get from too much caffeine. Like electrical impulses were racing through my body. I wondered if he could feel them in my arm.

Trying to keep the anxiety out of my voice, I said, "Okay."

He let go of my arm and went out the door. Mom came up and hugged me. She must not have known what to say, because she said nothing.

"It's okay, Mom," I said. "I'm sorry. I was going to take Ethan off your hands—"

"Don't be stupid," she said. "Just go with him." She let go and I could see tears welling up in her eyes. "David, I'm sorry, I think I may have said something—"

"What?"

"That detective, he looked at me funny when I said that Jan—"

"Mr. Harwood!"

I looked over my shoulder. Detective Duckworth had the passenger door of his unmarked car open, waiting for me.

"I have to go," I said. I gave my mother a hug and ran down to Duckworth's car, hopping into the front seat. He was going to close the door for me, but I grabbed the handle and slammed it shut myself.

When he got into the driver's seat, I said, "I could just follow you in. Then you wouldn't have to bring me back."

"Don't worry about that," he said, putting the car into drive, looking back, and then hitting the gas. "This will give us more time to talk."

"Why are we going to the station?"

Duckworth gave his head a small shake, his way of ignoring my question. "So you came back from Rochester, what, this morning?" he asked.

"Yes."

"And you went out there why again?"

"I was looking for Jan's parents."

"The ones she hasn't spoken to in years."

"Yes."

"Did you find them?"

I hesitated. "That's what I want to talk to you about. But let me ask you something first."

He glanced over. "Shoot."

"If the FBI or some other organization, if they put someone in the witness protection program, and they resettle them in your own backyard, do they give you a heads-up about it?"

Duckworth seemed to take a long time before answering, his tongue moving around the inside of his cheek. Finally, "What's that again?"

I repeated it.

"Well, I guess that might depend on the situation. But generally speaking, the FBI tends to view local law enforcement as a bunch of know-nothing hicks, so my guess is they'd not be inclined to share that kind of information. Also, in their defense, the more people know something like that, the more likely someone's going to find out."

I considered that. "That could be."

"And you're asking this because . . . ?" Duckworth asked.

"I'm not saying this is what's happened, but I think it's just possible that—"

"No, wait, let me guess," Duckworth said. "Your wife is a witness in hiding. And her cover's been blown, and now she's taken off."

"Is this a joke to you? I thought you'd want to know about this."

"No, no, that's a very serious thing," he said. "Very serious."

"You think I'm full of shit," I said.

I thought maybe he'd deny the accusation, and when he didn't, I said, "I think Jan may not be who she says she is."

Another glance. Then, "And just who is she, really? Tell me, I'm listening."

"I don't know," I said. "I've . . . I've found out some things in the last day that don't make a whole lot of sense to me. And they may have something to do with why Jan's missing."

"And what are these things you've found out?"

"I went to Rochester and found the people who are listed on Jan's birth certificate as her parents."

"And that's who?"

"Horace and Gretchen Richler. The thing is, they had a daughter named Jan, but she died when she was five."

The tongue was moving around inside Duckworth's cheek again. "Okay," he said.

"It was an accident. Her father hit her with the car, backing out of the driveway."

"Man," Duckworth said. "How do you live with that the rest of your life?"

"Yeah." I gave him a minute for it to sink in. "What do you make of that?"

"You know what? Let me make a call when we get to the station. And while someone's looking into that, we can talk about some other things."

\*　　\*　　\*

"Have a seat," he said, pointing to the plain chair at the plain desk in the plain room.

"Isn't this an interrogation room?" I asked.

"It's a room," Duckworth said. "A room is a room. I want to talk to you privately, it's as good a place as any. But hang on for a second while I make a call about that witness protection thing. You want a coffee or a soft drink or something?"

I said I was okay.

"Be right back, then." He slipped out of the room, closing the door behind him.

I walked over to the table, stood there a moment, finally sat down on one of the metal chairs.

This didn't feel right.

*Duckworth brings me in, says he wants to talk about something but doesn't say what, puts me in a room, leaves me alone.*

There was a mirror on one wall. I wondered whether Duckworth was on the other side, watching through one-way glass to see how I behaved. Was I fidgeting, pacing, running my fingers nervously through my hair?

I stayed in the chair, tried to calm down. But inside I was churning.

After about five minutes, the door opened. Duckworth had a coffee in one hand, and a bottled water tucked under his arm so he could turn the knob.

"Got myself a coffee," he said. "I grabbed you a water, just in case."

"I'm not an idiot," I said.

"Say what?"

"I'm not an idiot. The way this is going. Bringing me down here. Leaving me in here to sweat it out for a while on my own. I get it."

"I don't know what you're talking about," Duckworth said, pulling up a chair and setting the coffee and water on the table.

"Look, I'm not the greatest reporter in the world. If I were, I wouldn't be at the *Standard*. They stopped caring about journalism a long time ago. But I've been around long enough to know the score. You think I'm some kind of suspect or something."

"I never said that."

"So tell me I'm wrong. Tell me you don't think I have anything to do with this."

"How about you tell me about this trip you took up to Lake George two days ago?"

"What?"

"You've never mentioned it. Why's that?"

"Why would I? Jan went missing the following day. Why would I bring up what happened on Friday?"

"Why don't you tell me about it now?"

"Why is this important?"

"Is there some reason you don't want to tell me, Mr. Harwood?"

"No, of course not, but—fine. Jan and I drove up to Lake George to meet with a source. Actually, I was meeting with the source. Jan just came along."

"A source?"

"For a story I've been working on."

"What story is that?"

I hesitated before continuing. Could I discuss with the police stories I was working on for the *Standard*? Was it ethical? Did it violate journalistic principles?

Did I really, at this moment, give a flying fuck?

"I've been working on stories about Star Spangled Corrections wanting to come to Promise Falls. The company has been doing favors for at least one council member that I know of. Someone sent me an email, that there were others taking payoffs or kickbacks, or whatever, to buy their votes when the prison comes up before council for zoning approvals."

"Who sent you the email?"

"I can't tell you that."

"Oh," said Duckworth, looking like he wanted to roll his eyes but restraining himself. "Confidentiality. Protecting your source."

"No," I said. "The email was anonymous."

"But if you met with this person, you must know who it is."

"She didn't show up," I said.

"She?"

"She said in her email that I was to look for a woman in a white truck. No woman in a white truck showed up."

"Where was she supposed to meet you?"

"At a general store/gas station place north of Lake George. Ted's, it was called."

"So you drove up there?"

"That's right. Friday afternoon. She was supposed to come at five."

"And you took your wife with you?"

"Yes."

"Why'd you do that? Do you normally take your wife along when you're going to interview someone?"

"Not usually."

"Have you ever taken your wife with you before when you were on an assignment?"

I thought. "I'm sure I have, but I can't actually think of an instance. There was an awards dinner a couple of years ago."

"You were covering the awards? Or you were up for one?"

"I was up for one. For spot news reporting."

"So that wasn't really an assignment. That was the sort of thing anyone would take their spouse to."

"I suppose so," I conceded.

"Did you win?" Duckworth asked.

"No."

"So then, why did you take your wife on this outing?"

"Like I told you, she's been feeling depressed the last few weeks, and she told me she was going to take Friday off, so I suggested she come along for the ride. She could keep me company on the way up and back."

"Okay," Duckworth said. "What did you talk about on the way up?"

I shook my head in frustration. "I don't know, we just— What's the point of this, Detective?"

"I'm just getting a full picture of the events that led up to your wife's disappearance."

"Our drive to Lake George did not *lead up* to her disappearance. It's just something we did the day before Five Mountains. Unless—"

Duckworth cocked his head to one side. "Unless?"

*The car. The one Jan had spotted following us. The one that did a couple of drive-bys of the place where I was supposed to meet the woman.*

"I think we were followed," I said.

Duckworth leaned back in his chair. His eyebrows went up. "You were followed."

I nodded. "Jan noticed a car following us up. But I wasn't that sure. Then, when we were waiting in the parking lot for this contact to show up, the car drove by a couple of times. Went up the road, turned around and came back. I ran out to it at one point, trying to get a look at who it was, but then the car sped off."

Duckworth folded his arms across his chest. His forearms sat on his belly like it was a countertop. He hadn't touched his coffee yet, and I hadn't cracked the top of the bottled water.

"You were followed," he said again.

"I'm pretty sure," I said.

"Who would have followed you?"

"I don't know. At the time, I figured it was someone who found out this woman had arranged to meet me. I thought maybe that was what scared her off. She saw that car snooping about and chickened out."

"But now you have a different theory?"

"I don't know. You're so interested in what happened Friday, and after what I found out from these people I thought were Jan's parents, maybe the person in that car was following Jan. Maybe that's what this is all about. She's a relocated witness, someone figured out who she was, was following her, and she had to disappear."

Duckworth finally took a sip of his coffee. He smiled. "You're not going to believe this, but this coffee is fantastic. We've got this one guy, he works burglary, makes the best pot of coffee. Better than Starbucks. What are the odds, in a police station, you know? You sure you don't want a cup?"

"No thanks."

"So, what did you tell your wife about where you were going?"

"I told her what I've told you. That I was going up there to meet with this woman."

"Who was going to tell you all the council members who're taking payoffs from this prison outfit."

"That's what she suggested in her email."

"I guess you wouldn't have any trouble producing this email for me," Duckworth said. "When did you receive it?"

"Last Thursday," I said. "And . . . I deleted it."

"Oh," Duckworth said. "That seems like an odd thing to do. Why'd you do it?"

"Because," I said slowly, "I didn't want it left in the system."

"At your own office? Why?"

I thought before answering. "I don't think everyone at

the *Standard* shares my enthusiasm for pursuing this story."

"What's that mean?"

"Just that I'm learning not to present stories on this prison thing unless they're completely nailed down. I want to make it hard for my superiors to say no to printing something. I like to play my cards close to the chest. So I don't leave emails around for them to read."

Duckworth looked unconvinced but went in another direction. "Do you remember the email address?"

I took a look around the room and shook my head, disgusted with myself. "No. It was just random numbers and letters strung together. A Hotmail address."

"I see. Okay, then," Duckworth said, "tell me about this car that was following you. Make, model?"

"It was dark blue. It was a Buick with tinted windows. A four-door sedan."

Duckworth nodded, impressed. "Did you happen to get a plate number?"

"I tried," I said. "But it was covered with mud. But it was a New York plate."

"I see. Was the whole car covered in mud, or just the plate?"

"The car was pretty clean, actually. Just the plate was dirtied up. Doesn't that tell you they probably did it deliberately?"

"Absolutely," Duckworth said.

"Don't patronize me," I said. "You don't believe a word I'm saying. I can tell. I can see it in your face. But we were there. If you don't believe me, talk to whoever was working in the store that day. It's called . . ." I struggled to remember the exact name of the place. "Ted's Lakeview General Store. That was it. Jan went in to buy something to drink. Someone there might remember her."

Duckworth looked at me without saying anything.

"What?" I said.

"I believe you were there," he said. "I don't doubt that for a minute."

He was good at keeping me off guard. Just when I was sure he didn't trust what I was saying, he seemed to accept that last part.

"Then what's the problem?"

"So when did you drive home?"

"I stayed until around five-thirty, and when I was sure the woman wasn't going to show, we drove back."

"Both of you," Duckworth said.

"Of course both of us."

"Any stops along the way?"

"Just to my parents' place. To pick up Ethan."

"So both of you went to get your son."

I could tell he already knew the truth here. "No," I said. "I went alone to get Ethan."

"I'm confused," he said, although I doubted that. "How did you end up going to your parents' house alone?"

"Jan wasn't feeling well," I said. "She had a headache. She asked me to drop her off at our house first. She didn't feel well enough to see my parents. Or maybe she didn't want to see them, and just said she had a headache."

Duckworth nodded a little too hard. "Okay, okay. But isn't your parents' place on the way home? I mean, you'd have to pass your parents' house to get to yours coming back from Lake George, then double back to get your son."

"That's true," I said. "But sometimes my parents . . . they like to talk. They would have thought it rude not to at least come out to the car to talk to Jan. And she wasn't up to that. That's why I took her home first. What are you getting at? You think I left her up in Lake George?"

When Duckworth didn't say anything right away, I said, "Do I have to bring my son in here? Do I need Ethan as a witness? To tell you my wife came back with me that day?"

"I don't think there's any need for that," Duckworth said. "I wouldn't want to put a four-year-old through anything like that."

"Why's that? Because if he backed me up, you wouldn't believe it anyway? Because he's a kid? And you'd think I coached him?"

"I never said anything of the kind," Duckworth said, taking another sip of coffee.

"At least go up there," I said. "Talk to whoever was working at Ted's store that day."

Duckworth said, "There's no problem there, Mr. Harwood. Your wife's been identified as being in the store at the time you say."

I waited.

"Trouble is what she had to say when she was in there."

"Excuse me?"

"She said you'd driven up there for some sort of surprise. She said she had no idea what she was doing up there."

"What?"

"She didn't know why you were taking her up there. She seemed not to know what you had in mind."

It felt like a punch to the gut.

"That's crazy," I said. "Jan knew why we were going up there. Whoever told you that's lying."

"Why would someone lie about that?" Duckworth asked.

"I have no idea. But it's not true. Jan wouldn't have said that. It makes no sense for her to have said that."

"Why did Mrs. Harwood tell you that you'd be happier if she was gone? Maybe even dead?"

"What?" I said again.

"You heard me."

"What the hell are you talking about?"

"Are you denying she ever said that?"

I opened my mouth to speak, but nothing came out. Not for several seconds. Finally, quietly, I said, "Gina's."

"Yes?"

"Almost two weeks ago, I think. We were having dinner—we were going to have dinner—at Gina's. This is what you're referring to."

"Suppose you tell me."

"Jan was very distraught through dinner. She said some crazy things. And then she had this outburst— probably loud enough for anyone in the restaurant to hear—that I'd be happy to be rid of her. Something along those lines. But not that I wanted her dead. She never said that."

"So you would be happy if you could be rid of her, but not if it meant she had to die."

"No! None of it's true. I mean, yes, she said I'd be happier without her, but it's not true. I don't know why she'd think that, unless it's all tied in to her depression. Did you talk to Gina? Because if she's saying Jan said I wanted her dead, that's horseshit."

"About Jan's depression," Duckworth said, "it's kind of interesting that the only one who's noticed your wife has been suffering from that is you."

I was shaking my head violently. "That's not true. That's not true at all. Talk to her doctor. Talk to Dr. Samuels. He'll tell you."

Duckworth gave me a pitying look. "Your wife never went to see Dr. Samuels."

"For Christ's sake," I said. "Get him on the phone."

"I've talked to him," Duckworth said. "Jan Harwood never went to see him about her depression."

I think I did a pretty good impression of a slack-jawed

idiot at that moment. I stared at him, openmouthed, trying to make sense of the news.

Finally, I said, "That's a load of horseshit, too."

But it only took me another couple of seconds to realize it was possible Jan could have lied to me about going to see the doctor, just so I'd get off her case. But this clown at the Lake George store, suggesting Jan didn't know why I'd brought her along, that person was a goddamn liar, there was no doubt in my mind about that.

"So everyone's full of shit," Duckworth said. "What about the security cameras and the computers at Five Mountains? Are they full of shit, too?"

"The ticket thing?" I asked. "Is that what you mean?"

"Why were only two tickets charged to your wife's card, Mr. Harwood? One adult, one child. Was it because you knew you wouldn't be taking your wife with you? Did you take her card out of her purse when you were online, or had you written down the details earlier?"

"I didn't order them," I said. "Jan ordered them. And she was there, at the park. I can't explain the ticket thing. Maybe . . . maybe, when she came back from the car, she realized she'd printed out the wrong thing, that there wasn't a ticket for her, and she paid cash to get in."

"We've looked at all the security footage at the gates, and we can't find her. Not coming in, and not going out."

"Then there's something wrong with it," I said. "Maybe there's some footage that's missing."

I pointed at him, then started stabbing the table with my index finger to make a point. "Look, I see what you're doing here, and you've got it wrong. The first thing you need to do is check out this thing with Jan's birth certificate, these people I thought were her parents, but who turned out not to be."

"So show it to me," Duckworth said.

"I don't . . . have it."

"It's at your house?"

I shook my head. "It had been hidden. It was in an envelope, behind a baseboard in the linen closet. But I looked today, when I got back from Rochester, and it was gone."

"Well."

"Come on. Can't you call those things up anyway? The state has records. You can get a copy of it. Can't you do that?"

Duckworth nodded slowly. "I suppose I could."

"But you're not going to. Because you don't believe anything I've told you."

"Which story would you like me to believe, Mr. Harwood? The one about your wife wanting to kill herself, or the one about her being in the witness protection program? Or have you got a third one waiting in the wings?"

I put my elbows on the table and my head in my hands. "My wife's out there somewhere and you need to be looking for her."

"You know what would save me a lot of time in that regard?" Duckworth asked.

I raised my head. "What?"

"You could tell me where she is. What did you do with her, Mr. Harwood? What did you do with your wife?"

# TWENTY-FOUR

"I DIDN'T DO ANYTHING with her!" I shouted at Barry Duckworth. "I swear to God I didn't. Why the hell would I want to hurt her? I love her! She's my wife, for God's sake. We have a son!"

Duckworth sat expressionless, unruffled.

"I am not lying to you!" I said. "I'm not making this up! Jan's been depressed. She *told* me she went to the doctor. So maybe she didn't go, maybe she didn't tell me the truth about that. But that's what she told *me*."

Still nothing.

"Look, I don't know how to explain that no one else noticed how Jan was feeling. Maybe . . . maybe she could only be herself when she was with me. When she was with others, she put on this act, put on a happy face, to get by." I shook my head in frustration. "I don't know what to tell you." Then, an idea. "You should talk to Leanne. Have you talked to her yet? They work together. Leanne sees Jan day in and day out. Even if Jan was able to hide how she was feeling with most people, Leanne would pick something up."

"Leanne." Duckworth said the name slowly.

"Leanne Kowalski," I said. "She'd be in the book. Her husband's name, I'm trying to think. It starts with an 'L,' too. Lionel, or Lyall, something like that."

"I'll have to check that out," Duckworth said. There was something in his tone, like he either didn't think

Leanne was worth talking to, or he'd already done it. "How would you describe Jan's relationship with Leanne?"

"Relationship?"

"Good friends?"

"I've told you this. They just worked together. Leanne generally acts like she's got a pickle up her ass."

"They ever do things together?" Duckworth asked.

"Like what?"

"Lunch, shopping? Catch a movie?"

"No."

"They didn't hang out sometimes after work?"

"How many times do I have to tell you? No. Why's this important?"

"No reason," Duckworth said.

"Look, just talk to her. Talk to anyone. Talk to every goddamn person you can find. You're not going to find anyone who thinks I have anything to do with Jan's disappearance. I love her."

"I'm sure," Duckworth said.

"Fuck this," I said. "You have this so completely wrong." I pushed back my chair and stood up. "Am I under arrest or anything?"

"Absolutely not," Duckworth said.

"Do I need a lawyer?"

"Do you think you need a lawyer?" he asked.

There was no smart way to answer that. If I said yes, I looked guilty. If I said no, I looked like a fool.

"I'm going to need a ride back to my car and—no, forget it. I'll find my own way back to my parents' place."

"About that," Duckworth said. "Before we sat down for our little chat, I popped out to see about search warrants. We're seizing both of your cars, Mr. Harwood, and we're going to be conducting a search of your house."

"You're what?"

"So maybe getting in touch with a lawyer would be a good thing."

"You're going to search my house?" I said.

"We're already doing it," he said.

"You think I've hidden Jan in our house? Are you serious?"

As if on cue, my cell phone rang. I flipped it open, recognized my parents' number.

"Hello?"

"David?" My mother.

"Yes?"

"They're towing away your car!"

"I know, Mom, I just found out that—"

"I went out and told them they couldn't do that, that you can park for free for three hours on that side of the street, but—"

"Mom, there's nothing you can do about it."

"You need to get here fast! They're loading it onto the back of another truck right now! Your father's out there telling them they've made a mistake but—"

"Mom! Listen to me! I'm at the police station and I need a ride—"

"One of my men can give you a lift," Duckworth said.

I glanced at him. "Go fuck yourself."

"What?" said Mom.

"Send Dad down here," I said. "Can you do that?"

"Are you okay? Are you in some kind of—"

"Mom, just send Dad and I'll explain it when I get there." I closed the phone and slipped it back into my coat.

"You son of a bitch," I said to Duckworth. "You goddamn son of a bitch. I'm not the bad guy here. You're going to have people searching my house when they should be searching all over Promise Falls. What if my wife's tried to take her life? What if she's somewhere and needs help? What if she needs medical attention? And what are you doing? Turning my life upside down?"

Duckworth opened the door for me and I went through it. I was heading for the main lobby, with Duckworth following, making sure, I supposed, that I got out of the building without causing any trouble. I was nearly to the front doors, people going this way and that, when I stopped suddenly, turned, and said to him, "You didn't even ask anyone to check the witness protection thing, did you?"

Duckworth said nothing.

"You *have* to look into Jan's background. I know, at first, I thought maybe Jan had killed herself. That's the way it was looking to me. But there's more going on here than I realized. And I don't even know what the hell it is."

"I can assure you, Mr. Harwood, that I'll be following this investigation wherever it goes."

"I'm telling you," I said, leaning in close to him, getting right in his face, "I did not kill my wife."

"Well," said a familiar voice off to one side.

Duckworth and I both turned to see Stan Reeves, the city hall councilor, standing there. A grin was creeping across his face.

"I'll be damned," he said, looking at me. "If it's not the holier-than-thou David Harwood of the *Standard*. The things you hear when you're just dropping by to pay a parking ticket."

# TWENTY-FIVE

I BROKE AWAY FROM Duckworth and headed for the door, glancing back only once to see Stan Reeves talking to the detective.

Dad pulled up to the curb in his blue Crown Victoria about five minutes later. I got in the passenger side and slammed the door.

"Watch it, you'll shatter the glass," he said.

"What's happening at the house?" I asked.

"It's like your mother told you on the phone. They took it away."

I had the keys on me, but the police wouldn't need them to remove the car, or get into it.

"It wasn't parked illegally," Dad said.

"That's not why they towed it," I said.

Dad looked at me with disappointment. "They repossessed it? Jesus, you didn't keep up your payments?"

I suppose it was a sign of faith in me that Dad would suspect me of being a deadbeat before he'd think of me as a murderer.

"Dad, the police are looking for evidence."

"Evidence?"

"I think the police are . . . I think the police are looking at me as a suspect."

"A suspect in what?" he asked.

"They think maybe I did something with Jan."

"Jesus!" he said. "Why the hell would they think that?"

"Dad, take me by my house."

"She's your wife, David! What's wrong with them? You'd never hurt Jan. And why do they think something's happened to her?" Suddenly it registered. "Oh my God, son, they haven't found her, have they? Have they found a body?"

"No," I said. "Cops, they always look at the husband when a wife goes missing." Was I trying to make Dad feel better, or myself? Maybe my interrogation by Duckworth was just standard operating procedure. Something the cops did as a matter of course.

No. There was more to it than that. The circumstances of Jan's disappearance were working against me. The fact that only two tickets had been ordered online. The fact that no one—other than Ethan and me—had seen Jan since before the trip up to Lake George. The fact that Jan had not disclosed to anyone else how depressed she'd been feeling the last couple of weeks.

I believed most of those things could be explained. What I couldn't figure out was why the person working at Ted's Lakeview General Store was lying. Why would someone tell police Jan had said she didn't know where she was going, that her husband had brought her up there for some sort of surprise?

That was crazy.

Jan had gone in to buy a couple of drinks. Nothing more, nothing less. How likely was it that she would strike up a conversation with whoever was behind the counter about anything, let alone why she was up there with her husband? I could imagine a short exchange about the weather, but what possible reason could Jan have for telling someone she'd been brought up there for reasons unknown? Given that I'd gone up there to meet a source, it stood to reason that Jan would have said very little, even if asked what she was doing up at Lake George.

If that's what the proprietor at Ted's told the police, he or she was lying.

Unless, of course, Detective Duckworth was lying.

Was he making the whole thing up to rattle me? To see how I'd respond? But how did he know in the first place that we'd been up there, that Jan had gone inside to buy drinks? The person she'd bought them from must have contacted the police, after seeing the news reports about Jan.

"What?" Dad said. "What are you thinking?"

"I don't know what to think," I said. "Just get me home."

I saw the police cars out front as we turned the corner. Jan's car was no longer in the driveway, so they must have scooped it the same time as they were taking mine from my parents' house. Dad barely had the car stopped before I was out the door, running across the lawn and up the steps. The front door was open and I could hear people talking inside.

"Hello!" I shouted.

A woman, in uniform, appeared at the top of the stairs. I recognized her as the officer who had looked after Ethan at Five Mountains yesterday while I talked to Duckworth. Campion, her name was.

"Mr. Harwood," she said.

"I want to see the warrant," I said.

"Alex!" she called, and a small, slender man who couldn't have been much more than thirty emerged from the bedroom I shared with Jan. His hair was bristle short, and he was dressed in a sport jacket, white dress shirt, and jeans.

"This is Mr. Harwood," she told him.

The man came down the stairs but didn't extend a

hand. I supposed those sorts of pleasantries were dispensed with when you were turning a man's house upside down for evidence that he'd offed his wife. "Detective Alex Simpson," he said, reaching into his jacket. He handed me a paper folded in thirds. "This is a warrant to search these premises."

I took the paper from him and glanced at it, unable to see through my anger to the words on the page. "Just tell me what the hell you're looking for and I'll show it to you," I said.

"I'm afraid it doesn't work that way," Simpson said.

I bounded up the stairs. Campion was looking through my and Jan's dresser, rooting through socks and underwear. I saw her linger a moment on a garter belt in one of Jan's drawers, then keep going. "Is this necessary?"

Campion did not answer. I noticed that the laptop that had been in the kitchen was in the middle of the bed. "What's that doing there?" I asked.

"I'm going to be taking that with me," Campion said.

"You have to be kidding," I said. "That's got all our finances and addresses and everything—"

"David."

I turned. My father was standing in the doorway. "David, you have to see what they've done with Ethan's room."

I crossed the hallway. My son's bed had been stripped, and the mattress was up on its side, leaning against the wall. All the plastic bins where he kept his toys had been dumped and strewn across the floor.

"Come on!" I said. "Why the hell do you have to tear apart my son's room?"

Simpson came up the stairs. "Mr. Harwood, you have the right to be here while we do this, but you can't interfere as we do our work, or you will be removed."

I was speechless with rage. I was about to say something else when the cell in my jacket rang.

"Yeah?" I said.

"Hey, Dave, it's Samantha. What the hell is going on?"

"I can't talk right now, Sam."

"Dave, listen, I've got to be up-front with you. This isn't just a friend calling. I'm looking for a quote. I need something now."

The *Standard*'s Monday edition wouldn't go to press until tonight, so Sam was looking for something for the online edition. I hadn't had a chance to check the website today, but it was reasonable to assume something was on there, given that Jan had made the TV news the night before.

I took a look into Ethan's room, a glance back into mine. What I felt most like saying at that moment was that the Promise Falls police were a bunch of morons and assholes who were wasting time harassing me while my wife remained unfound.

But instead I said, "Go ahead, Sam."

"Is it true," she asked, "that you're a suspect in this investigation into what happened to your wife?"

It hadn't been thirty minutes since I'd left the station. How could the *Standard* already know that—

*Reeves.*

I doubted Duckworth would have told the councilor anything, and the detective wouldn't have had time to call any sort of news conference since I'd left him. But my stupid overheard comment would be all Reeves needed to put in a call to the paper. Undoubtedly an anonymous call. Reeves was a weasel if there ever was one. A simple call to the assignment desk to say that one of the *Standard*'s own people was spotted at police headquarters, angrily denying that he'd killed his wife, would be enough to get the newsroom buzzing.

The moment Reeves was finished with the *Standard*, his next calls were probably to the TV and radio stations.

"Sam, where did you get this?"

Dad was looking at me, mouthing, "Who is it?"

"Dave, come on," Samantha Henry said. "You know how this works. I'm sorry, really, but I have to ask. Is it true? Are you about to be arrested? Are you a suspect? Are you a *person of interest*? Has Jan's body been found?"

"Jesus, Sam. Look, just tell me this. What are the police saying? What's their official comment?"

"I don't have anything yet from—"

"So this is just a rumor. Someone phone in to the desk, not leave his name?"

"Dave, I'm not doing anything you wouldn't do. We got a tip, and I'm following it up. Look, if you're going to talk to anybody, you should talk to me. This is your own paper. If anyone's going to give you a good shake, it's going to be us."

I wasn't so sure about that.

Outside, I heard the squeal of brakes. Still holding the phone to my head, I slipped past my father and down the stairs and looked out the front door.

It was a TV news van.

"I have to go, Sam," I said, and ended the call.

"Isn't that News Channel 13?" Dad said.

"Yeah, thanks, Dad," I said. "We need to get out of here. If they start showing up at your place, I don't want them bothering Ethan."

"Okay."

"We're just going to walk out calmly and get in your car," I said.

"Gotcha."

We walked out together, paying little attention as a driver and reporter got out of the van. I recognized the reporter as Donna Wegman. Late twenties, brunette, always pulling hair away from her eyes during remote newscasts.

"Excuse me," she called over. "Are you David Harwood?"

I pointed back to the house. "Check with the cops. They might know where to find him."

On the way, Dad said, "I don't know if you've thought of this, son, but maybe you need to talk to a lawyer or something."

"Yeah," I said. "I might have to do that."

"You could try Buck Thomas. You remember him? When we were having that trouble with the Glendons' driveway encroaching onto our lot? He's a good man."

"I might need someone with a different area of expertise," I said.

Dad nodded, conceding the point. "Lawyers charge a pretty penny, you know. If money's a problem, your mom and I, well, we have a bit tucked away. If you need it."

"Thank you, Dad," I said. "The thing is, the police haven't actually charged me with anything. I think if Detective Duckworth really had something on me, he never would have let me walk out of that station."

Dad nodded again, not taking his eyes off the road. "You're probably right. And since you haven't done anything wrong, it's not like they're going to find any evidence against you after tearing apart your house and your cars."

If that comment was meant to put me at ease, it didn't work.

"Jesus," Dad said, looking ahead. "Son of a bitch didn't even signal."

# TWENTY-SIX

THEY WERE CRUISING ALONG the Mass Pike in Dwayne's tan pickup, which his brother lent to him when he was released from prison. It was a fifteen-year-old Chevy, and despite all the rust around the wheel wells, it ran okay. But it sucked gas, even with the air conditioner off, which was all the time, because it didn't work.

"Are you sure it's not working?" Kate asked.

"Just put the fan on."

"I did and it's nothing but hot air."

"You're nothing but hot air," Dwayne said. "Just open the window."

Kate said, "Your brother really hate you? That why he gave you this clunker?"

"You want to walk?"

At least, if his brother gave it to him, chances were the truck was legit. If they did happen to get pulled over—God knows Dwayne had a history of getting arrested at the most inopportune times—the plates were in order. Dwayne even had a renewed driver's license, praise the Lord.

"You know," Dwayne said, "I used to know a Kate in high school, used to wear this low-cut thing, and when she'd bend over, she'd know you were looking and didn't give a shit. Wonder what she's doing now."

"I'll bet she's not sitting in some antique pickup truck

driving on the Mass Pike with no A/C when it's a hundred degrees out. Maybe we should have hung on to the Explorer. It was old, but the air worked."

Dwayne shot her a look. "What's with you? You still pissed about what happened back there?"

At Denny's. She'd given him shit for that as soon as they'd gotten back into the truck and were on the highway.

"What the hell were you thinking?" she'd said. "Probably somebody's already called the cops."

"It was no big deal," Dwayne had said. "I did that guy a favor."

"What?"

"From now on, he'll get those kids to behave, they won't grow up to be monsters."

For thirty miles she kept looking back, expecting to see flashing red lights. Maybe no one saw them leaving in the truck from Denny's.

This habit Dwayne had of losing it just when they needed to keep a low profile, it definitely was a problem. She just hoped he could keep a lid on things until they got their business done in Boston.

"Look, I'm sorry about that," Dwayne said as they continued along the highway. "So put the bitch back in the box and cut me some slack."

She held her hand out the window, felt the wind blow between her fingers. They didn't speak for several miles. She was the one to break the silence.

"What was it like?" she asked.

"What was what like?"

"Prison."

"What are you asking, exactly?"

"Not that," she said. "I mean, just like, everyday life, what was it like?"

"Wasn't so bad. You always knew what to expect. You had a routine. You knew when to get up and when to go to bed and when it was lunchtime and when you got to go out in the yard. You had stuff to look forward to."

This was not the answer she was expecting. "But you couldn't go anywhere," she said. "You were, you know, a prisoner."

Dwayne hung his left arm over the sill. "Yeah, but you didn't have to make a lot of decisions. What should I wear? What should I eat? What should I do? That kind of stuff wears you down, you know? I don't know sometimes how regular people do it, having to make so many decisions. Every day you got up, you knew what to expect. It was kind of comforting."

"So, it was paradise."

"Not always," he said, missing the sarcasm. "The food was shitty, and there wasn't enough of it. If you got in line last, there might not be anything for you. They cut back on how many times they did laundry. Ever since the place went private, the fuckers were looking to pinch pennies every place they could."

"Private?"

"The place was run by a company, not the state. Some of the guards, you'd listen to them, they got paid so lousy, they'd be talking about whether they were going to make it to payday, what with kids and the mortgage and car payments and all that shit. Almost made you count your blessings. Not that that's going to be a problem for us very soon."

Dwayne moved into the passing lane, went around a bus.

"You get what I'm saying?" he said. "About all those decisions? Only decision I want to make is how big a boat I'm gonna get."

She was thinking about what he'd said. She actually got it. Wasn't that what her life had been like the last few years? Decisions? Endless decisions? Having to make them not just for yourself but other people?

It did get tiring.

"Let me ask you this," she said. "You feel free?"

Dwayne squinted. "Yeah, sure, of course. Yeah, I'm free. I wouldn't trade this for being inside, if that's what you're thinking."

The thing was, she felt like she'd just gotten out of prison, too. She'd escaped, gone over the wall. Here she was, heading down the highway, feet up on the dashboard, the wind blowing her hair all over the place.

*What a feeling. What a rush.*

She wondered why she didn't feel better about it.


The plan was pretty simple.

First, they had to go to the two banks. Then, once they had the merchandise from the safe-deposit boxes, they'd find this guy Dwayne heard about who'd assess the value of their goods, then make them an offer. If it wasn't good enough, Kate figured there'd be room for negotiation. Or they could go see another guy. Where was it written that you had to take the first offer?

She just hoped it would be worth the wait. Hard to figure how it wouldn't be. She—they—were going to be rich. The only question was how rich. It was the only thing that kept her going all these years. No doubt about it, money was a great motivator. Knowing that at the end, there was going to be—in all likelihood—millions of dollars.

Maybe, if she and Dwayne hadn't swapped keys, and the moron hadn't gotten himself thrown in jail on an assault charge, she'd have found a way to move the process along, even if it meant only getting a chance at her half. But when Dwayne got himself arrested, and the key to her safe-deposit box got tossed in with his personal effects where she couldn't get at it, what choice did she have, really, but to hang in?

Hang in, and hide out. That last part was particularly important. Because she knew someone was going to be looking for her. She'd read the news. She knew the courier had lived, against all odds. Once he recovered, it seemed a safe bet he'd go looking for the person who'd not only relieved him of a fortune in diamonds, but his left hand as well.

She'd always figured she was more at risk than Dwayne. The courier had seen her face. He'd looked right into her eyes before he passed out. She hadn't expected him to wake up.

*The blood.*

It wouldn't take long, she figured, before the courier figured out how she'd gotten onto him.

It had been through his girlfriend, or rather, his ex-girlfriend. Alanna was her name. She'd worked late nights with Alanna at a bar outside Boston. Grabbing a smoke out back during breaks, Alanna would rag on about this guy, what an asshole he turned out to be. How he was always away, going over to Africa and shit, and he'd never let her come to his place, how he was all fucking mysterious about what he did for a living. One time she's with him, they're in his Audi, he has to pop into a building to meet somebody, tells her he'll be back in ten minutes, and she decides to check out this gym bag he's got tucked down on the floor behind the driver's seat. She didn't even know he worked out. First thing she notices is, it sure smells good for a gym bag. Or rather, it sure doesn't smell *bad*. What kind of guy has a gym bag that doesn't smell bad? She starts rooting around in there, doesn't find any shorts or track shoes or sweatbands, but damned if she doesn't find these little velvet-lined boxes. One of them's got half a dozen diamonds in it, and she's thinking, holy shit, is this stuff real? He comes back out sooner than expected, catches her, has a shit fit, hasn't called her since.

And the woman who now called herself Kate thought: *Diamonds?*

She'd been hanging out with this guy Dwayne for a few weeks at that point, told him what she'd heard. They tracked down Alanna's ex, started watching him, figuring out his routine. Planned a bait-and-switch. They'd meet him with a limo when he came up from New York on Amtrak.

It wouldn't take the courier long, once the painkillers started wearing off, to figure out Alanna was the leak.

A couple of months after it all went down, there was a story on the *Globe* website about a woman named Alanna Dysart found floating off Rowes Wharf. There was every reason to think that before she died, she gave her killer the names of everyone she might ever have blabbed to about his line of work.

She might very well have given him the name Connie Tattinger.

And so she vanished.


"So you think you're on the news yet?" Dwayne asked.

She'd been so wrapped up in her thoughts she didn't hear him the first time he asked.

"Get off at the next major intersection where there's some hotels," she said.

Dwayne aimed the truck down an off-ramp west of where 91 crossed 90, found a hotel with a business office where you could go in and check your email if you were the one business traveler in a thousand who didn't travel with a laptop.

Kate strolled into the office, told the girl her husband was at the front desk seeing about a room. But first, she needed to check on her sick aunt Belinda. Every time she phoned, the line was busy or she got voicemail. Maybe someone had sent an update to her email address. If Belinda had taken a turn for the worse, she said, laying it on thick, they'd just have to turn right around and go back to Maine, no sense finding that out after they'd registered and—

Go ahead, the girl said. Use this computer, no charge.

She went first to the *Standard* website, as well as the sites of a couple of the local TV stations.

There were two things she wanted to know.

Was Jan Harwood's disappearance getting a lot of play?

Had they found the body?

She scanned all the stories she could find, then said to the woman at the desk, "Thanks. She's taken a turn for the worse. We're going to have to turn back."

"I'm so sorry," the woman said.

Back in the truck, she said to Dwayne, "They haven't found her yet."

"That's not good, is it?" he said.

"It's only a matter of time," she said.

Dwayne thought about that for three seconds, then said, "I could definitely go for something to eat."

# TWENTY-SEVEN

ETHAN RAN INTO MY arms as I walked through the front door of my parents' house. I hoisted him into the air and kissed both his cheeks.

"I want to go home," he said.

"Not yet, sport," I said. "Not yet."

Ethan shook his head. "I want to go home and I want Mom."

"Like I said, not right yet."

He squirmed angrily in my arms to the point that I had to put him down. He strode forcefully down the hall and out the front door.

"Where are you going?" I asked.

"I'm going home," he said.

"The hell you are," I said and went out after him, grabbing him around the chest and swinging him up into the air. I brought him back inside, plunked him on the floor, gave him a light swat on the butt, and said, "Go find something to do."

He vanished into the kitchen, where I heard him open the fridge. Ethan usually enjoyed his time here, but he hadn't been in his own house since early yesterday morning. And as much as my parents loved Ethan, he was probably wearing out his welcome.

"Sorry," I said to Mom.

"It's okay," she said. "He just misses her. David, what's going on? Why did they take your car away?"

Dad, who'd just come in, said, "You should see what they're doing at his house. Tearing the goddamn place apart, that's what they're doing."

I steered Mom outside onto the porch where Ethan couldn't hear. "The police think I did something to Jan," I said.

"Oh, David." She was more sorrowful than surprised.

"I think they think I killed her," I said.

"Why?" she said. "Why would they think such a thing?"

"Things are . . . things seem to be pointing in my direction," I said. "Some of it's just coincidence, like the fact that no one's actually seen Jan since I took her to Lake George Friday. This mix-up with the online tickets—"

"What mix-up?"

"But then there's other things, things that don't make sense, where people have been telling lies. Like up in Lake George, whoever runs that store up there."

"David, I don't know what you're talking about. Why would people tell lies about you? Why would someone want to get you in trouble?"

"The boy needs a lawyer, that's what he needs," Dad said through the screen door.

"I need to go up there," I said. "I need to find out why that person's lying."

"Is anyone listening to me?" Dad said.

"Dad, please," I said.

"Your father's right," Mom said. "If the police think you had something to do with whatever happened to Jan—"

"I don't have time now," I said. "I have to find Jan, and I have to find out why things are being twisted to look like . . ."

"What?" Mom asked.

"Reeves," I said.

"The councilor?" Mom said. "Stan Reeves?"

"I was thinking he only just found out about this when I ran into him at the police station. But what if he's known about it for a while?"

"What are you talking about?" Dad asked.

"And Elmont Sebastian," I said. "I can't believe—I know they've got it in for me, but they wouldn't . . ."

My mind raced. It didn't take long to connect the dots, but what sort of picture did they form, really?

If something happened to Jan, and if I could be framed for it, I wouldn't be able to write any more stories challenging Star Spangled Corrections' bid for a prison in Promise Falls.

There wouldn't be any more attempts by me to get stories into the paper about how Sebastian was bribing councilors—at least Reeves—to see things his way.

Was that possible? Or was I nuts?

Was it worth going to that much trouble to silence one reporter? I did work for the only paper in town, and despite its decline, the *Standard* still wielded some influence in Promise Falls. And I was the only one at the paper who seemed to give a shit about this issue. Not just whether for-profit prisons were a good idea, but what Star Spangled Corrections was willing to do to get its way.

And while taking me out of the picture wouldn't solve all of Elmont Sebastian's problems, it sure wouldn't hurt.

But even if it was true, and Elmont Sebastian was manipulating things behind the scenes to have me neutralized, how was I to explain what I'd learned in Rochester? About Jan's past, or lack of it?

"I need a glass of water," I said suddenly.

Mom led me into the kitchen, where Ethan was lying on the floor, his head pressed sideways to the linoleum, running a car back and forth in his field of vision, making soft, contented engine noises. Mom ran the tap until the water was cold, filled a glass and handed it to me.

I took a long drink and then said, "There's something else."

My parents waited.

"Something about Jan."

I led them out of the kitchen so Ethan wouldn't hear what I had to say.

I hit the road half an hour later in my father's car. Now, having done it, I wasn't sure telling my parents about what I'd learned in Rochester had been such a good idea. Dad had gone into a rant about incompetent civil servants who'd probably issued Jan the wrong birth certificate.

"I'll just bet," he said, "she sent in her particulars to get a birth certificate, and they gave her one for some other Jan Richler, and when she got it in the mail she never even looked at what it said. They pay these people a fortune and they have jobs for life so they don't care how good they do them."

But Mom was deeply troubled by the news, and spent much of her time looking out the window into the backyard where Ethan was now whacking croquet balls all over the place. At one point, she said, "What will we tell him? Who are we supposed to tell him his mother really is?"

I floated my theory about the witness protection program, which Dad found plausible enough that it distracted him from his tirade about government slackers. (It never seemed to occur to him that he had been a municipal employee himself.) His willingness to embrace the theory made me doubt its validity.

Dad was still going on about how I needed to get a lawyer even as I got behind the wheel of his car. On this,

I had to admit he was talking sense, but I couldn't bring myself at this point to explain everything that had happened in the last two days to someone new.

I had too much to do.

To placate him, I said, "You want me to get a lawyer? Go ahead and find me one. Just not someone who handles driveway disputes."

I kept watching my rearview mirror all the way up to Lake George. I wasn't expecting to see the blue Buick Jan had spotted the last time I'd driven up here, but I did have a feeling that Detective Duckworth, or one of his minions, would be keeping an eye on me. If Duckworth truly believed I was a suspect, it didn't make sense for him to let me out of his sight.

If I was being followed, they were doing a good job of it. No one car caught my eye the entire drive up. I pulled off the road and into the parking lot of Ted's Lakeview General Store shortly after three in the afternoon.

The place was far from jumping. No one was pumping gas, and there were only a couple of cars in the lot. Assuming one belonged to whoever was minding the store, that meant maybe one customer inside.

The door jingled as I went in. A thin man in his late sixties or early seventies was behind the counter. At first I thought he was standing, then saw he was perched on the edge of a tall stool. He gave me half a nod, and half a smile, as I came in.

A plump woman already in the shop reached the counter before I did and set down a bag of Doritos, a king-sized Snickers bar, and a bottle of Diet Coke before him. He rang up her purchases, bagged them, and sent her on her way.

Once she was gone, I said, "Are you *the* Ted?"

"That's me," he said. "What can I do for you?"

"I'm a reporter for the Promise Falls *Standard*," I

said. "The police, Detective Duckworth, he told me he was speaking to someone here about that woman who's gone missing. Would that be you?"

"One and the same," he said with a lilt in his voice. The suggestion that he was about to be interviewed had brightened him.

"So this woman, Jan Harwood, she was in here?"

"I'm as sure it was her as I am that you're standing right there," he said.

"And you called the police? Or were they in touch with you?"

"Well," he said, slipping off the stool and leaning across the counter, "I saw her on the news the night before, them saying she was missing, and right away I recognized her."

"Wow," I said, making notes in the pad I'd taken from my pocket. "But how could you recognize someone who was just in here for a minute?"

"Normally, you'd be right about that," he said. "But she was pretty chatty, gave me a chance to get a good look at her. Nice-looking lady, too."

Jan? Chatty?

"What did she have to say?"

"That she was up here for a drive with her husband."

"She just came out and said that?"

"Well, first, she said how beautiful it was up here, that she'd never been to Lake George before, and I said are you staying somewhere up around here, and she said no, she was just up for a drive with her husband."

That all sounded plausible. Some friendly conversation. Why was Duckworth trying to make that sound like more than it was?

"So then what?" I asked. "She bought something and left?"

"She bought some drinks, I remember that. Can't say

what they were off the top of my head. An iced tea, I think."

"And then she was gone?"

"She asked me if there was any interesting things to do around here. Something fun."

"Something fun?"

"Aren't you going to write all this down?" Ted asked.

I realized I hadn't been taking notes. I smiled and said, "Don't worry, I'll remember the good stuff."

"I just don't want to be misquoted or anything."

"Don't worry about that. So what did she mean, something fun?"

"She wondered if there was something to do around here, because her husband had brought her up on a little car trip, and she was wondering why. She thought maybe he was planning to surprise her with something."

"Did she give any other reason why they were up this way? Like, I don't know, that they were meeting someone?"

Ted thought about that. "I don't think so. Just that her husband had brought her up this way and wouldn't tell her why."

I set my notepad and pen on the counter and didn't ask anything else for a moment. Ted was confused.

"There a problem?"

"Why are you lying, Ted?" I asked.

"What's that?"

"I asked why you're lying."

"What the hell are you talking about? I'm telling you the truth. I'm telling you the same thing I told the police."

"I don't think so," I said. "I think you're making this up."

"Are you some kind of nut? She was here, standing right where you are. Only two days ago."

"I believe she was here, but I don't believe she said those things to you. Did someone pay you to tell the police those things? Is that what's going on?"

"Who the hell are you, anyway?"

"I told you. I'm a reporter, and I don't like it when people try to jerk me around," I said.

"For fuck's sake," Ted said, "if you don't believe me, get the police to show you the tape."

"Tape?"

"Okay, I call it tape, but it's on a disc or digital or some kind of shit like that. But look." He pointed over his shoulder. A small camera hung from a bracket that was bolted to the wall. "We got sound, too. It's not great, but you listen close you can hear what people say. I got robbed pretty bad here back in 2007, asshole even took a shot that went right past my ear and into the wall back here. That's when I got the camera and the microphone."

"It's all recorded?" I said.

"Ask the cops. They came up here earlier today, made a copy of it. Why the hell are you accusing me of lying?"

"Why would she say those things?" I said. But I was talking to myself, not Ted.

I grabbed my notepad, slipped it back into my jacket, and started heading for the door.

Ted called out, "When's this going to be in the paper?"

I was shaking my head, looking down as I went out the door, trying to come up with a reason why Jan would have told someone she didn't know why I'd brought her up here. Why she would have said I was planning some kind of surprise for her. It made sense that Jan wouldn't have told a stranger we'd taken a run up here so I could meet a confidential source. That would have been just plain dumb. But to actually start up a conversation for the purpose of saying those things—what the hell was that about?

Maybe, had I not been so preoccupied, I would have had some inkling that Welland, Elmont Sebastian's ex-con driver, was waiting to ambush me the moment I came outside.

# TWENTY-EIGHT

WELLAND GRABBED HOLD OF me by my jacket and threw me up against the wall of Ted's Lakeview General Store hard enough to knock the wind out of me.

"What the—"

It was all I managed to say before Welland had his face in mine. "Hey, Mr. Harwood," he said. As I tried to catch my breath I couldn't help noticing his was hot and smelled of onions.

"Get your hands off me," I said. Welland's arms, like a couple of shock absorbers, had me pinned to the building.

"Mr. Sebastian was hoping," he said with exaggerated politeness, "you might be able to have a word with him."

I glanced over and saw the limo only a few feet away, the motor running, the tinted windows all in the up position. I'd have to take Welland's word that his boss was in there.

"I said get your fucking hands off me," I said to Welland, still holding me against the building.

Welland, not letting up, said, "Let me ask you something."

I said nothing.

"Some guys, guys like you, can actually go their whole lives and never actually have to prove themselves. You know what I mean? I'm talking in a man-to-man context." He said that last word with pride. "You ever had to do that? Or was the last time you were in a fight when you were six years old?"

I still said nothing. The door opened and Ted stuck his head out. "Everything okay out here?"

Welland shot him a look. "Get lost, old man."

Ted went back inside.

Welland eased off on me, but placed a viselike grip on my arm and led me to the limo. He opened the back door and shoved me through the opening.

Elmont Sebastian sat on the far side of the thickly padded leather seat. In his hand was a Mars bar, the wrapper peeled back on it like it was a banana. I pulled my leg out of the way just in time to keep Welland from closing the door on it.

"Mr. Harwood, a pleasure," Sebastian said.

Welland came around the car and got behind the wheel. He put the car in drive and sped out of the lot so fast I felt myself thrown back into the seat.

"I think they call this kidnapping," I said.

Sebastian grinned. "Don't be ridiculous," he said, chewing. "This is a business meeting."

"I never saw you following me," I said. "Big car like this is kind of hard to disguise."

Sebastian nodded. "We were a couple of miles back."

"Then how did you—"

"We were sloppy last time, having you followed up here with one car, which, to your credit, you spotted. So this time, we used several to keep track of you. I brought in a few of my other staff. When you have a network of institutions such as mine, you have access to a large and varied workforce. Most of them know how to drive. Some of them probably took their driver's test in stolen cars." He chuckled at his own joke. "Anyway, once you stopped here again, that information was relayed to me."

"Where are we going?" I asked as Welland pushed the car north.

"Nowhere in particular," Sebastian said. "Just tootling about." He finished the candy bar, wadded the wrapper down into a tiny ball, and tossed it to the floor. There was no other trash there, so I guessed Welland's duties included more than just driving.

"This'll make quite a story," I said. "'Prison Boss Kidnaps *Standard* Reporter.'"

"I don't think you'll write that," he said, moving his tongue over his teeth, getting the last little bits of chocolate out of the way.

"Why not?"

"Because you haven't heard my proposal. Once you have, I think you'll be feeling more kindly toward me."

"What sort of proposal?"

He reached out and touched my knee. "First of all, I totally understand if you don't give me an answer today. I know you have a lot on your plate right now, what with this unfortunate business of your wife."

"You know all about that," I said.

"It would be difficult not to," he said. "I'm sure you've seen the news. I believe some reports are calling you a 'person of interest,' which has always struck me as a nice way of saying 'suspect.' Wouldn't you agree?"

"How soon did Reeves call you after he left the police station?" I asked.

Sebastian grinned. "I will grant you, the only thing that travels faster than good news is bad news. But then, in your line of work, you probably already know that. Tell me this. Why do the media only focus on the negative? It's so discouraging, dispiriting even."

"When a plane lands safely, it doesn't tend to warrant a headline," I said.

"Yes, that's true. Good point. But look at my situation. Here I am, offering a needed service, willing to bring jobs and prosperity to your little shithole town, and all I get is grief. At least from the likes of you."

"But not my paper," I said. "It's been very kind. Have you made a deal yet with Madeline to buy her land?"

Sebastian smiled. "Star Spangled Corrections is exploring a number of options, Mr. Harwood."

"What makes you think that my current problems will stop me from writing about your plans?"

"Well, I don't know a lot about journalism, but I think even a minor newspaper like the *Standard* would have qualms about having a murder suspect actively reporting on the news. My guess is you'll be on a leave before long."

Was that something he actually knew? Just a guess? Either way, he was probably right.

"And frankly, even if your current problems, as you call them, should happen to disappear, I don't think it's in your interests to pursue this any further."

"And why would that be?" I asked.

"Let's come back to that later," Sebastian said. "What I'd like to do now is get to my proposal."

"By all means," I said.

"I wondered how you'd feel about a career change."

"A what?"

"A career change. There's no future in newspapers. Surely you must be considering your options."

"What are you getting at?"

"When Star Spangled Corrections does set up here— and we will, let me assure you—we're going to need a sharp media relations officer. Someone to deal with the press. I think someone familiar with how the media operates is the way to go."

"You're serious."

"I am. Do I strike you as someone who likes to joke around, David?"

Up front, Welland snickered.

"No," I said.

"I'm being quite sincere here. I'd like you to be my media relations officer. I can guess what you're being paid at the *Standard*. Seventy, eighty thousand?"

Less.

"Your starting salary would be nearly double that. Not a bad wage for a man with a wife and young son."

He seemed to linger on "son."

"You haven't even broken ground yet," I said. "I guess, in the meantime, I'd still be doing stories about the opposition to your prison."

"As a matter of fact, there's so much prep work involved, I'd need you to start right away if you're agreeable," Sebastian said. When I didn't say anything, he continued, "Look, David, neither of us is stupid. I don't want to insult you. I'll be honest. If you take this job, you solve two problems for me. Your editorial campaign against my facility ends, and I end up with a bright young man with a lot of media savvy. It's the old axiom about having your enemies in the tent with you pissing out, instead of being outside pissing in. I'm asking you to come into the tent, David, and I'm prepared to compensate you well for your trouble."

After a moment, I said, "As you said, I have a lot on my plate right now."

He leaned back, nodded. "Of course, of course. What must you think of me, even making such a proposal when you're going through such a difficult time."

"But I can still give you an answer now," I said.

"Oh," Sebastian said, taken aback. "Well then, let's have it."

"No."

He looked disappointed, but it seemed feigned. "In that case, that leaves just one other item of business. I had hoped, had you accepted my proposal, this next thing would be a simple matter. But now I suspect it may be more difficult."

"What's that?"

"Who's your source?"

"I'm sorry?"

"Who was it you came up here to meet?"

"I didn't come up here to meet with anyone," I said.

Sebastian smiled at me as though I were a child who had disappointed him. "Please, David. I know that's why you came up here Friday. I know a woman was in touch with you. And I know she didn't show up. Now you're up here again, only two days later, and you'd have me believe it's not for the same reason? Were you stood up again?"

"I'm not here to meet with anyone."

Sebastian sighed and took in the scenery flashing past his window. Without looking at me, he said, "Do you have time for a story, David?"

"I'm something of a captive audience," I said as the limo continued down the road.

"One time, at our facility outside Atlanta, we were having trouble with an inmate who went by the nickname of Buddy."

Welland glanced at his mirror.

Sebastian said, "He got that name because everyone wanted to be his friend. It's not that he was the life of the party or anything. It's just that everyone thought it was in their interests to stay on his good side. He was a tough character. Buddy was a member of the Aryan Brotherhood, a white supremacist gang that's insinuated itself into correctional facilities across the country. Are you familiar with them?"

I just looked at him.

"Yes, of course you are," Sebastian said. He shifted slightly to the center of the seat and called up to his driver. "Welland, given that you are our resident expert, how would you characterize the Aryan chaps?"

Welland glanced into the mirror. "Scariest mother-fuckers who ever lived."

"Yes," Sebastian said. "A fair assessment. Welland, would you like to tell this? I'm always afraid when I do it sounds boastful."

Welland collected his thoughts a moment, licked his lips, and then said, "Mr. Sebastian had a problem with Buddy. He was an expert at piss-writing."

"At what?" I asked. All I could picture was taking a leak outside as a kid, writing my name in the snow.

"You can use piss to write, and it's like invisible ink. When you hold the paper up to the light or heat it, you can see the message. Mr. Sebastian found out Buddy was sending a lot of messages this way, communicating with his associates, and he didn't want him to do it anymore. It wasn't conducive to the smooth operation of the facility."

That made Sebastian smile.

"So Mr. Sebastian here had Buddy brought to his office, keeping him cuffed, of course. One of the guards, he undid Buddy's pants, pulled 'em down around his ankles." Welland coughed, cleared his throat, like maybe he didn't enjoy telling this story. "And that was when Mr. Sebastian put fifty thousand volts to his package."

I looked at Sebastian.

"A Taser," he said. "A stun gun."

"You stun-gunned the man's genitals?"

"Not a simple task," Sebastian said. "The wires that shoot out from a stun gun don't have pinpoint accuracy. But I was lucky."

A lot luckier than Buddy, I thought.

"You might as well tell the rest," Welland said.

Sebastian said, "I explained to Buddy that when you have blood in your urine, it makes it a lot trickier to use it for invisible ink. To be honest, I wasn't sure fifty thousand volts would do anything but make Buddy a candidate for state-supplied Viagra, but as it turned out, it achieved the desired effect."

There was a moment of quiet in the car. Finally, Sebastian said, "I never would have thought it was possible to make a member of the Aryan Brotherhood cry."

"I think it would be hard not to, having something like that done to you," I offered.

"Oh, it wasn't that," Sebastian said. "Once he'd recovered from the shock, I showed Buddy a picture of his six-year-old son, living with his girlfriend on the outside, and explained how unfortunate it would be if any of the recently released inmates he'd sodomized and otherwise terrorized were to find out where his little boy lived. That was when I saw that solitary tear run down his cheek."

"Well," I said.

"Indeed," said Elmont Sebastian. "So, I would very much appreciate it if you would tell me who wrote to you at the *Standard* and invited you up here to meet with her."

"I don't know how you know about that email," I said, although I had a pretty good idea. "But since you clearly do, you know it was anonymous."

He nodded. "Quite true. But there are countless other ways to get in touch with people. And I think even though your first rendezvous was unsuccessful, it's entirely probable that this woman found another way to contact you."

"She didn't," I said. "I think she must have had second thoughts."

"Then what are you doing back here again?"

"I drove up to talk to the manager of that store back there. I wanted to ask him about my wife. She went in there to buy some drinks when we came up here Friday.

I thought she might have said something to him that would help me find her."

Sebastian appeared to be mulling that one over.

"You see, David, I can't afford to have leaks in my organization. No company can. Not Apple, not Microsoft, and certainly not Star Spangled Corrections. I have to assume that email came from one of two places. From within my organization, or from within Promise Falls city hall, specifically someone connected in some way to Stan Reeves. Now, as I explained to you the other day, all of my dealings with political representatives have been totally aboveboard. But a false allegation can be as damaging, perhaps even more so, than one that turns out to be true."

Welland was slowing the car. I glanced ahead and saw no obvious reason to do so.

"So it's very important to me to find out who would contact you and suggest any kind of malfeasance on my company's part. The author of that email admitted to a couple of things. One, that she was female, and two, that she had a white truck. My own investigation has determined that Star Spangled has four female employees within a two-hour drive who either have, or have access to, a white truck. And at city hall, among those who might be privy to the correspondence of council members, perhaps half a dozen are women. What vehicles they have I'm in the process of nailing down. I am prepared to escalate my investigation of these women unless you're willing to save us all some trouble."

I heard Welland repeat the word "escalate" under his breath. He had the turn signal on, and a moment later was driving down a narrow gravel road slicing its way into a thick forest.

"Mr. Sebastian, my hat's off to you," I said. "You're no slouch at this whole intimidation thing. It would have been hard to miss the point of your little Aryan cry-baby story. I'd toss whatever journalistic standards I might have out the window in a minute if I believed, even for a second, that you were threatening my son."

Sebastian made a face of mock outrage. "David, is that what you took from that story? I just thought you'd find it interesting."

I continued, "If I really thought you might hurt my boy, and all it took to save him was to betray a source, well, I'd burn that source. I wouldn't much like myself for it, but blood runs thicker than newsprint ink."

Sebastian nodded.

I added, "And if you did harm him in any way, if you so much as took away one of his action figures, I would find you and I would kill you."

Sebastian smiled wearily. "You know what would be really interesting? What would be really interesting is if they nail you for this. If they find your wife's body and find a way to pin it on you, and they put you on trial and convict you and send you up for ten or twenty years, and it turns out to be one of my jails. If we get this thing fast-tracked, it might actually be the one in Promise Falls. Wouldn't that be something?" He chuckled softly. "Welland, wouldn't that be something?"

"You know what that would be, sir?" he said, bringing the car to a stop. "That would be ironic."

"Indeed."

I looked outside. We were in the middle of nowhere, surrounded by forest.

I asked Sebastian, "Don't you worry about yourself?"

"What do you mean?"

"All those other Aryan Brothers out there, aren't you afraid someone might want to get even for what you did to Buddy? Maybe pay a visit on a member of your own family?"

"If I had any family, that might be a concern. But a

man in my line of work functions best when he doesn't have the burden of loved ones."

I looked out the window again. I didn't want to ask, but couldn't stop myself. "What are we doing here? Why are we stopping?"

Welland shifted in his seat so that he could catch his boss's eye in the rearview mirror. He was awaiting instructions.

"It's beautiful out here, isn't it?" Sebastian said. "Only a mile off the main road, and it's like you're a hundred miles from civilization. Magnificent."

I put my hand on the door handle. I was getting ready to run. I didn't like my chances of escaping, out here in the middle of nowhere.

"But being out here, in the open, can be as dangerous as being kept behind bars in one of my facilities," he said. "Certainly for you. Right now. At this moment."

We locked eyes. I was determined not to be the first to look away, even though I was pretty much scared shitless. He could have Welland kill me and dump me here and my body might never be found.

Finally, Sebastian sighed tiredly, broke eye contact, and said to Welland, "Find a place to turn around and head back." To me, he said, "This is your lucky day, David. I believe you. About your source. I actually do."

I felt, briefly, tremendously relieved. Elmont Sebastian, by giving me something new to worry about—whether I might live to see the end of the day—and then giving me a reprieve, had made me forget, at least for a while, my other troubles.

"But we're not done," he said. "While you may not know who this source is, I would be most grateful if you'd make an effort to find out, and then let me know. You may be contacted again. There may be an opportunity for another meeting."

I said nothing. The limo was moving again. Welland

found a narrow intersection up ahead and managed to turn the beast around, then headed for the highway that would take us, I hoped, back to Ted's.

"So was it Madeline?" I asked.

"I'm sorry?" Sebastian said.

"Madeline Plimpton. My publisher."

"And what is it you think she did?"

"She fed you the email from that woman. It's not much of a stretch to think the publisher would have some kind of clearance that would allow her to read every message attached to one of the paper's email addresses. I deleted it as quickly as I could, but I guess I wasn't fast enough. Is that the deal? She betrays her staff, keeps the heat off you, and in return you buy her land?"

Sebastian's eyes seemed to twinkle.

"That's the trouble with you newspaper types," he said. "You're so incredibly cynical."

# TWENTY-NINE

"WHY THE HELL DO you keep staring at that picture?" Horace Richler asked his wife.

Gretchen was sitting on the front step of their Lincoln Avenue home, forearms resting on her knees, holding the picture David Harwood had left with them of his wife in both hands. It was a printout on regular paper, and if she held it with only one hand the breeze would catch it and flip it over.

Horace noticed that on the step next to his wife was the framed photo of their daughter, Jan.

"What's going on?" he asked.

"I'm just thinking," she said.

"You want a coffee or anything? There's still some left in the pot."

Gretchen said nothing. She looked up from the picture and stared out at the street. She could see them. The two little girls playing in the front yard. Running around in circles, laughing one minute, arguing the next.

Then Horace, running out the front door, getting into his car, throwing it into reverse and hitting the gas.

"Hey. Coffee?"

Gretchen craned her neck around. She couldn't move it all that far. She noticed it most when she was trying to back out of a spot at the grocery store. Couldn't turn around to see where she was going, had to rely on the mirrors. Always came out real slow, figured if she did hit something, she'd hear it, could step on the brakes right away.

"I don't want anything, love, thanks," she said.

"What's going on inside your head?"

When Gretchen didn't reply, Horace came down the steps and plunked himself down, not without some discomfort. Both his knees hurt like the devil. Once he was settled, he leaned his shoulder into his wife's.

He said, "I had a dream about Bradley last night. That Afghanistan never happened. That he never went over there, there never was any goddamn Taliban, that none of that ever even existed. I was dreaming that I was sitting right here, and you were sitting next to me the way you are right now, and I looked down the street that way and I saw him walking up the road in his uniform."

A tear ran down Gretchen's cheek.

"And he had Jan with him," Horace said, his voice breaking. "She was still a little girl, and she was holding on to her big brother's hand, and the two of them were coming home. Together."

Gretchen held on to the photo with one hand and dug a tissue out of her sleeve with the other. She put it to her eye.

"And then I realized that they weren't really alive," Horace said. "I realized that you and I, we were dead. That Lincoln Avenue was heaven."

Gretchen sniffed, blew her nose, dabbed her eyes.

"Sorry," Horace said. "I shouldn't have told you that. It was that fella coming here, I think that's what triggered it. He shouldn't have come here. He shouldn't have done that, bringing his troubles into our house when we got enough of our own. I don't know what the hell he was thinking, barging in here with a cockamamy, bullshit story like that."

Gretchen sniffed again, dabbed again, then wadded the tissue up into a ball.

Horace picked up the photo of his daughter. His body seemed to crumple around it.

"It wasn't your fault," Gretchen said for probably the thousandth time in all these years.

Horace didn't respond.

Gretchen got both hands again on the printout picture of Jan Harwood and stared at it.

Horace said, "The idea that somebody would go around using our daughter's name and birth certificate, it just . . . how can you steal a little girl's identity?"

"It happens," Gretchen said quietly. "It happens all the time. I saw, on TV, how someone went through a cemetery, found graves where they could tell from the dates that it was a child that died, and they'd use that name to make up a whole new person."

"Some people," Horace said under his breath. He glanced over at the picture his wife couldn't stop staring at. "She's pretty."

"Yes."

"It must be hard on that fella, not knowing what's happened to her. Not knowing if she's dead or alive. That has to be bad, the not knowing."

"At least with not knowing, there's always hope," Gretchen said, not taking her eyes off the picture. "I haven't stopped looking at this all day. I knew, when he first showed it to me last night. . . ."

"You seemed kind of upset," Horace said. "You went upstairs."

Gretchen was struggling to say something. "Horace . . ."

He slipped an arm around his wife's shoulders. "It's okay," he said.

"Horace, look at the picture."

"I've seen the picture."

"Look, look right here." She pointed.

"Hang on," he said, then sighed and took his arm from around her shoulders. He reached into the front pocket of his shirt, where he kept a pair of small wire-rimmed reading glasses. He opened them up, noticed they were smudged and dirty, but slipped the arms over his ears just the same.

"Where do you want me to look?"

"Right here."

"I don't know what you're looking at."

"*Here.*"

He grasped the picture with both hands. He studied it for a moment, and then his face began to fall.

"I'll be goddamned," he said.

# THIRTY

ONCE WELLAND HAD THE limo turned around and we were well on our way, I said to Elmont Sebastian, "Suppose, just for a moment, that I did find out who emailed me, and I told you who she was."

His eyebrows went up half an inch.

"What would you do to her?" I asked.

Sebastian said, "I would have a word with her."

"A word."

"I would tell her that she was lucky that no harm had been done, and I would explain to her that it's not a good thing to be disloyal to those you work for."

"Assuming she works for you," I said.

"Or Mr. Reeves. It's not a good thing to rat out your friends or employers."

"But it's okay if I rat her out."

Sebastian looked at me and smiled.

As we approached Ted's, I sensed the car slowing, but then it sped up. "You passed it," I said to Welland.

"Thanks for that," Welland said. "I never would have known."

I glanced at Sebastian. "What's going on?"

He didn't seem to know any more than I did. "Welland?" he said.

His driver said, "Didn't look safe to pull in, sir."

"What did you see?"

"Looked like someone was waiting for Mr. Harwood," Welland said.

Someone was waiting for me at Ted's?

"Pull over up ahead, once we get round that bend," Sebastian said.

The car maintained its pace for another few seconds, then Welland steered it over onto the gravel shoulder. Once the car was fully stopped, Sebastian said to me, "Always a pleasure, David."

These guys were pretty consistent at not returning me to my pickup point.

As I opened the door Sebastian said, "I hope you'll give due consideration to everything I've said."

I got out and started walking back to Ted's without closing the door. It wouldn't have killed Sebastian to lean over and deal with it, but when I glanced back I saw Welland getting out of the driver's seat, going around to the other side. I expected him to slam the door, but he leaned in briefly, came back out with what appeared to be a Mars bar wrapper in his hand, then slammed the door shut. He glanced my way, and for a second time, made his fingers into a gun and pointed at me.

This time, he fired twice.

As I walked along the shoulder my cell phone rang. It was my mother.

"It's getting bad here," she said.

"What are you talking about?"

"TV trucks and reporters. Everyone wants to talk to you, and if they can't get you, they want to talk to me or your father. Or they want to get a picture of Ethan."

"God, Mom, what's tipped everyone off?"

"I've been checking the websites, first your paper's, then others. It's starting to spread. The headlines say things like 'Reporter Questioned in Wife's Disappearance' and 'Reporter Tells Police: I Didn't Kill My Wife.'

But like I said, it's not just your paper. It's on the TV news websites, and I heard something on the radio, and, David, it's just terrible. I can't believe the things they're saying about you, well, not actually about you, but it's all the innuendo and suggestions and—"

"I know, I know. Once Reeves got the ball rolling, everyone joined in. Tell me about Ethan."

"We're keeping him inside, just putting him in front of the television. We've got some Disney DVDs and he's watching them. David, I went onto the CNN website, and even they had an item on it. It was short but—"

"Mom, just worry about Ethan. Does he know what's going on?"

"He looked outside a couple of times, but I've told him to stay away from the window, because if they can get a picture of him, they'll probably use it."

"Okay, that's good. Does he know why they're there?"

"No," Mom said. "I made up a crazy story."

"What kind of story?"

"I told him sometimes people come by to see the house because Batman used to live here."

In spite of everything, I laughed. "Yeah, your house is a regular Wayne Manor."

"I don't know why I said it. It was the first thing I could think of. Hang on, your father wants to talk to you."

"Okay, Mom, thanks—"

"Son?"

"Hi, Dad."

"Where are you?"

"Just walking along the highway north of Lake George."

"Why the hell are you doing that?"

"What is it, Dad?"

"I got somebody for you."

"Got somebody who?"

"A lawyer. Her name's Bondurant."

It rang a bell. "Natalie Bondurant?" I asked.

"That's the one. Is that French, you figure?"

"I don't know."

"I called the office and they had this weekend emergency number and I got hold of her. She said she's willing to talk to you."

"Thanks. That's great, Dad."

"You need to talk to her today. The shit's hitting the fan around here."

"I hear ya."

"I got her number. Can you write something down?"

I had my notepad in my pocket. "All right, fine." I got out the pad, flipped it open, wrote down the number Dad dictated to me.

"If you were smart, you'd give her a call right now," Dad said.

"When I get back on the road."

"Is my car okay?" Dad asked. Even with all that was going on, Dad never lost sight of the things that mattered to him.

"The car's fine," I said.

"If you're not going to call her now, she did have one piece of advice for you in the meantime."

"What's that?"

"She said not to say a goddamn thing to the police."

Ted's had come into view. Leaning up against Dad's car was Detective Barry Duckworth.

"Nice day for a walk," Duckworth said as I approached. His unmarked cruiser was parked off to one side. That must have been what Welland saw before he decided to keep on driving. Unmarked police cruisers had a certain look about them.

"Yeah," I said. Was there anyone who *hadn't* followed me up here?

I fished the car keys out of my pocket, hoping to send the message that I was on my way.

"What are you doing up here?" Duckworth asked.

"I might ask you the same thing."

"But if I don't answer, it doesn't look suspicious," he said.

"I came up to talk to Ted."

"What were you doing leaving your car here and strolling down the highway? Not much down there to see."

I wanted to tell him about my ride with Sebastian. But the prison boss had intimidated me to the point that I wasn't sure that was a good idea. Plus, I didn't think Duckworth would believe me anyway.

"I was just walking, and thinking."

"About what Ted told you?"

"So you've already spoken to him."

"Briefly," Duckworth said. "You shouldn't be doing that. Approaching witnesses, giving them a hard time. That's bad form."

"He told you things that didn't make any sense to me. I wanted to hear them for myself."

"And did you?"

"Yeah."

"Still think he's lying?"

"He says it's on the security video. What Jan said to him."

"That's right," Duckworth said. "It's a little muddy in places, but we got people who can clean that up. But what he said basically checks out."

"I don't get it," I said.

"I think I do," Duckworth said.

"You would," I said, "because you think I know what's happened to Jan. But I don't."

"Who was it took you for a ride and dropped you off down the road?"

So. He already knew about that, too. Ted must have told him about seeing Welland grab hold of me.

"It was Elmont Sebastian," I said. "And his driver."

"The prison guy?"

"Yeah."

"What's he doing up here?"

"He wanted to talk to me. I've been trying to get some quotes from him."

"And he drove all the way up here to give them to you?"

"Look," I said, "I want to get back home. Things don't sound good there."

"Yeah," Duckworth said. "There's a bit of a media frenzy building. I want you to know, for what it's worth, I didn't set it off. I think it was your pal Reeves. Once the media started calling, we've had no choice but to field their questions. It's not my style, to get something like this going."

"For what it's worth, thank you," I said. "So you followed me up here?"

"Not exactly," Duckworth said.

"Then what are you doing here?"

"I was on my way up to something else and decided to pop in and have a word with Ted myself. Another Promise Falls officer came up earlier to get the surveillance video off him, but I thought a face-to-face was in order. Ted mentioned you'd just been in, and that your car was still here."

"So you decided to wait for me."

Duckworth nodded slowly.

"What was the other thing you were coming up here for?" I asked.

Duckworth's cell phone rang. He put it to his ear and said, "Duckworth . . . Okay . . . Is the coroner there yet? . . . I don't think I'm any more than a couple of miles away. . . . See you shortly."

He ended the call and put the phone away.

"What is it?" I asked. "What was that about the coroner?"

"Mr. Harwood, there's been a discovery just up the road from here."

"A discovery?"

"A shallow grave just off the side of the road. Freshly dug and covered over."

I reached my hand out and used the car to support myself. My throat went dry and my temples began to pulse.

"Whose body's in it?"

Duckworth nodded.

"Who?" I asked. "Is it Jan?"

"Well, they don't know anything for sure yet," Duckworth said.

I closed my eyes.

*It's not supposed to end this way.*

Duckworth said, "Why don't we take my car."

We headed north, the way I'd been taken by Sebastian and Welland, but in under a mile Duckworth put on his blinker and turned down a narrow gravel road that went down, then up, winding all the time. The inside of Duckworth's car smelled of french fries. The smell made me feel sick to my stomach.

Not far up ahead, several police cars and vans blocked our path.

"We'll walk in from here," Duckworth said, slowing and putting his car into park.

"Who saw this grave?" I asked. I'd felt my hands shaking a moment ago, and had grabbed the door handle with my right and tucked my left under my thigh, hoping Duckworth wouldn't notice. I felt I needed to disguise how nervous I was, worried Duckworth would take that to mean I was guilty of something.

But wouldn't any man, especially an innocent man whose wife was missing, be distraught after learning a body had been found?

"What the locals tell me," Duckworth said, "is there's a couple of cabins down at the end of this road, and a guy who lives in one of them spotted something suspicious at the side, went to check it out, realized what was buried there, and he called the police."

"How long ago was this?"

"Couple of hours," Duckworth said. "Local cops secured the scene, then they contacted us. We'd already been in touch, putting them on alert about your wife."

"I told you nothing happened with Jan when we were up here," I said.

"You've made that very clear, Mr. Harwood," he said. He opened his door, then looked at me. "You can stay right here if you'd like."

"No," I said. "If it's Jan, I have to know."

"Absolutely," he said. "Don't think I don't appreciate your assistance."

*Fuck you.*

We got out of the car and started up the road, the gravel crunching beneath our shoes. A uniformed officer coming from the direction of the crime scene approached.

"You Detective Duckworth?" he said.

Duckworth nodded and extended a hand. "Thanks for the quick heads-up on this," he said. The cop looked at me. Before I had a chance to introduce myself, Duckworth said, "This is Mr. Harwood. He's the one whose wife is missing." The two of them exchanged a quick glance. I could only imagine what this cop had been told already.

"Mr. Harwood," he said. "My name is Daltrey. I'm very sorry. This must be a very difficult time for you."

"Is it my wife?" I asked.

"We don't know that at this stage."

"But it's a woman?" I asked. "A woman's body?"

Daltrey glanced at Duckworth, as though looking for permission. When Duckworth didn't say anything, Daltrey replied, "Yes, it's a woman."

"I need to see her."

Duckworth reached over and lightly touched my arm. "I really don't know that that's a good idea."

"Where's the grave?" I asked.

Daltrey pointed. "Just beyond those cars, on the left side. We haven't moved her yet."

Duckworth tightened his grip on me. "Let me go up there first. You wait here with Daltrey."

"No," I said, breathing in short gasps. "I have to—"

"You wait. If there's a reason for you to come up, I'll come back and get you."

I looked him in the eye. I couldn't get a read on him. I didn't know whether he was trying to be compassionate here, or whether somehow I was being played.

"Okay," I said.

As Duckworth went ahead, Daltrey positioned himself in front of me, in case I decided to run after him. He said, "Looks like it might rain."

I walked to Duckworth's car, ambled around it a couple of times, always glancing back for him.

He was back in about five minutes, caught my eye, beckoned with his index finger. I ran over to him.

"If you're up to it," he said, "I think it would help if you make an identification."

"Oh God," I said. I felt weak in the knees.

He gripped my arm. "I don't know for certain that this is your wife, Mr. Harwood. But I think you need to be prepared for that fact."

"It can't be her," I said. "There's no reason for her to be up here. . . ."

"Take a minute," he said.

I took a couple of breaths, swallowed, and said, "Show me."

He led me between two police cars that had acted as a privacy shield. Once we got past them, I looked to the left and saw that where the opposite side of the ditch sloped up, there was a five-foot ridge of earth. It was in full view of the road. Draped over the ridge was a pale, dirt-splotched white hand and part of an arm. Whoever that arm belonged to was on the other side of the dirt pile.

I stopped, and stared.

"Mr. Harwood?" Duckworth said.

I took another couple of breaths. "Okay," I said.

"I can't have you disturbing anything," he said. "You can't . . . touch her. Sometimes, people, when they're overcome with grief . . ."

"I understand," I said.

He led me up to the grave. When we were close enough that we could see beyond the ridge, Duckworth stopped me.

"Here we are," Duckworth said. I could feel him watching me.

I looked at the dirt-smeared face of the dead woman lying in that grave and fell to my knees, then pitched forward, catching myself with my hands.

"Oh God," I said. "Oh God."

Duckworth knelt down next to me, held on to my shoulders. "Talk to me, Mr. Harwood."

"It's not her," I whispered. "It's not Jan."

"You're sure?" he said.

"It's Leanne," I said. "It's Leanne Kowalski."

# THIRTY-ONE

IN THE SHORT TIME she'd been going by the name Kate, she'd never gotten used to it. Maybe she needed a few more days for it to feel like her own. Taking Leanne's middle name, shortening it, it was the first idea that came to her. Just seemed natural.

The funny thing was, she couldn't even think of herself by her own name these days. If someone called out "Hey, Connie!" she wasn't even sure she'd turn around. It had been years since anyone had known her as Connie.

Her worry now was if someone shouted out "Jan!," she'd turn around reflexively, wouldn't even think about it.

But that was still how she thought of herself. You spend six years with a name, you start to get comfortable with it. That was the name she'd been answering to for a very long time.

That, and "Mom."

When she'd told Dwayne Jan was dead, she'd been telling herself more than him. She wanted to put that person, that life, behind her. She wanted to lay Jan to rest. Give her the last rites. Say a few words in her memory.

But she wasn't really gone. A large part of her still was Jan. But now she was moving into something new. She was evolving. She'd always been evolving, moving through one stage to get to another. It was just that some of those stages took longer to get through than others.

She reached up, made another adjustment to the wig as they continued their journey to Boston.

It was the same wig Jan had worn when she walked in—and out—of Five Mountains. She'd worn it long enough to get through the gates, then went in a ladies' room stall to remove it before rejoining Dave and Ethan. The wig and a change of clothes had been stuffed into the backpack. The moment Dave had run off in search of Ethan, instead of heading straight to the gate as he'd instructed her, she'd turned in to the closest ladies' room, taken a stall, and stripped down.

She'd switched from shorts to jeans, traded the sleeveless top for a long-sleeved blouse. Even took off the running shoes and went with sandals. But the blonde wig was the accessory that really pulled it all together. She jammed her discarded outfit back into the backpack—couldn't leave her clothes around for someone to find—and strolled back out of that ladies' room like she hadn't just had her son snatched out from under her. Walked, real cool-like, through those gates, through the parking lot, met up with Dwayne and got into his car. He'd wanted to take off the fake beard right then, said it itched like crazy, but she persuaded him to keep it on until they were beyond the park grounds.

She'd never had to worry about Ethan. She knew that if Dave didn't find him, someone else would. He'd be okay. The abduction thing, that was all a distraction, a way to make David's story even more unbelievable. Ethan would be fine.

She hoped the Dramamine-spiked juice box she'd given him put him out for most of it. Sure, there'd be plenty of teary moments later, in the days and weeks to come, but at least he didn't have to go through the terror of an actual kidnapping.

It was the least a mother could do.

Having a kid, becoming a mother, that had never been part of the plan. But then, neither had getting married.

She'd picked Promise Falls more or less at random. She saw it on a map, checked it out online. Nice upstate New York town. Quaint. Anonymous. A college town. It didn't look like the kind of place where someone would hide out. New York, that was a place where someone would disappear. Buffalo, Los Angeles, Miami. Those were places where someone went to blend in, to vanish.

Who'd go looking for someone in a place called Promise Falls?

She had no ties there, no roots. There was no more reason for the courier to think she'd be in Promise Falls than in Tacoma, Washington.

She could go there, find a job, a place to live, and bide her time until Dwayne had done his time. When he was out, they'd go back to Boston, exchange keys, open the safe-deposit boxes, and make their deal.

It would be a long time to wait, but some things were worth it. Like enough money to go sit on a beach forever with nothing more to worry about than a bit of sand in your shorts. Living the dream like Matty Walker in *Body Heat*.

It's what she'd always wanted.

So she came to Promise Falls, found a room over a pool hall in what was clearly not the best part of town, and went looking for work at the employment office at city hall. And ran into David Harwood, Boy Reporter.

He was, she had to admit, adorable. Not bad-looking, very sweet. She didn't want any part of his story, however. She was here to keep a low profile. If you gave an interview, the next thing they were going to ask you for was a picture.

*No thank you.*

But she chatted with him a little, and darned if he wasn't out there when she came out, offering to give her a lift. Why not? she thought. When he saw where she lived, he just about had a fit. Can't live here, he said, unless your employment plans include dealing crack and turning tricks. He actually said that.

Don't worry, she said. I'm a big girl. And, she told him with a smile, it's good to have options.

Later, when she opened the door and found him there with a list of other apartments for her to check out, well, she almost cried, except that wasn't something she tended to do unless she was having to perform. But it was sweet, no doubt about it. Not the sort of thing she was used to.

She let him help her move. Then she let him take her to dinner.

Not long after that, she let him take her to bed.

After a couple of months, David, while not actually popping the question, made some vague comments along the lines of how there were worse things that could happen than spending the rest of their lives together.

Jan sensed an opportunity presenting itself. She said to David that he might just be onto something there.

The only thing more anonymous than living as a single woman in Promise Falls was living as a married woman in Promise Falls. She'd turn herself into June Cleaver, the mom in *Leave It to Beaver*, although Jan didn't believe June ever did for Ward the things she did for David. Mayfield never had a girl who could fulfill a man's dreams the way Jan could. (Jan had to admit, Cleaver would have been the perfect name for her, considering what she was running from.)

With David, she could be the perfect wife with a perfectly boring job. She'd live in their perfect little house, and make a perfect little life for them. As the wife of a small-town newspaper reporter, she didn't exactly fit the profile of a diamond thief.

No one was going to find her here.

And she'd been right. Not that the first year hadn't been hell. Every time there was a knock at the door, she feared it would be him. But it was the meter reader, or someone looking for a donation to the cancer society, or the neighbor coming over to tell them they forgot to close their garage door.

Girl Scouts selling cookies.

But never him.

After a year or so, she started to relax. Connie Tattinger was dead. Long live Jan Harwood.

At least until Dwayne got out.

She could do this. Play the role. Wasn't that what she'd been doing since she was a little girl? Moving from one part to another? Imagining herself to be someone she wasn't, even if the only one she was fooling was herself?

That was certainly what she did when she was little. It was the only way she got through her childhood. Her father ragging on her all the time, blaming her for fucking up their lives, her mother too pissed or self-absorbed to run interference and tell her old man to lay off.

She did what a lot of children do. She created an imaginary friend. But it was different in her case. She didn't hang out with this make-believe companion. In her head, she became her. She was Estelle Winters, the precocious daughter of Malcolm and Edwina Winters, stars of the Broadway stage. New York was her home. She was only living with this bitter, mean-spirited man and his drunken bitch of a wife as research for a role she was destined to play. She wasn't really their child. How could she be? She was much too special to be the daughter of such common, horrible people.

She knew the truth, of course. But imagining herself to be Estelle, it got her through until that day she walked out that door and never came back.

And then, after a very long run, Estelle Winters, her imaginary friend/defense mechanism, was allowed to die.

For some time, she was actually Connie Tattinger. But even as Connie, she could be whoever she needed to be. She could be a good girl, and she could be a bad girl. Whatever the situation demanded.

When she was living on the street, the bad-girl thing wasn't so much an act as it was a way to survive. You did what you had to do, and with whoever you had to do it with, to get a roof over your head, some food in your stomach.

If you got a lead on a half-decent job, in an office, say, what her mother would have called a "shave your legs" position, well, she could do that, too. She could turn herself from a street kid to a nice girl in a flash.

Whatever the part demanded.

When she met David, she fell easily into the role of small-town wife. It didn't take a lot of effort. It was actually fun to play. She could do as long a run here as she had to. And when the time came to pack it in, she could do that, too.

The thing Jan hadn't counted on was the kid. That was definitely not part of the plan.

They hadn't been married long before she suspected she was pregnant. Couldn't believe it, sitting there in the bathroom one morning after David had gone to work. Got out the test, waited ten minutes, looked at the result, thought: *Shit*.

Great day for David to have forgotten some notes. Suddenly appears upstairs. She'd been pretty good—

excellent, in fact—at keeping on the mask, but he caught something in the way she looked, saw the pregnancy-test packaging. She ended up telling him she was pregnant.

This doesn't have to be a bad thing, he says.

Part of her decision, she knew, was calculating. A child would make her blend in even more. Make her more invisible. And David wanted this child. Ending the pregnancy, it could send this new marriage—this terrific cover—off the rails. So far, this marriage thing was going very well.

And being a loving mother, well, wasn't it just another role? One of the most challenging of her career? If she could play all these other parts, she could play this one, too.

Once she started looking at it this way, Jan wanted the child. She wanted the experience. She wanted to know what it would be like. She didn't think about the future, what she would do when Dwayne got out. For once, she wasn't thinking long-term. She was *in the moment*. Like all great ladies of the stage.

But now Dwayne was out. And she'd stayed with the plan. She was going for the money, and once she had it, she'd move on to her final role. The independent woman. The woman who didn't need anyone else for anything. The woman who didn't have to pretend anymore. The woman who could just *be*.

She was going for the beach and piña colada. No more David. No more Dwayne.

But there was a hitch.

*Ethan.*

She'd really gotten into that whole mother act. So she knew she'd feel something. What she hadn't anticipated was how hard this role would be to walk away from.

Jan knew the Five Mountains thing was going to be tricky to pull off.

But she'd been out there a couple of times on her days off, scoped out where all the CCTV cameras were. There was the remote chance she'd see someone they knew, but Jan figured she had a couple of things in her favor. She wasn't going to be there long, and for much of the time she wasn't going to look anything like Jan Harwood, not once she came back out of the women's restroom.

And if she had been spotted at Five Mountains—by a friend, a neighbor, someone who'd come into Bertram's to get a furnace part—then they'd abort. She'd told Dwayne, if I don't show up, we'll try this another way, soon.

But it went well. It went perfectly.

It just never, not in a million years, occurred to Jan she'd run into someone she knew *after* they got away. Once they were miles from Promise Falls.

If only Dwayne had picked someplace else to get gas. The needle had been a quarter tank off empty. He could have gone another sixty, seventy miles, but he wanted to start off with a full tank. Psychological, he said.

So outside Albany, he gets off the highway near one of those big malls. And guess who's filling up right next to them?

"Jan?" Leanne Kowalski said. "Jan, is that you?"
*The dumbass.*

On cue, like he knew she was thinking about him, Dwayne said, "We're making good time. Should be in Boston pretty soon."

"Great," Jan said. The fact was, the closer they got to Boston, the more on edge she felt. She told herself she wasn't being rational. It was a big city. And she hadn't been there in half a decade. What were the odds anyone was going to recognize her? And it wasn't like she and Dwayne were planning to spend a lot of time there.

"So let me ask you this," Dwayne said. "You feel kind of bad for him?"

"I wouldn't be human if I didn't feel bad about leaving my son," she said.

"No, not the kid. Your husband. I mean, the poor bastard, he's not going to know what hit him."

"What do you think would be better?" she asked. "Would it be better to have every cop in the country wondering where I'd run off to, have them looking for me? Or would it be better to have them thinking I'm already dead?"

"Listen, I'm not saying you did the wrong thing. It's fucking brilliant, that's what it is. Acting all depressed, but just for him, letting him think one thing, setting it all up so the cops will think another. I'm in awe, okay? I'm in fucking awe. All I'm saying is, you did live with the guy for a long time. How'd you do that, anyway? Stick with him only as long as you needed him? Make him think you cared about him when you really didn't?"

Jan looked at him. "It's just something I do." She went back to looking out her open window, hot wind blowing in her face.

"Well, you did it good," Dwayne said admiringly. "You ask me, it's okay if you don't feel bad about it. That's probably even better. No sense striking off on a new life feeling all guilty about what you did to get it. But I just keep picturing the look on his face. When he finds out what you told the guy at the store. When he finds out you never went to the doctor. And when they can't find you on those park cameras. The guy's got to be shittin' himself."

"Let's talk about something else," Jan said.

"What do you want to talk about?"

"When's the last time you talked to your guy who wants to buy our stuff?"

"The day after I got out," Dwayne said. "I call him

up, I say, you're never going to guess who this is. He can't believe it. He says he gave up on me long ago. I never got a chance to call him after I got picked up for the assault thing, so when we didn't show years ago, he just kind of gave up on us. So I say, hey, I'm back, and we're still ready to deal. He goes, shit, are you kidding me? He figured maybe I was dead or something. The other thing he said that was kind of interesting was, there was never anything in the news about it, I mean, about the diamonds actually going missing. He said there was something in the paper about some guy got his hand cut off, but nothing about diamonds."

"That's not surprising," Jan said.

"How you figure?"

"You don't go reporting illicit diamonds stolen," Jan said. "There's not even supposed to be any of them anymore, not since that whole diamond certification thing got going back in 2000. The Kimberley thing. You never saw that movie because you were in jail, the one with Leonardo DiCaprio, all about Sierra Leone and—"

"Don't you mean the Sierra Desert?" Dwayne asked.

"That's the Sahara Desert."

"Oh yeah. Okay."

"Anyway, even with the certification thing going on, and the whole industry clamping down, there's still a big market in illicit diamonds, and you don't go to the cops whining about having some ripped off, even as many as we got. Did you know that al-Qaeda made millions off the sale of illicit diamonds?"

"No shit?"

"Yeah," she said, holding her hand out the window, pushing against the wind.

"So what we did, in a way, was help fight the war on terror." Dwayne grinned.

Jan didn't even look at him. You had to be careful, she

thought. You started thinking he was dumb as shit, it made you forget he could also be very dangerous.

Funny thing was, he didn't mind inflicting pain, but he couldn't stand the sight of blood. Complex, in his own stupid way.

"So who is this guy?" Jan asked.

"His name's Banura," he said. "Cool, huh? He's black. But *really* black. I think he's from that Sierra place you mentioned."

"How do you get in touch?"

"I got his number written down in my pocket. He lives on the south side, in Braintree."

"Does he know we want to do this tomorrow?"

"I didn't tell him an exact day. I was kinda just putting him on alert."

Jan said she thought it would be a good idea for him to get in touch. Banura might need time to start pulling the cash together, in anticipation.

"That's a good idea," Dwayne said.

Jan didn't want to be around the Boston area any longer than she had to. Get the merchandise, exchange it for cash, get the hell out.

They got off the turnpike and Dwayne went looking first for a place to fill up. While he was pumping gas, Jan wandered into the store to look around. She was twirling the sunglasses rack when she noticed the heavy-set woman next to her. The woman was leaning over, telling her daughter to stop whining, and she'd slung her purse over her shoulder and onto her back.

It was open. Jan was staring straight into it.

She didn't care about the woman's purse. She had enough cash to get to Boston, and once they delivered the diamonds, there was going to be more money than she knew what to do with.

But the woman's cell phone might come in handy.

Jan pulled it off in one clean move. She leaned over

the woman as if to reach for something on a shelf, one arm going for a package of two cupcakes, the other sliding down into the purse, grabbing hold of the slender phone, and slipping it into the front pocket of her jeans.

She bought the cupcakes—they were Ethan's favorite; he liked to eat around the little white squiggle across the chocolate icing and save it for last—and got back to the truck about the time Dwayne was done filling the tank. She tossed the cupcakes through the window, got in, and handed him the phone once he was behind the wheel.

"Phone your guy," she said.

By the time they decided to each have a cupcake, the icing had melted to the cellophane wrapper.

Jan worked carefully to peel it away, and she managed to free one cupcake with relatively little damage. She handed it over to Dwayne, who shoved the entire thing into his mouth at once.

The second one turned into a horror show. Most of the icing lifted off, so she bared her teeth and scraped it off the wrapper.

A technique she had learned from her son.

*"Look, Mommy."*

*Ethan's in the car seat, Jan's up front, driving home from the market. She glances back, sees that he's not only managed to peel the icing from the wrapper in one piece, like a layer of pudding skin, he's eaten along each side of the white squiggle. He's lined it up along the underside of his index finger. His mouth is a mess of chocolate icing, but he looks so proud of himself.*

*"I have a squiggle finger," he says.*

Dwayne snapped the phone shut. "We're good to go, tomorrow. I told him we should be there about noon. Maybe even earlier. The banks open at what, around nine-thirty, ten? We hit mine, we hit yours, and unless you stashed your half in fucking Tennessee or something, we should be done pretty quick. Sound good to you?"

Jan was looking away. "Yeah."

"What's going on? You okay?"

"I'm fine. Just drive."

# THIRTY-TWO

OSCAR FINE HAD PARKED his black Audi A4 on Hancock Street, looking south, the back of the State House up ahead to the left. From this side, parked on the downslope, the gold dome was not visible. But that wasn't what he was looking for, anyway.

He liked Beacon Hill. He appreciated it. The narrow streets, the sense of history, the beautiful old brick homes with their extraordinary window boxes full of flowers, the uneven sidewalks and cobblestone streets, the iron boot-scraper bars embedded into almost all the front steps, not quite so important now that the streets weren't full of mud and shit. But it was too crowded for him around here. Too jammed in. He didn't like having a lot of neighbors. He liked being on his own.

But still, it was nice when his work brought him up here.

He was watching an address about a dozen doors up, on the other side of the street. It was early evening. It was about this time that Miles Cooper got home from work. His wife, Patricia, a nurse over at Mass Gen, was, as usual, working the late shift. She'd left about an hour ago. She usually walked, although sometimes she'd only hoof it as far as Cambridge and then grab a bus part of the way, and occasionally she'd even grab a cab. Most nights, when she got off, she was dropped off by a coworker who drove and lived in Telegraph Hill and didn't mind taking Patricia on her way home.

Oscar had been watching their routine for a few days now. He knew he was being more cautious than he needed to be. He already had a good idea of what Miles Cooper did, day in and day out. He knew Cooper liked to spend his weekends on his boat, that he spent too much money on the horses, that he was a lousy poker player. Oscar knew that firsthand. The guy had so many tells it was laughable. If he was dealt a useless hand, he shook his head side to side. Not noticeably. A millimeter in each direction, if that, but enough for Oscar to notice. If he was holding a flush, you could feel the floor shifting underfoot because Miles's right knee was bobbing up and down like a piston.

There were other things Oscar knew about Miles. He was seeing his doctor about gastrointestinal pains. He went through a medium-sized bottle of fruit-flavored Tums every day. He had a storage locker outside of the city where he was hiding, for his younger brother, three stolen Harley-Davidson motorcycles. Every second Monday, he went to the North End and paid three hundred dollars to a girl who worked out of her apartment over an Italian bakery on Salem Street to take her clothes off very slowly and then blow him.

Oscar also knew he was stealing from the man they both worked for. And the man had figured out what Miles was up to.

"I'd like you to look after this for me," the man said to Oscar.

"Not a problem," Oscar said.

So he'd tracked Miles's movements for the better part of a week. Didn't want to drop in on him when the wife was home. Or their daughter. She was in her twenties, lived in Providence, but she often came to visit her parents on weekends. This being Sunday, there was a chance she could have been here, but Oscar had determined she was not. If Miles Cooper followed his usual routine, he'd be walking down the hill from the direction of the State House any moment and—

There he was.

Late fifties, overweight, balding, a thick gray mustache. Dressed in an ill-fitting suit, white shirt, no tie.

As he reached his home, he fished around in his pocket for his keys, found them, mounted the five cement steps to his door, unlocked it and went inside.

Oscar Fine got out of his Audi.

He walked up the street, crossed diagonally, reaching the other side out front of Miles Cooper's home.

Oscar rang the bell.

He could hear Miles's footsteps on the other side of the door before it opened.

"Hey, Oscar," Miles said.

"Hi, Miles," he said.

"What are you doing here?"

"Can I come in?" Oscar said.

Something flickered in Miles's eyes. Oscar Fine could see it. It was fear. Oscar had gotten a lot better at reading people the last five years or so. Back then, he'd been a bit cocky, overconfident. Sloppy. At least once.

Oscar knew Miles wouldn't close the door on him. Miles had to know that if Oscar didn't already suspect he was up to something, he surely would if Miles refused to let him into his house.

"Sure, yeah, come on in," Miles said. "Good to see you. What are you doing around here?"

Oscar stepped in and closed the door. He asked, already knowing the answer, "Patricia home?"

"She'll be at work by now. She's usually half an hour into her shift by the time I get home. What can I get you to drink?"

"I'm good," Oscar said.

"You sure? I was just going to get a beer."

"Nothing," Oscar said, following Miles into the kitchen. Oscar Fine did not drink, which Miles could never seem to remember.

Miles opened the fridge, leaned down, reached in for a bottle, and by the time he turned around, Oscar was pointing a gun at him, holding it in his right hand, his left arm stuck down into the pocket of his jacket. The gun had a long tubular attachment at the end of the barrel. A silencer.

"Jesus, Oscar, what the fuck. You scared me half to death there."

"He knows," Oscar said.

"He knows? Who knows? Who knows what? Christ, put that thing away. I nearly wet my pants."

"He knows," Oscar said again.

Miles twisted the cap off the bottle, tossed it onto the countertop. His mouth twitched as he said, "I don't know what you're talking about."

"Please, Miles, show some dignity. He knows. Don't play stupid."

Miles took a long swig from the bottle, then moved to a wooden kitchen chair and sat down.

"Shit," he said. He had to put the bottle on the table because his hand was starting to shake.

"You need to know why this is happening," Oscar said. "It would be wrong for you to die not knowing why this is happening."

"Oscar, come on, we go way back. You got to cut me some slack here. I can pay it back."

"No," Oscar said.

"But I can, with interest. I'll sell the boat. I'll sell it tomorrow. And I've got some other cash set aside. The thing is, it's not really all that much. He won't have to wait for his money. He'll get it back right away, and that's a promise. Plus, I've got some motorcycles. I was holding them for my brother, but I can sell them and give the money to him. Fuck my brother. Tough shit for him, right? I mean, it's not like he had to pay for them in the first—"

The gun went *pfft, pfft*. Oscar Fine put two bullets in his head. Miles Cooper pitched forward, hit the floor, and that was it.

Oscar let himself out, walked down the street, got in his Audi, and drove out of Beacon Hill.

Oscar Fine only had to slow as he approached the security gate at the shipping container yard. The guard in the booth recognized the car and driver and had hit the button to make the gate slowly shift to the right. Oscar waited until there was just enough of an opening, then guided the car into the compound.

There were thousands of the rectangular boxes, stacked like monstrous colorful LEGO blocks. They came in orange, brown, green, blue, and silver and were labeled Sea Land, Evergreen, Maersk, and Cosco. They were stacked six high in some places, and it was like driving through a narrow steel canyon. The compound took up a good ten acres on the outside of the city. Oscar drove his car to the far side, parked up against a ten-foot fence with coils of barbed wire adorning the top. He got out of the car, taking with him some milk he had bought at a 7-Eleven after driving out of Beacon Hill, and walked over to the square end of an Evergreen container that had two others stacked atop it. He reached into his right pocket, found a key, and unlocked the container door.

He swung it open, and about four feet inside was a secondary wall and a regular-sized door. He unlocked it with a second key, opened the door toward him, and stepped into what seemed to be almost total blackness, although there was a hint of light.

He reached along the inside of the secondary wall with his right hand and found a bank of switches. He flipped them all up, and instantly the inside of the container was bathed in light.

While one might have expected the inside walls to be exactly the same as the outside—metal and vertically ribbed—they were instead smooth and painted a soft moss green. The interior walls, perfectly drywalled, were adorned with large examples of modern art. Underfoot was not metal but gleaming wood flooring. Just inside the door were a leather couch, a matching leather reclining chair, and a 46-inch flat-screen TV mounted to the wall. About halfway down the container was a narrow, gleaming kitchen area with aluminum countertops and dozens of recessed pot lights. Beyond that, an elegant bathroom and bedroom.

Oscar Fine heard a sound. A second later, something brushed up against his leg.

He looked down as a rust-colored cat purred softly.

"I bought you some milk," Oscar said. It was for the cat that Oscar had left on a couple of night-lights. He set the bottle on the counter, hugged it to himself with his left arm while he uncapped it with his right, and poured some into a bowl on the floor. The cat slinked noiselessly to the bowl and lowered its head down into it.

Oscar took the gun from his jacket, set it on the counter, then opened an oversized kitchen cabinet door to reveal a refrigerator. Oscar set the milk inside and took out a can of Coke. He popped the lid with his index finger, then poured the drink into a heavy-bottomed glass.

"How was your day?" he asked the cat.

Oscar sat on a leather stool at the kitchen counter. A silver laptop lay there, its screen black. He hit a button on the side, and while he waited for the machine to get up and running, he reached for a remote and brought the flat-screen TV to life. It was already on CNN, and he left it there.

The laptop was ready to go and he checked his mail first. Nothing but spam. If only you could find those people, he thought. They had it coming even more than Miles. He checked a couple of his favorite bookmarked sites. One showed how his various investments were doing. Checking that tended to depress him these days. The other site, which always cheered him, featured short videos of kittens falling asleep.

He glanced up occasionally at the TV while he surfed around.

Onscreen, the news anchor was saying, ". . . in an unusual turn of events, a person who makes his living reporting the news finds himself at the center of it. Police are refusing to say whether they believe Jan Harwood is alive or dead, but they have indicated that her husband, David Harwood, a reporter for the *Standard,* a paper in Promise Falls, north of Albany, is what they are calling a person of interest. The woman has not been seen since she accompanied her husband Friday on a trip to Lake George."

Oscar Fine glanced up from his laptop to the television for only a second, not really interested, then back to his computer. Then he looked back up again.

They had flashed a picture of this missing woman. Oscar Fine only caught a glimpse of the image before the newscast moved on to a shot of a house where it was believed this David and Jan Harwood lived, then another shot of the reporter's parents' house, and an older woman coming to the door, telling the media to go away.

Oscar kept waiting for them to show the woman's picture again, but they did not.

He returned his attention to the laptop, and with his right hand did a Google news search of "Jan Harwood" and "Promise Falls." That took him to a couple of sites, including that of the Promise Falls *Standard,* where he found a full story, by Samantha Henry, as well as a picture of the missing woman.

He clicked on it, blew it up. He stared at it a good minute. The woman's hair was very different. He remembered her hair as red, but now it was black. And she'd worn heavy makeup, eyelashes like spider's legs. This woman here, she had a toned-down look. Looked like your average housewife. Okay, better than that. A MILF.

He clicked again, blew the picture up even more. There it was. The small scar, shaped like an L, on her cheek. She probably thought she'd pancaked it enough to make it invisible the one and only time they'd met. But he'd seen it.

That scar was all the proof he needed. That, and the throbbing at the end of his left arm, where his hand used to be.

Oscar Fine had some calls to make.

# PART FOUR

# THIRTY-THREE

DUCKWORTH AND I HAD moved away from the open grave containing the body of Leanne Kowalski. I was shaking.

I said, "I'm gonna be sick." And I was. Duckworth gave me a few seconds to make sure I wasn't going to do it again.

"How can it be her?" I asked. "What's she doing up here?"

"Let's go back to my car," Duckworth said. He was sweating. He'd been crouching next to me when I first looked at the body, and getting back up had left him short of breath.

"If Leanne's here . . . ," I started.

"Yes?"

I felt I had to ask. "Is there another grave? Is this the only one?"

Duckworth looked at me intently, like he was trying to see inside my head. "Do you think there's another one?"

"What?" I said.

"Come on."

We said nothing on the way back to his car. He opened my door for me and helped me into the car like I was an invalid, then got in around the other side. Neither of us spoke for the better part of a minute. Duckworth turned the key ahead far enough to let him put the front windows down. A light breeze blew through the car.

I turned and looked at him. He was staring straight ahead, hands on the wheel, even though the engine was off.

"Did you already know who it was?" I asked him. "Did you know it was Leanne Kowalski?"

Duckworth ignored the question and asked one of his own. "When you came up here Friday with your wife, Mr. Harwood, did you bring Leanne Kowalski with you?"

I rested my head on the headrest and closed my eyes. "What? No," I said. "Why would we do that?"

"Did she follow you up here? Did you arrange to meet her up here?"

"No and no."

For a moment I wondered whether Leanne Kowalski could have, somehow, been the woman who sent me the anonymous email, who wanted to meet me at Ted's. But I couldn't think of a way for those dots to connect.

"You don't think it's odd that Leanne Kowalski's body turns up within a mile or two of the place where you claim you were meeting this source of yours?"

I turned. "Odd? Do I think it's fucking odd? You're damn right I think it's odd. You want me to list the fucking odd things that have happened to me in the last two days? How about this. My wife goes missing. Some stranger tries to grab my son. I find out Jan has a birth certificate for some kid who got run over by a car when she was five, that my wife may not even be who she says she is. She goes into that store and tells the guy a story about not knowing why I've brought her up here, like I've tricked her. Why the hell did she do that? Why did she lie to him? Why was there no ticket for her to get into Five Mountains? Why did she lie to me about seeing Dr. Samuels about wanting to kill herself? So when you ask me if I think it's *odd* that Leanne Kowalski is lying dead over there, yeah, I find that pretty fucking odd. Just like everything else that's going on."

Duckworth nodded slowly. Finally, he said, "And would you think it odd if I told you that a preliminary examination of your car—the one you used to drive up here Friday with your wife—has turned up samples of blood and hair in the trunk, and a crumpled receipt for a roll of duct tape in the glove box?"

So talkative a moment earlier, I now could find no words.

"I got the call just before you came back for your car. It'll be a while before we get back the DNA tests. Want to save us some trouble, tell us what we're going to learn?"

It was time to get help.

Driving home from Lake George, I reached Natalie Bondurant, the lawyer my father had been in touch with, on my cell phone. Once we got the preliminaries out of the way, and she was officially going to act on my behalf, I said, "There's been a development since you spoke to my father. Actually, a few."

"Tell me," she said.

"Leanne Kowalski, the woman who worked in the same office as my wife, her body was found not far from where I had driven on Friday with Jan."

"So the cops already like you for this thing," she said, "and now they've got this."

"Yeah."

"Are they going to find a second body, Mr. Harwood? Are they going to find your wife, too?"

"I hope to God not," I said.

"Because if they do they'll be able to nail you for it? Or because you're still hoping to see your wife come home alive?"

She had a directness that was disarming.

"The latter," I said. "And Detective Duckworth said they've found blood and hair in the trunk of my car, plus a receipt for duct tape in the glove compartment."

"He may be trying to rattle you. Can you explain those things?"

"No," I said. "I mean, the hair? Sure, we're in and out of the trunk, I suppose some stray hairs could fall in, but the other things? No. I don't know why there'd be blood there, and I haven't bought a roll of duct tape in a long time."

"Kind of convenient that they've found those things, then," Natalie Bondurant said.

"What do you mean?"

"There's a lot of circumstantial evidence building up around you."

She had me take her through things from the beginning. I tried to tell everything as simply as possible, as though I were spelling it all out in a news story. Give her the overall picture first, then start zeroing in on the details. I told her about my trip to Rochester, the revelation that Jan might not be who she'd been claiming to be.

"How do you explain that?" she asked.

"I can't. I asked Detective Duckworth whether she might be one of those relocated witnesses, but I don't think he took me seriously, after I'd already told him Jan had been acting depressed the last few weeks, and he couldn't find anyone else to back up that story."

Natalie was quiet a moment, then said, "You're in a load of trouble."

"Thanks," I said.

"What the police don't have is a body," she said. "They've got this Leanne Kowalski's, but they don't have your wife's. That's good news. Not just because we want your wife to come back alive, but it means the police don't have a solid case yet. That doesn't mean they might not be able to build one without a body. Plenty of people have gone to jail for murder where a body was never found."

"You're not cheering me up."

"That's not my job. My job is to keep your ass out of jail, or if you end up going there, to make it for as short a time as possible."

If I hadn't been driving, I would have closed my eyes. We had been talking so long, I was nearly home. It was just after eight.

A thought occurred to me.

"There was something weird about the grave," I said. "About where they found Leanne's body."

"What?"

"That hole that was dug, to put Leanne into. It was right by the side of the road. It wasn't much of a grave, either. Just enough to put somebody into it and cover it with a bit of dirt. All somebody had to do was go a few more feet into the woods and they could have buried her where she wouldn't have been seen. Why someone would try to bury her that close to the road, even a road that's not very well traveled, seems stupid."

"You're saying she was meant to be found," Natalie said.

"It hadn't occurred to me until now, but yeah. I wonder."

"Come to my office tomorrow morning at eleven," she said. "Bring your checkbook."

"Okay," I said. I was driving back into my parents' neighborhood.

"And don't have any more conversations with the police without me present," she said.

"Got it," I said. I made the turn onto my parents' street. The house was just up ahead.

There was a mini media circus on the street out front.

Two TV news vans. Three cars. People milling about. *Shit*.

"And," Natalie Bondurant said, "no talking to the press."

"I'll see what I can do," I said, and ended the call.

I was guessing that if there were this many reporters at my parents' house, my own house was probably staked out as well. One of the news vans was half blocking the driveway, so I had to park at the curb on the opposite side of the street.

I didn't see any way around this. I wanted to see my parents, and I desperately needed to see my son.

I got out of my father's car and started striding across the street. A reporter and cameraman jumped out of each of the news vans and called out my name. Young people with notepads and digital recorders got out of the three cars. Samantha Henry emerged from a faded red Honda Civic that I'd thought looked familiar. She wore a pained, apologetic look on her face as she approached, one that seemed to say, *Hey, look, I'm sorry, I'm just doing my job*.

The reporters swarmed me, shouting out questions.

"Mr. Harwood, any word on your wife?"

"Mr. Harwood, do you know what's happened to your wife?"

"Why do the police consider you a suspect?"

"Did you kill your wife, Mr. Harwood?"

I resisted my first inclination, which was to push my way through them and run into the house. Natalie's advice was fresh in my mind, but I'd worked in newspapers long enough to know how guilty brushing past the press, refusing to say anything, would make me look. So I stopped, held up my palms in a bid to show I was willing to take their questions if they'd just hold up.

"I'll say a few words," I said as the two cameramen

maneuvered for good shots. I needed a moment to compose myself, collect my thoughts. Then I said, "My wife, Jan Harwood, went missing yesterday morning while we were at Five Mountains with our son. I've been doing everything I can to find her, and I'm hoping and praying that she's all right. If you're watching this, honey, please get in touch and let me know you're okay. Ethan and I love you, we miss you, and we just want you to get home safely. Whatever's happened, whatever it might be, we can work it out. We can work through it together. And to anyone else who's watching, if anyone has seen Jan or knows anything about where she might be or what might have happened to her, I beg you, please get in touch with me or with the police. All I want is for my wife to come home."

One of the more beautifully coiffed TV reporters pushed a microphone into my face and said, "We have information that you felt compelled to tell the police that you did not kill your wife. Why did you feel you had to say that? Are you officially a suspect?"

"I said it because it's the truth," I said, trying to keep my voice even. I glanced at the house, saw my mother watching me through the curtains. "I understand that the police have to consider every possibility in a case like this, including looking at the spouse of a missing person. I get that. That's just standard procedure."

"But are you a suspect?" she persisted. "Do the police believe your wife has been murdered?"

"There's no evidence anything's happened to my wife," I said.

"Is that because you've done a good job getting rid of the body?" she asked.

I tried very hard to stay calm. "I won't dignify that with a response."

The second most beautifully coiffed reporter, from the

other TV station, asked, "How do you explain the fact that there's no evidence your wife was even with you at Five Mountains?"

"I'm sure there were a thousand other people at Five Mountains yesterday who might have a hard time proving they were there," I said. "She was there with me, and then she disappeared."

"Have you taken a lie detector test?" asked a rumpled reporter I was pretty sure was from Albany.

"No," I said.

"Did you refuse to take it?"

"No one's asked me to take one," I said.

The more beautiful TV reporter jumped in, "*Would* you take one?"

"I just told you, no one's asked me—"

"Would you take one if we set it up?" the less beautifully coiffed TV reporter asked.

"I don't see any reason why I would sit down with you—"

"So you're refusing, then? You don't want to take any questions about your wife's disappearance while hooked up to a polygraph machine?"

"This is ridiculous," I said. I was losing control of this. I'd been a fool to think I could walk into this and escape unscathed. You think, because you're a reporter, you know the tricks. Then you find out you're no smarter than anyone else.

Samantha, sensing what was happening to me, tried to help by breaking in with a soft question: "David," she said, "can you tell me how you're bearing up under this? It must be a terrible strain for you and for your son."

I nodded. "It's horrible. Not knowing . . . it's terrible. I've never been through anything like this before. You have no idea until you're experiencing it yourself."

"How does it feel," she continued, "being the subject

of a story instead of the one covering it? All of us here, ganging up on you like this, it must seem kind of weird."

The TV reporters gave Sam a dirty look when she said "ganging up."

I almost smiled. "It's okay, I know how it works. Look, I really have to go."

The reporters opened a path for me as I moved forward. I took Sam by the elbow and brought her along with me, which brought some grumbles from the rest of the pack. What the hell was I doing? Giving her an exclusive?

"Dave, I feel real bad about this," she said as we went up the stairs to my parents' front door. "You know I'm just doing—"

"I get it," I said. Before I could open the door, Mom had swung it open. She'd aged a couple of years since I'd seen her earlier in the day, and she gave Sam a withering look.

"Hi, Mom," I said. "You remember Sam." They'd met several times when we were going together.

Mom didn't return Sam's nod. She clearly viewed Sam, in her professional role, as the enemy.

"Where's Ethan?" I asked.

Mom said, "Your father took him out. They went for something to eat and then he was going to take Ethan down by the tracks to see some real trains. I told him I'd call when things quieted down around here."

That seemed like a pretty good plan to me. I was glad Ethan had been taken away from all this.

I said to Samantha, "Look, thanks for that question out there. It helped smooth things over a bit."

"It's okay," she said. "I've got to do this story but I'm not out to get you."

"I appreciate that."

"I mean, I know you would never do anything to Jan." She studied me. "Right?"

"Jesus, Sam."

"I really don't think you would."

"Thanks for the halfhearted vote of confidence."

The corners of her mouth turned up. "I have to at least pretend to be objective. But I'm on your side, I swear. But I can't promise the desk won't have its way with this story once I turn it in. Which reminds me." She looked at her watch. It was ten after eight. I knew she had until about nine-thirty to turn in a story and still make the first print edition.

"What did you want to tell me?" she asked. "I mean, if you're giving me some kind of exclusive, I'll take it. This is your paper, after all."

"You need to watch your back," I said.

"What?"

"I don't mean you're in any danger or anything, but you have to be careful. I think Madeline's monitoring all the email."

"What?" Sam's jaw dropped. "The publisher is reading my personal email?"

"If it's through the paper's system, yeah, I think so."

"Holy shit," she said. "Why? Why do you think that?"

"I received an anonymous email the other day, a woman wanting to talk to me, about the prison proposal, about members of council taking bribes or whatever in exchange for a favorable vote."

"Okay."

"It landed in my mailbox. I only had it there for a few minutes before I purged it from the system. But Elmont Sebastian, he knew about it. He knew someone had tried to get in touch with me. I wondered at first whether he got tipped at the other end, from where this woman got in touch with me, but I don't think so. I think he got the tip from the *Standard*. And who else but Madeline would have the authority to read everyone's email?"

"Why would she want to do that?"

"She might not be interested in yours, but she'd have a reason to be interested in mine. The Russell family, they've got land they want to sell to Star Spangled Corrections for that prison. It's not in our own paper's interest to take a run at them. I think when Madeline saw that email, she let Sebastian know."

"What about Brian?" she asked. "Maybe Madeline's got him looking into the emails. She's in his office all the time."

I thought about that. "That's possible. The bottom line is, our publisher can't be trusted. You just need to know that."

"I was kind of kidding when I said the desk might have its way with this story, but now I think they really might. Are they going to slant this thing with Jan to make you look even worse? Because you owned that prison story. Once you're out of the picture, how likely is it someone else is going to take it up?"

"I don't know." I didn't tell her the lengths to which Elmont Sebastian had already gone to stop me. A job offer. Veiled threats against my son. I hadn't given up on the theory that he had something to do with what had happened to Jan, but I couldn't put it together in a way that made sense.

"I gotta go," Sam said. "I've got to file this thing."

"I didn't have anything to do with Jan's disappearance," I said one last time.

She put a hand softly on my chest. "I know. I believe you. I'm not going to sell you out with this story."

She left.

Mom said, "I don't like her."

By the time I pulled into the driveway of my own house, it was nine. There were no media types camped out there. They'd all gotten what they needed at my parents' place and were going to give me some peace, at least for the rest of this evening.

Ethan had fallen asleep on the way home. I carefully lifted him out of his seat and he rested his head on my shoulder as I took him into the house. The moment I came through the door, I was instantly reminded that the house had been searched by the police earlier in the day. Sofa cushions were tossed about, books removed from shelves, carpets pulled back. It didn't look as though anything was actually damaged, but there was a lot of straightening up to do.

I laid Ethan gently on the couch and covered him with a throw blanket. Then I went upstairs and made some sense of his room. I put the mattress back in place, toys back in bins, clothes back in drawers.

It looked bad when I started, but only took fifteen minutes to tidy it up. I went back down, picked him up off the couch, and brought him up to his bed. I placed him on his back and undressed him. I'd have thought pulling a shirt up over his head would have awakened him, but he slept through all the jostling. I found his Wolverine pajamas and got them on him, then slipped him under the covers, tucked them in around him, and kissed him lightly on the forehead.

Without opening his eyes, he whispered sleepily, "Good night, Mommy."

# THIRTY-FOUR

ROLLING OFF HER, DWAYNE said to Jan, "I always like to start a big day like this with a bang."

She got out of the motel bed, slipped into the bathroom, and closed the door.

Dwayne, on his back and looking at the ceiling, laced his fingers behind his head and smiled. "This is it, baby. A few hours and we'll be set. You know what I think we should do later today? We should look at boats. I'll bet there are all kinds of people selling their boats. Just when everyone else is unloading their goodies because of the recession, we're going to be doing just fine. We'll be able to pick up some twenty- or thirty-foot cabin cruiser for a song, not that we couldn't pay full price if we wanted to. But if this money is going to last us the rest of our lives, we don't want to be really stupid with it, am I right?"

Jan hadn't heard anything after "baby." She had turned on the shower after taking a moment to figure out how the taps worked in this one-star joint, which was about five miles from downtown Boston. Plenty close enough, considering her nervousness about being anywhere around here.

Dwayne threw back the covers and stood naked in the room. He grabbed the remote and turned on the television. He was flipping through the channels at high speed.

"They don't get any of the good stations here," he said. "Why do they make you pay extra for the adult stuff? Don't they already charge enough for the room?"

He landed on a cartoon network that was running an animated Batman episode, got bored with that, and kept on surfing. He'd gone past a news channel and was already onto a stand-up comedy show when he said, "The fuck?" He went back a couple of stations and there was Jan. A photo of her.

"Hey!" he shouted. "Get out here!"

She didn't hear him from under the shower.

Dwayne banged the door open and shouted, "You're on the fucking TV!"

He tapped the volume up so high the television cabinet began to vibrate. The anchor was saying, "—yet when invited by the station to take a lie detector test, Mr. Harwood flatly refused. The journalist for the Promise Falls *Standard* says his wife went missing from the Five Mountains amusement park Saturday, yet police sources have said that no one has actually seen Jan Harwood since late Friday afternoon. And there's a new development this morning. The body of a coworker of the missing woman was found in the Lake George area, not far from where Jan Harwood and her husband were seen before she went missing. Looks like we're going to have some sunshine this afternoon in the greater Boston—"

Dwayne killed the TV and went back into the bathroom. He reached through the shower curtain and turned off the water. Jan's hair was in full lather.

"Dwayne! Shit!"

"Didn't you hear me?"

"What is it?"

"It was on the news. They were chasing your husband, asking him to take a lie detector test, and they found the body."

Jan squinted at him through soapy eyes. She was instantly feeling cold as the water dripped from her naked body. She said, "Okay."

"That's good, right?"

"Let me finish up in here," Jan said.

"Want me to get in with you?"

She answered by pulling the curtain shut. She went back to fiddling with the taps. The water blasted out cold at first, and she huddled, as though that would somehow protect her. She swore under her breath, adjusted the knob and then nearly scalded herself. She dialed it back and found the right temperature, then stuck her face into the spray to get the shampoo out of her eyes.

But they'd been stinging before this.

She'd found herself—she could hardly believe it when it happened—crying at one point in the night. Dwayne was snoring like a band saw, so there was no risk of waking him.

Not that she was sobbing uncontrollably. She hadn't been bawling her eyes out or anything undignified like that. But there was this moment when she felt, well, *overwhelmed.*

A couple of tears got away before she fought them back. You didn't want to slip out of character.

You didn't want people thinking you cared.

But as she lay there in bed, she imagined putting her hand on Ethan's head, feeling the silky strands of his hair on her palm. She imagined the smell of him. The sounds his feet made padding on the floor when he got up in the morning and walked into their bedroom to see if she was awake. The way his fingers picked up Cheerios, how he stuffed them into his mouth, the sounds he made when he chewed. How he sat, cross-legged, in front of the television when he watched Thomas the Tank Engine.

The warmth of his body when he crawled into bed with her.

*Think about the money.*

She tried to push him out of her thoughts as she lay there in the middle of the night. The way some people might count sheep, she counted diamonds.

But Ethan's face kept materializing before her eyes.

From the moment she started going out with David, she'd convinced herself it was about the money. This façade, this marriage, this raising a child, it was all part of the *job*. This was how she was earning her fortune. She just had to do the time, until Dwayne got out, and she'd be out of there. She'd walk away and not look back. And once she'd exchanged the diamonds for cash, she'd be rid of Dwayne, too.

One last costume change.

With any luck, the way she'd left things in Promise Falls, no one would be looking for her. At least not alive. And when they didn't find her body, the police would figure David had done a very good job of disposing of it. Oh, he'd tell them he had nothing to do with it, that he was an innocent man, but wasn't that what all guilty men said?

Maybe he'd even, at some point, suspect what it was that had really happened. When and if it finally dawned on him that his wife had set him up, what exactly was he going to do about it from a jail cell? He'd have spent everything he had on lawyers trying to beat the charges. He wasn't going to have anything left to hire a private detective to track her down.

At least Ethan would be okay. His grandparents would look after him. Don, he was a bit loopy at times, but his heart was in the right place. And while Jan never much cared for the way Arlene looked at her some-times—it was like she knew Jan was up to something, but she couldn't figure out what it was—there was no doubt she'd be able to raise that boy. She had a lot of years left in her, and she loved Ethan to death.

Jan struggled to find some comfort in that.

Maybe, once she had her money, once she really knew there was a new life waiting for her, a new life where she could do anything she wanted, she'd be able to forget about the last few years, pretend they never happened, make believe the people she'd known—and the one she had brought into the world—during that time never really existed.

Once she had the money.

The money would change everything.

Money had a way of healing all sorts of wounds, of helping one move on. That's what she'd always believed.

Dwayne stopped the truck on Beacon Street, just west of Clarendon.

"Here you go," he said.

Jan looked to her right. They were parked out front of a MassTrust branch sandwiched between a Starbucks and a high-end shoe store.

"This is it?" she said.

"This is it. Your key opens a box right here."

This had been the way they'd worked it. They'd each picked a safe-deposit box to store their half of the diamonds, kept the location secret, and then swapped keys. That way, they'd need each other when they wanted to cash in.

"Let's do it," she said.

They got out of the truck together and walked through the front doors of the bank and went up to a service counter.

Jan said, "We'd like to get into our safe-deposit box."

"Of course," said a middle-aged woman. She needed a name, and for Dwayne to sign in a book, and then she

led them into a vault where small, rectangular mailbox-
like doors lined three walls.

"Here's yours right here," the woman said, producing
a key and inserting it into a door. Jan took out the key
she'd been holding on to for five years, inserted it into
the accompanying slot. The door opened and the
woman slid out a long black box.

As she tipped it, something inside rattled softly.

"There's a room right here for your convenience," she
said, opening the door so Dwayne and Jan could enter.
She set the box down on a counter and withdrew, closing the door on her way out. The room was about five
by five feet, well lit, with a padded office chair in front
of the counter.

"This place is even smaller than my cell," Dwayne
said. He hooked his fingers under the front of the box lid
and lifted. "Oh boy."

Inside was a black fabric bag with a drawstring at the
end, the kind that might hold a pair of shoes or slippers.

Jan reached and took out the bag, feeling the contents
inside first without opening.

"Feels like teeth," she said nervously.

She loosened the drawstring and tipped the bag over
on the counter.

The diamonds began spilling out. Much smaller than
teeth, but far more glittery. They hit the counter and
scattered. Dozens and dozens of them. More than they
could count at a glance.

"Jesus fucking Christ," Dwayne said, like he'd never
seen these gems before. He picked them up randomly,
rolled them around in his palm, held them up to the
fluorescent light as though that would tell him anything
about their worth.

Jan was shaking her head slowly in disbelief.

"And this is just half of them, sugar tits," Dwayne
said. "We are so fucking rich."

"Calm down," Jan said. "We need to keep it together. We start getting all crazy, we'll do something stupid."

"What do you think I'm going to do? Take one of these next door and buy a latte with it?" Dwayne asked.

"I just . . . I didn't remember there was this many," she whispered.

She started collecting them, slipping them back into the bag. "I think one of them fell on the floor," she said.

Dwayne dropped down to his hands and knees, running his palms across the surface of the short-pile industrial carpet. "Got it," he said, and then he wrapped his arms around Jan's legs, pulling her toward him, burying his face in the crotch of her jeans.

"We should do it in here," he said.

"We can think about celebrating later," she said. "After we get our money. Then, we'll fuck our brains out." *Give 'em what they want,* she thought.

Dwayne stood up, took the bag from Jan's hand.

"I'll put it in my purse," she said.

"No, it's okay," he said, stuffing the bag into the front pocket of his jeans, which created an unsightly, off-center bulge. "I got it."

Jan gave directions to Dwayne that took them north across the Charles on the Harvard Bridge, then over to Cambridge Street.

"Stop anywhere around here," she said.

"Where is it?" he asked, pulling over to the curb and putting the truck in park. He'd spotted a Bank of America and figured that was the place, but Jan pointed across the street to a Revere Federal branch.

"Fucking awesome," he said, feeling in his other front pocket for the safe-deposit box key he'd been hanging on to for so long.

He had his hand on the door when Jan reached over

and held his arm. "This time," she said, "I'll hold on to them."

"Yeah, sure, no big deal," he said, pulling his arm away.

"I mean it," she said.

They crossed the street on the diagonal, nearly getting hit by an SUV as they stood on the centerline waiting for traffic to pass. *Terrific,* Jan thought. *Moments away from getting your fortune and you get hit by a Tahoe.*

Once they were safely across, they entered the bank and followed much the same routine. This time, a young East Indian man led them into the vault, then ushered them into a private room so that they could inspect the contents of the box.

"This never gets old," Dwayne said when Jan opened the bag and spilled its contents onto the table.

Once the diamonds were back in the bag, and the bag safely tucked into Jan's purse, they walked out of the bank and back to the truck.

All of their loot, recovered.

Jan thought, *In a perfect world, there'd be a way to hang on to Dwayne's half, without hanging on to Dwayne.*

She wondered whether he might be thinking something similar.

# THIRTY-FIVE

SAM DIDN'T SELL ME out. As best as I could tell, the city desk had not had their way with the story. It hadn't been jazzed up, slanted, or twisted. It was a factual, direct, straightforward account of what had been going on for the last two days. It didn't ignore the fact that the police had been talking to me at length about Jan's disappearance, but it did not go so far as to name me as a suspect. Neither Detective Duckworth nor anyone else with the Promise Falls police had said anything as direct as that.

Sam had also managed to get into her story the discovery of a woman's body in Lake George. An astute reader would put it together, that maybe I'd killed Jan and buried her up there, but the story didn't spell it out. The police had not identified the body as Leanne Kowalski's, at least not by Sam's Sunday night deadline. I was betting, however, that that information might be on the website version of the story by now, but I wasn't able to check, considering that the police had taken our laptop when they'd searched the house the day before.

I had a lot to do that Monday, and needed to get Ethan up and over to my parents' house. I woke him shortly after eight, sitting on the edge of the bed and rubbing his shoulder.

"Time to get moving, sport," I said, pulling back his

covers. The inside of the bed was littered with cars and action figures.

"I'm tired," he said, grabbing one of the toy cars and drawing it toward his face like it was a teddy bear.

"I know. But soon you'll be starting school. You'll be getting up early almost every morning."

"I don't want to go to school," he said, turning his head into the pillow.

"That's what everyone says, at first," I said. "But then once they start going, they really start to like it."

"I just want to go to Nana and Poppa's."

"Yesterday you didn't even want to be there," I reminded him. He buried his face in his pillow, an interesting debating strategy. "You'll still see lots of them. But you'll get to see other people, too. And lots of kids your own age."

He turned his head, coming up for air. "What's Mommy making for breakfast?"

"I'm making breakfast. What do you want?"

"Cheerios," he said, then added, "and coffee."

"I don't think so," I said. "Although it might be just the thing to wake you up."

"What does it taste like?"

"Pretty awful, most of the time."

"Then why do you drink it?"

"Habit," I said. "You drink it enough times, you stop noticing how bad it is."

"Get Mommy."

I left my hand on his shoulder, rubbed it softly. "Mommy's still not here," I said.

"She's been away for . . ." He closed his eyes for a few seconds. "She's been away for two sleeps."

"I know," I said.

While he gathered together his bed toys, he asked, "Did she go fishing?"

"Fishing?"

"Sometimes people go away fishing." He looked at Robin, smoothed out his cape. "Poppa goes away fishing sometimes."

"That's true. But I don't think your mom has gone fishing."

"Why?"

"I don't think fishing is really her thing," I said.

"Then where would she go?" He had Robin in one hand, Wolverine in the other. They were facing each other, about to engage in combat, or just shoot the shit. It was hard to know.

"I wish I knew," I said. "Listen, I need to talk to you about something."

Ethan looked at me, his face all innocent, like maybe I was going to tell him we were out of Cheerios and he was going to have to eat toast. He still had the action figures in his fists, and I pushed them down to get his full attention.

"Even though you're going to be at my parents' house, you still might hear some things, maybe on TV or on the radio, or maybe from someone coming by their place, about your dad that aren't very nice."

"What kind of things?"

"That I was mean to your mother." How did you tell your son that people might think you killed his mother?

"You aren't mean to her," he said.

"I know that and you know that, but you know how, sometimes, your friends will tattle on you, even though you didn't do anything?"

He nodded.

"That's kind of what might happen to me. People saying I did bad things to your mom. Like the TV news people, for one."

Ethan thought a moment, then reached out and patted my hand. "Do you want *me* to talk to them and tell them it's not true?" he asked.

I had to look away for a moment. I made as though I had something in my eye, both of them.

"No," I said. "But thank you. You just have a good time with your grandparents."

"Okay." Now he was thinking about something else. "That's like what Mom told me."

"What do you mean?" I asked. "What did she tell you?"

"She said that people might say awful things about her, but that she wanted me to remember that she really loves me."

I remembered that.

"Is everybody going to start saying bad things about me, too?" he asked.

"Never," I said, leaning in and kissing Ethan's forehead.

When I walked out the door with Ethan, Craig, my neighbor to the right, was getting into his Jeep Cherokee to head off to work. Since moving in three years ago, I'd never known Craig not to say hello, comment on the weather, ask how we were doing. He was a friendly guy, and when he borrowed your hedge trimmer, he always returned it the minute he was finished.

I saw Craig glance my way, but he said nothing. So I said, "Morning."

Not even a grunt. Craig got into his car, put on his seatbelt, and turned the ignition without looking my way. He backed out and took off briskly.

While I was getting Ethan buckled into the back seat, I heard a car that had been driving up the street slow down as it reached the end of my driveway.

I looked up. A man in a Corolla had put down his window and shouted as he drove by, "Who you gonna kill today?" Then he laughed, stomped on the gas, and disappeared up the street.

"What did he say?" Ethan asked.

"It's just like I told ya, sport," I said, snapping his strap into place.

After I had dropped him off at my parents', I drove to the newspaper. I had time to pop in before my appointment with Natalie Bondurant.

I went up to the newsroom first. As I walked through, what few people were there stopped whatever they were doing to watch me. No one called out, no one said anything. I was a "dead man walking" as I proceeded to my desk.

There were several phone messages—most from the same media outlets that had already tried to reach me at home. One call, which I was unable to determine whether it was a joke—was from the *Dr. Phil* show. Did I want to come on and give my side of the story, let America know that I had not killed my wife and disposed of her body?

I erased it.

When I tried to sign in to my computer, I couldn't get it to work. My password was rejected.

"What the fuck?" I said.

Then, a voice behind me. "Hey."

It was Brian. When I spun around in the chair, he said to me, "I didn't expect you to come in today, what with, you know, all you got to deal with at the moment."

"I'm just popping in," I said. "You're right, I have a lot on my plate right now."

"Got a sec?" he said.

Once we were both inside his office, he closed the door, pointed to a chair. I sat down and he settled in behind his desk.

"I really hate to do this," he said, "but I—we're—I mean, they're putting you on suspension. Actually, more like a leave. A leave of absence."

"Why's that, Brian? Did you think I wanted to write a book?" It was a reporter's usual reason for taking a leave.

I knew what was going on, and understood it, but even in my current circumstances it was hard to pass up an opportunity to make Brian squirm. Particularly when I considered him to be a first-class weasel.

"No, not anything like that," he said. "It's just, given your current predicament, being questioned by the police about your wife, it kind of compromises your ability as a journalist at the moment."

"When did the paper start worrying about its journalistic integrity being compromised? Does this mean we've fired our reporters in India and plan to send our own people to cover city hall?"

"Jesus, Dave, do you always have to be a dick?"

"Tell me, Brian. Was it you?"

"Huh?"

"Was it you who got into my emails?"

"What the hell are you talking about?"

"You know what? Forget it. Because even if it was you, you'd just have been doing Madeline's bidding."

"I really don't know what this is about."

"So, am I on a paid suspension or unpaid?"

Brian couldn't look me in the eye. "Things are kind of tight, Dave. It's not like the paper can afford to pay people for not doing anything."

"I've got three weeks' vacation," I said. "Why don't I take that now? I still get paid, but I'm not writing. If my problems haven't gone away in three weeks, you can suspend me then without pay."

Brian thought about that. "Let me bounce that off them."

"Them" meaning Madeline.

"Thanks," I said. "Do you want me to ask *them* myself?"

"What do you mean?"

I stood up and opened the door. "See you later, Brian."

On the way out of the newsroom, I went past the bank of mailbox cubbyholes, scooped three or four envelopes out of my mailbox—one of them my payroll deposit slip. I wondered whether it would be my last. I stuffed the envelopes into my pocket and kept on walking.

From there, I went to the publisher's office. Madeline Plimpton's executive assistant, Shannon, was posted at her desk just outside Madeline's door.

"Oh, David," she said. "I'm so sorry. . . ." She struggled. Sorry that my wife was missing? Sorry that the cops liked me for it? Sorry that the publisher wanted to help me through my difficult time by bouncing me from the payroll?

I went straight past her and opened the door to Madeline's oak-paneled office despite Shannon's protests.

Madeline sat behind her broad desk, looking down at something, a phone to her ear. She raised her eyes and took me in, not even blinking.

"Something's come up. I'll have Shannon reconnect us shortly." She cradled the receiver and said, "Hello, David."

"I just dropped by to thank you for your support," I said.

"Sit down, David."

"No thanks, I'll stand," I said. "I saw Brian, found out I'm on the street for the duration."

"I'm not without sympathy," Madeline said, leaning back in her leather chair. "Assuming, of course, that you had no involvement in your wife's misfortune."

"If I told you I didn't, would you even believe me?"

She paused. "Yes," she said. "I would."

That threw me.

"I've heard the whispers," Madeline said. "I've asked around. I know people in the police department. You're much more than a person of interest. You're a suspect. They think something has happened to your wife and they think you did it. So I feel doubly bad for you. I feel badly that something may have happened to Jan. My heart goes out to you. And I feel sick at the witch hunt whirling around you. I think I know you, David. I've always thought you were a good man. A bit self-righteous at times, a bit idealistic, not always able to see the big picture, but a man who's always had his heart in the right place. I don't know what's happened to Jan, but I would find it hard to believe you've had anything to do with it."

I sat down. I wondered whether she was being sincere or playing me.

"But it's not possible for you to work as a reporter at the moment. You can't be doing stories when you are a story."

"I asked Brian if I could take all the vacation that's owed to me."

She nodded. "That's a good idea. Of course, do that."

"I have to ask you something else, and I need an honest answer," I said.

She waited.

"Did you go into my emails, find one from a source offering to tell me about Star Spangled payoffs to council members, and pass it on to Elmont Sebastian?"

She held my stare for several seconds. "No," she said. "And, when and if you get back to work, if you get something on him or anyone whose votes he's allegedly buying, I'll see that it makes the front page. I don't like that man. He frightens me, and I don't want to do business with him."

I got up and left.

* * *

When I walked into Natalie Bondurant's office and she came around from behind her desk, I was expecting her to shake hands with me. But instead, she reached for a remote and turned on the television that was recessed into the far wall.

"Hang on," she said. "I just had it cued up here a second ago. Okay, here we go."

She hit the play button and suddenly there I was, making my way through a small media scrum, denying that there was any need for me to take a lie detector test.

She hit pause, threw the remote onto a chair, and turned on me.

"My God, you really want to go to jail, don't you?"

# THIRTY-SIX

THE THING WAS, JAN didn't know whether she could pull off the role of a murderer. You needed some real acting chops for that. The motivation for most of her performances had been coping, or blending in. Biding time.

But killing? Not so much.

If an opportunity did present itself where she could take off with Dwayne's half of the loot from the diamonds, she'd take it. No question. She'd pulled off a vanishing act on David and she could do it with Dwayne, too. But was she prepared to kill him to do it?

To put a bullet in his brain or a knife in his heart?

She'd never actually killed anyone, at least not on purpose.

But she wasn't stupid. She knew the law would already see her as a murderer. Even though she hadn't been the one who clamped a hand over Leanne Kowalski's mouth and nose and kept it there until she stopped flailing about, she didn't exactly do anything to stop it, either. Jan watched it happen. Jan knew it had to be done. And it was her idea to take Leanne's body back up to Lake George—a way to tighten the noose on David, who police would know had already been up in that neck of the woods with her—and bury it in that shallow grave in plain view, using a shovel in the back of Dwayne's brother's pickup. Any jury would see that they hung for that one together.

And she knew it was only luck—or divine intervention, if you believed in that kind of thing—that Oscar Fine hadn't died when she cut off his hand to steal the briefcase he had cuffed to his wrist.

That had been—let's face it—a pretty desperate moment. They thought he'd have a key on him. Or a combination to the briefcase. And the chain that linked the case to his cuff was some high-tensile steel that the tools they'd brought along wouldn't cut. But at least they could go through flesh and bone.

The bastard hadn't left them much in the way of options.

So, once he was out cold—and that hadn't taken long after Dwayne shot the dart into him—she did it. If you'd asked her the day before whether she had it in her to cut off a man's hand, she'd have said no way. Not a chance. Not in a million years. But then there you are, in a limo parked in a Boston vacant lot, not knowing whether someone's going to come by at any moment, and suddenly you're doing things you'd have never thought yourself capable of. Of course, millions in diamonds was a great motivator.

Wasn't that what it was all about? Knowing your motivation? So she got into the role. She became the kind of woman who could do this, who could cut off a man's hand. She played the part long enough to get the job done.

Too bad he got that one long look at her face before passing out. Even tarted up with enough lipstick and eye shadow to paint a powder room, she never stopped worrying that he might remember her. Would have been a lot better—truth be told—if the son of a bitch had bled to death. Then she wouldn't have had to put her life on hold for five years, marry a guy, have a kid, work at a goddamn heating and cooling business, for Christ's sake, live a lie—

*Focus,* she told herself.

*Let's just take this a step at a time. We have all the diamonds. Now we just have to convert them to cash. Let's see how things play out.*

They'd driven south out of Boston, and already Jan was feeling slightly more at ease. She knew the odds of running into Oscar Fine in a city as big as Boston were remote, but it didn't make her feel any less nervous. Now that they were out of downtown, she felt she could breathe a little. They had to find this Banura-of-Braintree dude, find out what the jewels were worth, negotiate a price, get their cash, start their new life together.

Start *her* new life. One way or another, Dwayne was going to be history.

Not that he didn't have his merits. He had a fabulously taut, sinewy body, and if he could stop fucking like he was expecting the warden to walk in at any moment, he might have some actual potential in that department. And he'd been the perfect one to help her out when she got wind of the diamond courier. He had the guts—or lack of sense, depending on how you looked at it—to help her set it up, get the dart gun, drive the limo. So maybe she was the only one with the balls to cut the guy's hand off. You couldn't have everything.

But she'd needed him to get into the safe-deposit boxes. And she needed him now to connect with Banura.

But after that, well, Dwayne really wasn't what Jan was looking for in a man. The only man she wanted to see in her future was the one delivering her drink to her cabana.

One thing you had to give David, he was a hell of a lot

smarter than Dwayne. There was no denying that. Smart enough to be working at a paper better than the Promise Falls *Standard*. He'd had that one offer, a couple of years back, to go to Toronto to work for the largest-circulation paper in the country, but Jan was nervous about moving to Canada. Her phony credentials were rock solid, but the idea of crossing a border when she wasn't who she said she was, that gave her pause. Jan had told David she didn't think it was a good idea to move so far away from his parents, and he had come around to her way of thinking.

Once she had her money, she'd start this identity thing all over again and invest in some foolproof passports—real high-class stuff—and then get the hell out of the States. Maybe this Banura guy could put her onto someone who did good work. Then, off to Thailand, or the Philippines. Someplace where the money would last forever. Shit, it might be enough money to last right here in the good ol' US of A, but you'd always be looking over your shoulder, never able to relax.

*David, you poor bastard.*

The guy thought he was some hotshot reporter, but how hotshot could you be at the *Standard*? Not exactly a risk taker. Always played it safe. Made sure there were new batteries in the smoke detectors, a fresh filter in the furnace. Paid the bills on time. When a shingle came loose, he got up there on the roof—or got his dad up there with him—and nailed it down. He remembered anniversaries and Valentine's Day and brought home flowers some days for no reason at all.

The guy was goddamn perfect.

Perfect husband.

Perfect father.

*Don't go there.*

Dwayne, driving south on Washington and peering

through the windshield at street signs, shifted in his seat and ripped off a fart.

"Where the fuck is Hobart?" he said.

They found the house. A small story-and-a-half with white siding. Dwayne wheeled the truck into the driveway behind a Chrysler minivan.

"See?" Dwayne said. "The guy's smart, doesn't attract attention. He could afford a goddamn Porsche, but then the neighbors are going to say, hey, where's he get off driving a car like that? And he could live in a bigger house than this, right? But again, he knows how to keep a low profile."

"What's the point getting rich if you have to live the way you've always lived?" Jan asked.

Dwayne shook his head, like the question was too deep. "I don't know. Maybe he's got another place. In the Bahamas or something."

Dwayne had his hand on the door. Half the diamonds were still tucked into his jeans, while Jan had her share in her purse.

"He said come in around the back," Dwayne said, nodding toward the end of the drive, which ran down the side of the house.

"You're not worried, us walking in here with everything we've got?" Jan asked. "What if he decides to take the diamonds off us? What are we supposed to do then?"

"Hey, he's a businessman," Dwayne said. "You think he's going to throw away his reputation, fucking over a client like that?"

Jan wasn't convinced.

"Okay, if you're worried . . ." Dwayne reached under the seat and pulled out a small, short-barreled revolver.

"Jesus," Jan said. "How long you had that?"

"Pretty much since I got out," he said. "Got it from my brother when he let me have the truck."

*One more thing that could have sunk us if we'd gotten pulled over,* Jan thought. But knowing they had a weapon did offer some comfort.

He reached into the small storage area behind the seats and grabbed a jean jacket. Awkwardly, he slipped it on while still behind the wheel, then tucked the gun into the right pocket. "Don't want to walk in waving the thing. But you're right, it's good to have it along. Okay, let's go get rich."

They got out of the truck and walked up the drive past the minivan. Dwayne turned at the back of the house, found a ground-level wood door with a peephole, and pressed a tiny round white button to the left of it. They didn't hear the buzz inside through the thick door, but seconds later there was the sound of a substantial deadbolt being turned back.

A tall, wiry man with very dark brown skin opened the door. His T-shirt was several sizes too large, and a rope belt cinched around his waist kept his baggy cargo pants up. He smiled, exposing two rows of yellowed teeth. "You are Dwayne," he said.

*Great,* Jan thought. *Real names.*

"Banura," Dwayne said, shaking hands. He went to introduce Jan. "This is . . . Kate?"

She smiled nervously. She couldn't be Jan. And she couldn't be Connie. So Kate it was. "Hi."

Banura extended a hand to her and drew them both into the house. Inside the door was a narrow flight of stairs heading down. There was no access, at least from the back door, to any other part of the house. Once inside, they watched as Banura returned to position a massive bar that spanned the width of the door. He led them down the stairs, hitting a couple of light switches on the way.

The stairway wall was lined with cheaply framed photos—some in color and some, mercifully, in black and white. Most of them were of young black men, some just children, barefoot and dressed in tattered clothes, photographed against bleak African landscapes of ruin and poverty. They were wielding rifles, raising hands together in victory, mugging for the camera. In several, the men posed over bloody corpses. One that made Jan look away showed a black child, probably no more than twelve, waving a severed arm as though it were a baseball bat.

Banura took them into a crowded room with a long, brilliantly lit workbench. Spread out on the bench was a black velvet runner, and over it three different magnifiers on metal arms.

"Have a seat," Banura said in his thick African accent, gesturing to a ratty couch that was half-covered in boxes and two IKEA-type office chairs that probably cost five bucks new.

"Sure," Dwayne said, dropping onto a narrow spot on the couch.

"You won't be needing your gun," Banura said, his back to Dwayne as he sat on the stool at the workbench.

"What's that?"

"The one in your right pocket," he said. "I'm not going to take anything from you. And you are not going to take anything from me. That would be totally foolish."

"Hey, sure, I get that," Dwayne said, laughing nervously. "I just like to be cautious, you know?"

Banura pulled his magnifiers into position, flicked another switch. They had lights built into them.

"Let me see what you have," he said.

Jan, who had chosen not to sit, reached into her purse and withdrew her bag. Dwayne leaned back on the couch to make it easier to reach into his pants and fished out his half. He tossed the bag over to Jan, like having a bag of diamonds was no biggie, and she presented both of them to Banura.

Delicately, he opened both bags and emptied them onto the black velvet. He examined no more than half a dozen of the stones, putting each one under bright light and magnification.

"So, you know this stuff is pretty good, huh?" Dwayne said.

"Yes," Banura said.

"So whaddya think?"

"Just a moment, please."

"Dwayne, let the man do his job," Jan said.

Dwayne made a face.

Once he'd finished looking at the half dozen stones, Banura slowly turned on his stool and said to them, "These are very good."

"Well, yeah," said Dwayne.

"Where did you get these?" he asked. "I'm just curious."

"Come on, Banny Boy, we went through this before. I'm not telling you that."

Banura nodded. "That's fine, then. Sometimes it is better not to know. What counts is the quality of the merchandise. And this is superb. And you have a lot of it."

"So, what do you think it's worth?" Jan asked.

Banura turned his head and studied her. "I am prepared to offer you six."

Jan blinked. "I'm sorry?"

"Million?" Dwayne said, sitting up at attention.

Banura nodded solemnly. "I think that's more than generous."

Jan had never expected to be offered anything remotely close to six million dollars. She thought maybe two or three million, but this, this was unbelievable.

Dwayne stood, struggled not to look excited. "You'll never guess what my lucky number happens to be." He slapped his own ass where he'd been tattooed. "Well, you know, I think that's a figure that my partner and I can work with. But we'll need to talk about it."

"We'll take it," Jan said.

Banura nodded again, then turned back to his table. He began selecting more of the diamonds at random for study. "The quality is consistent," he said.

"Fuckin' A," Dwayne said. "So, where's the money?"

Banura frowned without taking his eyes off the jewels. "I don't keep funds of that nature around here," he said. "I will have to make some arrangements. You may take your product with you, and later this afternoon we can make an exchange."

"Here?" Dwayne said. "We come back here?"

"Yes," Banura said. "And I should tell you that for a transaction of this size, I will have an associate present, and you will not be permitted to enter my premises with that gun on you."

"No problem, no problem," Dwayne said. "We want to do everything straight up."

Banura glanced at his watch. It looked, to Jan, like a cheap Timex. "Come back at two," he said.

Dwayne said, "So it'll be cash, right? I don't want a check."

Banura sighed.

"I'm sorry," Jan said. "We're just . . . a little excited, to be honest."

"Of course," Banura said. "You have plans?"

"Yes," Jan said, without elaborating.

"Oh yeah," Dwayne said.

Banura gathered the jewels and returned them all to one bag, since they fit easily enough. "That's okay?" he asked.

"Sure," Jan said.

He held out the bag and Jan took it before Dwayne could get his hands on it. She dropped it into her purse.

"So, two o'clock, then," Jan said.

Banura followed them up the stairs, peered through the peephole, then pulled back the bar across the door.

"Goodbye," he said. "And when you come back, you don't bring your gun in here. I won't have it."

The bar could be heard clinking back in place once they were outside.

"Six mil!" Dwayne said. "Did you hear the man? Six fucking mil!"

He threw his arms around her. "It was all worth it, baby. All fucking worth it."

Jan smiled, but she wasn't feeling it.

It was too much money.


When he was back at his workbench, Banura picked up a cell phone, flipped it open, and dialed a number.

He put the phone to his ear. It rang once.

"Yes?"

"It was them," Banura said.

"When?"

"Two o'clock."

"Thank you," Oscar Fine said and ended the call.

# THIRTY-SEVEN

NATALIE BONDURANT SAID, "EITHER somebody's setting you up, or you killed your wife."

"I didn't kill my wife," I said. "I don't know for sure something's even happened to her."

"*Something* has happened to her," Bondurant said. "She's gone. She may very well be alive, but *something* has happened to her."

I'd told my new lawyer everything I knew, and everything that had happened to me in the last couple of weeks. That included my chats—and rides—with Elmont Sebastian.

Natalie sat behind her desk and leaned back in her chair. She appeared to be looking up at the ceiling, but her eyes were closed.

"I think it's a stretch," she said.

"What?"

"That Sebastian is somehow setting you up to take the fall for this. That he's done something to her and found a way to make everything point your way."

"Because it's a lot of trouble to go to just to silence one critic," I said.

She shook her head. "Not so much that. It's not his style. From everything you've told me, Elmont Sebastian has a more direct approach. First, a cash inducement. The job offer. When you turned that down, he moved on to simple scare tactics. Mess with me and something'll happen to you, or worse, to your child."

"Yeah," I said.

"I think there's a more obvious answer," she said.

"That's staring us in the face?" I said.

Natalie Bondurant opened her eyes and leaned forward, elbows on the table. "Let's review a few things here. The ticket thing, going into Five Mountains."

"Yeah," I said.

"One child ticket, one adult ticket ordered online," she said.

"Right."

"You're the only one who seems to know about your wife's recent bout of depression. Jan says she went to the doctor but didn't."

"Yeah."

"No one sees Jan from the time you left that store in Lake George. She didn't go with you to your parents' house to pick up your son. She tells that shopkeeper some tale about not knowing why you've driven her up there."

"Supposedly."

Natalie ignored that. "And Duckworth wasn't lying to you. They've found hair and blood in the trunk of your car, plus a recent receipt for duct tape in the glove box, which is a kind of handy item to have around if you're planning to kidnap someone and get rid of them."

"I didn't buy any duct tape," I said.

"Somebody did," Natalie said. "And guess what they found in the history folder of your laptop?"

I blinked. "I don't know. What?"

"Sites that offered tips on how to get rid of a body."

"How do you know this?"

"I had a chat with Detective Duckworth before you arrived. Full disclosure and all."

"That's crazy," I said. "I never looked up anything like that."

"I told Duckworth the planets are all in alignment for him on this one. That should be his first clue that you're being set up."

"Set up? Is that what he thinks?"

"Hell no. The more obvious the clue, the more the cops like it. There's also this business of the life insurance policy you recently took out on your wife."

"What? How do you know about that?"

"I'll give Duckworth this much. He can be thorough. Tell me about the policy."

"It was Jan's idea. She thought it made sense, and I agreed."

"Jan's idea," Natalie repeated, nodding.

"What?" I said.

"You're not getting this, are you?"

"Getting what? That I'm in a shitload of trouble? Yeah, I get that. And don't talk to the press. I get that now, too."

She shook her head. "Just how well do you really know your wife, David?"

"Really well. Very well. You don't spend more than five years with someone and not know them."

"Except you're not even sure what her real name is. Clearly it's not Jan Richler. Jan Richler died when she was a child."

"There has to be an explanation."

"I've no doubt there is. But how can you claim to know your wife well if you don't even know who she is?"

The question hung there for several seconds.

Finally, I said, "Duckworth may be covering for the FBI. She might be a relocated witness. Maybe she testified against someone and no one can say, for the record, that she had to take on a new identity."

"You told this to Duckworth," she said.

I nodded. "I don't think, when I told him, he believed a word of it. I'd already told him about Jan's depression, but that story was falling apart whenever he talked to anyone else."

"So he may not even have checked the FBI thing."

"I don't know."

"How do you explain the fact that you're the only one who witnessed your wife's change in mood?"

"I don't know. Maybe I was the only one she felt she could be that honest with."

"Honest?" Natalie said. "We're talking about a woman who's been hiding from you, since the day she met you, who she really is."

I had nothing for that.

"What if this depression thing was an act?" she asked.

I had nothing for that, either.

"An act just for you."

Slowly, I said, "Go on."

"Okay, let's rewind a bit here. Forget this business about the FBI getting your wife a new name and life. The FBI doesn't have to troll around looking for people who died as children to create new identities for people. They can make them right out of thin air. They've got all the blank forms for every document you could ever need. You want to be Suzy Creamcheese? No problem. We'll make you up a Suzy Creamcheese ID. So what I'm asking is, has it occurred to you that your wife might have gone about getting a new identity all on her own?"

I took a second. "I've thought about it, but I can't come up with a reason why she'd do such a thing."

"David, it wouldn't surprise me that as we sit here the police are drawing up a warrant for your arrest. Finding Leanne Kowalski's body only a couple of miles from where you were seen with your wife will have shifted them into overdrive. All they've wanted is to find a body, and now they've got one. Don't think that just because it isn't your wife's, that's going to slow them down. They probably figure you killed Jan, that Leanne found out or witnessed it, so you killed her, too. They don't even need to find your wife's body now. They'll be able to put together some kind of case with Leanne's. Maybe you did a better job at hiding Jan's body, but you screwed things up and panicked and did a shitty job with Leanne's. If I were them, that's how I'd be putting this together."

"I didn't kill Leanne," I said.

Natalie waved her hand at me, like she didn't want to hear it. "You're in a mess, and there's only one person I can think of who could have put you there."

My head suddenly felt very heavy. I let it fall for a moment, then raised it and looked at Natalie.

"Jan," I said.

"Bingo," she said. "She was the one who ordered the Five Mountains tickets. She was the one who fed you—and you alone—a story about being depressed. Why? So when something happened to her, that's the story you'd tell the cops. A story that would look increasingly bogus the more the police looked into it. Who had access to your laptop to leave a trail of tips on how to get rid of a body? Who could easily have put her own hair and blood in the trunk of your car? Who went in and told the Lake George store owner that she had no idea why her husband was taking her for a drive up into the woods? Who persuaded you to take out life insurance, so that if she died you'd be up three hundred grand?"

I said nothing.

"Who's not who she claims to be?" Natalie asked. "Who took on the identity of some kid who got hit by a car way back when?"

I felt the ground starting to swallow me up.

"Who the hell is your wife, really, and what did you

do to piss her off so badly that she'd want to frame you for her murder?"

"I didn't do anything."

Natalie Bondurant rolled her eyes. "There isn't a husband on the planet whose wife hasn't thought of killing him at one time or another. But this is different. This takes things to a whole new level."

"But why?" I asked. "I mean, if she didn't love me anymore, if she wanted out of the marriage, why not just leave? Tell me it's over and walk away? Why do something as elaborate as what you're suggesting?"

Natalie mulled that one over. "Because there's more to this. Because it isn't enough for her to get away. She doesn't want anyone to come looking for her. She doesn't want anyone to know she's alive. No one's going to come looking for her if they figure she's dead."

"But I'd come looking for her," I said. "She'd have to know I'd do everything I could to find her."

"Kind of hard to do from a jail cell," Natalie said. "And if the cops think they've closed this thing, so what if they haven't actually got a body? They've got you, their work is done. And your Jan's off living a new life somewhere."

I sat, numb, in Natalie's leather chair.

"I can't believe it," I said. "She couldn't have set it all up." I struggled to get my head around it. "What about that Lake George trip? How could she have known I was going to go there Friday to meet that source?"

Natalie shrugged. "Who knows? And who the hell ran off with Ethan at Five Mountains? Who caused that distraction? How does Leanne Kowalski fit in? No idea. But right now, based on what you've told me, the only thing that makes sense is that your wife is behind this. She wanted to get away, and she wanted you to be her cover story. Her patsy. Her fall guy. And she's done a pretty fantastic job of it, if you don't mind my saying so."

"Why would she do this to me?" I whispered. But there was a bigger question. "Why would she do this to Ethan?"

Natalie crossed her arms and thought about that a moment.

"Maybe," she said, "because she's not a very nice person."

# THIRTY-EIGHT

"SOMETHING'S WRONG," JAN SAID.

They were sitting in a Braintree McDonald's on Pearl Street. Dwayne had ordered two double-sized Big Macs, a chocolate shake, and a large order of fries. Jan had bought only a coffee, and even that she wasn't touching.

His mouth full, Dwayne said, "What's wrong?"

"It's too much."

"What are you talking about?"

"It's too much money."

Jan could see fries and bun and special sauce when Dwayne said, "If you don't want your half, I'll take it off your hands."

"Why would he offer us so much right away?" she asked.

"Maybe," Dwayne said, continuing to talk with his mouth full, "he knew the stuff was worth a hell of a lot more and he's actually cheating us."

A woman about Jan's age, with a small boy in tow, sat down two tables over. The boy, maybe four or five years old, perched himself on the chair and swung his legs a good foot above the floor. Jan watched as his mother put a Happy Meal in front of him and unwrapped his cheeseburger. The boy put a single fry into his mouth like he was a sword swallower, leaning back, pointing the fry in slowly.

Jan was just turning to look at Dwayne again when she heard the woman say, "Don't be silly, Ethan."

Jan whipped her head to the side. Did she hear that right?

The mother said, "Can you open your milk, Nathan, or do you want me to do it?"

"I can do it," he said.

"You just worry too much," Dwayne said. "We've been waiting years for this moment and now you're getting all antsy."

"I never expected that kind of money," Jan said quietly. "Come on. The stuff is hot. You're never going to get retail value for it, you're not even going to get whole-sale. Best you can expect is maybe ten percent, okay, maybe twenty."

"That's probably what he was offering us," Dwayne said. "What we got could be worth way, way more than we can even imagine."

"He didn't even look at all the diamonds," she said. "He only looked at a few."

"He did a random sampling, and he was impressed," Dwayne said authoritatively, putting his mouth over the end of the straw and sucking hard. "Fuck, these are hard to get up."

The mother glanced over at Dwayne.

"Watch your language," Jan said. She looked over and smiled apologetically. The mother was not pleased. Nathan did not appear to have noticed. He was holding his cheeseburger firmly with both hands as he took his first bite.

"Chill out," Dwayne said. "You think the kid's never heard that word before?"

"He might not have," Jan whispered. "If she's a good mother, watches who he hangs out with, makes sure he doesn't watch anything bad on TV."

She thought about how upset David had gotten when his mother allowed Ethan to watch *Family Guy*. A smile crossed her lips ever so briefly.

"What?" Dwayne asked.

"Nothing," she said and refocused. "I just don't like it."

"Okay," Dwayne said, actually allowing his mouth to empty before continuing. "What exactly is the downside? So maybe he's offering us more than you were expecting. What are you worried about? That he's going to come after us later and ask for some of his money back?"

"No, I don't think he's going to ask for some of his money back," she said. "Did you see the photos on his wall?"

Dwayne shook his head. "I didn't notice."

Jan thought, *There's a lot you don't notice.*

Dwayne glanced at his watch. "Couple of hours, we go pick up our money. I was thinking, to kill time, we go find some place that sells boats."

"I want to find a jewelry store," Jan said.

"What? If you want a diamond, I'm sure you could keep one of the ones we've got. There's so fucking many, Banny Boy won't even notice if he's one short."

The woman shot Dwayne another look. He returned it and said, in an exaggerated fashion, "*Sorry.*"

"I don't want to buy something," Jan said. "I want a second opinion."

The woman was gathering up her son's lunch onto the tray and moving them to another table on the other side of the restaurant.

Dwayne, shaking his head, said to Jan, "You know, if you don't allow your kids to be exposed to certain things, they're not going to grow up ready to face the world."

* * *

"This is a dumb idea," Dwayne said as they sat in the truck out front of Ross Jewelers, a storefront operation with black iron bars over the windows and door.

"I want someone else to have a look at them," Jan said. "If this guy in here looks at a few and says they're worth such and such, then I'll know what we're being offered isn't out of whack."

"And if we find out they're worth even more, when we go back we'll just have to renegotiate," Dwayne said. "We'll tell him the price has gone up."

Jan still had the bag of diamonds in her purse.

"Don't you go thinking about sneaking out a back door," Dwayne said. "Half those diamonds are mine."

"Why would I run off with them now when someone has promised to give us six mil for them?"

"Did I tell you that was my lucky number?"

Only for about the hundredth time.

Jan got out of the truck, opened the outer door of the jewelry store, and stepped into a small alcove. There was a second door that was locked. Through the iron bars and glass, Jan could see into the store, but not get in. There was a woman in her fifties or sixties, well dressed with a hairdo that appeared to have been pumped up with air, behind the counter. She pressed a button and suddenly her voice filled the alcove.

"May I help you?" she asked.

"Yes," said Jan. "I need a quick appraisal."

There was a loud buzz, Jan's cue to pull on the door handle. Once inside, she approached the counter.

"What were you looking to have appraised?" the woman asked politely.

Jan set her open purse on the counter and discreetly picked half a dozen diamonds from the bag inside. She held them in her hand for the woman to examine.

"I was wondering if you could give me a kind of ball-park idea what these might be worth. Do you have someone who can do that?"

"I do that," the woman said. "Is this for insurance purposes? Because the way it usually works is, you leave these with me, I'll give you a receipt for them, and when you come back in a week I can give you a certificate of appraisal—"

"I don't need anything like that. I just need you to give them a quick look and tell me what you think."

"I see," the woman said. "All right, then. Let's see what you have."

On the glass counter was a desktop calendar pad, about one and a half by two feet, a grid of narrow black rules and numbers on a white background. The woman reached for a jeweler's eyepiece, adjusted a counter lamp so it was pointing down onto the calendar, then asked Jan to put the diamonds in her hand onto the lit surface.

The woman leaned over, studied the diamonds, picked a couple of them up with a long tweezerlike implement to get a closer look.

"What do you think?" Jan asked.

"Let me just get a look at all of them," she said. One by one, she studied each of the six stones. She never said a word or made a sound the entire time.

When she was done, she said, "Where did you get these?"

"They're in the family," Jan said. "They've been passed down to me."

"I see. It sounded as though you had more of them in your purse there."

"A couple more," Jan said. "But they're all pretty much the same."

"Yes, they are," the woman said.

"So what do you think? I mean, just a rough estimate,

what would you say they were worth? Individually, that is."

The woman sighed. "Let me show you something."

She set one of the diamonds on its flattest side directly on one of the black rules on the calendar. "Look at the stone directly from above." Jan leaned over and did as she was told. "Can you see the line through the stone?"

Jan nodded. "Yes, I can."

The woman turned and took something from a slender drawer in a cabinet along the wall. She had in her hand a single diamond. She straddled it on the black line beside Jan's stone. The two diamonds looked identical.

"Now," the woman said, "see if you can see the line through this stone."

Jan leaned over a second time. "I can't make it out," she said. "I can't see the line."

"That's because diamonds reflect and refract light unlike any other stone or substance. The light's being bounced in so many directions in there, you can't see through it."

Jan felt a growing sense of unease.

"What are you saying?" Jan asked. "That my diamonds are of an inferior quality?"

"No," the woman said. "I'm not saying that. What you have here is not a diamond."

"That's not true," Jan said. "It is a diamond. Look at it. It looks exactly like yours."

"Perhaps to you. But what you have here is cubic zirconium. It's a man-made substance, and it does look very much like diamond, no question. They even use it for advertisements in the diamond trade magazines." To prove it, she reached for one sitting atop the cabinet and turned through the pages. Each one was filled with dazzling photos of diamonds. "That's fake, that's fake. This one, too. The security costs for photo shoots would be astronomical if they used real diamonds for everything."

Jan wasn't hearing any of this. She hadn't taken in anything after the woman said what she had were not diamonds.

"It's not possible," she said under her breath.

"Yes, well, I suppose it must be a bit of a shock if your family's been leading you to believe these are real diamonds."

"So this stone," Jan said, pointing to the real diamond and thinking ahead, "wouldn't break if I hit it with a hammer, but mine would."

"Actually, they both would," the woman said. "Diamonds can chip, too."

"But my diamonds, my cubic . . ."

"Cubic zirconium."

"They must be worth something," Jan said, unable to hide the desperation in her voice.

"Of course," the woman said. "Perhaps fifty cents each?"

# THIRTY-NINE

BARRY DUCKWORTH PULLED HIS car over to the shoulder. Fifty yards ahead, police cars were parked on either side of this two-lane stretch of blacktop northwest of Albany. The road had been built along the side of a heavily wooded hill. The ground sloped down from the left, then, just beyond the shoulder where Duckworth had parked, it dropped off steeply into more forest.

That was where a passing cyclist had noticed something. An SUV.

When the first rescue team had shown up, ropes were used to get down to the vehicle safely. The rescue team members knew it was going to be tricky, moving an injured person back up the hill to the ambulance, but it turned out that wasn't going to be a problem.

There was no one in the Ford Explorer, and nothing to indicate that an occupant had been injured inside it. No blood, no matted hair on the cracked windshield.

A check of the plates showed that the Explorer belonged to Lyall Kowalski, of Promise Falls. Soon the locals learned that the wife of the man who was the registered owner of the vehicle was missing. And that was when someone put in a call to Barry Duckworth.

The night before, about twelve hours before getting the call about the SUV, Duckworth had paid a visit to the Kowalski home to tell Lyall that his wife, Leanne, had been found in a shallow grave near Lake George.

The man wailed and banged his head against the wall until it was raw and bloody, and then his dog began to howl.

Duckworth didn't get in touch with the man when he heard about the car being found. He decided to take a drive down, see it for himself, and learn what he could before informing him of the development.

Standing at the top of the hill, he could see the path the SUV had taken. Grass had been flattened, dirt dug up. The Explorer had nicked a couple of trees on the way down, judging by the missing bark. A towering pine had brought the car's trip to an end when it plowed into it head-on.

The first thing Barry thought was, *Huh?*

What was the Explorer doing here? If you looked at a map, Promise Falls was here in the middle, Lake George was up here to the north, and Albany was down here to the south. How did Leanne's car end up at the bottom of this hill, but her body up in Lake George?

"Someone ditches the car here hoping it won't be found," he said to himself, "but leaves Leanne's body so somebody's sure to find it."

The local police, who'd been down to the car several times before Duckworth arrived, said they'd found a gas station receipt on the floor for early Saturday afternoon. An Exxon just off the interstate north of the city. Duckworth took note of the location, then made sure everyone at the scene understood that the Explorer was linked to a homicide, and that it needed to be sent to a lab as soon as they figured a way to get it back up that hill.

On his way to the Exxon, Duckworth's cell rang, interrupting thoughts about what sort of snack foods they might sell at the gas station. He was thinking maybe a Twinkie. He hadn't had a Twinkie in weeks.

"Yeah?"

"Hey, Barry. How's it hanging?"

"Natalie. How you doin', my dear?" His encounters with Natalie Bondurant were often antagonistic, but he liked her.

"I'm doing just fine, Barry. Yourself?"

"Couldn't be better. Your client decided to make a full confession yet?"

"Sorry, Barry, not just yet. I have a question for you."

"Shoot."

"When your clowns did a search of the Harwood house, did they dust for prints?"

Barry scratched his ear with the cell. "No," he said. "They looked for any signs of violence, but not finger-prints."

"Why not?"

"Natalie, it's not officially a crime scene. We were looking for other things. Like what we found on the lap-top."

"Anyone could have done those Internet searches, Barry."

He ignored that. Instead, he asked, "Why do you care about fingerprints?"

"I want a set of the wife's," she said. "If you're not planning to get a set, then I'm going to have someone go into the house and pull a set."

"It's not exactly going to be a surprise to find the wife's fingerprints all over that house, Natalie," Barry said cautiously.

"I want to see if they're in any database. I want to know who she really is."

"So you're buying your guy's story. Is this the one where his wife is in the witness protection program, or is he now thinking she got replaced by a pod person?"

"You never checked the FBI angle, did you?"

"In fact, I did," Barry said. "If she's a witness, they're not copping to it."

"What about this fake name she was going by? You looked into that?"

He hadn't, but rather than admit it, he said, "Even if she did turn out to be somebody else, it doesn't mean her husband didn't do her in."

"You're going in the wrong direction on this one, Barry. Isn't your sizable gut telling you that yet?"

"Always a pleasure, Natalie," Barry said and ended the call.

That last comment of hers had taken all the fun out of thinking about a Twinkie. The hell of it was, there was something going on down there, in that sizable gut of his.

# FORTY

I DIDN'T EVEN REMEMBER driving home from Natalie Bondurant's office. By the time I walked out of her building, I was so shaken by her interpretation of recent events I was in a walking coma. I was traumatized, shell-shocked, dumbstruck.

*Jan had set me up.*

At least that was how it looked. Maybe, I kept telling myself, there was some other explanation. Something that didn't force me to reassess my life for the last five years. Something that didn't transform Jan from a loving wife and mother to a heartless manipulator.

But the part of me that had been trained to deal with the facts as they presented themselves—a part of me I'd been successfully suppressing lately—found it hard to reject Natalie's theory out of hand.

If one bought into the premise that I had something to do with Jan's disappearance, as Detective Duckworth no doubt did, the circumstantial evidence was substantial. My story that Jan had been depressed and might well have killed herself didn't hold up to scrutiny. The more that story fell apart, the more it looked as though I'd made it up.

And suddenly I was a prime suspect.

*Jan had set me up.*

Those five words kept playing on a loop in my head the entire way home. Somehow, without being aware I was doing it, I'd taken the keys from my pocket, started my father's car, driven it from one side of Promise Falls to the other, pulled into my driveway, unlocked my front door, and stepped into my home.

Our home.

I tossed Dad's keys onto the table by the front door, and as I stood in that house it suddenly felt very different, like someplace I'd come into for the first time. If everything that had happened here for the last five years was built on a lie—on Jan's false identity—then was this a real home? Or was this place a façade, a set, a stage where some fiction had been playing out day after day?

"Just who the fuck are you, Jan?" I said to the empty house.

I mounted the stairs and went into our bedroom, which I'd so carefully tidied after the house had been turned upside down by the police. I stood at the foot of the bed, taking in the whole room: the closet, the dresser, the end tables.

I started with the closet. I reached in and hauled out everything of Jan's. I tore blouses and dresses and pants off their hangers and threw them on the bed. Then I attacked the shelves, tossing sweaters and shoes into the room. I don't know what I was looking for. I don't know what I expected to find. But I felt compelled to take everything of Jan's and toss them, disrupt them, expose them to the light.

When I was done with the closet, I yanked out all the drawers on Jan's half of the dresser. I flipped them over, dumped their contents onto the bed, much of the stuff falling onto the floor. Underwear, socks, hosiery. I tossed the empty drawers into a pile, then tore into the items on the bed in a frenzy.

I was venting rage as much as I was looking for anything. Why the hell had she done this? Why had she left? What was she running from? What was she running to?

Why was disappearing so important to her that she was willing to sacrifice me to do it? Who was the man who'd run off with Ethan at Five Mountains? Was that why she'd left? For another man?

And the question I kept coming back to: Who the hell was she?

Abruptly, I walked out of the bedroom—leaving it in a much worse state than the police had—and traveled down two flights to the basement. I grabbed a large screwdriver and a hammer, then came back up to the second floor, taking the steps two at a time.

I opened the linen closet, hauled everything out that was on the floor, got down on my knees, and started ripping out the baseboards. I set the end of the screwdriver where the wood met the wall and drove it in with the hammer.

There was nothing delicate about the way I was going about this.

Once I had the wood partly pried from the wall, I forced the claw of the hammer in there and yanked. The wood snapped and broke off. I did it all the way around the closet, cracking wood, throwing it into the hallway behind me.

When I was finished with that closet—having found nothing—I started in on the one in Ethan's room. I tossed out any toys and small shoes in the way and ripped out all the molding around the closet base. When I struck out there, I tackled our own bedroom and again came up empty.

I did a walkabout of the upstairs, took in all the damage I'd created so far.

I was just getting started.

Dropping down to my hands and knees again, I started tapping on the wood floors throughout the house, looking for any planks that appeared loose or

disturbed. I threw back the carpet runners in the upstairs hallways and started there. A couple of the boards
looked as though they might have been tampered with,
so I drove the screwdriver down between them and
pried up. The flooring cracked and snapped as the nails
were ripped out.

I got my nose right into the hole I'd created, then
rooted around with my hand. I came up with nothing.

When I was done prying up a few other boards on the
top floor, I moved down to the main floor. I dragged rugs
out of the way, continued to tap on boards, pried them
up here and there. Then I removed the baseboards from
the inside of the front hall closet. In the kitchen, I emptied every drawer, flipped it over. Pulled out the fridge
and looked behind it, dumped out the flour and sugar
containers, took out every saved plastic grocery store
bag from a storage unit in the pantry. Opened the lids on
rarely used baking dishes. Got on a chair and looked on
top of all the kitchen cabinets.

Nothing.

Then I had an idea and rounded up every framed family photo in the house. Pictures of Ethan. Jan. Jan and
me together, pictures of the three of us. A photo of my
parents on their thirtieth anniversary.

I took apart all the frames, removed the pictures,
looked to see whether anything had been slipped in between the photo and the cardboard backing.

I turned up nothing.

In the living room, I tossed cushions, unzipped and removed covers, flipped chairs over, tipped the sofa on its
back and tore the filmy fabric that covered the underside,
stuck my hand in and cut my palm on a staple.

When I'd looked into every possible hiding spot on
the main floor, I moved down to the basement.

That meant opening up countless boxes of things. Old

books, family mementos—exclusively from my side—small appliances we no longer used, sleeping bags for camping trips, stuff from my days in college.

As in the rest of the house, the search was feverish, reckless. Items scattered everywhere in haste.

I was desperate to find something, anything, that might tell me who Jan really was or where she might have gone.

And I didn't find a single goddamn thing.

Maybe that birth certificate that had been hidden behind the baseboard in the upstairs linen closet had been it. The only thing Jan had hidden in this house. Or if there had been other things, she'd been smart enough to take them with her, too, when she disappeared.

The birth certificate, and the envelope.

There'd been a key in that envelope, too. A strange-looking key, not a typical door key. A different kind of key.

Then it hit me what it probably was. A safe-deposit box key.

Before Jan had met and taken up with me, she'd put something away for safekeeping. And the time had come for her to go and get it.

And leave Ethan and me behind.

Slowly, I walked through our home and surveyed the damage I'd wrought. The house looked like a bomb had hit it.

There weren't many places to sit down save for the stairs. I set my ass down on one of the lower steps, put my face into my hands, and began to cry.

If Jan really was dead, my life was shattered.

If Jan was alive, and had betrayed me, it wasn't much better.

If Natalie Bondurant's take on everything was right, it meant Jan was alive, and to save my own neck, I needed to find her.

But it didn't mean I wanted her back.

As I wiped the tears from my cheeks, trying to focus through my watery eyes, I looked for something in all of this that was good. Something that would give me some hope, some reason to carry on.

Ethan.

I had to keep going for Ethan.

I had to get through this, find out what was going on, and stay out of jail, for Ethan.

I couldn't let him lose his father. And I wasn't about to lose my son.

# FORTY-ONE

WHEN JAN CAME OUT of the jewelry store and got into the pickup truck, she didn't say anything. But Dwayne sensed something was wrong. Jan's face was set like stone and her hand seemed to shake when she reached for the handle to pull the door shut.

"What's going on?" Dwayne asked. "What'd they say?"

Jan said, "Just go."

"Go where?"

"Just go. Anywhere. Just go."

Dwayne turned the ignition, threw the truck into drive, and pulled out in front of a Lincoln that had to hit the brakes.

"What the hell's wrong?" Dwayne said as he drove. "You look like you just saw a ghost. Or you're constipated." When Jan didn't laugh, Dwayne said, "Come on, I'm trying to make a joke. What'd they say in that store?"

Jan turned and looked at him. "It's all been for nothing."

"What? What are you talking about?"

"All of it. What we did, the waiting, everything. It's all been for nothing."

"Jesus, Connie, would you mind telling me what the fuck you're talking about?"

"They're worthless," she said.

"What?"

"They're fake, Dwayne!" she screamed at him. "They're all cubic fucking something or other! They're not diamonds! They're fucking worthless! Do you understand what I'm telling you?"

Dwayne slammed on the brakes in the middle of the street. Behind him, a horn blared.

"What are you fucking telling me?" he said, foot on the brake.

"Are you deaf, Dwayne? Are you fucking hard of hearing? Let me tell it to you real slow so you'll understand. They. Are. Worthless."

Dwayne's face had gone crimson. His hands were gripping the steering wheel so hard his knuckles were going white.

Another honk of the horn, and then the Lincoln pulled up alongside, hit the brakes, and a man shouted, "Hey, asshole! Where'd you learn to drive?"

Dwayne tore his hand off the wheel, reached under the seat for his gun, whirled around and pointed it out the window.

"Why don't you give me a lesson?" he shouted.

The driver of the Lincoln floored it. The car squealed off.

Dwayne turned back to face Jan, gun in hand. "Tell me."

"I showed this woman half a dozen of the diamonds. Picked them at random. She said they were all fake."

"That is *not* possible," Dwayne said through clenched teeth.

"I'm telling you what she said. They're worthless!"

"You're wrong," he said.

"It's not me who's saying it," Jan said. "She got out her fucking eye thing and studied them all."

Dwayne was shaking his head furiously. "She's

wrong. Fucking bitch is playing some sort of game. Figured if she said they were worth next to nothing, she could make you a lowball bid. That's what she was doing."

"No, no," Jan said, shaking her head. "She didn't make any offer. She didn't—"

"Not *now*," Dwayne said. "But you can bet she's just waiting for you to come back in and say, 'What would you give me for these? A thousand, five hundred?'"

Jan screamed at him, "You're not getting it! They're not—"

He lunged across the seat and with his left hand—the gun was still in his right—he grabbed her around the throat and pushed her up against the headrest.

Jan choked. "Dwayne—"

"Now you listen to me. I don't give a fucking rat's ass what you were told by some stupid bitch back there. We have a guy who is prepared to give us six million for these diamonds, and I am quite prepared to accept his offer no matter what you say."

"Dwayne, I can't brea—"

"Or maybe . . . let me guess. Did she say the diamonds were actually worth more? But you figure, you'll come back out and tell little ol' Dwayne that they're worth nothing, so I'll figure; fuck it, let's forget the whole thing and hit the road, while you go back and negotiate an even better deal and keep all the money for yourself? I had a sneaking suspicion this was always your game."

Jan gasped for air as Dwayne maintained his grip on her neck. She tried to bat his arms away, but they were like steel rods.

"You were able to play your little husband for all these years, so how hard could it be to play me for a few days, am I right? You wait till I get out, get the other key, get all the diamonds, and then figure out a way to get all the money, cut me out of the picture."

Jan felt herself starting to pass out.

"You think I'm stupid?" Dwayne asked, his face in hers, his hot McDonald's breath enveloping her. "You think I don't know what you're doing?"

Jan's eyelids started to flutter, her head started to list to one side.

Dwayne took his hand away.

"Fuck this," he said. "I'm trading these diamonds for our six million, and when I've got the money I'll make a decision about what your share is going to be."

Jan coughed and struggled to get back her breath. She put her own hand to her neck and held it there as Dwayne put the truck in gear and sped off down the street.

It was the closest she'd ever come to dying. Two thoughts had flashed across her mind before she thought it was all over.

*I could do it. I could kill him.*

And: *Ethan.*

Dwayne was driving around in circles, waiting until it was two o'clock and time to return for his money. Jan had sat quietly in the seat next to him, waiting until she thought he'd calmed down.

Finally, she whispered, "You need to listen to me."

He poked his tongue around inside his cheek, not turning to look at her.

"All I want you to do is listen. Do what you want, but hear me out." He didn't tell her to shut up, so she continued. "If something seems too good to be true, it's probably because it is."

"Oh, please."

"I know you think I'm lying about what the lady in the jewelry store said. But let's just say I'm telling you the truth. If I am, why did Banura look at them and say they were first-rate?"

Dwayne shook his head. "Okay, if you're not lying, then maybe that woman doesn't know shit."

"It is her business," Jan said. "It's what she does."

Dwayne thought about that. "Then maybe Banura doesn't know shit."

Now Jan was shaking her head. "It's his business, too."

Dwayne made a snorting noise. "Well, if they both know so fucking much, how come one of them is wrong? Clearly, one of them doesn't know what the fuck they're talking about."

"I think they both know what they're doing," Jan said. "But one of them's lying. And it doesn't make any sense that the woman in the jewelry store is lying."

"It might. If you'd decided to sell everything to her for a song, she'd make out like a bandit."

"I don't think so."

Dwayne's eyes narrowed. "What are you saying? You saying Banny Boy is lying to us?"

"Yeah."

"About how much he's going to give us? You think we show up, he's going to have three million for us instead of six?"

"He's not going to pay anything for stones that are worthless," Jan said. Even as she said it, she could hardly believe it. All the time invested, the waiting . . .

Dwayne's face was darkening again. The anger was returning. Jan knew what was going on. He was so close to the money he could taste it. He didn't want anyone ruining his dream.

"If they're worthless, then why didn't he tell us that when he first saw them?" Dwayne said. "Why put us through all this, make us come back at two?"

"I don't know," Jan said.

"I'll tell you why," Dwayne said. "Because it's not safe to keep that kind of cash around. He probably had to go someplace to get it. Or have some courier come by with it. Maybe he's got a safe-deposit box, too, and he had to go get the cash out of it. That's what's going on."

Suddenly, Dwayne veered the truck over to the curb.

"Give me a diamond," he said.

"What?"

"Any diamond. Just give me one."

Jan reached into the bag in her purse, picked out one small stone, and handed it to Dwayne. He closed his palm on it, got out of the truck, and went around to the sidewalk, just beyond Jan's window. He bent over, placed the stone on the sidewalk, stood upright, then stomped on the stone with the heel of his shoe. When he lifted his foot, the stone was gone.

"Shit," he said. "Where the fuck did it go?"

Then he examined the bottom of his shoe, and found the stone embedded in the rubber sole. Bracing himself with one hand on the truck, he dug the stone out with his finger and held it up to Jan's nose.

"There, look," he said. "It's perfectly fine."

Jan knew the test didn't prove a damn thing, but she knew Dwayne was beyond convincing at this point.

He handed her the stone before going around the truck and getting back in behind the wheel.

He said to her, "When I get my boat, I'm using you for a fucking anchor."

# FORTY-TWO

FOR OSCAR FINE, IT was about rehabilitating his image.

Of course, it was about respect. Self-respect, and keeping the respect of others.

No question, it was about revenge.

But more than anything, it was about redemption. He needed to redeem himself. He had to set things right, restore some personal order, and the only way he could do that, no matter how long it took, was to find the woman who took his hand.

It was more than an injury, more than a physical disfigurement. It was a humiliation. Oscar Fine had always been the best. When you wanted something done, he was the man you called. He was a fixer. He took care of things.

He didn't screw up.

But then he did. Big-time.

The thing was, he knew something might be up. That was the whole point of toting a briefcase full of bogus jewels. They were worried about a leak, that maybe their system for moving jewels into the country, and then to their various markets, had been compromised.

It had been Oscar Fine's idea. Do a decoy delivery, he said. Let me do the regular run, he said, but bring the real stuff in some other way, a route that hasn't been done before. If someone makes a move on me, if the jewels are taken, or if the shipment is somehow damaged—Oscar Fine had imagined a scenario where he might have to send someone, briefcase and all, down to the bottom of the Boston Inner Harbor—we're not out merchandise.

For theatrical effect, he hooked himself to the briefcase with the handcuff. Any other time, he transported goods in a gym bag. A handcuff, it was like carrying a big sign that said "Rob me."

The gems were inside several cloth bags. One of them had a GPS transmitter stitched into the lining. Say someone got the drop on him. He'd give up the combination so they could open the briefcase, take the bags. Then he'd just see where they went, using the cell phone–sized receiver in his pocket.

His bosses weren't so sure. "What if they just kill you?"

"They need me for the combination. I plan on being obliging. They got nothing to gain by killing me."

Oscar Fine knew right away something was up when the limo arrived and the driver did not get out to open his door. Let him do it himself.

*Okay,* he thought, *I can play along. That's the whole point of this, after all.*

So he opened the back door on his own, and there she was. This woman with red hair, sitting on the far side, not bad looking, all lipstick and low-cut top and a skirt up to here and sheer black stockings and hooker heels, and right away he knew this was not right, this was a trap, this was all bullshit, and it almost made him grin, how amateur hour it all was.

She said, "They said you deserved a bonus."

Yeah, fuck, like that would happen. But he could play along with this. Let them think they're pulling a fast one. Pretty soon a gun will come out, he gives up the code and the briefcase, lets them drop him off somewhere.

Too bad about the dart.

It came from where the driver was sitting. Caught him below the right nipple, went through his jacket, pricked the skin.

*Son of a bitch.*

The effect was almost instantaneous. As he began to weave, the woman lurched toward him, grabbed the briefcase, yanked. Since he was attached to it by the wrist, he stumbled forward and into the back of the car.

Not good, he told himself. Not good at all. His arms and legs started going numb. Couldn't even reach out to break his fall. But the leather upholstery gave him a soft landing.

He started to say "What the fuck," but all that came out was "Wawawa."

How did he fail to anticipate something like this? While the dart had numbed and dizzied him, made it difficult to speak, it hadn't totally slowed his thought process. *No one's supposed to get the drop on me,* he thought. *Suddenly, I'm an amateur again.*

He started wondering how this was going to work. They were going to want the briefcase, no doubt about that. And he was more than happy to let them have every piece of cubic zirconium that it held. But if he couldn't talk, how the hell was he going to tell them the combination? The case had a lock on its side, next to the handle. A series of five numbers that had to be lined up for it to open. There was no key.

He couldn't see the driver, but the woman, he'd gotten a good look at her.

The two of them, once they couldn't open the case or release it from the handcuff that attached it to his wrist, started yelling at each other. First, he heard metallic clinking. They'd brought tools. Several of them, on the car floor. His wrist, being grabbed, examined, thrown down, picked up again. A search of his pockets, the inside of his jacket. The woman found his phone, the GPS receiver, pocketed both.

Then she found the gun strapped to his ankle. "Jesus," she said. She took it as well.

Then they were both shouting at him, asking for the combination. He tried to say something, but the words would not come. He continued to be aware of what was happening around him, even if he couldn't talk or move.

He thought he felt some tingling in his fingers, like maybe his feeling was coming back. Maybe whatever was in that dart wasn't all that powerful.

*He's really out of it,* the woman said.

*Look for a key,* said the driver.

*I told you, I've been through his pockets. There's no goddamn handcuff key,* said the woman.

*What about the combination? Maybe he wrote it down somewhere, put it in his wallet or something,* said the driver.

The woman: *What, you think he's a moron? He's going to write down the combination and keep it on him?*

*So cut the chain,* the driver said. *We take the case, we figure out how to open it later.*

*It looks way stronger than I thought,* the woman said. *It'll take me an hour to cut through.*

The driver: *You can't get the cuff over his hand?*

The woman: *How many times do I have to tell you? I'm gonna have to cut it off.*

*I thought you said it would take forever to cut the cuff,* the driver said.

The woman: *I'm not talking about the cuff.*

Oscar Fine tried to will some feeling back into his arms. He had a pretty good idea now what they were going to do.

He was a bit surprised when he realized it was the woman who was going to do it.

He tried to form the word "Wait." If they could hold off long enough for the tranquilizer to wear off, if only slightly. Not to the point where he'd be any threat to them, but enough that he could articulate the words, the numbers they needed to open the briefcase.

Then maybe they'd decide against the amputation.

"Wu," he said.

"What?" said the woman.

"Dwer," he said.

She shook her head and looked down at him. A change seemed to come across her face, like a mask. He would never forget that face, not if he lived through this.

"Sorry," she said.

And then she began to cut.

The injury was so horrendous, so traumatic, that while it might normally have caused Oscar Fine to pass out, it also had the effect of rousing him from the effects of the mild tranquilizer.

Once the woman and the driver had bolted with the case, he managed to summon enough strength to slip off his necktie and, with his remaining hand, wrap it a couple of inches above the ragged stump. A memory flashed through his brain, something he'd seen on one of the morning news shows, about that kid who'd gone exploring in a canyon, got trapped when a rock fell on his hand. How he went days without being found, and eventually had to cut the hand off with his penknife.

*I can be that kid,* Oscar Fine thought. *Shit, half the work's been done for me.* The woman had done the hard part. All he had to do was stanch the blood flow.

With what little reserves of will he had left, he started twisting the ends of the tie, tightening it on his wrist, attempting to stop the rate at which his blood was flowing out of him.

It wasn't enough. The blood was still coming.

*He was going to die.*

If he'd still had his phone, he'd have called for help. But the woman had taken it. He didn't have the strength to open the door, get to his feet, try to flag someone down.

*This was it.*

"Would you step out of the car, please?"

Huh?

Banging on the window. "Hello? Police! You can't park your limo here. Would you step out of the car, please? I'm not going to ask again."

He wasn't able to offer the cops much help.

Didn't see them, he said.

Never mentioned the briefcase.

Said he had no idea why they cut off his hand.

His guess? Mistaken identity. No one would have any reason to do such a thing to me, he said. They must have thought I was someone else.

The cops didn't buy it for a second.

And Oscar Fine knew it. So fuck 'em.

The hell of it was, someone hit the other courier, the one with the real diamonds. And that courier didn't fuck things up. He shot the guy, and before he died, learned he'd been tipped by someone from inside.

The hit on Oscar Fine, it appeared, came out of left field.

His employers said not to worry, we'll look after you.

They covered his medical expenses, even when he said no. Why should they be on the hook for this, he said, when he was the one who screwed up? But they insisted. His recovery took several months. Even though the paramedics had found the hand right there on the car floor, the doctors had been unsuccessful in reattaching it.

Sure, Oscar Fine felt pain. But mostly, he felt shame.

He'd fucked up a job. He'd been outwitted. He'd allowed others to cover his health costs.

I can still do this, he said. I'm not asking to get out. They said don't worry about it. When we need you for something, we'll be in touch, pay the going rate.

He knew they'd never call. You couldn't trust a guy who couldn't hang on to all his body parts.

So he said, the next five jobs are free. Just tell me what you need. And his employers thought, what the hell, let's see if the guy can get back on the horse.

And he did.

In many ways, even minus a hand, he was better at this than he'd ever been before. Less cocky, more cautious.

Less forgiving. Not that he'd ever been a softy. But sometimes, he used to actually listen when someone pleaded for his life. Not that it was going to change anything, but Oscar Fine thought maybe it made them feel better. Gave them, if only for a few seconds, a glimmer of hope.

Now he just did the job.

And there was never a moment, not in the last six years, when he wasn't looking for her. Watching faces, scanning crowds, searching the Net. He only had one real lead. A name: Constance Tattinger. He'd gotten it from that crazy bitch Alanna, the one who'd gone snooping in his gym bag when he'd left her in the car for only a few minutes. She was the only one he could think of—other than those who employed him—who had any inkling of what he did.

He needed to know who she might have talked to.

And before she died, Alanna came up with that one name.

The only Constance Tattinger he was able to find any record of was born in Rochester, but her parents moved when she was a little girl after some incident in which a playmate got run over by a car backing out of a driveway. From there they moved to Tennessee, then Oregon, then Texas. The girl had left home when she was sixteen or seventeen, and her parents, speaking to Oscar Fine in the kitchen of their El Paso home, had told him that they'd never heard from her again.

He was pretty sure they were telling him the truth, considering the mother and father were bound to kitchen chairs at the time, and Oscar Fine was holding a knife to the woman's neck. It was too bad they didn't have any useful information for him.

He slit both their throats.

Oscar Fine figured she'd been going by other names since his encounter with her. That made it difficult, but he'd never given up. He was pretty sure she and her accomplice had never tried to unload the fake diamonds. Oscar Fine and the rest of the organization he worked for had put the word out to everyone they knew to be on the lookout for them. That many diamonds—real or not—had a way of attracting attention.

And years had gone by without anyone trying to turn them into cash.

Maybe they knew they were fake, Oscar Fine thought. But even if they figured that out, he guessed they'd still try to unload them to someone who didn't know any better.

Something must have gone wrong. A change in plan. He could imagine any number of scenarios. But he never gave up hope that—someday—they'd try.

When he saw the face of Jan Harwood—all scrubbed up and wholesome—on television, he just knew.

It was *her*.

Constance Tattinger.

And knowing the kind of person she was, what she was capable of, he was betting she was fit as a fiddle. This was a girl who knew how to look out for herself. Oscar Fine was betting she was going to be needing some cash.

That was when Oscar Fine started making some calls.

"I really appreciate this," Oscar Fine said to Banura, sitting in his basement workshop.

"No problem, my friend," Banura said. "Fucker called me Banny Boy."

"That's just rude," Oscar Fine said.

"No shit."

"You're sure this is the stuff I've been looking for?"

"No question."

"And they're expecting how much?"

"Six."

Oscar Fine smiled. "I'll bet he got a hard-on when he heard that."

Banura nodded. "Oh yeah. The girl, though, she looked a bit, I don't know."

"Dubious?"

"Yeah, dubious. I was thinking, maybe I oversold it."

"Not to worry." Oscar Fine looked at his watch. "Almost two."

Banura grinned. "Showtime."

# FORTY-THREE

THE PHONE IN THE kitchen rang. I'd been sitting on the stairs for some time, feeling sorry for myself, not knowing what to do next now that I'd torn the house to pieces and found nothing.

I got up and, stepping carefully around the boards I'd pried up here and there, went into the kitchen.

"Hello," I said. I glanced down at the phone screen, but the caller's name and number were blocked.

"You should rot in hell," a woman said.

"Who's this?"

"We don't like having wife killers in the neighborhood, so you better watch your back."

"Thanks for your support. I'll bet you thought when you made this call your number wouldn't show. Now you'll have to watch *your* back, too."

"What?" Then, a hurried hang-up.

Give her something to think about.

I'd barely hung up the phone when it rang again. Perhaps she'd figured out I was bluffing. But this time, there was a number showing, if not an actual name, so I picked up.

"Mr. Harwood?"

"Speaking," I said.

"This is Annette Kitchner. I'm a producer with *Good Morning Albany*. We'd very much like to have you on our program. You wouldn't have to come to the studio, we'd be more than happy to come to you to talk about your current situation, and give you a chance to tell your side."

"What side would that be?" I asked.

"It would be an opportunity for you to refute allegations that you had a role in your wife's disappearance."

"Unless you know something I don't," I said, "I haven't been charged with anything."

In the back of my mind, I heard Natalie Bondurant saying, *Hang up, you idiot.*

So I hung up.

I took another slow walk through the house, stepping over the ripped-off planks, the dislodged baseboards, the tossed cushions, and wondered what the hell had gotten into me. I'd lost my mind for the better part of an hour.

I heard someone trying the front door, which I had locked behind me when I'd come home. I made my way to it.

"David?" It was my father, shouting through the door.

I turned back the deadbolt and opened the door. His eyes went wide when he saw the damage.

"Jesus, David, what the hell happened here?" he said, stepping in. "Have you called the police?"

"It's okay, Dad," I said.

"Okay? You gotta call the police—"

"I did it, Dad. It was me."

He looked at me, his mouth open. "What the hell's gotten into you?"

I led him back through the debris into the kitchen. "You want a beer or something?" I asked him.

"There's thousands of dollars in damage here," he

said, looking at sugar and flour dumped out on the counter, cereal boxes emptied. "And your insurance isn't going to cover it if you did it yourself. Are you nuts?"

I opened the fridge. It was still pulled out from the wall, but I hadn't unplugged it. "I got a can of Coors in here. You want that?"

Dad shook his head, looked at me, and extended his hand. "Yeah, sure." He took the can, popped the top, and took a swig. "Beer kind of upsets my system a bit more than it used to, if you get my drift, but maybe half a can."

I found one more can tucked in behind a carton of orange juice and opened it. After I took a long drink, I looked at my father and said, "So, I've been thinking of doing a few things around the house. You up to helping me with that?"

Dad was still too stunned to appreciate the joke. Maybe that was because it really wasn't much of one.

"Why did you do this?" he asked.

"I thought Jan might have hidden something else in the house. She hid that birth certificate and a key in an envelope behind a baseboard upstairs. I thought maybe she'd done that someplace else."

"Jesus H. Christ," Dad said. "What exactly did you think you were going to find?"

"I don't know," I said. "I have no idea."

The phone rang again. I glanced at it, didn't recognize the number calling. After two rings, Dad said, "You going to get that?" When I didn't say something immediately, he added, "What if it's your wife?"

I picked up. I wasn't expecting it to be Jan. I was guessing more abuse.

"Hello."

A voice I recognized. "Mr. Sebastian would like to speak with you." It was Welland.

I sighed. "Sure."

"Not on the phone. Out front."

I replaced the receiver, ignored Dad's quizzical look, and went out the front door and down the steps to the limo I was now becoming far more familiar with than I wanted to be. Instead of following me outside, Dad went upstairs, no doubt curious about just how much damage he was going to feel obliged to help me fix.

As I approached the curb, Welland, looking thuggish as ever, his eyes hidden behind a pair of Serengetis, came around the front of the car to greet me. The limo windows were so heavily tinted I couldn't even see Elmont Sebastian's silhouette inside.

Welland reached for the rear door handle to open it for me.

"I'm not getting inside and I'm not going anywhere," I said. "If he wants to talk to me, he can put his window down."

Welland, evidently prepared to accept that, rapped the window lightly with his knuckle, and a second later it powered down. Sebastian leaned forward slightly in his seat so he could see me.

"Good day, David."

"What do you want?"

"The same thing I wanted the last time we spoke. I want to know who was going to meet with you. I was hoping you'd made some progress in this regard."

"I told you. I don't know."

"You need to find out," Sebastian said calmly. "That woman, whoever she is, is a threat to my organization. It makes it difficult to move forward with things knowing that someone is prepared to pass on proprietary information."

"My plate is full," I said. "But I do have an idea for you."

Sebastian's eyebrows went up a notch.

"You could go fuck yourself."

Sebastian nodded solemnly, said no more, and put the window back up. Once it had sealed him off from the rest of the world, Welland looked at me.

"He's not going to ask you again," he said.

"Good," I said.

"No," Welland said. "Not good. It means that Mr. Sebastian is prepared to *escalate*."

He got back behind the wheel of the limo and took off quietly down the street. I watched the car go until it made the turn at the end, then slowly walked back to the house.

As I went in I could hear Dad mucking about upstairs.

"Dad!" I called.

"Yeah?"

"What are you doing?"

"Starting to figure out how we're going to get this all fixed up. Goddamn, you really went to town."

I found him in the upstairs hallway, on his hands and knees, straddling an open stretch in the floor where I'd ripped up a board.

"You can't let Ethan come back here to this," Dad said. "There's a hundred places he could catch his foot and get hurt real bad. There's nails sticking up all over the place. Damn it, David, I know you're going through a lot right now, but there's some really nice hardwood here you've gone and ruined."

I didn't care about that, but I did feel badly that I had made the house dangerous for my son.

"It was a stupid thing to do," I conceded.

Dad was collecting boards and putting them to one side. "I should be able to figure out, through trial and error, which boards go where. But some places, you're going to have to spring for some new wood. And it's going to take a few days. I can go home and get my tools."

"You don't have to do that right now," I said.

Dad turned and yelled, "What the hell else am I supposed to do? Tell me that! What the hell else!"

I leaned up against a wall, feeling defeated.

"Honest to God, what a fucking stupid thing to do," he said, padding farther up the hall, watching for nails as he approached the linen closet.

"That was where I started," I said. "That was where I found the envelope, in there."

"But you didn't find anything else," he grumbled.

He reached for a piece of white baseboard I'd pried away from inside the linen closet, turned it over to look for nails, and said, "Hello."

"What?" I said.

"What's this?"

I moved closer. It was an envelope, similar to the one I'd found before, taped to the back side of the baseboarding. When I'd ripped the boards off, I'd been looking for what might be left behind them, not what might be taped to the back of them.

Dad peeled the tape away. It was yellowed and brittle. When he had the envelope free, he handed it to me. It was sealed. I ripped open the end, blew into it, and pulled out the single piece of paper that had been placed inside. It was folded in thirds.

I unfolded it.

It was another birth certificate, for a child named Constance Tattinger.

"What is it?" Dad asked.

"A birth certificate," I said.

"Whose?"

Slowly, I said, "I'm not sure." I knew I'd heard that name. At least the first name, Constance. Recently, within the last couple of days.

"Well, whose name is on it?" Dad asked.

"Dad," I said, holding up my hand to tell him to keep quiet. "Please."

I tried to think.

The name had come up at the Richlers'. Constance was the name of Jan's playmate. The little girl who had been playing with her in the yard when Horace Richler backed his car too quickly out of the driveway.

The little girl who had pushed Jan Richler into the path of the car.

I looked back at the birth certificate, checking for a date of birth for Constance Tattinger.

April 15, 1975. Just a few months before the date of birth on the Jan Richler birth certificate.

I scanned the rest of the document. Constance Tattinger had been born in Rochester. Her parents' names were Martin and Thelma.

"Jesus," I said.

"What?" Dad said.

"It all fits."

"What are you talking about?"

"If you were the grown-up Constance Tattinger, and you needed a new identity, and you were looking for someone who'd died as a child, you could save yourself a lot of time by picking one you already knew about."

"Constance who?"

"Not just someone you knew," I said. "But someone whose death you had a hand in."

"I don't know what the hell you're talking about," Dad said.

I needed to confirm this. I went to the phone, got the number again for the Richlers in Rochester, and dialed.

"Hello?" Gretchen Richler.

"Mrs. Richler," I said. "It's David Harwood."

"Oh, yes."

"I'm sorry to bother you, but I have a question."

"Okay." Tiredly.

"You mentioned the first name, I think, of the little girl who was playing in your yard when . . . the accident happened."

"Constance," she said. Gretchen made the name sound like ice.

"What was her family's name?"

"Tattinger," she said without hesitation.

"Do you know what happened to her family? Didn't you say they moved away?"

"That's right. Not long after."

"Do you know where they moved to?"

"I have no idea," she said.

"Do you know anyone in the Rochester area who might know?"

"I have no idea. I really don't." She paused. "Why are you asking?"

I didn't want to reveal to Gretchen Richler things I didn't know for certain. So I fudged. "I'm just looking into every angle I can think of, Mrs. Richler, that's all."

"I see." Another pause. "Have you found your wife, Mr. Harwood?"

"Not yet," I said.

"You sound hopeful."

It was my turn to pause. Finally, I said, "Yes."

"You think she's alive."

"I do. But I don't yet understand all the circumstances behind why she disappeared."

"I see," she said.

"Thank you, Mrs. Richler. I appreciate this. I'm sorry to have disturbed you. Please pass on my regards to your husband."

"Perhaps I'll be able to do that when he gets home from the hospital," Gretchen Richler said coldly.

"I'm sorry? Something's happened to your husband?"

"He tried to kill himself this morning, Mr. Harwood. I think your visit, and your news, were all a bit too much for him."

# FORTY-FOUR

"I'M NOT GOING IN," Jan said. "I'm not going down into that basement."

They were sitting in the pickup, parked in the driveway up close to Banura's nondescript Braintree house. A couple of houses down, a black Audi was parked at the curb.

"Look," said Dwayne. "Is it because I lost my cool back there? Is that it?"

*Lost your cool? You nearly killed me,* Jan thought.

"If that's what this is about, I'm sorry," he said, laying it on so thick she could tell he wasn't. "We're minutes away from becoming millionaires, you know? You gotta keep your eye on the prize."

"I'll keep a watch out here," she said. "If there's a problem, I'll lay on the horn." Dwayne eyed her suspiciously, prompting Jan to add, "What? You've got the goods, you're going in to get the money. What am I going to do? Drive off?"

That mollified him. "Okay, I guess not." He appeared thoughtful.

The thing was, she'd been thinking about it. She didn't give a shit about what might happen to Dwayne, but she needed to know how this was going to play out. If there was still a chance, even one in a million, that she was wrong, that there might be some money in this for her, she was hanging in.

"What if Banny Boy decides to give the stones another inspection?" Dwayne asked. "What if they don't pass the inspection this time?"

"So, what, now you believe me?" Jan said. "You believe what that woman said?"

Dwayne suddenly looked trapped, less sure of himself. "I don't know." He shook his head, as if to cast off any doubts. "No, this is good. Everything's fine. He looked at the diamonds, he liked them, he offered us money for them. That's good enough for me. If you want to sit out here and be a big pussy, that's fine."

"Good," Jan said. "Because this is exactly where I'm staying."

Dwayne glanced at his watch. It was five minutes to two. "This shouldn't take long, unless he wants me to count the money. How long do you think it would take to count six million?"

"A long time."

"I don't want him cheating me."

"If he's got a bag of money for you, take it. We'll go somewhere and count it, and if he shortchanged us, we'll come back and pay him a visit." Not that she believed that for a second. If they got away from this house with anything reasonable, she wasn't coming back. She didn't ever want to see those photos on the wall again. The picture of that kid, probably Banura, waving a severed arm about. Made her think maybe she had more in common with him than she wanted to admit.

"Yeah, okay." Dwayne grabbed the bag of diamonds, opened the truck door, the key chiming in the ignition, and started getting out.

"Wait," Jan said. "Take the gun."

Dwayne looked at her scornfully. "You heard what the man said. He said not to bring any weapons into his house. He was pretty clear about that."

Jan leaned across the front seat and reached under it.

She pulled out the gun. "Seriously, you should take it."
It wasn't Dwayne she was worried about. But if things
went south in that basement, it was best that Dwayne
took care of them before someone came charging out
looking for her. And she'd rarely handled guns. At least
Dwayne knew how to point and shoot.

Dwayne said, "You need to lighten up." He put both
feet on the ground, slammed the door shut, and said
through the open window, "Think about where we're
going to go to celebrate. I am going to get fucking
wasted."

As Dwayne walked down the left side of the house,
Jan shifted over behind the wheel and kept the gun on
the seat next to her.

"So let me ask you this," Banura said to Oscar Fine. "I
know you don't give a flying fuck about the diamonds,
since they're worth shit, so I'm guessing, if you don't
mind my saying, that this has something to do with
that."

Banura pointed to the end of Oscar Fine's left arm.

"Yes," he said. "That's right."

"So these two, these are the people who did this to
you."

"One of them," he said. "The woman. You described
her perfectly."

Banura nodded. "That must have hurt like a son of a
bitch."

Oscar Fine nodded. He didn't like to talk about it all
that much.

"I seen a lot of that kind of thing, where I come from.
It's a little more common there than it is here."

"I can imagine. I've seen your photos."

Banura nodded. "I was eleven."

"To do something like that, at eleven, it must stay
with you," Oscar Fine said.

Banura appeared thoughtful. "Yes." It was difficult to discuss such things with a man who had had his hand chopped off.

There was a loud rapping on the door above them. Oscar Fine took a position around the corner from the bottom of the stairs while Banura went up to answer it. Oscar Fine took his gun from inside his jacket and held it firmly in his right hand.

Oscar Fine listened as Banura moved the bar out of position and opened the door.

"Hey," Banura said.

"How's it going," said Dwayne.

"Raise your arms, please." Dwayne did as he was told, allowing Banura to pat him down.

"You can trust me," Dwayne said. "You said not to carry, I don't carry."

"Where is your friend?" Banura asked.

"She's just waiting for me in the truck," he said. "I didn't come too soon or nothin', did I? You got the money?"

"Everything is all set to go," Banura said, closing the door and putting the bar back in position. "You brought the same number of diamonds back, I hope?"

"Fuck yeah." Dwayne laughed. "That'd be a pretty dickish thing to do, get a generous offer from you and then come back with half the goods."

Banura chuckled along with him as they came down the stairs. As Dwayne entered the room, he glanced right, saw Oscar Fine standing there, left arm tucked into his pocket, right arm extended, pointing the gun directly at his head.

"Hey, whoa, the fuck is this?" Dwayne said. To Banura, he said, "Okay, you said you might have a whatchamacallit, an associate, here, that's cool, but you got no call to threaten me."

"Do you remember me?" Oscar Fine asked.

"Huh? You his banker or bodyguard or what? I'm not looking for any trouble. I'm just here to pick up what's owed me."

Banura stood at the bottom of the stairs, blocking Dwayne's way should he decide to bolt.

"I asked, do you remember me?" Oscar Fine said.

"I got no idea who the fuck you are," Dwayne said.

The man with the gun took his left arm out of his pocket. Dwayne looked down, maybe expecting to see another weapon, then noticed the missing hand.

He paled instantly. A moment later, the crotch of his jeans darkened.

"Aw, shit, don't piss on my floor, man," said Banura, although he had to know that a puddle of urine on his basement floor was going to be the least of his worries in a few minutes.

"I take that to mean that you do remember me," Oscar Fine said, pointing the gun below Dwayne's waist.

"Yes," Dwayne said.

"Tell me your name."

"Dwayne. Dwayne Osterhaus."

"Well, Dwayne Osterhaus, it's very nice to meet up with you at last. Although we didn't have a real face-to-face, I believe you were the driver."

"You shoulda had a combination or something," Dwayne said. "Then, you know, things would have been different. Wouldn't have had to, you know, with the hand."

"It was difficult to communicate a combination to you once you'd shot me with the dart," he said.

"I'm really sorry, man, honest to God," Dwayne said. "And I know you kind of passed out and everything, but you understand, I wasn't the one who actually did it, you know that, right?"

"I remember who did it," Oscar Fine said. "Where is she?"

Dwayne hesitated.

Oscar Fine said, "Please, Dwayne, you must see where this is going. It's in your interest to be cooperative. Here, let me show you something." He held up his left arm. The shirt cuff was tucked around the stump, and Oscar Fine slipped it up his arm with the index finger looped through the trigger of his gun.

"No, that's okay," Dwayne said.

"Not at all, my pleasure," Oscar Fine said. He pulled away the fabric and displayed the ragged, but healed, end of his arm.

"Jesus," Dwayne said.

"He can't help you," Oscar Fine said. Satisfied that Dwayne had had a good look, he tucked his shirtsleeve back around the wound. He asked, "Are you left- or right-handed?"

The spot on Dwayne's pants broadened. Oscar Fine repeated the question.

Dwayne swallowed. "Right."

"Then I shall take your left. No sense making this any more difficult than it needs to be. And I trust Banura here has something that will allow me to make a cleaner cut than the one I was left with."

Sweat droplets were forming on Dwayne's forehead. "You don't need to do anything like that. If you let me go, I'll tell you anything you want to know."

"Where is she?"

"She's in the truck."

"Why didn't she come in with you?"

"She's nervous," Dwayne said.

"And why would that be?"

"She thinks Mr. Banura here was offering us too much money. She got suspicious. So she took some of the diamonds to someone else to look at, and they said they're worthless."

Oscar Fine nodded. "But yet you're here."

Dwayne appeared on the verge of tears. "I took Mr. Banura here at his word."

"So it's 'Mister' now," Banura said. "No more 'Banny Boy.'"

"Hey," Dwayne said, smiling nervously. "No disrespect."

"So she thought something was wrong," Oscar Fine said. "Does she suspect I'm here?"

"She never said that. She's just spooked, is all." Dwayne brightened, wiped the tears from his eyes. "I got an idea. You don't take my hand off, you let me walk away from this, and I'll go out to the truck, and I'll tell her there's a problem, that some of the money, it's in some weird currency, like euros or Canadian, and she needs to help me count it, and I'll get her in here, and then you can let me go. Because, swear to God, I never wanted her to cut your hand off. I was all, hey, let's go someplace, get some stronger tools. What we brought wasn't good enough, to cut through the chain? You know what I'm saying? I'd drive the limo somewhere where we could take some time, do it right, so you wouldn't get hurt. But she got all kind of caught up in the moment and went crazy, but you need to know, I was totally opposed to that shit."

Oscar Fine nodded, as though considering the proposal.

"So you bring her to me, and then I let you go."

Dwayne nodded furiously, offered up a nervous smile. "Yeah, that's right. That's the deal. I wanna help you out here."

"I have some questions," Oscar Fine said.

"Oh yeah, sure, no problem."

In fact, Oscar Fine had quite a few. About where the

two of them had been the last six years. About who Constance Tattinger had become. Where she'd been living, and with whom. Dwayne tried to be as obliging as possible. He told Oscar Fine everything he knew.

"You've been very helpful," Oscar Fine said.

"Yeah, well, you know, it's the least I can do, considering." Dwayne attempted another smile. "So, whaddya say, I bring her in here, and you let me go?"

"I don't think so," Oscar Fine said, and shot Dwayne Osterhaus in the center of his face. "There's no reason I can't go out and talk to her myself."

# FORTY-FIVE

OSCAR FINE OFFERED HIS apologies to Banura. "I have made a mess, and I accept full responsibility for that."

Banura was looking at the blood and brain matter on the wall behind where Dwayne had been standing. The bullet had gone through his head and out the back.

"I seen worse," Banura said.

Oscar Fine wrote a number on a piece of paper on Banura's worktable. "Call that number, tell them Mr. Fine told you they'd handle things. They'll come and take care of all this. Cleanup as well as removal."

"Appreciate it," Banura said.

"But you might as well wait a few minutes until I have the other one," he said, and Banura nodded.

"Do you have any other way out of here?" Oscar Fine asked. "Someone could be watching this door."

"No," he said. "This is all walled off from the rest of the house, only access is from the back door. You can't even get to the furnace from here. There's another set of stairs down in the regular part of the house. But there are cameras."

"Show me."

Banura led Oscar Fine over to the worktable, where in addition to his jeweler's tools there was a keyboard and an ultra-thin flat-screen monitor. Banura tapped a couple of keys, and suddenly the screen was divided into equal quadrants, each one offering a different view of Banura's property.

"There's a wide-angle camera on each side of the house," he said.

Oscar Fine leaned in, looking at the upper right corner, which was a view of the street out front of the house, with the driveway off to the far right. He could see the pickup, but given the angle and the way the light was reflecting off the windshield, it was difficult to make out who, if anyone, was inside. There was no one on the passenger side, and too much glare to determine whether anyone was behind the wheel.

"Hmmm," he said.

The camera mounted at the back door showed no one in the yard, which appeared to be empty by design. No storage shed to hide behind, no trees with broad trunks. Just a flat yard of dead grass bordered by a six-foot plank fence.

Banura pointed to the lower left quadrant.

"You see that?"

Oscar Fine had missed it. "What?"

"There was—look."

In the upper right image, the pickup truck was starting to back up.

The moment after Dwayne disappeared around the corner of the house, Jan thought, *I'm outta here.*

She was working out possible scenarios in her head for what was going on:

*Banura was a moron and didn't know the first thing about diamonds.* Unlikely.

*The woman in the jewelry store was a moron and didn't know the first thing about diamonds.* Ditto.

*Banura knew they were fake, didn't like being conned, and was going to teach them a lesson when they returned.* Possible, but why wait until 2 p.m.? Why not teach them a lesson earlier?

*Banura needed time to set something up.* That seemed likely. But Jan didn't think it had anything to do with getting the money together.

Could he have been in touch with Oscar Fine? After all these years, could that man still be putting the word out, reminding those in the business to be on the look-out for a large quantity of fake diamonds? And a particular woman who matched her description?

*Get out of here,* she told herself.

She had her hand on the key, got ready to turn it. All she had to do was start the engine, put the truck in reverse, get on the interstate, put as much distance as possible between herself and the greater Boston area.

And go where?

All these years, she'd had a plan. Get out of Promise Falls, head to Paradise. But she needed the cash from those diamonds to buy her ticket.

*Worthless.*

She waited all that time to get what she wanted, never stopping to think for a moment she might already have something.

That phony life was a real life.

A real house.

A real husband.

*A real son.*

All traded away for this. A long shot. A chance to have enough money to live the rest of her life on her own terms, playing only herself. All so she could head to that mythical beach. She'd never even figured out where it was. Tahiti? Thailand? Jamaica?

Did it matter?

And when she got there, she could dream of telling her mother and, especially, her father, *Fuck you. I'm here, living the life, and you're not.*

The beach seemed far away now.

She was sitting in a pickup truck outside Boston, waiting for some clueless ex-con to show up with six million dollars, wondering whether her entire world was about to go to shit.

She took her fingers off the keys and reached into her purse. Tucked into a side pocket was a photo, creased and tattered. She took it out, held it carefully, the photo as light and fragile as a fallen autumn leaf. She looked into the face of her young son.

"I'm sorry," she whispered. She set the photo on the seat next to her.

She sat there another moment, her hand on the keys, ready to bail. But there was part of her that still wondered: *What if.*

What if, by some fluke, Dwayne had called it right?

Everything told her he had it wrong. But what if he walked out with the money and she wasn't there?

She needed a sense of how things were going.

Jan left the keys in the ignition and got out of the truck, first grabbing the gun she'd been unable to persuade Dwayne to take. She walked down the side of the house, rounded the corner, and went up to the door.

Didn't knock. Just looked at it. Wanted it to open. Didn't want it to open.

Very faint noises, muffled by the heavy door, came from inside. The hint of a voice, high-pitched, whiny. The kind of noise she could imagine Dwayne making.

She caught a few phrases.

". . . swear to God, I never . . . I was all, hey, let's . . . get some stronger tools . . . know what I'm saying? I'd drive the limo. . . ."

Jan didn't need to hear any more. She'd been sold out. They'd be coming for her next. Any second now that door would be opening.

Should she wait, shoot whoever came out? No, not

good, just standing there. It was just as likely she'd be the one to end up taking a bullet. She moved off the door, pressed herself up against the house, and in doing so happened to look up and saw the tiny camera mounted below the eaves.

She'd spent so much time at Five Mountains, scoping out where all the closed-circuit TV cameras were, she thought she might have noticed that one sooner. If there was one there, there was probably one on each side of the house.

They might already know she was out there, waiting by the door.

She had to run.

She bolted, rounded the corner of the house, grabbed the handle on the driver's door with her left hand, the gun still in her right. She jumped in, dropped the gun onto the seat, and turned the ignition.

The engine didn't catch the first time.

As she turned the key a second time, she noticed a figure coming out from behind the house. A man in a long jacket, wielding a gun in his right hand. It was pointed in her direction.

The engine caught and she threw the column shifter into reverse and had her foot on the gas even before she'd turned to make sure no one was there. She threw her right arm over the seat, turned around, bounced from the driveway to the street, and cranked the wheel.

The windshield shattered.

For a millisecond she looked back in the direction of the shot, saw the man with the gun.

Saw the left arm with no hand at the end.

A blue Chevy coming down the street laid on the horn as the back end of the pickup lurched into its path. The car swerved, a man shouted "Asshole!" and the car kept on moving.

As Jan slammed on the brake and put the truck into

drive, Oscar Fine fired again. The shot didn't hit the truck, but Jan had the sense it went in through the passenger window and out the driver's door.

Oscar was running into the street now, his face set in grim determination. Jan cranked the wheel hard again and stomped on the accelerator, narrowly missing him with the truck's right front fender. He pivoted so hard he went down to the pavement, even though he hadn't been hit.

The gun was still on the seat next to her, but there was no time to use it. And what kind of shot could she get off anyway, driving flat out, Oscar Fine directly behind her?

She raced past the black Audi, guessing that was his car. But he was still a good fifty feet away from it. By the time he reached it, got in, fired it up, she could be a block or two away.

It might be just enough of a head start.

She heard a sharp ping, above and behind her head. Sounded like a bullet had gone into the cab, above the back window.

It just made her drive faster. She glanced into her mirror, saw the man running for the black car. It was the last image she had of him before she hung a hard right and kept on going.

She never noticed that, in all the excitement, the wind had swept up her picture of Ethan and carried it out the window.

Oscar Fine was about to take chase when he saw the piece of paper fluttering through the air.

He was almost glad for an excuse not to get in the car and go after Jan Harwood. Chases invariably ended badly. A crash. Attracting the attention of the police. And with only one hand, it was difficult for Oscar Fine to perform quick steering maneuvers.

If he could find her once, he could find her again. Especially with everything Dwayne had told him. He let the car door close and walked up the street to pick up the piece of paper. It appeared to be nothing more than a simple white square, but after he bent over, picked it up, and flipped it over, he saw that it was a photograph.

A picture of a small, smiling boy. Oscar Fine slid it into his pocket.

That was when it occurred to him that if he was going to have to go out of town, he was going to have to call someone to feed his cat.

# FORTY-SIX

NOT LONG AFTER MY talk with Gretchen Richler, there was an unexpected call.

I grabbed the phone before the first ring was finished. "Hello?"

"Mr. Harwood?" A woman's voice. Something about it was familiar.

"Yes?"

"You're not the person to do this story anymore."

"What? Who is this?"

"I sent you the information about Mr. Reeves's hotel bill. So you could write about it. Why didn't you do a story?"

I took a second to focus. "He paid Elmont Sebastian back," I said. "My editor felt that killed it."

"Well, then give that list to someone else, someone who can get the story done. I called the paper and they told me you were off or suspended because your wife is missing. I don't want anyone who might have killed his wife working on this story, no offense."

"List? What are you talking about? A list?"

She sighed at the other end of the line. "The one I mailed to you."

I patted my jacket side pocket, felt the envelopes I'd stuffed in there when I'd passed my mailbox on the way out of the *Standard*. I dug them out. One of them was from payroll, another was a useless news release from a soap company, and the third was a plain white envelope addressed to me, in block printing, with no return address. I tore it open, took out the single sheet of paper and unfolded it.

"Mr. Harwood?"

"Hang on," I said, scanning the sheet. It was a handwritten list of names of people on Promise Falls council, with dollar amounts written next to them. They ranged from zero up to $25,000.

"Jesus," I said. "Is this for real? Is this what Elmont Sebastian's been paying these people?"

"You're just looking at this now?" the woman said. "That's what I mean. That's why someone else should be looking into this. That son of a bitch Elmont has screwed me over one time too many, and I want to see him nailed. You want to do a story, ask women at Star Spangled Corrections how they like getting felt up every day by the male employees and no one at the top giving a damn."

So she did work for Elmont. And the hell of it was, considering my current situation, she was right. Someone else should be doing this story.

I asked, "Why didn't you show up at Lake George?"

"What?" she said. "What are you talking about?"

"The email you sent me. To meet you up there."

"I don't know what you're talking about," she said. "I'm not meeting you or anyone else face-to-face. You think I'm stupid?"

She hung up.

I sat there a moment, slid the paper back into the envelope and stuffed it back into my pocket. Any other time, this would have made my day, but getting a great story wasn't exactly a priority at the moment.

But one thing my anonymous caller had said stuck with me. She had not emailed me to meet her in Lake George. Someone else had lured me up there. It was all part of the setup. It fit in perfectly with Natalie Bondurant's theory.

*Jan.*

I spent pretty much all of the rest of that day trying to find out everything I could about Constance Tattinger. I didn't have a lot to work with. There must have been a Tattinger family living in Rochester in the 1970s and 1980s, but after that, according to Gretchen Richler, they had moved away.

I explained to Dad that I had some work to do, and he said he did as well. He was going to get started on repairing all the damage I'd done in the house.

He phoned my mother and explained, quietly, what had happened, and that he was going to stay there for the rest of the day, if that was okay with her. It would mean she'd have to look after Ethan without any assistance.

Mom said that was fine. She asked to speak to me.

"Tell me how you are," she said.

"I'm losing my mind, but otherwise, okay," I said.

"Your father says you've ripped your house apart."

"Yeah. And I felt pretty stupid about it, until Dad found something I missed. I think I have a lead on Jan."

"You know where she is?"

"No, but I think I know *who* she is. I could really use a computer. I need to search for people named Tattinger."

"Your father says he's coming home for more tools. I'll send him back with my laptop."

I thanked her for that, and said, "Something bad happened, something I feel responsible for."

Mom waited.

"Horace Richler—he tried to kill himself. I stirred things up. And finding out that someone was out there—my wife—using his daughter's name, it was too much for him."

"You're doing what you have to do," Mom said. "It's not your fault, what happened to that man's daughter. Whatever it is that Jan may or may not have done, that's not your fault, either. You need to find out the truth, and that may be difficult for some people."

"I know. But they're good people, the Richlers."

"Do what you have to do," Mom said.

I told Dad to make sure he came back with Mom's laptop. He was already making a list of things he needed and added "laptop" to the bottom.

"Be back in a jiff," he said.

I called Samantha Henry at the *Standard*. "Can you do me a favor?" I asked her.

"Shoot," she said.

"I need you to check with the cops, whoever else you can, see what you can get on the name Constance Tattinger."

"Spell it."

I did.

"And who's this Constance Tattinger?"

"I'd rather not say," I said.

"Oh, okay," she said. "So you're on suspension, the cops think you may have killed your wife, and we're actually writing *stories* about you, one of our own employees, and you want me to start trying to dig up info for you without telling me why."

"Yeah, that's about right," I said.

"Okay," said Sam. "Can you give me any more than a name? D.O.B.?"

"April 15, 1975."

"Got it. Anything else?"

"Not really. Born in Rochester. I think her parents left there when she was just a kid."

"I'll call you if I get anything."

"Thanks, Sam. I owe you."

"No shit," she said. "If we had any journalistic ethics around here, I might be troubled by this."

"One more thing," I said. "The story about Sebastian and Reeves I've been working on?"

"Yeah?"

"It's yours. I've got something that'll finally break this story wide open. A list of payouts to various councilors."

"*What?*"

"I can't sit on this. I don't know when I'm coming back. This story needs to be told ASAP. You should do it. I'll hang on to this list, give it to you next time I see you, see if you can find a way to confirm the numbers."

"Where'd you get this list?"

"I can fill you in later, okay? I've got to go."

"Sure," Sam said. "I really appreciate this. I'll nail this thing for you."

"Right on," I said and hung up.

Dad was back within the hour. He dragged in his toolbox, a table saw, some scraps of baseboarding he must have been keeping in his garage since God invented trees, and went upstairs. It wasn't long before I heard him banging around.

I took Mom's laptop, got it up and running, and started with the online phone directories. There weren't all that many people with that name in the U.S.—about three dozen—and only five listings for an "M. Tattinger." They were in Buffalo, Boise, Catalina, Pittsburgh, and Tampa.

I started dialing.

People answered at the Buffalo and Boise numbers. Not necessarily the actual people who had the phone listing, but the Buffalo Tattinger was a Mark, and the Boise Tattinger was a Miles.

I was looking for a Martin.

In both cases, I asked if they knew of a Martin Tattinger who, with a woman named Thelma, had a daughter named Constance.

No, and no.

No one answered at the Catalina and Pittsburgh numbers, and the Tampa listing had been disconnected.

I figured I might be able to raise someone later in the day at the other numbers, once people were home from work. In the meantime, I tried to figure out what school Jan Richler and Constance Tattinger might have attended—they must not have gotten any further than kindergarten or first grade together. I studied a Google map of where the Richlers lived, found the names of nearby elementary schools and scribbled down their numbers.

As I began dialing, I realized it was August. The schools would be empty for a few more weeks. But I also knew, from friends who were teachers, that staff were often there in the month leading up to that first day, preparing.

At the first school, I reached a vice principal, but her school, she explained, didn't even exist in the 1980s. It had been built in the mid-'90s.

While I waited for someone to pick up at the next school, I tried to replay in my head the conversation I'd had with the Richlers when I was in their house. Gretchen had been talking about how devastated everyone had been by their daughter's death, including her kindergarten teacher.

She'd mentioned a name. Stevenson? Something like that.

An older woman picked up. "Diane Johnson, secretary's office."

I told her, first, that I was relieved to find someone at the school, then launched into my story about looking for information about a Constance Tattinger who had attended the school—briefly—back in 1980.

"Who's calling?" she asked.

I was reluctant to say, considering that even CNN had carried an item on Jan's disappearance, and my face and name had been plastered across the tube. But my name and number were very likely displayed on Diane Johnson's phone.

"David Harwood," I said. "I didn't go to school in the Rochester area, but I'm trying to track down Constance, or her parents, because of a family emergency." I put a special emphasis on the last two words, hoping they sounded grave enough that Diane Johnson would help me and not ask a lot of questions.

She said, "Well, that was the year before I started here, so I can't honestly say I remember the name."

"I think she only attended kindergarten there," I said. "Her parents took her out of school and moved away. She was friends with a girl named Jan Richler."

"Oh now, hang on," said Diane Johnson. "That name I know. We have a plaque dedicated to her memory in the hall right outside the office. She was the child who got run over by a car."

"That's right."

"It was her father driving. I think he was backing out of the driveway."

"Yes, you've got it."

"What a terrible thing. Even though I wasn't here yet, I remember a bit about that. There was talk that she got pushed into the car's path."

"Yes," I said. "That's the girl I'm calling about. Constance Tattinger."

"Oh my, that was so long ago."

"As you can guess, it can be hard to find someone when you lose track of someone that far back."

"I don't really know how I can help you."

"Would you have any school records? That might have any information about Constance? Where she might have moved to?"

A bell rang in the background for several seconds. When it finished, Diane Johnson said, "They're just trying them out today." Then, "We don't have records that old here. They might be with the central office, but I'm not sure they'd release them to you."

"Oh," I said.

"Do you remember her teacher's name?"

I struggled. "I want to say Stevenson."

"Oh. Could it have been Stephens? With a P-H?"

"That's possible."

"Tina Stephens was the kindergarten teacher here when I arrived. She was here for a couple of years and then transferred to another school."

"Do you have the name of that school?"

"I don't remember offhand, but there's a good chance she's taught in half a dozen places since then. Teachers move around a lot."

"Maybe if I called your central office."

"I can tell you this. She got married. Let me think . . . she met the nicest man. He worked for Kodak, I think. But then, who hasn't at some time or other?"

"Do you remember his name?"

"Hang on a minute, there's someone else in the office here who might know." I heard her put down the receiver. I clung to the phone, kept it pressed to my ear, while Dad hammered and sawed upstairs.

Diane Johnson got back on and said, "Pirelli." She spelled it for me. "Like the tires? I never heard of tires called that. The only kind of tires I've ever heard of are Goodyear, but that's what they said it's like. Frank Pirelli."

I wrote it down. "Thank you," I said. "You've been very helpful."

I quickly found a listing for an "F. Pirelli" in Rochester and dialed. The phone rang three times before it went to message: "Hi. You've reached the voicemail of Frank and Tina Pirelli. We can't come to the phone right now, but please leave a message."

I didn't leave one. I was starting to feel like I was spinning my wheels.

The day dragged on.

At one point, Dad said he needed something to eat, so he went out and bought us a couple of submarine sandwiches stuffed with meatballs and provolone. We took a break and ate them sitting at the kitchen table.

I said, "Thanks."

"No big deal," Dad said. "Just a couple of sandwiches."

"I'm not talking about the sandwiches."

Dad looked embarrassed and opened the fridge to see whether there was any more beer.

Late afternoon, not long after I'd tried the Catalina listing a second time with no luck, the phone rang. Mom said, "Ethan wants to talk to you." Some receiver fumbling, then, "Dad?"

"Hey, sport, how's it going?"

"I wanna come home."

"Soon," I said.

"Nana says I have to stay here all day."

"That's right."

"I've been here for days and days."

"Ethan, it's only been a couple."

"When's Mommy coming home?"

"I don't know," I said. "Are you being a good boy for Nana?"

A hesitation. "Yes."

"What did you do?"

"She yelled at me about jumping on the stairs."

"Is that all?"

"Yes. Now I'm playing with the bat."

"Bat?"

"The okay bat."

I smiled. "Are you playing *croquet* with Nana?"

"No. She says it makes her back hurt to hit the ball."

"So how do you play by yourself?"

"I hit the wood ball through the wires. I can make it go really far."

"Okay," I said. "Is Nana making anything for dinner?"

"I think so. I smell something. Nana! What's for dinner?" I heard Mom talking. Then Ethan said, "Pot roast." He whispered, "It's got carrots in it."

"Try to eat just one carrot. It's good for you. Do it for Nana."

"Okay."

"What time's Nana serving dinner?"

Ethan shouted out another question. "Seven," he said.

"Okay, I'll see you then, okay?"

"Okay."

"I love you," I said.

"I love you, too," he said.

"Okay. Bye, sport."

"Bye, Dad."

And he hung up.


I tried the Rochester Pirelli number again.

"Hello?" A woman.

"Hi," I said. "I'm trying to find Tina Pirelli."

"Speaking."

I tried to hide the excitement in my voice. "Would this be the Tina Pirelli who once taught kindergarten in Rochester?"

"That's right." A suspicious tone in her voice. "Who's calling?"

"My name is David Harwood. I'm trying to find someone who I think was a student of yours, very briefly, back then."

"David who?"

"Harwood. I'm calling from Promise Falls."

"How did you get my number?"

I told her, briefly, about the steps I'd taken to find her.

"And who are you trying to find?" she asked.

"Constance Tattinger."

There was silence at the other end of the line for a moment. "I remember her," Tina Pirelli said quietly. "Why are you trying to find her?"

I'd thought about whether to make up a story, but decided it was better to play it straight. "She grew up to become my wife," I said. "And she's missing."

I could hear Tina draw in her breath. "And you think I'd know where she is? I haven't seen her in probably thirty years, when she was just a little girl."

"I understand," I said. "But when her parents moved away from Rochester, did they say where they were moving to?" Having had no luck so far tracking down a Martin Tattinger in the United States, I wondered whether they could have moved to Canada or overseas.

"Considering the circumstances," Tina Pirelli said, "they didn't really have much to say to anyone. They just moved away."

"The circumstances being . . . the accident?"

"So your wife has told you about that," she said.

"Yes," I lied.

"Poor Constance, everyone blamed her. Even though she was just a child. Her parents pulled her out of school and eventually moved away. I don't have any idea where. I'm sorry. You say she's missing?"

"She just disappeared," I said.

"That must be terrible for you," she said.

"It is."

"I only had Constance for a couple of weeks. The accident was in September. But she was a good girl. Quiet. And I saw her only once after the accident."

"How was she then?" I asked.

Tina Pirelli took so long to answer, I thought the connection had been broken. "It was like," she said, "she'd stopped feeling."

I called the Pittsburgh listing for M. Tattinger.

"Hello?" A man. Sounded like he could be in his sixties or older.

"Is this Martin Tattinger?" I asked.

When the man didn't respond right away, I asked again.

"No," the man said. "This is Mick Tattinger."

"Is there a Martin Tattinger there?"

"No, there isn't. I think you must have the wrong number."

"I'm sorry," I said. "But maybe you can help me. My name is David Harwood. I'm calling from Promise Falls, north of Albany. I'm trying to find a Martin Tattinger, who's married to Thelma. They have a daughter Constance, and last I heard, they were living in Rochester, but that was some time ago. You wouldn't by any chance be a relative, know anything about how I might find Martin?"

"The Martin Tattinger you're looking for is my brother," he said flatly.

"Oh," I said, suddenly encouraged.

"He and Thelma, they moved around a lot, ending up in El Paso."

I'd seen no Tattinger listing for El Paso. "Do you have a number for him there?" I asked.

"Why you trying to get in touch with him?" Mick Tattinger asked.

"It's about their daughter, Constance," I said, not disclosing, this time, my relationship to her. "There's reason to believe she might be in trouble, and we're trying to contact her parents."

"That's going to be hard," Mick said.

"Why's that?"

"They're dead."

"Oh," I said. "I'm sorry. I didn't realize they'd passed on."

Mick snorted. "Yeah, passed on. That's a nice way to put it."

"I'm sorry?"

"They were murdered."

"What?"

"Throats slit. Both of them. While they were tied to the kitchen chairs."

"When was this?"

"Four, five years ago? It's not like I circle the date on my calendar, if you know what I mean."

"Did they catch who did it?" I asked.

"No," Mick Tattinger said. "What's this about Connie?"

"Constance—Connie is missing," I said.

"Yeah, well, there's nothing exactly new about that. She's been missing for years. Martin and Thelma, when they died, they hadn't heard from her for ages, had no idea what happened to her. She took off when she was sixteen or seventeen. Not that I could blame her. You telling me she's turned up?"

"It looks that way," I said.

"Son of a bitch," he said. "Where the hell is she? She probably doesn't even know her parents are dead."

"I think you might be right," I said.

"She might get some satisfaction from knowing," Mick Tattinger said. "Martin was my brother and all, but he was an ornery son of a bitch. We hadn't been close for years. Him and Thelma wouldn't ever have won any Parent of the Year awards. His bitchin' and her drinkin' and mopin' about, they were a pair. But still, that doesn't mean they deserved what they got. Martin was fixing cars, running a garage in El Paso. Far as I know, he was keeping his nose clean. So why does someone come and kill them? Nothing was stolen."

"I don't know," I said quietly.

"But Connie's alive? That's a kick in the head. I figured she was probably dead, too."

"Why do you say that?"

"I don't know. She was so screwed up, you know? It all goes back to something that happened when she was little, but no sense getting into that."

"The girl that got run over in the driveway."

"Oh, so you already know about that? Martin was a prick even before that, but after the accident, things really turned sour. He was working for a dealership that was owned by the dead girl's uncle. He took it out on Martin, fired him. Martin blamed Connie, which to a degree I suppose you could understand, but she was just a kid, right? But he never did let up on her. Found another job at a dealership in another town, ended up taking the fall when someone broke in and stole a bunch of tools. Wasn't Martin that did it, but management thought it was and fired him. Now he'd been fired from two jobs and things got worse. He finally found some other work, but it didn't matter what happened, he always put the blame on Connie, like she was their own bad luck charm." Mick paused, trying to recall something. "What was it he used to call her? He had a name for her."

"Hindy," I offered.

"Yeah, that was it. For 'Hindenburg.'"

"How'd she handle it?" I asked.

"The few times I saw them all together, it was kind of strange."

"What do you mean?"

"It was like . . . it was like she was in another place."

"Excuse me?"

"Like she wasn't there. It was like she was imagining she was someplace else, or *someone* else. I think it was her way of surviving."

I was listening, nodding my head.

"Who'd you say you were?" he asked, and I told him my name again. "If and when you find Connie, you tell her to get in touch. Would you do that?"

"Sure," I said.

"What are you? Some kind of private investigator?"

"A reporter," I said. "I'm a reporter."

Dad came down to the kitchen.

"It must be dinnertime," he said, looking at the clock. It was 6:40 p.m. "When did your mother say we were supposed to go over?"

I said, "Huh?"

"What's wrong with you? You look like you've seen a ghost or something."

"Something like that," I said.

The phone rang. I glanced down at the display. Mom. Or possibly Ethan, who had learned some time ago how to use the speed dial on his grandparents' phone.

I picked up. "Yeah."

"I can't find him," Mom said, her voice shaking. "I can't find Ethan."

# PART FIVE

# FORTY-SEVEN

FOR THE BETTER PART of half an hour, Jan drove randomly. Go a few miles, turn left. Go a few more, turn right. Get on the interstate, go two exits, get off. She hoped the more randomly she drove, the harder she'd be to follow.

And she hadn't noticed any black Audis in the pickup truck's rearview mirror. When she got on the interstate, and was able to see a good mile or so behind her, and when there was no sign of the Audi, she started to feel more confident that Oscar Fine was not on her tail.

But that was not a great comfort.

If he could find her once, it seemed likely he could find her again.

She must have looked like a madwoman to other motorists who happened to glance her way. Wide-eyed, her hair a mass of tangles from the wind blowing through the open side windows and the new crack in the windshield. She was holding on to the steering wheel as hard as she could not just to maintain control, but to keep from shaking.

She was a disaster.

Dwayne had to be dead. No way Oscar Fine was letting him walk out of that basement alive.

The question was, how much had Dwayne said before he died?

Did Oscar know who she was?

Did Oscar know who she'd been?

Had he already known before Dwayne walked in to trade his fake diamonds for six million?

*Think*, she told herself, heading west on the Mass Pike. *Think*.

One thing was a no-brainer. Banura had turned them in. Once they'd been to see him, and he'd examined what they had to sell, he must have tipped off Oscar Fine. But why was Oscar on alert now, after all this time? Had he been checking in with everyone in the diamond trade regularly for the last six years, reminding them to be on the lookout for those worthless stones as a way of tracking Dwayne and her down?

Maybe. But it was also possible something had triggered Oscar Fine to start looking now, perhaps more vigorously than he had been lately.

Had he seen a news report about her disappearance? Even if he had, those stories carried pictures of her looking like Jan Harwood, and Jan Harwood didn't look anything like that girl who got the drop on him in the back of the limo. But maybe, when you've had someone cut off your hand, you remember a little more than hair color and eye shadow. . . .

Jan let go of the steering wheel long enough to bang it several times with her fist. Was there any part of this that she hadn't fucked up?

Where to start?

Pulling the stupid job in the first place. Hooking up with Dwayne Osterhaus. Being so incredibly dumb as to not know the value of the goods they'd stolen. Coming back to Banura's when she knew the deal was too good to be true.

*Walking away from what she had.*

She glanced down at the dash, saw that the truck was nearly out of gas. Now she had a practical matter to contend with. She took the next exit, which was littered with gas stations and fast-food joints. She put thirty dollars' worth into the tank, then crossed the street and parked in a McDonald's lot.

She bypassed the ordering counter, went straight to the ladies' restroom, rushed into a stall, and vomited before she could get the seat up. She had her hands on the stall walls, steadying herself. She was sweating and dizzy.

And then she was sick again.

She flushed the toilet and stood in there, blotting her face with toilet tissue. Once she was sure she was ready, she opened the door, went to the sink, and splashed water on her face, trying to cool herself down. A woman helping her daughter wash up at the sink next to hers gave Jan a cautious look.

Jan knew what she was thinking. *You're some sort of crazy lady.*

There were no paper towels, just those confounding hot-air blowers, and the last thing Jan wanted blowing on her face was hot air. So she walked out of the restroom, and out of the restaurant, droplets of water running down her face.

She leaned up against the brick wall of the restaurant, keeping an eye on the pickup and the traffic, always on the lookout for a black Audi. She stood there for a good half hour, as though paralyzed, not knowing what she should do next.

A restaurant employee emptying trash cans asked if he could help her. Not really wanting to help, but wanting Jan to move on. She got back behind the wheel of the truck, sat there a moment.

A cell phone rang, making Jan jump. She didn't even have a cell phone. Then she remembered the one she'd stolen from the woman's purse at the gas station. She reached into her own purse, found the phone, looked at the number.

There was no way anyone knew how to get in touch with her, was there?

But Dwayne had used the phone to call Banura. He probably had it on his phone's log.

She flipped it open. "Hello?"

"Who is this?" a woman asked. "Have you got my cell phone? I've spent all morning looking for it and—"

Jan broke the flip phone, like she was snapping its spine, got out of the truck, and threw the two pieces into a garbage can.

When she got back into the truck, she was shaking.

And thinking. Thinking all the way back to the very beginning. Back to when she pushed the Richlers' daughter into the path of that car.

Wasn't that when it all started, really? If she hadn't done that—and God knows she never meant for that to happen—then her parents would never have had to move away. And then her father's work might not have gone down the toilet, and he might not have hated her quite so much, and she might not have been so desperate to leave home so young, taken up with someone like Dwayne Osterhaus and—

No, she never meant to kill the Richler girl. She was just angry, that was all. Angry about something she'd said. Constance Tattinger was jealous of Jan Richler. Jealous of the things she had. Jealous of how much her parents adored her. Gretchen and Horace Richler bought her Barbies, and pretty shoes, and on her birthday let her order in Kentucky Fried Chicken. They'd even bought their girl a necklace that looked like a cupcake. It was the most beautiful necklace Constance had ever seen, and she had coveted it from the moment she first laid eyes on it.

One day, when Jan Richler wore it to school, and took it off briefly when it was itching her neck, Constance Tattinger reached into her jacket pocket and took it. Jan Richler cried and cried when she couldn't find it, and became convinced Constance had taken it. Two days later, on Jan Richler's front lawn, she told Constance what she believed she'd done, and Constance, angry and defensive, shoved the girl out of her way.

Right into the path of the car.

All these years, the woman who would steal Jan Richler's identity hung on to that necklace. She'd been tempted many times to throw it away, but could never bring herself to do it. It wasn't that she loved the piece of jewelry. Far from it. The necklace was a reminder of a terrible thing she'd done. It signified not only the moment Jan Richler's life ended, but the moment Constance Tattinger's own life changed forever.

She was pulled out of school.

Her parents moved away.

Her father began his never-ending resentment of her.

The day she took that necklace was the day it was determined she would leave home at seventeen and never get in touch with her parents again. She wondered, sometimes, whatever had happened to them. And then she realized she didn't much care.

She hung on to the necklace for what it represented. A defining moment in her life. Even though it was a bad one.

One day, Ethan would see it in her jewelry box and ask if he could have it—cupcakes were his favorite snack in the whole wide world—and his mother would say no, it really wasn't something a boy would wear, so he begged her to wear it when they went on a trip to Chicago.

She agreed to wear it for a day, and then never wore it again.

She thought about all these things, about her life,

about Ethan, about David, as she sat in that truck. She thought about the life she'd had with them and—

*Focus.*

The woman known as Jan gave her head a small shake. There'd be plenty of time later to wallow in self-pity, immerse herself in it like a hot bath.

Something more urgent was nagging at her.

There was every reason to believe Oscar Fine knew that she had been living the last few years as Jan Harwood. He could have learned this from Dwayne, or he could have figured it out from the news reports of her disappearance.

If he knew about Jan Harwood, it wasn't going to take him any time at all to figure out where she was from.

If she were Oscar Fine, she told herself, wouldn't Promise Falls be her next stop?

She reached down next to her, looking for the photograph of Ethan she had taken from her purse only an hour or so earlier.

It wasn't there.

Jan put the key into the ignition and started the engine. Without even realizing it, she'd already been driving in the direction of the place she'd called home the last five years.

She had to go back.

And she had to get there before Oscar Fine did.

She made no further pit stops on the way to Promise Falls, even when she was rounding Albany and saw that she had less than a quarter of a tank left. She felt she could make it.

She wondered where Ethan would be. It made sense that, considering the predicament she'd left David in, their son would not be at their house. David, if he hadn't already been arrested, would probably be at the police station, or meeting with a lawyer, or driving all over hell's half acre trying to figure out what had happened to her.

Jan almost laughed when it hit her: *I wish I could talk to David about this.*

She knew that wasn't possible. There would be no room for forgiveness there, even though all she had to do was walk into a police station to put him in the clear. The things she'd done—you didn't put that kind of stuff behind you and start over. Maybe, someday, some evidence might come along that would clear him. So be it.

By then she and Ethan would be long gone.

Ethan was her son. She was going to come out of all this with something that was hers.

It was most likely he was with Nana and Poppa.

She'd take a drive by there first.

# FORTY-EIGHT

BARRY DUCKWORTH WAS DRIVING back from Albany in the late afternoon, approaching the Promise Falls city limits, when his cell rang.

His last stop had been north of the city at the Exxon station where whoever had been using Lyall Kowalski's Ford Explorer—and Duckworth couldn't begin to guess whether it had been his wife, Leanne, or someone else—had bought gas. The receipt that had been found in the SUV indicated that the purchase had been a cash sale, which made sense, since Lyall Kowalski had told Duckworth that their cards had been canceled.

When he got to the station, he showed a picture of Leanne to staff who'd been on duty at the time, but no one had any recollection of seeing Leanne Kowalski, or the Explorer, even though she would have had to come inside to pay. That didn't surprise Duckworth. With the hundreds of customers coming in here in a single day, the odds that anyone would remember Leanne were slim. Even though Duckworth knew, from the receipt, the time of the purchase, there was no surveillance tape to check. The equipment was broken.

For good measure, he showed them pictures of Jan Harwood and David Harwood. No joy there, either.

So he got back into his cruiser and began the trek back home. It gave him some time to think.

Just about from the beginning, he'd liked David Harwood for this. You always look to the husband first, anyway. And there were so many parts of his story that didn't hold together. His wife's so-called depression certainly didn't. The ticket that was never purchased. The evidence from Ted, the store owner in Lake George. And if you were looking for motive, there was that $300,000 life insurance policy. Just the sort of safety net a guy working in newspapers—or anywhere else these days, for that matter—might be glad to have.

It looked very much like Harwood took his wife to Lake George and killed her. After all, no one had seen her since, so long as you didn't count the boy, Ethan. But Duckworth had been having doubts about his initial theory ever since the discovery of Leanne Kowalski's body. From the moment David Harwood had looked into that shallow grave and seen her there, Duckworth had been watching closely for the man's reaction.

Duckworth had not anticipated what he saw.

*Genuine surprise.*

If David Harwood had killed that woman and put her into the ground, he might have been able to feign shock. He could have put on an act and looked shattered. And faking tears, lots of people could pull that off. All of those things the seasoned detective would have expected.

But why had Harwood looked so surprised?

It had flashed across the man's face for a good second. The eyes went wide. There was a kind of double take. There was no mistaking it. Leanne Kowalski's body was not the one he had been steeling himself to see.

That told Barry Duckworth a couple of things. Harwood was not Kowalski's killer. And it wasn't very likely that he'd killed his wife, either.

If Harwood had killed Jan Harwood, and disposed of

her elsewhere, he wouldn't have looked so taken aback. He'd have known he was going to be looking down at someone other than his spouse. Even if he had killed Kowalski, and knew she was going to be there, he might have acted surprised, but that's what it would have been: an act. What Duckworth saw was the real deal.

And then there was the business of the Explorer.

Harwood might have had time to kill Leanne Kowalski between taking his wife up to Lake George and going to Five Mountains the next day, but Duckworth couldn't for the life of him figure out how the Explorer got all the way down to Albany and ended up at the bottom of an embankment. When did Harwood have time to do that? How did he manage it alone? Wouldn't you need one person to drive the Explorer, and another for the car that you'd need to get back to Promise Falls?

Duckworth wasn't liking Harwood for this nearly as much as he once had. Maybe there was something to the reporter's claims that his wife had taken on a new name, changed her identity, after all. It had seemed pretty outrageous to him at first, but now he was feeling obliged to give it a look-see. He could find out again the names of those people Harwood had been to see in Rochester. See what they had to say.

He was starting to get a new feeling in that gut of his that Natalie Bondurant had so maligned.

And that was when his cell rang.

"Duckworth."

"Yeah, Barry, it's Glen."

Glen Dougherty. Barry's boss. The Promise Falls police chief.

"Chief," he said.

"It wouldn't normally be me calling you with this, but some lab results just got copied to me and I wondered if you had them yet."

"I'm on the road."

"This Jan Harwood disappearance. You're handling that."

"As we speak," he said.

"You asked for tests on some hair and blood samples in the trunk of the husband's car."

"That's right."

"They're back. They both match the missing woman, based on the hair samples you took from the house when you had it searched."

"I hear ya."

"I think you need to move on this," the chief said. "Looks like this clown moved her body in the trunk."

"Maybe," Duckworth said.

"Maybe?"

"There's parts of this I don't like," the detective said.

"Looks to me like you've got this son of a bitch dead to rights now. Time to bring him in again, sweat him out. Once you lay this out for him, he's gonna fold."

"I can bring him in again, but I'm not sure."

"Look, Barry, I'm not going to tell you what to do. But I am going to tell you this. I'm getting a lot of pressure on this one. From those fucking amusement park people, from the tourism office, and the mayor's office. As well as that weasel Reeves. God, I hate that guy. The bottom line is, Five Mountains makes a lot of money not just for Five Mountains, but for the area. People start thinking there's someone snatching kids there, they're going to stay away. And from the sounds of it, this guy may have made up all that shit about his kid getting abducted there. You hearing me?"

"Absolutely," Duckworth said.

"If I were you, I'd bring him in again."

"He's hired Natalie Bondurant."

"Well, by all means, bring her in, too. Once she sees

what you've got on her client, she may just tell him to take some kind of deal."

"Got it," Duckworth said. "I—"

But the chief had ended the call.

Duckworth was getting another feeling in his gut. He didn't like this one at all.

# FORTY-NINE

DAD AND I DROVE over in two cars as fast as we could. Mom was standing on the porch, waiting for us, and ran over to the driveway as we each pulled in.

She was at my door as I was getting out.

"There's still no sign—"

"Start from the beginning," I said as Dad got out of the other car and came over.

Mom took a moment to catch her breath. "He'd been out in the backyard off and on all day. Playing with the croquet set, just whacking the ball around."

"Okay," I said.

"I was doing some things in the kitchen and around the house, checking outside for him every few minutes, but the thing was, I was always hearing *whack, whack, whack,* so I knew what he was up to. And then I realized it had been a while since I heard it, and I was pretty sure I hadn't heard him come in, so I went out to make sure he wasn't getting into anything he shouldn't, like your father's tools in the garage. And I couldn't find him."

"Dad," I said, "call the police."

He nodded and headed for the house.

Mom reached out and held my shoulders. "I'm sorry, I'm so sorry, David, I'm just so—"

"Mom, it's okay. Let's—"

"I swear, I was watching him. I only let him out of my sight for a few minutes. He was—"

"Mom, right now we have to keep looking. Have you tried the neighbors?"

"No, no, I've just been looking everywhere. I thought maybe he was hiding in the house, under a bed, something like that, maybe playing a trick on me. But I can't find him anyplace."

I pointed to the houses next door and across the street. "You start knocking on doors. I'll make one last check of the house. Go. Go."

Mom turned and ran to the house on the left as I ran up the porch stairs and into the house.

"His name is Ethan Harwood," Dad was saying into the phone. "He's four years old."

I shouted, "Ethan! Ethan, are you here?"

I ran downstairs first, checking behind the furnace, moving back the door to the storage compartment under the stairs. A four-year-old boy, he could hide in a lot of places. I could remember, when I was Ethan's age, getting out my parents' suitcases and curling myself up inside them. One time, one of them latched shut on me, and Mom heard my screams before I ran out of air.

The flashback made me dig out the larger cases—a different set, all these years later—from under the stairs and give them a shake.

Satisfied that Ethan was not in those cases, or anywhere else in the basement, I scaled the stairs and faced Dad as I came into the kitchen. He was off the phone.

"They said they're going to have a car swing by in a while," he said.

"A while?" I said. *"A while?"*

Dad looked shaken. "That's what they said. They asked how long he'd been gone and when I said under an hour, they didn't seem all that excited."

I moved Dad aside and grabbed the phone, the receiver still warm to the touch, and punched in 911.

"Listen," I said once I had hold of the dispatcher

who'd spoken to my father. "We don't need some car coming by in *a while* to help us find my son. We need someone right fucking *now*." And I slammed the receiver down.

To Dad I said, "Go help Mom knock on doors."

For the second time in almost as many minutes, Dad turned and did what I told him.

I ran upstairs and opened closet doors, looked under beds. There was an access to the attic, but even with a chair, there was no way Ethan could hope to reach it.

"Ethan!" I shouted. "If you're hiding, you better come out right now or there's going to be trouble!"

Nothing.

By the time I got out front of the house, about a dozen neighbors were on the street, milling about. My parents' door-knocking had brought people out, wondering what was going on and whether they could do anything to help.

"Everyone!" I shouted. "Everyone, please, can you listen up for a second?"

They stopped gossiping among themselves and looked at me.

"My boy, Ethan, you've probably seen him around here a lot the last couple of years. We can't find him. He was in my parents' backyard, and now he's gone. Could you please all check your properties, your backyards, your garages? Any of you with pools, God forbid, please check them first."

My mother looked as though she might faint.

Some of them started nodding, like *Sure, that's a great idea*, but they weren't moving with any speed.

"Now!" I shouted.

They started to disperse, save for one man in his twenties, a tall but doughy, unshaven lout with a tractor hat on. He said, "So what'd you do, Harwood? Getting rid of the wife wasn't enough? You got rid of the kid, too?"

Something snapped.

I ran at him, got him around the waist, and brought him down on a front yard. All the others who'd been heading off to hunt for Ethan stopped in their tracks to watch the show. Straddling the man, I took a swing and caught the corner of his mouth, drawing blood instantly.

"You motherfucker," I said. "You goddamn son of a bitch."

Before I could take another swing, Dad had his arms around me from behind. "Son!" he shouted. "Stop it."

"You fucker!" the man with the hat said, rolling onto his side, feeling his mouth for blood.

Dad shouted at everyone, "Please, just look for Ethan." Once he had me off the man, Dad leaned over him and said, "And you get your sorry ass home before I take a kick at it myself."

The man got up, dusted himself off, and started to walk away, but not before looking at me and saying, "You watch it, Harwood. They're going to get you."

I turned away, my face hot and flushed. Dad came up alongside me. "You okay?"

I nodded. "We have to keep looking."

Even though Mom had said she'd already done it, Dad and I searched the backyard and his garage. The croquet set wires were shoved into the lawn randomly, striped wooden balls scattered about. There was one mallet lying on the grass. I went over, picked it up, as though it could tell me something, then dropped it back to the ground.

"Ethan!" I shouted as dusk began to fall. "Ethan!"

Down at the end of my parents' street, and then a block to the left, was a 7-Eleven. Could Ethan have wandered down there on his own, looking to buy a package of his favorite cupcakes? Would he have attempted something like that? Did he even have any money on him?

I started running. Dad shouted, "Where you going?"

"I'll be right back!"

Running flat out, it only took a minute to reach the store. I burst through the front door so quickly the guy behind the counter must have thought I'd come to rob the place.

Breathlessly, I asked if a small boy had been in within the last hour, all by himself, to get a package of cupcakes. The man shook his head, but said, "There was a lady here, she bought some, but no kid."

I ran back to my parents' house, both of them standing out front.

"Anything?" I asked.

They both shook their heads no.

"Where would he go?" Dad asked. "Where do you think he would go?"

"Would he try to go to your house?" Mom asked.

I looked at her. "Shit," I said. "That's brilliant. He kept asking me if he could come home. Maybe he just decided to start walking." I recalled when he had stormed out the door, threatening to do just that.

Although only four, Ethan had already demonstrated a keen sense of direction, correcting me from his backseat perch anytime I took us on a route to my parents' that wasn't the most direct. He'd probably be able to find his way to our house, even though it was a couple of miles away. And the thought of him crossing all those streets on his own . . .

"We need to trace our way back," I said.

"I didn't see him on the way over," Dad said.

"But we weren't looking," I said. "We were in such a rush to get here, we might not have noticed."

I had the keys to Dad's car in my hand and was heading over to it when an unmarked police car came tearing up the street.

"Good," I said. "Cops."

The car pulled over to the curb, blocking the end of my parents' driveway, and Barry Duckworth got out, his eyes fixed on me.

"They sent *you*?" I said to him. "I thought they'd send a regular car, and uniformed officers. But, whatever."

"What?" he said.

"Aren't you here about Ethan?"

"What's happened to Ethan?" Duckworth asked.

My heart sank. The cavalry hadn't arrived after all. "He's missing," I said.

"Since when?"

"The last hour or so."

"You've called it in?"

"My dad did. Look, you need to get your car out of the way. He might have gone back to our house."

Duckworth didn't make any move to get back in his car. "We need to talk," he said.

"What?" I thought maybe he had news about Jan, or maybe even about Ethan. "What is it? What's happened?"

"Nothing. But I need you to come downtown. I want to go over a few things again." He paused. "You might want to have your lawyer meet us there."

My jaw dropped. "Are you listening? My son is missing. I'm going to look for Ethan."

"No," said Duckworth. "You're not."

# FIFTY

MY FIRST IMPULSE WAS to start shouting, but I knew if I overreacted, Barry Duckworth might very well have me on the ground and in handcuffs in a matter of seconds. So I tried to keep my voice even and controlled.

"Detective Duckworth, I don't think you understand," I said. "Ethan may be wandering around all by himself, trying to get from one side of town to the other, crossing streets he's not old enough to cross. He's four years old, for Christ's sake."

Duckworth nodded, giving me hope maybe he actually did understand. "Have you searched the house, and out behind—"

"We've searched everywhere. We've got neighbors checking their properties. But he could be trying to get back to our house, and I need to check."

"When other officers get here, they'll be able to mount a systematic search," Duckworth said. "They can get the word out, every officer out there in a car will be looking for your son. They're good at this sort of thing."

"I'm sure they are, but he's my son, and if you'll move your goddamn car out of the way, I'm going to try to find him myself."

Duckworth's jaw tightened. "I have to bring you in, Mr. Harwood."

The air around us was charged, like an electrical storm was imminent. "This is not a good time," I said.

"I appreciate that," the detective said. "But those are my instructions."

"Are you arresting me?" I asked.

"My instructions are to bring you in for more questioning. I suggest you get in touch with Natalie Bondurant. She could meet us at the station."

"I'm not going," I said.

"I'm not asking," Duckworth said firmly.

"Come on," Dad said. He and Mom were standing just behind me. "What the hell are you doing? You have to let him find Ethan."

"I'm sorry, sir, but this does not involve you," Duckworth said.

"Doesn't concern me?" Dad said, outrage growing in his voice. "We're talking about my grandson. You got the nerve to tell me it doesn't concern me?"

Duckworth blinked, the first hint that maybe he could see this wasn't going well.

"As I just said, sir, when the other officers get here, they'll be able to conduct a thorough search."

Dad raised his arms in frustration. "You see any here now? Huh? How long are we supposed to wait? What if Ethan's in some kind of trouble right this very second? Is my son supposed to sit around answering your damn fool questions while his boy's in trouble? What the hell's so important that you have to talk to him now?"

Duckworth swallowed. Instead of looking at Dad, he spoke to me. "Mr. Harwood, there are developments in your wife's disappearance that we need to go over."

"What developments?"

"We can talk about that at the station."

There was no way I was going to that station. I had a feeling if Duckworth managed to get me there, I wouldn't be leaving. Not any time soon.

"Hey!" someone across the street shouted.

We all looked. It was the guy with the tractor hat, the one I'd punched in the mouth. There was still blood on his chin.

"Hey!" he shouted a second time, looking at Duckworth. "You a cop?"

"Yes," the detective said.

"That asshole assaulted me," he said, pointing a finger my way.

Duckworth tilted his head at me.

"It's true," I said. "We were asking all the neighbors to help us look for Ethan, and he . . . he accused me of killing my son. And my wife. I lost it."

Duckworth turned back and said to the man, "I'm sure an officer will be along shortly, and he can take your statement."

"Fuck that," the man said, walking across the street toward us. "You need to put the cuffs on him right now. I got witnesses!"

Even with Duckworth standing there, the guy was ready to get into it with me all over again, striding right up, pointing that finger. He got close enough to poke me in the shoulder. I hadn't noticed it when I'd tackled him, but this time I was getting a strong whiff of booze off him.

Duckworth quickly pulled the man's arm down and off me and said, forcefully, "Sir, if you'll just go stand over there and wait for the officers to arrive, they'll be more than happy to take your statement."

"I seen this guy on the news," he said. "He's the one killed his wife. Why isn't he in jail already? Huh? If you guys were doing your fucking job, he wouldn't be out walking around attacking people like me."

Duckworth had no choice now but to turn away from me and deal with the guy. "What's your name?"

"Axel. Axel Smight."

"How much have you had to drink tonight, Mr. Smight?"

"Huh?" He looked offended.

"How much have you had to drink?"

"Not very much. What the fuck is that supposed to mean anyway? If I've had a bit to drink, I'm not entitled to police protection?"

"Mr. Smight, I'm only going to tell you this one more time. Go stand over there and wait for the officers to arrive."

"You're not going to arrest him? What else do you need? I'm telling you, the guy attacked me." He touched his hand to his bloody chin. "What the fuck do you think this is?" He was shouting now. "Strawberry milk shake? The fucker hit me right in the mouth!"

Duckworth pulled back his jacket, revealing a set of handcuffs clipped to his belt.

"There you go!" Axel Smight said. "Now we're getting somewhere. Cuff the fucker!"

Duckworth, with more skill and speed than his bulk might have suggested, took hold of Smight, spun him around, and forced him down onto the hood of his unmarked cruiser. He twisted Smight's left arm behind him, slapped one cuff on the wrist, and then grabbed the right arm to do the same.

I didn't stay to watch the whole procedure. I ran for Dad's car, slipped the key into the ignition, and turned over the engine. There looked to be just enough room to squeeze past Duckworth's car if I ran over onto the grass.

"Mr. Harwood!" Duckworth shouted, trying to hold a squirming Axel Smight onto the hood. "Stop!"

I put it in reverse and hit the gas, clipping the corner of the front bumper of Duckworth's car on the way out. I heard it scrape along the entire side of Dad's car.

"You dumb bastard!" Duckworth shouted.

I didn't know what the hell he meant by that, but I wasn't hanging around to find out. I got the car onto the street, stopped with a screech, threw it into drive, and sped off.

A person might normally be inclined to keep speeding away from a scene like that, but the moment I turned the corner I slowed down, scanning both sides of the street, looking for any signs of Ethan.

"Come on," I said under my breath. "Where the hell are you?"

It was tricky, watching both sidewalks and the traffic in front of me all at the same time, and I had to hit the brakes hard and fast a couple of times to keep from rear-ending someone. I was turning in to my street when my cell went off. I was nosing the car in to the curb and getting out as I put the phone to my ear.

"Yeah?"

"Dave, it's Sam."

"Hey," I said.

"Where are you? You sound kind of out of breath."

"I'm kind of busy, Sam," I said.

"I need you to come by the paper," she said.

"I can't," I said. I was walking down the side of the house. Ethan didn't have a key to the house, at least not that I knew of. I supposed it was possible he'd taken the one my parents keep on a nail at their place.

"It's really important," Samantha Henry pleaded.

I stood in the backyard and shouted, "Ethan!"

"Shit," Sam said. "You just blew out my eardrum."

I used my key to open the back door, and while I didn't expect my son to be in the house, I called out his name anyway.

There was no answer.

"Dave?" Sam asked. "Dave, are you listening?"

"Yeah," I said.

"I need you to come by the paper."

"This is not a good time, Sam. What's this about?"

"Elmont Sebastian," she said. "He's here. He wants a word with you."

I felt a chill run the length of my spine. I remembered the story about the Aryan Brotherhood prisoner whose genitals he'd Tasered. The one nicknamed Buddy. The one Sebastian had made cry when it was suggested to him something might happen to his six-year-old son on the outside if he didn't play by Sebastian's rules.

# FIFTY-ONE

IT WAS GETTING DARK when I wheeled into the Promise Falls *Standard* parking lot. I spotted Elmont Sebastian's limo parked at the far end, near the doors to the production end of the newspaper building, where the presses were housed. There was no one standing around.

I parked a couple of car lengths away from the limo and got out. As I did, Welland appeared from behind the driver's seat and motioned for me to get in the back.

"No thanks," I said. He opened the door anyway. I was expecting to see Sebastian, and he was there, but sitting next to him was Samantha Henry. She appeared to have been crying.

She shifted over to get out of the car and said to me, "I'm really sorry."

"Sorry?"

"I just, I was doing it for my kid."

"What are you talking about?"

"Do I have to tell you times are tough? I've got bills. I'm raising a child. I know it was wrong, David, but what the fuck am I supposed to do? Tell me that? End up on the street? And newspapers are screwed, anyway. There's no future here. It's only a matter of time before we all lose our jobs. I'm looking out for myself and my kid while I can. Mr. Elmont's offered me a job with Star Spangled Corrections."

"Writing press releases or midnight guard duty?" I asked. From what I'd gathered from my source, women didn't fare too well in Sebastian's empire.

"Deputy assistant media relations officer," she said, trying to hold her head high without success.

"It was you," I said. "You saw the email before I deleted it." She'd have had time. When the anonymous email landed, I went for a coffee before making the decision to delete it. "You went on my computer and told Sebastian about it."

"I said I was sorry," she said. "And I told him you're trying to find someone named Constance Tattinger, that she's probably the one who just sent you that list. That's what he wants to talk to you about." She turned and walked away, got into her car and drove out of the lot.

My face felt hot.

"Come on in," Sebastian said, patting the leather seat. "Help me out here and I might still be able to find a spot for you, too. It might not be media relations. I've promised that to Ms. Henry, and I'm a man of my word. But you'd be perfect for writing up our proposals. You have a nice turn of phrase."

"Do you have my son?" I asked.

Sebastian's eye twitched. "I'm sorry?"

"If you have him, just tell me. If there's something you want in exchange, name it. You hold the cards. I'll tell you anything I know." I allowed myself to get into the car, the door still open, one foot still on the pavement.

"All right, then," he said. "Tell me about Constance Tattinger. You asked Ms. Henry to check into that name. That's your source? I'm puzzled, because I've never heard of her. There's no one working for me or Promise Falls with that name."

"She's not the source," I said. "Constance Tattinger is, as far as I know, my wife."

Sebastian's eyes narrowed. "I don't follow. Why would your wife have a list of names of people—"

"She didn't. I called Sam about two different things. I guess she thought they were related when she called you."

Sebastian leaned back into the leather seat and sighed. "I have to admit, I'm a bit confused. I thought your wife's name was Jan."

"Jan Richler's the name she was using when we met, but I think she was born Constance Tattinger. I've been trying to find out everything I can about her, hoping it will lead me to her. I'm pretty sure she's the one who set up the meeting at Lake George. It was a trick."

Elmont Sebastian looked like he was getting a headache. "So your wife's not the source, but you think she's the one who emailed you to say she had all this information to give you about my company?"

"Yeah."

"Why the hell would she do that?" Sebastian asked.

"It doesn't matter," I said. "Not as far as you're concerned. She wouldn't know the first thing about your company, or what you're doing to buy votes on council. Now what about my son?"

"I don't know a damn thing about your kid," Sebastian said. "And I don't care."

I felt deflated. As frightening as it would be for Ethan to have been picked up by this pair, I was hoping they had him to trade.

"You really don't have Ethan," I said.

Sebastian shook his head in mock condolence. "All my years running prisons, I don't think I ever had an inmate in more shit than you."

I took a moment. "If you don't know anything about my son, then we're done here," I said, swinging my other leg back out of the car.

"I don't think so," Sebastian said. "Regardless of

whoever your wife is, something was mailed to you. Something you have no business possessing."

The list in my pocket. The one I'd foolishly told Sam about.

"I think you're mistaken," I said, now fully out of the car.

It would have been easy to give him the envelope. God knows I had enough to worry about right now. I could have handed Sebastian what he wanted and walked away. But I also knew there was a chance I might—just might, somehow—come out the other side of this hell I was currently living through, and actually return to work as a reporter. If not at the *Standard,* then someplace else. And if I did, I wanted to bring down Elmont Sebastian.

There wasn't any chance of that happening if I handed over what was in my jacket.

"Really, David, you need to consider your position," Sebastian said.

Welland was coming around the car. When he reached the open door, he and Sebastian exchanged a look. Sebastian said, "If you're not going to hand it over, I'll have to ask Welland to get it for me."

I bolted.

Welland's right arm shot out, got hold of me by the wrist, but I was moving quickly enough that my hand slipped out of his grasp. As I ran I reached into my pocket for my keys, thinking, naïvely, that maybe I could get behind the wheel of my car before Welland was on me.

As I felt him closing in on me, I abandoned the idea of my car and instead hightailed it across the lot for the *Standard* building. Welland was snorting like an angry bull in pursuit. While he had me beat in the muscle and bulk department, he wasn't all that fast, and I felt myself pulling ahead of him.

I mounted the five steps up to the back door and had it open before Welland could get hold of me, but there was no time to pull it shut. I was overwhelmed by the sound of running presses, a heavy, loud, humming that went straight to the center of my brain. This time of night, only one of the three presses was running, producing some of the weekend sections. The other two presses wouldn't be set into motion for a couple more hours, when the newsroom finished putting together the first edition.

I was running wildly at this point, heading down any path that presented itself to me. Ahead and to the right was a set of steep metal stairs leading up and onto the boards that ran down along the sides and through the presses.

I grabbed hold of the tubular handrails and scurried up them. Even over the din, I heard some pressmen shouting, telling me to get off. This was their domain, and they didn't care for trespassers. They could tolerate Madeline in here to check on press repairs, but I was just some dumbass reporter.

Once up on the boards, I had a good fifty feet of cat-walk ahead of me. I looked back, expecting to see either a pressman or Welland appear at the top of the stairway, but no one materialized.

But there was still a lot of indistinct shouting going on.

I stopped for a moment, wondering if it was possible I'd lost Welland. I debated doubling back, then concluded it was safer to keep going in the same direction, to the set of stairs at the far end of the presses.

To my left, the press was going at full bore, endless ribbons of newsprint going past at blinding speed, trekking up and down and through the massive apparatus. Every few feet there was an opening where the boards cut through to the other side.

I started moving again, my hands running along the top of the railing, and then there he was. At the far end of the walkway, Welland loomed into view at the top of the other set of stairs.

"Shit," I said, although I barely heard the word myself for the humming of the press.

I whirled around, planning to double back, but standing where I'd been seconds earlier was Elmont Sebastian. He wasn't the youngest guy in the world, but he'd scaled those steps in no time. He looked down at his hand, smeared with ink residue from the railing. He gave his suit a worried look, probably wondering how soiled it had already become.

I thought I had a better chance of bulldozing my way past him than heading the other way toward Welland.

I started running at Sebastian. He broadened his stance, but I didn't slow down. I slammed into him, but instead of just him going down, he grabbed me around the neck and we went down together.

"You son of a bitch!" he shouted. "Give it to me!"

We rolled on the boards. I brought up a knee and tried to get him in the groin or stomach. I must have hit something, because he loosened his hold on my neck long enough for me to start scrambling back onto my feet.

But Sebastian was up almost as quickly, and leapt on my back. The tackle threw me to one side, into one of the walkways that went through the presses. Newsprint flew past us on both sides, the words and images an indistinct blur.

As I stumbled to one side, Sebastian was pitched up against the railing. He was facing it, and his upper body leaned over with the impact. He threw his hands out in front of himself, but there was nothing there to catch on to.

But there was something to catch on to him.

It happened so blindingly fast that if you'd caught it

on video, and had the chance to play it back in slow motion, you still probably wouldn't be able to see how it went down.

But what happened, basically, is Sebastian's right hand bumped up against the speeding newsprint, which flung his arm upward and into the spinning press. It was moving so quickly there was no opportunity for Sebastian to react.

His arm was torn off in a second. And it just disappeared.

Elmont Sebastian screamed and collapsed onto the boards, reaching over with his left arm, hunting for his right.

I looked down, horrified and aghast, and God help me, thought of Ethan's joke.

*Black and white and red all over.*

Welland came up behind me, saw his boss, and said, "Jesus."

Sebastian thrashed about for a second or two, then stopped. His eyes were open and unblinking, but I wasn't sure that he was dead. Not yet.

I said to Welland, "We've got to call an ambulance."

I started to move, knowing no one would be able to hear me on my cell with the roar of the press—which had not stopped—in the background.

Welland grabbed hold of my arm. Not quite the way he had before. Not in a menacing way. He was just holding me.

"No," he said.

"He hasn't got long," I shouted.

"Let's wait a bit," he said.

"What the hell are you doing?"

Down below, pressmen were pointing, shouting. From their viewpoint, I wasn't sure they could see what had happened to Sebastian.

"We're gonna let him go," Welland said.

"What?"

"The fucker never should have zapped me in the balls, or threatened my son."

I stared at him, speechless.

Welland added, "We didn't take your boy. I'd never have let him do that."

# FIFTY-TWO

SOMEONE HAD KILLED THE press. It was slowing, the noise receding.

Welland—or Buddy, as I now knew him to be—squeezed past me on the catwalk.

"I'm outta here," he said.

An alarm was ringing now, and pressmen were coming up on the boards from all directions.

"Where are you going?" I asked Welland. I was, in the midst of everything, thinking about how I was going to explain Elmont Sebastian, the CEO of Star Spangled Corrections, getting torn apart in the Promise Falls *Standard* pressroom.

"I got people who can help me disappear," he said. "You tell whatever story you want." He glanced up, pointed. "Those look like cameras. Whole thing's probably on closed circuit. You're in the clear. By the time they start looking for me, I'll be gone."

He didn't waste another word on me. He was a big, intimidating presence, and none of the pressmen stood in his way as he made for the stairs and slid down them navy-style, feet braced on the outside of the railings. I watched him run for the door, and then he was gone.

One of the pressmen, who recognized me from around the building, said, "What happened?" Then he spotted Sebastian, and looked away almost as quickly. "Oh, man."

"Call an ambulance," I said. "I don't think it's going to matter, but . . ."

"I've seen guys lose fingers, but God almighty, never anything like that." He shouted down to someone to call 911.

I didn't want to hang around and explain. I made my way to the stairs and down and was about to head for the door to the parking lot when I saw Madeline Plimpton striding in my direction. She looked past me and barked at the pressman, "Talk to me."

"Ask him," he said.

Madeline fixed her gaze on me. "I thought you were using up vacation time."

"Elmont Sebastian's up there," I said, pointing at the rollers. "If he's not dead yet, he will be before anyone gets here. I hope selling him land for a prison wasn't your only plan for keeping the paper afloat."

"Dear God," she said. "Why—"

"It may be on the monitors," I said. "I hope to God it is." I moved around her, heading for the door. "And I guess I owe you an apology. Sam Henry was reading my emails. She's sold out you and me and everyone else at the paper. However much time it's got left, she shouldn't be here for it."

"David, start from the beginning."

I shook my head. "Ethan's missing. I have to go."

"Ethan—for Christ's sake, David, what's going on?" Madeline said. "You come back here now and—"

I didn't hear the rest as the door closed behind me. Sebastian's limo was already long gone. Welland, knowing the authorities would soon be after him, would have to ditch it at the earliest opportunity. After I got into my car and turned the key, I had to think a moment about where I was going to go next. I'd been left shaken by what had just happened and felt disoriented.

Samantha Henry's phone call luring me to the *Standard* had prevented me from doing a search of my own house for Ethan. I'd gotten the door open, and I'd called out his name, but I hadn't been through the house room by room.

I hadn't actually expected him to be there. The house was locked, and Ethan certainly didn't have his own key, unless, as I'd considered earlier, he'd taken a spare from my parents' house.

But I had no memory of locking the house after getting Sam's call. It was possible that even if Ethan had no key, and hadn't been in the house when I was last there, he could be there now.

It made sense to check in with my parents to see whether anything had happened since I'd fled in such a hurry. I took out my phone and saw there was one message. I wouldn't have heard it ring with the press rolling.

I checked it.

"Mr. Harwood, this is Detective Duckworth. Look, I'm willing to overlook what happened, but I'm not kidding around here. You have to come in. I'm going to call your lawyer and tell her to bring you in. I'm not out to screw you over, Mr. Harwood. There are things about this case that don't make sense, things that are in your favor. But we need to sort them out, and we need to sort them out now if—"

I no sooner had deleted the message than the phone rang in my hand.

"Yeah?"

"Tell me you didn't do what the police say you did," Natalie Bondurant said.

"Unless you have news about my son," I said, "I don't have time to talk to you."

"Listen to me," she said. "You're making things worse for yourself by—"

I ended the call, then speed-dialed my parents' house. Mom answered on the first ring.

"Has Ethan turned up?" I asked.

"No," Mom whispered. She sounded as though she'd been crying when the phone rang, and was trying to pull herself together. "Where are you? That detective, he was gone and now he's back. I think he went by your house and couldn't find you and now he's back here. I think he's going to arrest you if you show up."

"I just have to keep looking," I said. "If you hear any-thing—*anything*—let me know."

"I will," she said.

I slipped the phone back into my coat and sped out of the lot, heading for home.

I was worried Duckworth or other members of the Promise Falls police might be watching my place, so I parked around the corner and walked up. I saw no sus-picious cars on the street. After a while, you get to know the cars of your neighbors and their friends. Nothing out of the ordinary jumped out at me.

I came down the side of the house and entered through the back door. As I'd suspected, I'd left it un-locked.

I came in through the kitchen. The house was in dark-ness, and I was reluctant to flip on a light just in case someone was out there that I'd missed. But I needed to let my eyes adjust to be able to see where I was going. I knew my way around in the dark, but there were still several boards out of place. The house was full of booby traps, and I was suddenly worried that if Ethan had come home, he might have caught his foot in one of the holes where boards were missing.

"Ethan!" I said. "It's Dad! It's okay! You can come out!"

Then I listened. I stood there, just inside the door, and held my breath, hoping to catch some faint sound of movement in the house.

"Ethan?" I called again.

I let out a long, discouraged sigh. And then thought I heard a board creak, overhead, in the area of Ethan's room.

I went through the kitchen, stepping carefully. Dad had put all the boards I'd ripped up to one side, and pried the nails from them, but he hadn't covered over the long, narrow holes I'd left behind.

I went through the living room to the stairs and mounted them slowly in the dark. "Ethan?" I said.

Surely Ethan wouldn't be moving through the house in total darkness. After all, he was still a little boy, and, like most kids, had a fear of the dark, even in his own home.

"Are you up here?" I asked.

The door to Ethan's room was ajar. Sidestepping the few openings in the floor of the upstairs hall, I got to the door and pushed it open.

A glow from a streetlamp fell through Ethan's window.

There was a dark shadow on the far side of his bed. Someone was standing there, someone far too tall to be Ethan.

I reached over to the wall switch and flipped it up.

It was Jan.

The shock of seeing her, standing there, was overtaken by the shock of seeing the gun in her hand, which she was pointing directly at me.

"Where's Ethan?" she asked. "I've come for Ethan."

# FIFTY-THREE

ETHAN'S DRESSER DRAWERS WERE open and his clothes had been tossed onto the bed, next to a soft-sided flight bag, the one we kept in his closet for trips.

I couldn't recall Jan ever looking worse. Her hair was scraggly, her eyes bloodshot. It had only been two days since I'd seen her, but she looked as though she'd lost ten pounds, aged ten years. The gun was shaking in her hand.

"Put that down, Jan," I said. "Maybe you'd rather I called you Constance, but it's hard for me to think of you as anyone but Jan."

She blinked. The gun didn't move.

"Or maybe I've got it wrong, and Constance isn't your real name, either."

"No," she whispered. "That's my real name."

"I guess I can understand why you never wanted to introduce me to your parents," I said. "One set was fake, and the other was dead."

Her eyes widened. "What?"

"Martin and Thelma? Your real parents?" Something in her eyes said yes. "You don't know? Someone killed them a few years ago. Slit their throats."

If she was troubled by this news, she didn't show it. "Where's Ethan?" she asked.

I said, "He's not here."

"Is he with Don and Arlene?"

"No," I said.

"Oh no . . . ," she said. "No, no . . ."

I took a step closer to her. "Put that gun down, Jan."

She shook her head. "No, he has to be here," she said dreamily. "I've come for him. We're going away."

"Even if he was here," I said, "I would never, ever let you take him. Give me the gun." I inched closer.

"We have to find him," Jan said.

"I know," I said. "But you're not going to be looking for him with a gun."

"You don't understand," she said. "I need it. I need this gun."

"You don't need it with me," I said, taking another step toward her. "What do you think I'm going to do to you? I'm your husband."

Jan stifled a laugh. "I think you'd probably like to do plenty to me. But you're not the one I'm worried about."

"Who are you talking about?"

"So my parents are dead," she said, ignoring my question, her mind drifting, a slightly crazed look in her eye. "He must have thought they knew something. He must have thought they'd know where I was. He must have killed them when they couldn't tell him anything."

"Are you talking about who killed your parents? Is that who you're worried about?"

"I did a bad thing," Jan told me. "I did something. . . ."

"What did you do? What's all of this about?" I was less than two feet away from her now.

"Everything's been for nothing," she said. "The diamonds weren't real."

"Diamonds?" I said. "What diamonds?"

"They were worthless. Fucking worthless." Another stifled laugh. "It's like some huge cosmic joke."

I grabbed her wrist.

I'd thought maybe she'd let me wrest the gun away

from her, but as soon as I tried to twist it out of her hand she reacted, trying to pull her arm away. I wouldn't let go. She swung at me with her left hand, hitting me in the side of the face. I swung my right arm up, knocked her hand away as I held on to her right. Then her free hand was clawing at me, her nails digging into my cheeks, but instead of trying to block that hand I turned in to her and got both hands on her wrist, doubling the pressure on it to make her drop the weapon.

As I turned I threw my body into it and forced Jan up against the wall, hard, knocking the wind out of her. While the move may have had the effect of weakening her, it also prompted her to pull the trigger.

The shot, which sounded like a sonic boom in Ethan's small bedroom, went into the floor. I jumped, but I didn't loosen my grip. I slammed her wrist against the wall. Once, twice. The third time, the gun fell from her hand and clattered to the floor. I was terrified it might go off again, but it bounced harmlessly up against the base-board.

I let go of Jan's hand and dived down to get it, but the moment I let go and turned, she jumped onto my back.

"No!" she screamed.

I rolled, forcing her up against the metal frame of Ethan's bed. The beam jammed into her back and she yelped in pain. I scrambled ahead, crablike, to get my hands on the gun, got it, then rolled and pointed it straight at her.

"Just shoot me, David," she said, winded and getting up onto her hands and knees. "Just put a fucking bullet in my head. It'd be easier."

"Who are you?" I shouted, both hands wrapped around the gun. "Who the hell *are* you?"

She rose up, sat on the side of the bed, and put her head in her hands. After a moment, she looked up, tears running down her cheeks. "I'm Connie Tattinger," she said. "But . . . I'm also Jan Harwood. No matter who I am, I'm Ethan's mother." She paused. "And I was your wife. For a time."

"What's all of this been?" I asked her. "These last five years? Some kind of goddamn joke?"

She shook her head. "Not a joke . . . not a joke. I was, I've been . . . waiting. And hiding."

"Waiting for what? Hiding from whom?"

Jan took a few breaths, ran a finger under her wet nose, and said, "We hijacked a diamond shipment."

"What? We?"

Jan dismissed the questions with a wave. "Six years ago. Then, my partner, he got sent away for something else. The diamonds were in a safe place, but it was going to be a few years before we could get at them. The man we took them from . . . he's been looking for us, for me, all that time."

I was trying to take it all in. Those few short sentences, summing up years of deception. I grabbed on to something Jan had already said. "But you said they were worthless. Why would this man, why would he want them back?"

She summoned some more strength to continue. "Because of what I did to him."

I waited.

"I cut off his hand," she said. "To get the briefcase he was attached to." She sniffed. "He lived."

I was so stunned that I lowered the gun, letting it rest on the floor next to me, but still within reach. "I don't know who you are," I said.

She nodded. "No, you really don't. You never have."

"Where did this all happen?" I asked.

"Boston," she said.

"So after it happened, you had to hide out," I said. "You came to Promise Falls."

She nodded, her eyes glistening.

"And married me. Why? Why do that?"

She couldn't find the words. I took a shot at helping her out. "It was like camouflage. You figured I could help you blend in. Who'd guess the nice little wife down the street had anything to do with a diamond heist?"

She nodded again.

"Did you really need to have a child to complete the picture?" I asked. "Is that what Ethan's been for you? Part of a cover story?"

"No," she whispered.

I shook my head. I had more questions. "So let me figure this out. When your partner got out of jail, you'd recover the diamonds?"

"Yeah," she said. "We expected to get a lot of money for them."

"Enough to go away and live happily ever after," I said.

She closed her eyes and nodded again.

"And I was dumb enough to think you already were. God, I'm such an idiot."

Jan swallowed, wiped away a tear, and said, "But they weren't worth anything. The man whose hand I cut off—his name's Oscar Fine—he'd been putting the word out. When we showed up at this guy's place, this guy Dwayne—"

"Dwayne?"

"He was the one I stole them with," she said. "Dwayne knew a man who'd give us cash for the diamonds. But he must have called Fine. When we went back for the money, Fine was there. He must have killed Dwayne. And he tried to kill me before I got away."

I rested my head up against Ethan's closet door.

Jan said to me, "What the hell happened to the floors? All the boards ripped up?"

"I found the birth certificate, the one for Jan Richler," I said. "Behind the baseboard in the linen closet."

"You couldn't have," she said. "I took it with me."

"I found it a long time ago, but put it back. After you disappeared, I wondered what else you might have hid. I found the other one, the real one. Why didn't you take it, too?"

"I needed the other envelope for the key that was in it," she said. "It didn't occur to me to get the other one. So . . . you knew about the Richlers?"

"I knew of them, but I only went to see them after you disappeared. I found out about their daughter."

Jan looked away.

"I guess that was handy in getting a new ID," I said, not able to keep the sarcasm out of my voice. "Knowing someone personally who died as a child. So you applied for a copy of the birth certificate and—"

"No," she said.

"What? But I found—"

"It was the original. I tried applying for a copy but didn't have enough substantiating information. So I watched the Richlers' routine for a few days, figured out when they did their groceries, got in when they went out. People generally keep those kinds of documents in one spot. A drawer in the kitchen, the bedroom. Only took me an hour to find it. Once I had it, everything else—driver's license, Social Security—was a breeze."

I was actually impressed, but only for a moment. "You have any idea what you've done to those people? Bad enough what happened when you were a little girl."

Jan shot me a look, evidently figuring out I knew she'd pushed the other girl into the path of the car.

"But to use their daughter's name now, all these years later, that—"

"Okay, so I'm a shit," she said. "I'm poison. Anyone who comes in contact with me, their life eventually goes into the toilet. Jan Richler, her parents, my parents, Dwayne."

"Me," I said. "Ethan."

Jan met my eye and looked away again.

"The whole depression thing, it was masterful," I said.

"My mother," Jan whispered. "She spent most of her life down in the dumps. Can hardly blame her, considering what she was married to, the bastard. I just modeled myself on her, without the booze."

"Well, you set me up beautifully. I was the perfect patsy, wasn't I? Your sole audience. So when you disappeared, it looked like I was lying. Like I was trying to make them think you killed yourself, and the cops would figure I'd killed you. The trip to Lake George, the horseshit you told that guy in the store. Everything pointed to me. And it was you who sent the email."

Half a nod. "You'd already heard from that woman. I knew you'd fall for the email."

"And the tickets you ordered online. How'd you get into the park?"

"I paid cash," she whispered.

"Was Dwayne the one who ran off with Ethan? So I'd have this crazy story to tell the cops, and give you time to slip away?"

"I'm sorry," she whispered.

"Please," I said. "How'd you pull it off?"

"I had a change of clothes, a wig, in the backpack. When you ran after Ethan, I went into the restroom and changed, then walked out of Five Mountains."

My fingers touched the gun resting on the floor.

"There's more," she said quietly. "Sites you supposedly visited on the laptop, blood in the trunk, a receipt for duct—"

"Yeah," I said. "I know. And talking me into the life insurance policy. About the blood. Did you really cut your wrist?"

"No. I nicked my ankle so I could leave a sample in the trunk."

"You're really something," I said. "The thing I don't get—the thing I will probably never get—is why?"

Jan wiped a finger under her nose again. "They wouldn't be looking for me if they thought I was already dead," she said. "Even if they never found a body, if they figured you'd killed me . . ."

"That's not what I meant," I said. "I'm asking *why*."

She didn't seem to follow.

"Why would you do this to me?" I asked her. "How could you do this? How could you do this to me? How could you do this to Ethan?"

Her eyes moved about for a second, as though searching for the answer. Then they stopped abruptly, as though the answer had been right in front of her.

She said, "I wanted the money."

# FIFTY-FOUR

"WHAT DID YOU THINK was going to happen?" I asked. "After I ended up going to jail for killing you?"

"I figured, maybe, because there was no body, you'd end up getting off," she said. "But they'd still think you did it, and they wouldn't come looking for me."

"And if they convicted me?"

"Your parents would look after Ethan," she said. "They love him. He'd be safe with them."

"But you had to know," I said, "that if I did get off, I wouldn't rest until I found you."

"I'd already had someone looking for me," Jan said. "And he hadn't, until now, found me. I figured I could deal with that, once we had the money from the diamonds."

The word "we" had triggered something in me. "This Dwayne," I said. "Were you in love with him?"

She didn't need time to think. "No," she said. "But he was useful."

I nodded. "Like me." I couldn't stop myself from asking, "And what about me? Did you ever love me?"

"If I said yes, would you even believe it?" she said.

"No," I said. "What about Leanne? How'd she end up dead?"

Jan shook her head tiredly. "That wasn't supposed to happen. But Dwayne and I, we ran into her, outside Albany. She saw me in the truck, came over, wondered what I was doing there, who Dwayne was. Dwayne did what he had to do. We got rid of her car, and took her up to Lake George, in the pickup, under the cover."

"That meant a lot of backtracking."

"I had this idea," she said, looking down into her lap, "that if we left her body up there, it would . . . it would build the case against you."

I ran my fingers across the gun again, slowly took it into my hand.

"I never knew you for a minute," I said.

She looked at me. "No, you never did."

"Why did you have him?" I asked.

"What?"

"Why did you have Ethan? When you got pregnant, why did you go ahead with it? Why didn't you get an abortion?"

She bit her lip. "I was going to," she said. "I thought about it. Having a child, it was never part of the plan. I couldn't believe it when it happened. I thought I'd taken precautions, but . . . I lay awake at nights, convinced I was going to do something about it. I made some calls, went to a clinic in Albany. I had an appointment." She wiped tears from her eyes. "I couldn't do it. I wanted to have him. I wanted to have a baby."

Now I was shaking my head. "You're something else. You know what you are?"

She waited.

"A monster. A psychopath. The goddamn devil in a dress. I loved you. I really loved you. But it was all an act. None of it real. Not for one fucking minute."

Jan struggled to find the words she wanted to say. "I came back because of love," she said.

"No, you didn't."

"I came back for Ethan," she said. "You, I figured you could find a way to fend for yourself. But with Oscar Fine out there, looking for me, looking for ways to get to me, I knew I had to come back for Ethan, to protect him. He's my son. He *belongs* to me. I'm his *mother*, for Christ's—"

I'd had enough.

I picked up the gun, pointed it, and pulled the trigger, felt the gun kick back in my hand.

Jan screamed as the shot filled the room.

The bullet went into the wall over Ethan's headboard, a good two feet to the left of Jan. She looked around, saw the hole in the wall.

"That's what kind of mother I think you are," I said.

Shaking, Jan said, "It's true. I came here for him. I drove by your parents' house first, didn't see any sign of him, then I came here. It was dark, so I let myself in, decided to pack his things, then when you came home, I was going to leave with him."

"Jesus, Jan, what were you going to do? Kidnap him at gunpoint? Wave this in my face and drag him off? Is that really what you were going to do?"

She was shaking her head. "I don't know."

"Jan, it's over. Everything's over. You have to turn yourself in. You have to tell the police what you did, how you set me up. If you love Ethan, the only way to prove it, at this point, is to make it possible for me to raise him. You're going to go to jail. There's no way around it. Probably for a very, very long time. But if you mean what you say, if you love your son, you have to make things right so that he has his father there for him."

A calm seemed to come over her. "Okay," she said quietly. "Okay."

"But the first thing we have to do," I said, "is find him."

It was as though I'd thrown cold water on her. She became, suddenly, focused. "Find him? You don't know where he is? He's missing?"

"This afternoon. He was playing with the croquet set in the backyard and Mom stopped hearing—"

"When?" Jan asked urgently. "When did she notice he was gone?"

"Late. Like, five or six o'clock."

Jan seemed to be computing something in her head. "He could have gotten there by then," she said.

"Tell me," I said. "Are you talking about this Oscar person?"

She nodded. "I think he knows where I've been living, who I've been these last six years. Either from the news, or from Dwayne, before he killed him. Fine would have had time to get here. He's driving a black Audi, something he could make good time in. He might have gotten to Promise Falls before I did. I pulled off the highway for a while, trying to gather myself together."

"Jesus Christ, Jan, how would he even know where to find Ethan?"

"You think he's stupid? All he has to do is look up your name. He'll find this address, your parents' address, plus . . ."

"Plus what?"

Jan's face crumpled like paper. "He may even have a picture of Ethan."

It was all dizzying. Finally encountering Jan, learning about her past, coming to grips with the realization that Ethan might not just be missing, but in real danger. As I went to get up off the floor, my hand caught on the rough edge of a long piece of hardwood flooring shaped like a jagged icicle.

"Fuck," I said. Still not trusting Jan, I tucked the gun under the edge of my butt while I pried out a splinter with my thumb and forefinger. Blood bubbled out of the wound.

Jan made no move for the weapon, and I took hold of it again as I got to my feet.

"This guy," I said, "whose hand you cut off, what would he do with Ethan if he had him?"

Jan shuddered. "I think he'd do anything," she said. "I think he'd do anything he had to, to get back at me."

The words "eye for an eye" came to me. But I wasn't thinking about eyes. I thought of the feel of Ethan's hand in mine.

"Do you have a way to reach this man?" I asked, feeling frantic. "Some way to find him? So we could try to work something out? Make some sort of deal?"

Jan said, "He might be willing to trade Ethan for me."

There was nothing in that plan that troubled me. Not at this moment. But I didn't think it was our only option.

"I'll call Duckworth," I said.

"Who?"

"The detective who's been trying to find you, to nail me for your murder. He can put the word out. Get everyone looking for Oscar Fine. You can give them a description, tell them about the car he's driving. If the police find him, they find Ethan. I don't think he's going to do anything to him before he's found you. He probably figures as long as he has Ethan, alive, he'll have some leverage with you."

Jan, resigned, nodded. "You're right. You're right. You're right. Call him. Call the detective. I'll tell him anything he needs to know to find Ethan. I'll tell him anything he needs if it'll help find Oscar Fine, if it'll lead us to Ethan."

I took out my phone.

Jan reached out, touched my arm. "I don't expect you to forgive me."

I moved my arm away. "Gee, you think?" I said.

I flipped open the phone, started searching the list of incoming calls so I could find Detective Duckworth's

number, and was hitting the button to connect when a
voice said, "Stop."

I looked up. There was someone standing in the doorway to Ethan's room.

A man with one hand.

# FIFTY-FIVE

"DROP THE GUN, AND the phone," Oscar Fine said to me. He had a weapon of his own pointed at me. It had a long barrel, slightly wider at the end. I was guessing that was a silencer. There'd already been two unsilenced shots fired off in this room. With any luck, maybe the neighbors had heard them and dialed 911.

My gun was aimed at the floor, and I was pretty sure I'd be dead before I could raise my arm to use it. So I let the gun fall down along the side of my leg to the floor and tossed the phone, still open, onto the bed.

"Kick it over here," Oscar Fine said. "Carefully."

I lined up the edge of my shoe with the gun and slid it toward him. It narrowly missed one of the holes in the floor. Never taking his eyes off either of us, he knelt down, and using his stump and the weapon in his one hand like a set of chopsticks, picked up the gun and slipped it into his pocket.

The color had drained from Jan's face. I'd never seen her look more frightened, or more vulnerable. Maybe, if there'd been a mirror around, I would have felt the same about myself. *This is it,* her expression said. *It's over.*

"Where's my son?" I asked.

Oscar Fine didn't look at me. His eyes were fixed on Jan. "It's been a long time," he said.

"Please," Jan said. "You have the wrong person."

He smiled wryly. "Really. Show a little more dignity

than your boyfriend did at the end. You know what he did? He pissed himself. The poor bastard pissed himself. I'm guessing you're made of stronger stuff than that. After all, you were the one who had it in you to cut off my hand. He just sat up front. Did he piss himself then, too?"

Jan licked her lips. I was guessing her mouth was as dry as mine. She said, "You should have had a key on you. If you'd had a key, we could have taken the briefcase without hurting you."

Oscar Fine momentarily looked solemn. "I can't argue with you there. But you know what they say about hindsight." He smiled and then said, with no hint of irony in his voice, "You have to play the hand you're dealt."

Jan said to him, nodding in my direction, "Please let him go. Tell him where our son is so he can go get him. He's just a boy. Please don't make him pay for anything I've done to you. I'm begging you. Is Ethan outside? Is he in your car?"

Oscar Fine's tongue moved around inside his mouth, like he was thinking something over.

And then, in an instant, his arm went up and the gun in his hand went *pfft*.

I shouted, "No! God, no! *Jan!*"

Jan was tossed back against the wall. Her mouth opened, but she didn't make a sound. She looked down at the blossom of red above her right breast, put her right hand up and touched it.

I ran to Jan, tried to hold her as she started her slide down the wall. I eased her down, tried not to look at the blood trail she'd left behind her. Her eyes were already glassy.

"It's going to be okay," I said.

The front of her blouse was already soaked with blood. Her breathing was short and raspy.

"Ethan," she whispered to me.

"I know," I said. "I know."

I looked at Oscar Fine, who hadn't moved since firing the shot. It struck me that he looked at peace.

"I have to call an ambulance," I said. "My wife . . . she's losing a lot of blood."

"No," he said.

"She's dying," I said.

"That's the idea," Oscar Fine said.

Jan struggled to raise her head, looked at him and, with considerable effort, said, "Ethan. Where is Ethan?"

Oscar Fine shook his head. "I have no idea," he said. "But if you'd like, I'd be happy to look for your son. Once I find him, who would you like his hands sent to?" He smiled sadly at me. "It won't be you."

"You don't have him," I said.

"I wish," Oscar Fine said.

Jan's eyelids fell shut. I slipped my arm around her, pulled her to me. I couldn't tell whether she was still breathing.

In the distance, we heard a siren.

"Shit," said Oscar Fine. He glanced at the open phone on the bed, shook his head in disgust, reached over and snapped it shut. He sighed as the siren—it sounded like only one—grew louder. In another few seconds, I could hear steps pounding on the front porch.

"Change of plan," Oscar Fine said. He waved the barrel at me. "Come."

I took my arm from around Jan and walked across the room, past Oscar Fine and through the door. He stayed close behind me. I could feel the barrel of the gun touching my back.

"Stay very close," he said.

From downstairs, I heard Barry Duckworth yell, "Mr. Harwood?"

"Up here," I said, not shouting, but in a voice loud enough to be heard.

"Are you okay?" Lights started coming on downstairs.

"No. And my wife's been shot."

"I've already called an ambulance." Duckworth had reached the bottom of the stairs. Oscar Fine and I were standing behind the short upstairs hall railing, about to turn and come down the stairs.

Duckworth, who had his weapon drawn, looked up. I could see the puzzlement in his face, wondering who the man behind me could be.

Oscar Fine said, "I'm going to shoot Mr. Harwood if you don't let us leave together."

Duckworth, his gun angled upward, took a moment to assess things. "There's going to be a dozen officers out front in about two minutes," he said.

"Then we have to move quickly," Oscar said, moving me down a step at a time. "Lower your weapon or I'll shoot Mr. Harwood right now."

Duckworth, seeing the gun at my back, lowered his gun but held on to it. "You need to give yourself up," he said.

"No," he said. We were halfway down the stairs now. "Please back away."

Duckworth took a couple of steps back toward the front door.

We reached the first floor. Keeping me in front of him as a shield, Oscar Fine started easing me toward the kitchen. He was going to take me out the back door. Maybe his car was parked a block over, and we'd be heading through the backyard and between the houses to get there.

Duckworth watched in frustration. His eyes met mine.

We were under the railing when I noticed Duckworth glancing up.

Oscar Fine and I both craned our necks upward at the same time, too.

It was Jan. She was standing at the railing, leaning over it at the waist. A drop of blood touched my forehead like warm rain.

She said, "You will never hurt my son."

And then her body pivoted forward. She wasn't leaning on the railing, she was pitching herself right over it.

As she started to come down, I saw that she was clutching firmly, in both hands, the two-foot daggerlike plank of hardwood flooring I'd caught my hand on.

She plunged over the side, the plank pointing straight down ahead of her.

Oscar Fine had no time to react before its sharp, ragged end caught him where neck meets shoulder. The force of Jan's fall rammed the plank deep into his torso, and that, combined with the weight of Jan's body, put him down on the floor in an instant.

Neither of them moved after that.

# FIFTY-SIX

JAN AND OSCAR FINE were both declared dead at the scene. Once the initial panic was over, I couldn't bring myself to go back into the front hall and look at the tangled wreckage that was my wife and her killer.

I spent the better part of an hour with Barry Duckworth, explaining everything to him as best I could. Broad strokes, mostly. Many of the details I didn't know, and didn't expect I ever would.

I had the sense he believed me.

But even before we got into that, I had something more urgent to discuss with him.

"Ethan's still missing," I said. "Jan was certain Oscar Fine had taken him, but upstairs there, just before everything happened, he said he didn't know anything about him."

"Was he lying, you think?" Duckworth asked. "Messing with you?"

"I don't think so," I said. "If he'd had Ethan, I think he would have enjoyed taunting us with the fact."

But to be certain, we found a black Audi—registered to Oscar Fine—one street over. We checked the back seat and trunk for any signs of Ethan.

We came up empty.

"We have everyone working on this," Duckworth assured me as the two of us sat together at the kitchen table. "Every single available member of the department is looking for your boy. We've brought people in on their days off. We're doing a block-by-block search."

"What if Ethan's disappearance . . . what if it has nothing to do with any of this?" I asked. "What if he just wandered off? Or some sick son of a bitch just happened to be driving through the neighborhood and—"

"Regardless," Duckworth said, "we're doing everything, exploring all those angles. We're interviewing everyone on your parents' street and your street, doing a door-to-door right now."

None of this made me feel any better.

"She did it for Ethan," I said. "And for me."

"She did what?" Duckworth said.

"She pulled it together long enough to kill that man so I'd be there for Ethan."

"I guess she did," Duckworth said.

"She said she didn't expect my forgiveness," I said.

"Maybe, if she could ask you now . . ."

I said nothing and looked down at the table.

Mom and Dad arrived shortly after that. There was hugging and crying, and as I had done with Duckworth, I tried to tell them what I knew about the events of the last three days.

And the last six years. And even before that.

"Where could Ethan be?" Mom asked. "Where would he go?"

While Duckworth went off to help oversee the crime scene, the three of us sat at the table, not knowing what to do.

We were tired, depressed, traumatized.

Part of me was grieving.

Sometime around midnight, the phone rang. I picked up.

"Hello?" I said.

"Mr. Harwood?"

"Yes?"

"I've done a terrible thing."

I was there by 3 a.m.

Detective Duckworth put up some objections at first. First, he didn't want me leaving the crime scene. Second, if I knew who had taken my son, if he'd been kidnapped, Duckworth had to send in the police.

"I don't know that it's exactly a kidnapping," I said. "At least not now. It's kind of complicated. Just let me go and get my boy. I know where he is. Let me bring him home."

He mulled it over a moment, then finally said, "Go." He said he'd try to pave the way for me with the New York Thruway authorities, maybe save me the trouble of getting pulled over for speeding.

When I pulled up in front of the Richlers' house on Lincoln Avenue in Rochester, the living room lights were on. I didn't have to knock. Gretchen Richler was standing at the door waiting for me, and had it open as I came up the porch steps.

"Let me see him," I said.

She nodded. She led me upstairs and pushed open the door to what I presumed to be the bedroom she shared with her husband, who was not around. Ethan was under the covers, his head on the pillow, sound asleep.

"I'll let him sleep for a bit more," I said.

"I've put on some coffee," Gretchen said. "Would you like some?"

"Yes," I said, following her back downstairs. "Is your husband . . ."

"Still in the hospital," she said. "They have him in the psychiatric ward, I guess they call it. They've got him under observation."

"How do you think he's going to be?"

"It's a kind of wait-and-see situation," she said.

"With any luck, he could be home in a few days, although I . . . I don't know how he'll fend on his own."

She filled two mugs with coffee and set them on the kitchen table. "Would you like some cookies?" she asked.

I shook my head. "Coffee's fine."

Gretchen Richler took a seat across from me. "I know what I did was wrong," she said.

I blew on the coffee, took a sip. "Tell me what happened."

"Well, first of all, we were looking at that picture you left with us, the one of your wife. It was the necklace she was wearing. The cupcake."

"Yes?"

"It had been our daughter's. She'd lost it just before she died. She'd accused Constance of stealing it. When I saw it on your wife, it all came together. I knew."

"It was the only time I remember seeing her wear it," I said. "She had it in her jewelry box but never put it on. But just before that trip, Ethan found it. He loves cupcakes and begged her to wear it."

"That last time you called, just after Horace tried to take his own life, when you said you thought your wife was still alive, that you thought maybe you were going to find her, I went . . . I went a little crazy."

"Go on," I said.

"I was so angry. Here's this woman, she'd taken my daughter's life not once but twice. I couldn't get it out of my mind, what she'd done to us. I wanted her to know how it felt."

I nodded, had another sip of the hot coffee.

"I just, I just thought that she deserved it. That if she could take a child from us, if she could take her from us, and then take her identity, something bad had to happen so she'd understand. So, with Horace in the hospital, I drove to Promise Falls. I found your parents' house and

I saw your son playing in the backyard. I told him I was his aunt Gretchen, and that it was finally time for him to come home."

"And he went with you."

"That's right. He was so excited about going home, he never questioned me for a minute."

"He didn't think it was odd that he had an aunt he'd never heard of before?"

Gretchen shook her head. "He never questioned it."

"So he got in the car with you," I said.

She nodded. "I'd stopped around the corner, before I got to your place, and bought some treats to keep him happy. Then I started driving back here, and he was telling me I was going the wrong way. I had to explain to him that before I could take him home, he was going to stay with me for a little while."

"How'd he take that?"

Gretchen choked up and a tear formed at the corner of her eye. "He started to cry. I told him not to, that everything was going to be okay. That he wouldn't have to stay with me all that long."

"What were you planning to do?" I asked.

Gretchen looked into my eyes. "I don't know."

"You must have some idea."

"On the way to Promise Falls, I'd made up my mind. I was going to . . . I was going to . . ."

"You wouldn't have hurt him."

She couldn't look at me. "I hope not. It's like, for a while there, I was possessed or something. I wasn't my-self. I was going to get even, make things right. But when I saw him, once I had him in the car . . ."

"You couldn't do it," I said.

"He's a lovely boy," she said, looking at me again. "He really is. You must be so proud of him."

"I am," I said.

"But once I'd taken him, I didn't know what to do."

"So you just came back to Rochester."

She nodded sadly. "I'm very ashamed of myself. I am."

"You have no idea what you've put us through," I said.

"I know."

"My mother, I don't know that she can ever forgive herself for letting Ethan out of her sight."

"I'll tell her I'm sorry. I will. Don't you get a chance to make some sort of statement when they sentence you? Don't you get to say something to the family?"

I felt so tired.

"I don't think that will be necessary," I said.

Gretchen was confused. "I don't understand. I kidnapped your son. I have to be punished for that."

I reached across the table and put a hand on hers. "I think you've been punished enough. You and your husband." I paused. "By my wife."

"Even if you don't want me arrested, she might," Gretchen said.

"No," I said. "She won't. She's dead."

Gretchen gasped. "What? When?"

"About four hours ago," I said. "Her past—one of them—caught up with her. So there's no one to get even with anymore. She's gone. And the truth is, you may have saved Ethan by taking him away when you did."

"That doesn't excuse me," she said.

"All that matters to me, at this moment, is that my son is okay, and that he's not in any danger. I'll do what I can to persuade the police not to charge you. I won't cooperate if they want me to testify."

"I made him a late dinner," Gretchen said, not hearing me. "He settled down after a while, and I made him some macaroni and cheese."

"He likes that."

"I knew I was going to have to call you. I was going

to do it in the morning. But I knew you wouldn't be able to sleep, not knowing where he was, so I decided to call when I did."

"I'm glad." I took my hand off hers. "I'd like to get my son now."

"You'd be welcome to sleep on the couch again, go in the morning."

"Thank you for the offer," I said, "but no."

Gretchen led me upstairs. I sat on the edge of the bed. Ethan stirred, rolled over.

"Ethan," I whispered, touching his shoulder gently. "Ethan."

He opened his eyes slowly, blinked a couple of times to adjust for the light spilling in from the hall.

"Hi, Dad," he said.

"Time to go," I said.

"Back to our house?" he said hopefully.

"Not for a while yet," I said. Maybe never. "Probably Nana and Poppa's. But I'm going to be with you."

I pulled back the covers. He was still dressed, his shoes on the floor next to the bed.

"I didn't have any pajamas for him," Gretchen said apologetically.

I nodded. As I helped Ethan sit up, Gretchen handed me his shoes. While I was slipping them on his feet and securing them with the Velcro straps, he said, "That's Aunt Gretchen."

"That's right," I said.

"She picked me up at Nana's."

"I hear she made you macaroni and cheese."

"Yup."

Once I had his shoes on, I picked him up, let him rest his head on my shoulder, and went back downstairs.

"I hope Horace will be okay," I said as Gretchen opened the door for me.

"Thank you," she said. "But you just worry about your boy." She patted Ethan on the head. "Bye-bye."

"Bye, Aunt Gretchen," he said, rubbing his eyes.

I carried him to Dad's car and belted him into the safety seat in the back. I was about to turn the key when Ethan asked, "Did you find Mommy?"

"Yes," I said.

"Is she home?" he asked.

I took my hand away from the key, got out of the front seat and into the back. I closed the door behind me and snuggled in close to Ethan, taking his hands into mine.

"No," I said. "She's gone away. She won't be coming back to us. But you have to know she loves you more than life itself."

"Is she mad at me?" he asked.

"No, of course not," I said. "She could never be mad at you." I paused, then found the words I wanted. "The last thing she did, she did for you."

Ethan nodded tiredly, cried a little, then yawned and fell back asleep. I kept holding him. We were still there like that when the sun came up.

# ACKNOWLEDGMENTS

LET'S START WITH BOOKSELLERS. You wouldn't have this in your hands—or on your eReader—without them. I am most grateful for the enthusiasm shown by those people who've turned their love of books into a life's work. It doesn't matter how many ads you may see or reviews you may read, nothing sells a novel better than a bookseller putting it in your hands and saying, "You really should try this."

Thank you.

I'd be nowhere without my good friend and agent, Helen Heller. She knows a good story, and she knows a bad one, and she's never afraid to tell me which kind I'm writing. Her instincts and advice are invaluable.

I am deeply indebted to Gina Centrello, Nita Taublib, Danielle Perez, and everyone else at Bantam for their dedication and support.

Keith Williams, of Williams Distinctive Gems, filled me in on diamonds. At the Vaughan Press Centre, where the *Toronto Star*—my terrific employer for twenty-seven years—is printed, Sarkis Harmandayan and Terry Vere kindly gave me a refresher course on how presses operate.

Speaking of newspapers, I'd like to thank them, too. Most of what I know comes from reading them, and working for them. They're having a tough time these days. If they end up going totally online, so be it, but we need to pay for it, or stories that need to be told won't be.

And, as always, none of this would matter without Neetha, Spencer, and Paige.

If you enjoyed *Never Look Away,*
you won't want to miss any of Linwood Barclay's
electrifying suspense novels.
Read on for an exciting early look at

# THE ACCIDENT

## Coming soon from Bantam Books

IF I'D KNOWN THIS was our last morning, I'd have rolled over in bed and held her. But of course, if it had been possible to know something like that—if I could have somehow seen into the future—I wouldn't have let go. And then things would have been different.

I'd been staring at the ceiling for a while when I finally threw back the covers and planted my feet on the hard-wood floor.

"How'd you sleep?" Sheila asked as I rubbed my eyes. She reached out and touched my back.

"Not so good. You?"

"Off and on."

"I sensed you were awake, but I didn't want to bug you, on the off chance you were sleeping," I said, glancing over my shoulder. The sun's first rays of the day filtered through the drapes and played across my wife's face as she lay in bed, looking at me. This wasn't a time of day when people looked their best, but there was something about Sheila. She was always beautiful. Even when she looked worried, which was how she looked now.

I turned back around, looked down at my bare feet. "I couldn't get to sleep for the longest time, then I think I finally nodded off around two, but then I looked at the clock and it was five. Been awake since then."

"Glen, it's going to be okay," Sheila said. She moved her hand across my back, soothing me.

"Yeah, well, I'm glad you think so."

"Things'll pick up. Everything goes in cycles. Recessions don't last forever."

I sighed. "This one sure seems to. After these jobs I'm doing now, we got nothin' lined up. Some nibbles, did a couple of estimates last week—one for a kitchen, one to finish off a basement—but they haven't called back."

I stood up, turned and said, "What's your excuse for staring at the ceiling all night?"

"Worried about you. And . . . I've got things on my mind, too."

"What?"

"Nothing," she said quickly. "I mean, just the usual. This course I'm taking, Kelly, your work."

"What's wrong with Kelly?"

"Nothing's wrong with her. I'm a mother. She's eight. I worry. It's what I do. When I've done the course, I can help you more. That'll make a difference."

"When you made the decision to take it, we had the business to justify it. Now, I don't know if I'll even have any work for you to do," I said. "I just hope I have enough to keep Sally busy."

Sheila'd started her business accounting course mid-August, and two months in was enjoying it more than she'd expected. The plan was for Sheila to do the day-to-day accounts for Garber Contracting, the company that was once my father's, and which I now ran. She could even do it from home, which would allow Sally Diehl, our "office girl," to focus more on general office management, returning phone calls, hounding suppliers, fielding customer inquiries. There usually wasn't time for Sally to do the accounting, which meant I was bringing it home at night, sitting at my desk until midnight. But with work drying up, I didn't know how this was all going to shake down.

"And now, with the fire—"

"Enough," Sheila said.

"Sheila, one of my goddamn houses burned down. Please don't tell me everything's going to be fine."

She sat up in bed and crossed her arms across her breasts. "I'm not going to let you get all negative on me. This is what you do."

"I'm just telling you how it is."

"And I'm going to tell you how it will *be*," she said. "We will *be* okay. Because this is what *we* do. You and I. We get through things. We find a way." She looked away for a moment, like there was something she wanted to say but wasn't sure how to say it. Finally, she said, "I have ideas."

"What ideas?"

"Ideas to help us. To get us through the rough patches."

I stood there, my arms open, waiting.

"You're so busy, so wrapped up in your own problems—and I'm not saying that they aren't big problems—that you haven't even noticed."

"Noticed what?" I asked.

She shook her head and smiled. "I got Kelly new outfits for school."

"Okay."

"Nice ones."

I narrowed my eyes. "What are you getting at?"

"I've made some money."

I thought I already knew that. Sheila had her part-time job at Hardware Depot—about twenty hours a week—working the checkout. They'd recently installed these new self-checkout stations people couldn't figure out, so there was still work there for Sheila until they did. And since the early summer, Sheila had been helping our next-door neighbor—Joan Mueller—with her own books for a business she was running from her home. Joan's husband, Ely, had been killed on that oil rig off the coast of Newfoundland when it blew up about a year back. She'd been getting jerked around by the oil company on her settlement, and in the meantime had started running a daycare operation. Every morning four or five preschoolers got dropped off at her door. And on school days when Sheila was working, Kelly went to Joan's until one of us got home. Sheila had helped Joan organize a bookkeeping system to keep track of what everyone owed and had paid. Joan loved kids, but could barely finger count.

"I know you've been making some money," I said. "Joan, and the store. Everything helps."

"Those two jobs together don't keep us in Hamburger Helper. I'm talking about better money than that."

My eyebrows went up. Then I got worried. "Tell me you're not taking money from Fiona." Her mother. "You know how I feel about that."

She looked insulted. "Jesus, Glen, you know I would never—"

"I'm just saying. I'd rather you were a drug dealer than taking money from your mother."

She blinked, threw back the covers abruptly, got out of bed, and stalked into the bathroom. The door closed firmly behind her.

"Aw, come on," I said.

By the time we reached the kitchen, I didn't think she was angry with me anymore. I'd apologized twice, and tried to coax from Sheila details of what her idea was to bring more money into the house.

"We can talk about it tonight," she said.

We hadn't washed the dishes from the night before. There were a couple of coffee cups, my scotch glass, and Sheila's wine goblet, with a dark red residue at the bottom, sitting in the sink. I lifted the goblet onto the counter, worried the stem might break if other things got tossed into the sink alongside it.

The wineglass made me think of Sheila's friends.

"You seeing Ann for lunch or anything?" I asked.

"No."

"I thought you had something set up."

"Maybe later this week. Belinda and Ann and me might get together, although every time we do that I have to get a cab home and my head hurts for a week. Anyway, I think Ann's got some physical or something today, an insurance thing."

"She okay?"

"She's fine." A pause. "More or less."

"What's that mean?"

"I don't know. I think there's some kind of tension there, between her and Darren. And between Belinda and George, for that matter."

"What's going on?"

"Who knows," she said.

"So then, what are you doing today? You don't have a shift today, right? If I can slip away, you want to get lunch? I was thinking something fancy, like that guy who sells hot dogs by the park."

"I've got my course tonight," she said. "Some errands to run, and I might visit Mom." She shot me a look. "*Not* to ask her for money."

"Okay." I decided to ask nothing further. She'd tell me when she was ready.

Kelly walked into the room at the tail end of the conversation. "What's for breakfast?"

"You want cereal, cereal, or cereal?" Sheila asked.

Kelly appeared to ponder her choices. "I'll take cereal," she said, and sat at the table.

At our house, breakfast wasn't a sit-down family meal like dinner. Actually, dinner often wasn't, either, especially when I got held up at a construction site, or Sheila was at work, or heading off to her class. But we at least tried to make that a family event. Breakfast was a lost cause, however. I had my toast and coffee standing, usually flattening the morning *Register* on the countertop and scanning the headlines as I turned the pages. Sheila was spooning in fruit and yogurt at the same time as Kelly shoveled in her Cheerios, trying to get them into herself before any of them had a chance to get soggy.

Between spoonfuls she asked, "Why would anyone go to school at night when they're grown up and don't have to go?"

"When I finish this course," Sheila told her, "I'll be able to help your father more, and that helps the family, and that helps you."

"How does that help me?" she wanted to know.

I stepped in. "Because if my company is run well, it makes more money, and *that* helps you."

"So you can buy me more stuff?"

"Not necessarily."

Kelly took a gulp of orange juice. "I'd never go to school at night. Or summer. You'd have to kill me to get me to go to summer school."

"If you get really good marks, that won't happen," I said, a hint of warning in my voice. We'd already had a call from her teacher that she wasn't completing all her homework.

Kelly had nothing to say to that and concentrated on her cereal. On the way out the door, she gave her mother a hug, but all I got was a wave. Sheila caught me noticing the perceived slight and said, "It's because you're a meanie."

I called the house from work mid-morning.

"Hey," Sheila said.

"You're home. I didn't know whether I'd catch you or not."

"Still here. What's up?"

"Sally's dad."

"What?"

"She was calling home from the office and when he

didn't answer she took off. I just called to see how he was and he's gone."

"He's dead?"

"Yeah."

"Oh jeez. How old was he?"

"Seventy-nine, I think. He was in his late fifties when he had Sally." Sheila knew the history. The man had married a woman twenty years younger than he was, and still managed to outlive her. She'd died of an aneurysm a decade ago.

"What happened to him?"

"Don't know. I mean, he had diabetes, he'd been having heart trouble. Could have been a heart attack."

"We need to do something for her."

"I offered to drop by but she said she's got a lot to deal with right now. Funeral'll probably be in a couple of days. We can talk about it when you get back from Bridgeport." Where Sheila took her class.

"We'll do something. We've always been there for her." I could almost picture Sheila shaking her head. "Look," she said, "I'm heading out. I'll leave you and Kelly lasagna, okay? Joan's expecting her after school today and—"

"I got it. Thanks."

"For what?"

"Not giving up. Not letting things get you down."

"Just doing the best I can," she said.

"I love you. I know I can be a pain in the ass, but I love you."

"Ditto."

It was after ten. Sheila should have been home by now.

I tried her cell for the second time in ten minutes. After six rings it went to voicemail. *"Hi, you've reached Sheila Garber. Sorry I missed you. Leave a message and I'll get back to you."* Then the beep.

"Hey, me again," I said. "You're freaking me out. Call me."

I put the cordless receiver back onto its stand and leaned up against the kitchen counter, folded my arms. As she'd promised, Sheila had left two servings of lasagna in the fridge, for Kelly and me, each hermetically sealed under plastic wrap. I'd heated Kelly's in the microwave when we got home, and she'd come back looking for seconds, but I couldn't find a baking dish with any more in it. I might as well have offered her mine, which a few hours later still sat on the counter. I wasn't hungry.

I was rattled. Running out of work. The fire. Sally's dad.

And even if I'd managed to recover my appetite late in the evening, the fact that Sheila still wasn't home had put me on edge.

Her class, which was held at the Bridgeport Business College, had ended more than an hour and a half ago, and it was only a thirty-minute drive home. Which made her an hour late. Not that long, really. There were any number of explanations.

She could have stayed after class to have a coffee with someone. That had happened a couple of times. Maybe the traffic was bad on the turnpike. All you needed was someone with a flat tire on the shoulder to slow everything down. An accident would stop everything dead.

That didn't explain her not answering her cell, though. She'd been known to forget to turn it back on after class was over, but when that happened it went to voicemail right away. But the phone was ringing. Maybe it was tucked so far down in her purse she couldn't hear it.

I wondered whether she'd decided to go to Darien to see her mother and not made it back out to Bridgeport in time for her class. Reluctantly, I made the call.

"Hello?"

"Fiona, it's Glen."

In the background, I heard someone whisper, "Who is

it, love?" Fiona's husband, Marcus. Technically speaking, Sheila's stepfather, but Fiona had remarried long after Sheila had left home and settled into a life with me.

"Yes?" she said.

I told her Sheila was late getting back from Bridgeport, and I wondered if maybe her daughter had gotten held up at her place.

"Sheila didn't come see me today," Fiona said. "I certainly wasn't expecting her. She never said anything about coming over."

That struck me as odd. When Sheila mentioned maybe going to see Fiona, I'd figured she'd already bounced the idea off her.

"Is there a problem, Glen?" Fiona asked icily. There wasn't worry in her voice so much as suspicion. As if Sheila's staying out late had more to do with me than it did with her.

"No, everything's fine," I said. "Go back to bed."

I heard soft steps coming down from the second floor. Kelly, not yet in her pajamas, wandered into the kitchen. She looked at the still-wrapped lasagna on the counter and asked, "Aren't you going to eat that?"

"Hands off," I said, thinking maybe I'd get my appetite back once Sheila was home. I glanced at the wall clock. Quarter past ten. "Why aren't you in bed?"

"Because you haven't told me to go yet," she said.

"What have you been doing?"

"Computer."

"Go to bed," I said.

"It was homework," she said.

"Look at me."

"In the *beginning* it was," she said defensively. "And when I got it done, I was talking to my friends." She stuck out her lower lip and blew away some blonde curls that were falling over her eyes. "Why isn't Mom home?"

"Her thing must have run late," I said. "I'll send her up to give you a kiss when she gets home."

"If I'm asleep, how will I know if I get it?"

"She'll tell you in the morning."

Kelly eyed me with suspicion. "So I might never get a kiss, but you guys would say I did."

"You figured it out," I said. "It's a scam we've been running."

"Whatever." She turned, shuffled out of the kitchen, and padded back upstairs.

I picked up the receiver and tried Sheila's cell again. When her greeting cut in, I muttered "Shit" before it started recording and hit the off button.

I went down the stairs to my basement office. The walls were wood-paneled, giving the place a dark, oppressive feel. And the mountains of paper on the desk only added to the gloominess. For years I'd been intending to either redo this room—get rid of the paneling and go for drywall painted off-white so it wouldn't feel so small, for starters—or put an addition onto the back of the house with lots of windows and a skylight. But as is often the case with people whose work is building and renovating houses, it's your own place that never gets done.

I dropped myself into the chair behind the desk and shuffled some papers around. Bills from various suppliers, plans for the new kitchen we were doing in a house up in Derby, some notes about a freestanding double garage we were building for a guy in Devon who wanted a place to park his two vintage Corvettes.

There was also a very preliminary report from the Milford Fire Department about what may have caused the house we'd been building for Arnett and Leanne Wilson on Shelter Cove Road to burn down a week ago. I scanned down to the end and read, for possibly the hundredth time, *Indications are fire originated in area of electrical panel.*

It was a two-story, three-bedroom, built on the site of a postwar bungalow that a strong easterly wind could have knocked down if we hadn't taken a wrecking ball to it first. The fire had started just before one p.m. The house had been framed and sided, the roof was up, electrical was done, and the plumbing was getting roughed in. Doug Pinder, my assistant manager, and I were using the recently installed outlets to run a couple of table saws. Ken Wang, our Chinese guy with the Southern accent—his parents emigrated from Beijing to Kentucky when he was an infant, and we still cracked up whenever he said "y'all"—and Stewart Minden, our newbie from Ottawa who was living with relatives in Stratford for a few months, were upstairs sorting out where fixtures were going to go in the main bathroom.

Doug smelled the smoke first. Then we saw it, drifting up from the basement.

I shouted upstairs to Ken and Stewart to get the hell out. They came bounding down the carpetless stairs and flew out the front door with Doug.

Then I did something very, very stupid.

I ran out to my truck, grabbed a fire extinguisher from behind the driver's seat, and ran back into the house. Halfway down the steps to the basement, the smoke became so thick I couldn't see. I got to the bottom step, running my hand along the makeshift two-by-four banister to guide me there, and thought if I started spraying blindly from the extinguisher, I'd hit the source of the fire and save the place.

Really dumb.

I immediately started to cough and my eyes began to sting. When I turned to retreat back up the stairs, I couldn't find them. I stuck out my free hand and swept it from side to side, looking for the railing.

I hit something softer than wood. An arm.

"Come on, you stupid son of a bitch," Doug growled,

grabbing hold of me. He was on the bottom step, and pulled me toward it.

We came out the front door together, coughing and hacking, as the first fire truck was coming around the corner. Minutes after that, the place was fully engulfed.

"Don't tell Sheila I went in," I said to Doug, still wheezing. "She'd kill me."

"And so she should, Glenny," Doug said.

Other than the foundation, there wasn't much left of the place once the fire was out. Everything was with the insurance company now, and if they didn't come through, the thousands it would cost to rebuild would be coming out of my pocket. Little wonder I'd been staring at the ceiling for hours in the dead of night.

I'd never been hit with anything like this before. It hadn't just scared me, losing a project to fire. It had shaken my confidence. If I was about anything, it was getting things right, doing a quality job.

"Shit happens," Doug had said. "We pick ourselves up and move on."

I wasn't feeling that philosophical. And it wasn't Doug's name on the side of the truck.

I thought maybe I should eat something, so I slid my plate of lasagna into the microwave. I sat down at the kitchen table and picked away at it. The inside was still cold, but I couldn't be bothered to put it back in. Lasagna was one of Sheila's specialties, and if it weren't for the fact that I had so much on my mind, I would have been devouring it, even cold. Whenever she made it in her browny-orange baking pan—Sheila would say it was "persimmon"—there was always enough for two or three meals, so we'd be having lasagna again in a couple of nights, maybe even for Saturday lunch. That was okay with me.

I ate less than half, rewrapped it, and put the plate in the fridge. Kelly was under her covers, her bedside light on, when I peeked into her room. She'd been reading a Wimpy Kid book.

"Lights out, sweetheart."

"Is Mom home?" she asked.

"No."

"I need to talk to her."

"About what?"

"Nothing."

I nodded. When Kelly had something on her mind, it was usually her mother she talked to. Even though she was only eight, she had questions about boys, and love, and the changes she knew were coming in a few years. These were, I had to admit, not my areas of expertise.

"Don't be mad," she said.

"I'm not mad."

"Some things are just easier to talk to Mom about. But I love you guys the same."

"Good to know."

"I can't get to sleep until she gets home."

That made two of us.

"Put your head down on the pillow. You might nod off anyway."

"I won't."

"Turn off the light and give it a shot."

Kelly reached over and turned off her lamp. I kissed her forehead and gently closed the door as I slipped out of her room.

Another hour went by. I tried Sheila's cell six more times. I was back and forth between my office basement and the kitchen. The trip took me past the front door, so I could keep glancing out to the driveway.

Just after eleven, standing in the kitchen, I tried her friend Ann Slocum. Someone picked up long enough to stop the ringing, then replaced the receiver. Ann's husband, Darren, I was guessing. That would be his style. But then again, I was calling late.

Next I called Sheila's other friend, Belinda. They'd worked together years ago, for the library, but stayed close even after their career paths went in different directions. Belinda was a real estate agent now. Not the greatest time to be in that line of work. A lot more people wanted to sell these days than buy. Despite Belinda's unpredictable schedule, she and Sheila managed to get together for lunch every couple of weeks, sometimes with Ann, sometimes not.

Her husband, George, answered sleepily, "Hello?"

"George, Glen Garber. Sorry to call so late."

"Glen, jeez, what time is it?"

"It's late, I know. Can I talk to Belinda?"

I heard some muffled chatter, some shifting about, then Belinda came on the line. "Glen, is everything okay?"

"Sheila's really late getting back from her night class thing, and she's not answering her cell. You haven't heard from her, have you?"

"What? What are you talking about? Say that again?" Belinda sounded instantly panicked.

"Has Sheila been in touch? She's usually back from her course by now."

"No. When did you last talk to her?"

"This morning," I said. "You know Sally, at the office?"

"Yeah."

"Her dad passed away and I called Sheila to let her know."

"So you haven't talked to her pretty much all day?" There was an edge in Belinda's voice. Not accusing, exactly, but something.

"Listen, I didn't call to get you all upset. I just wondered if you'd heard from her is all."

"No, no, I haven't," Belinda said. "Glen, please have Sheila call me the minute she gets in, okay? I mean, now that you've got me worrying about her, too, I need to know she got in okay."

"I'll tell her. Tell George I'm sorry about waking you guys up."

"For *sure* you'll have her call me."

"Promise," I said.

I hung up, went upstairs to Kelly's door and opened it a crack. "You asleep?" I asked, poking my head in.

From the darkness, a chirpy "Nope."

"Throw on some clothes. I'm going to look for Mom. And I can't leave you alone in the house."

She flicked on her bedside lamp. I thought she'd argue, tell me she was old enough to stay in the house, but instead she asked, "What's happened?"

"I don't know. Probably nothing. My guess is your mom's having a coffee and can't hear her phone. But maybe she got a flat tire or something. I want to drive the route she usually takes."

"Okay," she said instantly, throwing her feet onto the floor. She wasn't worried. This was an adventure. She pulled some jeans on over her pajamas. "I need two secs."

I went back downstairs and got my coat, made sure I had my cell. If Sheila did call the house once we were gone, my cell would be next. Kelly hopped into the truck, did up her belt, and said, "Is Mom going to be in trouble?"

I glanced over at her as I turned the ignition. "Yeah. She's going to be grounded."

Kelly giggled. "As if," she said.

Once we were out of the driveway and going down the street, I asked Kelly, "Did your mom say anything about what she was going to do today? Was she going to see her parents and then changed her mind? Did she mention anything at all?"

Kelly frowned. "I don't think so. She might have gone to the drugstore."

That was only a trip around the corner. "Why do you think she was going there?"

"I heard her talking to someone on the phone the other day about paying for some."

"Some what?"

"Drugstore stuff."

That made no sense to me and I dismissed it.

We weren't on the road five minutes before Kelly was out cold, her head resting on her shoulder. If my head was in that position for more than a minute, it would leave me with a crick in my neck for a month.

I drove up Schoolhouse Road and got on the ramp to 95 West. It was the quickest route between Milford and Bridgeport, especially at this time of the night, and the most likely one for Sheila to have taken. I kept glancing over at the eastbound highway, looking for a Subaru wagon pulled off to the side of the road.

This was a long shot, at best. But doing something, anything, seemed preferable to sitting at home and worrying.

I continued to scan the other side of the highway, but not only didn't I see Sheila's car, I didn't see any cars pulled over to the shoulder at all.

I was almost through Stratford, about to enter the Bridgeport city limits, when I saw some lights flashing on the other side. Not on the road, but maybe down an off-ramp. I leaned on the gas, wanting to hurry to the next exit so I could turn around and head back on the eastbound lanes.

Kelly continued to sleep.

I exited 95, crossed the highway and got back on. As I approached the exit where I thought I'd seen lights, I spotted a police car, lights flashing, blocking the way. I slowed, but the cop waved me on. I wasn't able to see far enough down the ramp to see what the problem was, and with Kelly in the truck, pulling over to the side of a busy highway did not seem wise.

So I got off at the next exit, figuring I could work my way back on local streets, get to the ramp from the bottom end. It took me about ten minutes. The cops hadn't set up a barricade at the bottom of the ramp, since no one would turn up there anyway. I pulled the car over to the shoulder at the base of the ramp and got my first real look at what had happened.

It was an accident. A bad one. Two cars. So badly mangled it was difficult to tell what they were or what might have happened. Closer to me was a car that appeared to be a station wagon, and the other one, a sedan of some kind, was off to the side. It looked as though the wagon had been broadsided by the sedan.

Sheila drove a wagon.

Kelly was still sound asleep, and I didn't want to wake her. I got out of the truck, closed the door without slamming it, and approached the ramp. There were three police cars at the scene, a couple of tow trucks and a fire engine.

As I got closer, I was able to get a better look at the cars involved in the accident. I began to feel shaky. I glanced back at my truck, made sure I could see Kelly in the passenger window.

Before I could take another step, however, a police officer stood in my way.

"I'm sorry, sir," he said. "You have to stay back."

"What kind of car is that?" I asked.

"Sir, please—"

"What kind of car? The wagon, the closest car."

"A Subaru," he said.

"Plate," I said.

"I'm sorry, sir?"

"I need to see the plate."

"Do you think you know whose car this is?" the cop asked.

"Let me see the plate."

He allowed me to approach, took me to a vantage point that allowed me to see the back of the wagon. The license plate was clearly visible.

I recognized the combination of numbers and letters.

"Oh Jesus," I said, feeling weak.

"Sir?"

"This is my wife's car."

"What's your name, sir?"

"Glen Garber. This car, it's my wife's car. That's her plate. Oh my God."

The cop took a step closer to me.

"Is she okay?" I asked, my entire body feeling as though I were holding on to a low-voltage live wire. "Which hospital have they taken her to? Do you know? Can you find out? I have to go there. I have to get there right now."

"Mr. Garber—" the cop said.

"Milford Hospital?" I said. "No, wait, Bridgeport Hospital is closer." I turned to run back to the truck.

"Mr. Garber, your wife hasn't been taken to the hospital."

I stopped. "What?"

"She's still in the car. I'm afraid that—"

"What are you saying?"

I looked at the mangled remains of the Subaru. The cop had to be wrong. There were no paramedics there; none of the nearby firefighters were using the Jaws of Life to get to the driver.

I pushed past him, ran to the car, got right up to the caved-in driver's side, looked through what was left of the door.

"Sheila," I said. "Sheila, honey."

The window glass had shattered into a million pieces the size of raisins. I began to brush them from her shoulder, pick them from her blood-matted hair. I kept saying her name over and over again.

"Sheila? Oh God, please, Sheila . . ."

"Mr. Garber." The officer was standing right behind me. I felt a hand on my shoulder. "Please, sir, come with me."

"You have to get her out," I said. The smell of gasoline was wafting up my nostrils and I could hear something dripping.

"We're going to do that, I promise you. Please, come with me."

"She's not dead. You have to—"

"Please, sir, I'm afraid she is. There were no vital signs."

"No, you're wrong." I reached in and put my arm around her head. It nodded over to one side.

That was when I knew.

The cop put his hand firmly on my arm and said, "You have to move away from the car, sir. It's not safe to stand here." He pulled me forcibly away and I didn't fight him. Half a dozen car lengths away, I had to stop, bend over, and put my hands on my knees.

"Are you okay, sir?"

Looking down at the pavement, I said, "My daughter's in my truck. Can you see her? Is she asleep?"

"I can just see the top of her head, yes. Looks like she is."

I took several shaky breaths, straightened back up. Said "Oh my God" probably ten times. The cop stood there, patiently, waiting for me to pull it together enough for him to ask me some questions.

"Your wife's name is Sheila, sir? Sheila Garber?"

"That's right."

"Do you know what she was doing tonight? Where she was going?"

"She has a course tonight. Bridgeport Business College. She's learning accounting and other things to help me in my business. What happened? What happened here? How did this happen? Who the hell was driving that other car? What did he do?"

The cop lowered his head. "Mr. Garber, this appears to have been an alcohol-related accident."

"What? Drunk driving?"

"It would appear so, yes."

Anger began to mix in with the shock and grief. "Who was driving that car? What stupid son of a bitch—"

"There were three people in the other car. One survived. A young boy in the back seat. His father and brother were the two fatalities."

"My God, what kind of man gets behind the wheel drunk with his boys in the car and—"

"That's not exactly how it looks, sir," the cop said.

I stared at him, trying to figure out what he was getting at. Then it hit me. It wasn't the father driving. It was one of the sons.

"One of his boys was driving drunk?"

"Mr. Garber, please. I need you to calm down for me. I need you to listen. It appears it was your wife who caused the accident."

"What?"

"She'd driven up the ramp the wrong way, then just stopped her vehicle about halfway, parking it across the road, no lights visible. We think she may have fallen asleep."

"What the hell are you talking about?"

"And then," he said, "when the other car came off the highway, probably doing about sixty, he'd have been almost on your wife's car before he saw it and could put on the brakes."

"But the other driver, he was drunk, right?"

"You're not getting me here, Mr. Garber. If you don't mind my asking, sir, did your wife have a habit of drinking and driving? Usually, by the time someone actually gets into an accident, they've been taking chances for quite some—"

Sheila's car burst into flames.